D1215078

Someone To Cherish

Book 2 of the Lost Girls Trilogy

CHERYL HOLT

Praise for *New York Times* Bestselling Author
CHERYL HOLT

"Best storyteller of the year . . ."
Romantic Times Magazine

"Cheryl Holt is magnificent . . ."
Reader to Reader Reviews

"Cheryl Holt is on my 'favorite authors' list. I can't wait to see what she'll write next."
The Reading Café

"A master writer . . ."
Fresh Fiction

Here's what readers are saying . . .

"OMG! I just started reading this series yesterday. It was hard for me to close my Kindle and go to bed. So, so good!"
Artemis

"Cheryl Holt has packed in so much action that the reader is constantly spellbound. So many characters, so vividly portrayed! Rogues, unfaithfulness, loyalty, and delightful dialogue. You will love this book!"
Gladys

"It was fabulous! I laughed, I cried, I got angry, and I smiled. I read the whole book without stopping."
Robin

"Action, drama, and intrigue. I read it in one afternoon. I couldn't put it down!"
Gina

"You just can't wait to turn the page to see what happens next. Outstanding!"
Margaret

"This book is such an emotional roller-coaster. I cried and laughed and cheered. It was so good!"
Colleen

BOOKS BY CHERYL HOLT

Someone to Cherish
Copyright 2020 by Cheryl Holt
All rights reserved under International and Pan-American Copyright Conventions.

ISBN: 978-1-64871-173-2 (Paperback)
ISBN: 978-1-64871-171-8 (eBook)

By payment of required fees, you have been granted the non-exclusive, non-transferrable right to access and read the text of this book. No part of this text may be reproduced, transmitted, downloaded, decompiled, reverse engineered, stored in, or introduced into any information storage and retrieval system, in any form or by any means, whether electronic or mechanical, now known or invented in the future, without the express written permission or the copyright holder.

Please Note

The reverse engineering, uploading, and/or distributing of this book via the internet or via any other means without the permission of the copyright owner is illegal and punishable by law. Please purchase only authorized editions, and do not participate in or encourage the piracy of copyrighted materials. Your support of the author's rights is appreciated.

No part of this book may be reproduced or transmitted in any form or by any electronic or mechanical means, including photocopying, recording, or by any information storage and retrieval system, without the written permission of the author, except where permitted by law.

Thank you.

Cover Design: Angela Waters
Interior Design & eBook formatting: Dayna Linton • Day Agency • www.dayagency.com

Someone To Cherish

Prologue

"ARE THEY BAD MEN?"

Caro peered at Libby, waiting to hear her decision. Libby was their leader. Libby was in charge. She was very bossy and liked to tell them how to behave, and Caro was happy to let her. They were only five, and there were too many huge problems to solve. Libby liked to pretend she knew what was best.

Caro didn't bother to seek Joanna's opinion. Joanna hadn't talked in ages, so it was pointless to expect a response.

"They might be bad," Libby said, "or they might not."

"How can we be sure?"

When Joanna's mother had still been alive, she'd warned them to watch out for strangers. The Caribbean was awash with pirates and other criminals who would be eager to kidnap a little girl. They had to constantly be vigilant.

They were up on the promontory, the highest point on the island. Earlier that morning, sails had appeared on the horizon, and gradually, a large ship had come closer and closer. Finally, it had dropped anchor out in the bay.

Sailors scurried about, tying down the canvas and seeing to various chores. A man in a blue coat studied the island through a brass spyglass.

He gestured toward their dilapidated hut, then orders were shouted, and two long boats were lowered.

A dozen sailors scampered down the rope ladder and jumped into the boats, then they rowed for shore.

"What should we do?" Caro asked Libby.

"Hide," was Libby's quick reply.

"Where?"

Joanna slipped her hand into Caro's and gripped it tight. She was trembling, but then, she was younger than Libby and Caro. She frightened more easily and fretted more intensely.

"In the hut," Libby said. "In the traveling trunks."

Many objects from their sunken ship had washed ashore, including several trunks filled with adult clothes and other personal items.

"It's the first place they'll look," Caro complained.

"Do you have a better idea?"

"Let's sneak into the jungle."

"The traveling trunks are safer."

"No, they're not."

The long boats were getting nearer, the man in the blue coat perched at the front like an angry statue. His coat was covered with medals, ribbons, and gold braids.

Joanna was tired of listening to them argue. She started off, dragging Caro away from the cliff and out of sight of the men who were swiftly approaching. Libby and Caro glared at each other, then Libby ran in one direction, while Caro and Joanna ran in the other.

The island was very small, so there weren't many spots where they could conceal themselves. Caro chose a tree in the center where rain had carved a hole around the roots. They snuggled into it, Joanna still fiercely gripping her hand.

"Don't worry," Caro whispered. "They won't find us."

Joanna stared, wide-eyed with alarm. From the minute so many months prior when the storm had struck their own ship, people had been telling Joanna that she'd be fine. She didn't believe it anymore, and neither did Caro.

They hovered under the tree forever, but ultimately, three sailors stomped toward them. One of them blustered over and knelt down.

"Out with you," he said, but they didn't move. "Come out. Do you understand me? Do you speak English?"

They still didn't move, but gaped at him as if he were a peculiar creature they'd never observed previously. For an eternity, it had just been Caro, Libby, and Joanna, and the encounter seemed to be occurring in a dream, as if they'd never seen another human.

He grabbed Joanna's ankle and pulled her out. She wailed with dismay, and her fear galvanized Caro. She always yearned to be more like Libby who wasn't afraid of anything, and Libby and Joanna were Caro's only friends, her only family. They were like sisters, only closer than sisters. She wouldn't permit anybody to harm Joanna.

She burst from the hole like a wild animal, and she attacked the man, wrestling and clawing to yank Joanna away from him, but the other men seized her and pinned her arms to her sides until she lost the energy to keep fighting.

"We won't hurt you," a sailor repeated over and over. "You don't have to be scared of us. We'll help you."

"Is your mother here?" another asked. "Or your father?"

"No." Caro's voice sounded rusty and rough.

"Are there any grownups with you?"

"No."

"Where are they? What happened to them?"

"They died. What would you suppose?"

"Were you in a shipwreck?"

"Yes. In a really, really big storm."

The men exchanged glances Caro couldn't decipher. What were they thinking?

"We should take them to the captain," one of them said. "He'll be stunned. They're like a couple of orphaned wolf pups."

"We're not wolves," Caro protested. "We're girls. Can't you tell the difference?"

"Yes, you're girls, very pretty little girls."

Caro figured he was simply being polite. At the moment, they weren't pretty, but were incredibly bedraggled.

Their hair was knotted and bleached white from the sun. They were scrubby and barefoot, their dresses faded and bleached white too. Their skin was bronzed though, the slow, lazy days on the tropical beach burnishing them so they were the color of copper coins.

The men marched off, with Joanna and Caro encircled so they couldn't dash away. They walked out of the jungle and onto the sand where their meager hut sagged under a palm tree. Joanna's mother had built it before she'd passed away. It was merely some logs they'd scrounged and stacked together, and they'd covered them with palm fronds. It wasn't much, but it provided shelter from the occasional rain squalls.

For a brief instant, she hoped Libby had escaped, but no. She'd been found too. The man with the medals and ribbons on his coat was standing beside her. While Caro watched, he picked up Libby and balanced her on his hip—as if she were a baby.

Caro's first reaction was jealousy. She wished the man would pick her up too; she'd feel so much better if he would. Her second reaction was that the men weren't bad or dangerous. They might actually fix what was wrong.

As she realized adults would be in charge, that adults would begin making the decisions, tears flooded her eyes and dripped down her cheeks. Maybe everything would finally be all right.

Chapter

1

Twenty years later...

CAROLINE GREY STROLLED DOWN the lane, her heavy basket banging against her thigh. She'd been to the village, having offered to complete some errands for their housekeeper, Mrs. Scruggs. She was on her way back to the manor, but she was in no hurry.

It was a beautiful July afternoon, the sky blue with fluffy clouds drifting by. The temperature was so warm she hadn't needed a shawl, and she'd left her bonnet behind too, enjoying the chance to have the sun shine on her face.

Though it was considered unladylike to have her skin darken even the tiniest bit, she always worried that she looked much too pale. It was an exasperating affectation she'd adopted after she'd been rescued from her deserted island where she'd lived with Libby and Joanna.

When those navy sailors had stumbled on them—quite by accident, she'd been told—she'd been bronzed as a penny. Over the subsequent weeks and months, as her tanned hue had faded, she'd suffered from the constant perception that she was becoming invisible and that, shortly, no one would be able to see her.

As with so many aspects of that terrible period, she'd never shared the story with others. Her relatives didn't like to be reminded of her history, so at an early age, she'd learned not to talk about it, but whenever she could revel in the sun, she did.

She wasn't invisible. She hadn't disappeared. She'd survived the very worst ordeal a person could survive, and it had imbued her with odd quirks and old fears she kept carefully hidden.

If her uncle or cousins had the slightest inkling of some of the musings that consumed her, they'd probably lock her in an asylum. Her family liked to blend in and never be noticed for any peculiarity, so they didn't like people gossiping about what had happened to her.

Then of course, there was the issue with her parents who'd perished in the shipwreck. Her father had been a wastrel who'd driven her Puritanical grandfather to fantastic levels of outrage. The last straw had occurred when he'd wed Caroline's mother without permission, so at the time of his death, he'd been disowned and disinherited.

Her grandfather had never forgiven her parents. In his stern, unbending opinion, not even their violent demise absolved them of the sins they'd committed. She'd been exhaustively lectured over how she had their tainted blood flowing in her veins and that she would have to fight the immoral urges that would rule her if she wasn't cautious.

She thought it was all very silly. She didn't remember her parents and couldn't guess if they'd been wildly immoral.

When she, Libby, and Joanna had arrived in England from Jamaica, they'd been dubbed the *Lost Girls* and the *Mystery Girls of the Caribbean*. Shocking articles had been printed in the newspapers about their being abandoned and alone on their tiny island.

They'd been too young to provide much information about their kin, and the authorities had struggled to locate their relatives. In the process, they'd fended off charlatans and liars as various criminal types had stepped forward to claim connections.

She'd been sent to live with her Grandfather Walter who hadn't wanted to have her thrust on him. To her great dismay, there had been no more dour, grim man in the whole kingdom, so it had been a horrific spot for her, and it had guaranteed her recuperation from the tragedy was very slow.

His household had been a quiet, miserable place, so even though she'd returned to England with a myriad of emotional problems, there had been no kindly aunties or even any servants who might have helped her adapt.

Every adult had pretended that no unusual incident had transpired, so she'd had to pretend too. With it being the twentieth anniversary of their rescue, she was more overwhelmed than ever, but putting on a good show.

She spent every second trying to fit in, to prove she'd overcome the dreadful event, but she hadn't really. Who would have?

A horse's hooves clopped on the gravel behind her, and she glanced over her shoulder, curious as to who was approaching. Over the next week, they had company arriving, with numerous people scheduled to roll in from London, so it could be anyone.

She wasn't nearly as excited about the pending festivities as she should have been, which was the main reason she'd gone to the village for Mrs. Scruggs. Caroline was the *lady* of the house, serving as hostess for her widowed Uncle Samson, and she should have been pacing in the front parlor and eager to greet their guests.

Yet she was conflicted about what was occurring, conflicted about her role, conflicted about her future. When she was distressed, she felt very claustrophobic, so she'd had to get outside, knowing she would calm down once she could breathe the fresh air.

The walk had been beneficial. It had settled her down, so she could display a modicum of civility. She forced a smile and spun toward the horse.

A man was on its back, and she caught herself gawking at him. She couldn't stop.

He was incredibly handsome in a way that was stirring. His hair was blond, the color of golden wheat, and he had aristocratic features—high cheekbones, strong nose, generous mouth. He was thin and muscular, his shoulders broad, his waist narrow, his legs muscled and impossibly long.

His eyes were the most riveting. They were very blue, very direct and probing. They seemed to cut right through her and catalogue every detail.

He reined in and studied her too, and she didn't have to wonder what he saw. Her grandfather had relentlessly scolded her about pride, but she wasn't blind.

With her black hair and blue eyes, she was very pretty and, in a world where practically everyone was blond, she was unique. It was a fact that had always thrilled her. She wasn't curvaceous though, as an adult female should be. She was short and too slender, her body never fully recovering from her ordeal on the island.

She'd been in England for two decades, but they hadn't been easy decades. She never ceased fretting over the most trivial things, and she had worry lines that made her appear older than she was.

"Hello," he said, his voice a deep baritone that tickled her innards. "I'm bound for Grey's Corner. Have I ridden down the correct lane? Or am I lost?"

"You're on the correct lane."

"Praise be. I'm a Londoner, and all these country roads look exactly the same to me. I was afraid I might never reach my destination."

"You're almost there."

He dismounted and came over to her. He had a confident swagger, as an army soldier might have, and she suspected he was a veteran. He was that impressive and imposing.

He was very tall, six feet at least, so he towered over her. He was dressed casually, in leather trousers and black boots. As a bow to the temperate weather, he'd shed his coat as she had her shawl. He wore a flowing white shirt, the sleeves rolled to reveal his powerful forearms.

"Are you headed to the manor?" he asked.

"Yes."

"May I accompany you?"

"Of course."

"And may I carry your basket?"

The request had her momentarily taken aback. She ran the house for her Uncle Samson, and she was in charge of the servants and the daily operations, but it was a rare circumstance when she was offered even the most paltry assistance.

"Why, yes," she said, "you may carry it for me."

He shifted it from her hand to his, and for the briefest instant, their fingers touched. It was very strange, but she felt that light caress clear down to her toes.

She introduced herself. "I am Miss Grey. Are we expecting you?"

"I hope I'm expected. I'm Mr. Caleb Ralston."

On learning his surname, she tamped down a blanch of surprise. The captain who'd rescued them in the Caribbean had been a Captain Miles Ralston. They'd spent a few days on his ship, then he'd delivered them to the authorities in Jamaica. They'd never seen him again, and Caroline occasionally pondered him.

Might he still be alive? At the time, he'd seemed very old to her, but she'd been so young. She couldn't guess what his current age might be, but she'd love to correspond with him, to thank him for saving her. She never had. When they'd parted from him, she hadn't realized it would be forever.

She possessed such an intense fondness for him, and whenever she heard his name, she wondered if she'd stumbled on a relative. But because her grandfather had forbidden her to discuss her past, she never raised the topic, so she never inquired about Captain Ralston, and it was probably for the best.

If she was revealed to be a *Lost Girl*, people stared as if she had two heads or blue skin, so her history remained a dear and private secret.

Fortunately, Mr. Ralston hadn't noticed her heightened interest over his identity. She smiled up at him, and when he smiled back, it was so dazzling that she was practically knocked over by it.

She warned herself to buck up and stop acting like a ninny, and she calmly said, "I'm very pleased to meet you, Mr. Ralston. I'm delighted that so many of Gregory's London friends could attend."

"My brother, Blake, will be here too, but not until tomorrow. Gregory tells me the manor will be filled with beautiful women."

"Gregory told you that? I can't imagine him boasting about it. He's not exactly the type to wax poetic."

"No, not usually, but in this case, he was very vocal on the subject. He claims to have gorgeous female kin, so which Miss Grey are you?"

She chuckled, but with exasperation. "I am his cousin, Caroline."

He assessed her cryptically, then murmured, "Ah...the blushing bride-to-be."

"Yes."

Gregory was her Uncle Samson's only son and heir, with Samson having sired a daughter too, Caroline's other cousin, Janet. Caroline had been engaged to Gregory since she'd turned seventeen, with her Uncle Samson announcing the plan and giving her very little latitude to object.

And she hadn't objected. Not really. It made sense for her and Gregory to wed—cousins always did—and it wasn't as if she'd had a thousand suitors lined up and demanding to marry her instead. She had no dowry or prospects, and she was considered to be very odd due to her being a famous Lost Girl.

Gregory was the sole nuptial choice ever presented. Why wouldn't she wed him? Why wouldn't she have agreed?

If she'd refused the match, he'd have ultimately picked someone else. He was thirty and had to get on with the business of starting a family. If he'd selected a different bride, Caroline would have had to let a stranger take over in the manor. She might even have been asked to move out, but where would she have gone?

She had no funds of her own, and she was a very aged twenty-four and about to be twenty-five, so she'd been waiting to tie the knot for seven long years.

Gregory had never been in much of a hurry to proceed. He lived in London and reveled in the sort of excitement all gentlemen pursued there. It had begun to seem as if she wasn't betrothed, as if she wasn't destined to be her cousin's bride, but during his last visit, Uncle Samson had put his foot down and insisted Gregory set the date.

So...a week hence, she would be Mrs. Gregory Grey rather than Miss Caroline Grey.

After the ceremony, not much would change. Gregory would still carouse in town, while she resided in the country. She'd still manage the servants and the house, but she'd have the security and respect that came from being a wife.

She was trying to be happy about what was approaching. It was her *wedding*. It was the event every girl supposedly dreamed about, but she didn't feel much of anything. Not elation. Not joy. Not even much interest, if she was being truly honest.

Once they spoke the vows, she would formally bind herself to Grey's Corner. She loved her home and wanted to stay in it, but bubbling just below the surface, she had her father's wanderlust.

On occasion, her world was so small that she yearned to scream at the fetters shackling her to it. She yearned to run away and experience the kind of escapades her father had relished. Why, he'd even journeyed to Africa with the notorious explorer, Sir Sidney Sinclair! But it was madness to think she could have a bigger life than what had been provided.

Females weren't allowed to travel and engage in wild antics, and she'd had plenty of *dangerous* adventure when her ship had sunk in the Caribbean. She had to remember that there was great solace in the quiet passing of the decades, where there were no huge swings of circumstance.

She was *glad* she was finally marrying. She was relieved. Wasn't she?

"I will admit to being the bride-to-be," she said, "but I won't admit to blushing. I'm not the blushing type. I'm much too confident and composed."

"Wonderful. I can't abide trembling maidens, so I'm sure we'll get on famously."

"Since you'll be at my wedding, I should probably learn a bit about you. How are you acquainted with Gregory?"

Mr. Ralston paused for an eternity, then said, "We're friends."

"It took you long enough to select the term to describe your relationship with him."

"I'm not exactly a *friendly* person. Gregory and I frequently socialize. Does that make us friends? I'm not certain."

It was a peculiar reply. Their wedding guests would be neighbors, the larger tenant farmers, and the important merchants in the village. There would be several pews filled with distant cousins and their spouses too. The only attendees who would raise her curiosity in the least would be Gregory's companions from London.

He'd distributed invitations to his London circle, but Caroline didn't know any of them. In fact, she had scant notions of how he carried on in the city—except that he spent money like an aristocrat. Considering the fiscal condition of the family when her Grandfather Walter was still with them, it was bizarre to see Gregory with money *and* to watch him fritter it away with such a reckless abandon.

Grandfather Walter had been exhaustively pious. As a result, he'd eschewed frivolity and ostentation so, under his iron thumb, they might have been monks laboring under vows of poverty. Once he'd died though, her Uncle Samson had quickly proved that he and Gregory didn't subscribe to his father's parsimonious ways.

They'd both inherited fortunes from her grandfather, and they were happy to use them so all their lives would be more pleasant. They often scoffed at how her grandfather had been so determined to be miserable. *They* didn't intend to be.

She and her cousin, Janet, hadn't benefited from the inheritances though. Janet had a small trust fund from her maternal grandmother, but no bequests had been delivered to them from their Grandfather Walter. They blundered on fairly much as they always had, although they were now able to buy a new gown or slippers when the mood struck them.

She'd even been permitted to have a dress specially sewn for the wedding. Gregory had sent a modiste from town to take her measurements and show her fabric samples. It was a sweet gesture and one that was surprising from a man as self-centered as Gregory had always been.

Obviously, he wanted them to get off on the right foot. Perhaps he even felt a tad guilty about the lengthy delay between proposal and ceremony, and the gown was his method of telling her that he was delighted to proceed. She had to cease being so negative about every little issue.

"How long have you known Gregory?" she asked.

"A few months."

"Months? I assumed it would be years. Gregory told me his London guests were his dearest chums."

"Gregory doesn't have *chums*. I met him at a faro parlor that's run by a good friend of mine."

She scowled. "Faro is gambling."

"Yes, it is."

"Gregory doesn't gamble."

Mr. Ralston stared at her with a pitying look that indicated he deemed her a naïve fool.

Was Gregory a gambler? She had no idea. He received quarterly disbursements from his trust fund, and he regularly overspent and had to borrow from the next disbursement. He and Uncle Samson repeatedly argued about it, but she'd figured he wasted his money on ordinary expenses such as food and clothes.

Was he throwing it away in the gambling hells? Excessive wagering was a scourge among a fast crowd in town, with men losing their properties and fortunes. For many, it was like an addiction that couldn't be controlled.

Was Gregory addicted? Was that it? And if he was, had she the right as his wife to have an opinion about it? Then again, since he would continue to reside in the city and rarely visit Grey's Corner, did it matter how he carried on?

It wasn't as if she'd ever have to be confronted by his mischief. If he disgraced himself, why would she care?

A thousand questions flew to the tip of her tongue, and she was anxious to pry into the details about Gregory's life in London. It seemed Mr. Ralston knew secrets to which she desperately needed to become privy. If she inquired, would he reply candidly?

He realized he'd revealed a fact he shouldn't have. He pointed down the lane, cutting off her chance to delve into several topics that ought to be addressed.

"Is the house close?" he asked.

"Yes, yes, and I'm preventing you from arriving. Let me show you the way."

They walked side by side, his horse plodding behind and nudging him in the back as if urging him to hurry.

It should have been a companionable stroll, but she was suddenly overwhelmed by problems she should have been contemplating for ages. Her wedding to Gregory was an inevitable conclusion, and there hadn't ever been a reason to worry about him or his antics. Should she start worrying?

"I don't want to call you Miss Grey," he said, breaking the awkward silence. "With the manor full of your relatives, there will be numerous *Miss* Greys traipsing about. I'd hate to have to keep explaining which one I mean."

"It's fine with me if you call me Caroline."

"Thank you, but I don't like Caroline either. It's too much name for you."

She snorted with amusement. "It's the only one I have."

"You're such a tiny sprite of a woman, so it doesn't suit you. I believe I shall shorten it to Caro. Caro would be much better."

She sighed and chuckled. "Little Caro..."

"Why is it funny?"

"I haven't been thought of as *Caro* in a very long time. An old friend used to use Caro, and I've missed it."

On their deserted island, she'd been Caro to Libby and Joanna. She'd been Caro to Captain Ralston too. The whole trip to England, she'd been Caro, but once she'd been ensconced in her grandfather's grim, sad home, she'd been referred to correctly.

Little Caro had vanished, and quiet, bewildered Caroline had emerged instead.

They reached the end of the trees, and the house loomed in the curved driveway. It wasn't the grandest mansion in the land, but nonetheless, it was quite imposing. Three stories high and constructed of a tan-colored stone, there were dozens of windows and a set of fancy stairs leading to the front doors.

The property had been in the family for two centuries, and under her grandfather, it had fallen into an embarrassing state of disrepair.

Her Uncle Samson had swiftly rectified her grandfather's neglect. The roof had been replaced, the window trim repainted, the chimneys modernized.

He'd permitted her to hire more servants too, so there were many more people to help maintain the enhanced condition.

She was inordinately proud of it. It was a bucolic abode, sitting in a grassy meadow with woods and hills beyond. It was the sort of pastoral scene a painter might have captured: *Rural England on a Summer Day...*

"It's not nearly as impressive as I was expecting," he suddenly said, then he winced. "That was a horrid comment, wasn't it? Please pardon my awful manners."

"You're pardoned, but why is it less impressive than you anticipated?"

"With how Gregory waxes on, I figured it would be second only to Buckingham Palace."

"You have to forgive him. He likes to brag."

"Yes, he does."

She peeked over at him, and he was standing with his feet apart, his legs straight, his hands clasped behind his back. It was how sailors stood as they balanced against the roll of the waves.

"By any chance, Mr. Ralston," she said, "were you ever in the navy?"

"I served for over a decade. How can you tell?"

"Your posture gave you away."

"I guess a man never really stops being a sailor."

"Are you retired?"

"You could describe it that way."

He didn't add any details, leaving her with the distinct opinion that he wasn't keen to discuss his separation from the navy.

She tiptoed out onto a limb and inquired, "I'm acquainted with a navy captain from when I was a girl. Miles Ralston? Might you be related to him?"

He pulled his gaze from the manor and stared at her for an eternity. She could practically see the thoughts flitting around as he decided how to answer.

Finally, he said, "I've never heard of him."

She suspected he was lying, but why would he deny knowing Captain Ralston? She wanted to scoff with disgust. It was the sole time she'd ever uttered Captain Ralston's name aloud, and it hadn't proved satisfying in the least.

"Your wedding is almost here," he said, deftly switching subjects.

"One week from today."

"Has Gregory arrived?"

"Last night."

"How long have the two of you been engaged? I remember him telling me it's been a few years."

She wasn't about to admit that she'd agreed when she was seventeen, that she'd been waiting for Gregory to get on with it, and he'd only proceeded after significant nagging from his father. He hadn't been very eager to become a husband. Or maybe he wasn't eager to become *her* husband, which was too humiliating to consider.

"We've been betrothed for awhile," she blithely replied. "We're both busy, and there was never a reason to hurry."

"You're about to tie the knot. Are you excited?"

"What a strange question. Yes, I'm excited."

"Well then... good. I'm happy for you."

"Gregory and I are cousins. It's the best ending we could have devised."

She had no idea why she'd offered the justification, but under his heightened scrutiny, she felt a desperate need to clarify the situation. She'd consented to the betrothal when she'd been too young to wonder if she should refuse. With her having no dowry, she'd assumed she would never marry, that she'd dodder around at Grey's Corner forever as an unwanted spinster.

Her uncle had saved her from that fate, and she'd been glad of it, but she was more mature now and more accustomed to speaking up for herself. She could have told her uncle she'd changed her mind, but she hadn't changed it. Not really.

She was about to be a wife. It was the normal path for every woman. She'd be fine. Wouldn't she?

The worst wave of dread swept over her, and her anxiety spiraled. She took several deep breaths, struggling to calm herself.

He studied her even more intently. "I've distressed you."

"No, you haven't. I'm just...ah...tired. We have a full house, and I'm overwhelmed by chores."

"How old are you?"

"Twenty-four. Almost twenty-five."

"You've been valiantly marching toward this destiny, but you don't have to go through with it. Not if you don't want to."

For the briefest instant, there was the most outlandish perception in the air, as if Time had stopped ticking so she could ponder his suggestion.

Not go through with it...

The words sounded so thrilling, and a potent surge of relief flooded her. She nearly twirled in ecstatic circles, but as rapidly as she was riveted by the sensation, it vanished.

Of course she'd wed Gregory. Why wouldn't she? It was silly to mull any other conclusion.

Mr. Ralston shook himself as if he'd been in a stupor. "I can't believe I said that to you."

She grinned to lighten the mood. "Neither can I."

"I can't figure out what's come over me. Will you pardon me again?"

"Certainly. There's no harm done."

"I will confess that I am a terrible insomniac. I never sleep."

"Never?" she asked.

"Well, not often and not for any useful length of hours. I fear fatigue is making me act like an idiot, and I can't control my unruly tongue."

"You're not acting like an *idiot* precisely. I find you to be quite odd, but that isn't necessarily bad. I'm very sheltered at Grey's Corner, and it's a rare occasion when I hear a comment that's new or different."

His expression sobered. "Seriously, Miss Grey. Caro. Don't listen to me. I would never presume to advise you in your personal choices. I wish you all the happiness in the world."

"I'm sure you do, and I thank you for it."

She stared up into his magnificent blue eyes, and he stared back, his gaze fantastically enthralling. She'd met so few handsome men in her life, and there'd definitely never been one who assessed her so meticulously.

It felt as if he was cataloguing every detail for subsequent reflection. It was an exhilarating realization, and she caught herself leaning toward him, as if she might simply fall into his arms.

Any marvelous thing could have happened, but from over by the manor, Gregory called, "Ho, ho! Ralston! Is that you?"

They glanced over to see Gregory standing on the stairs. He'd been nervous and jumpy, watching for his guests and as eager as a boy on Christmas morning.

"It appears I've been summoned," Mr. Ralston said, as he slipped her the basket.

"Let's get you inside," she told him. "Once you're settled in your room, perhaps you should take a nap. If you rest for a bit, it might prevent you from uttering indiscreet remarks."

"I would *try* to take a nap, but it would probably be pointless."

"Good luck with your socializing then. I predict you'll step in numerous holes."

"Just for you, I vow to be exhaustingly polite."

"I shall keep hope alive, Mr. Ralston."

He sauntered off, his long legs covering the ground much quicker than hers could, so she was left alone to observe as he greeted her cousin.

To her great exasperation, he'd immediately forgotten that they'd been strolling together and that they'd shared a...a...

There was no term to describe what had occurred. Whatever it had been, it had seemed important and vital—and even a tad dangerous. The hottest fire had ignited in her chest, as if his arrival would spark changes she'd been waiting for forever. But had she been waiting for changes?

One fact was certain: The days leading up to her wedding would be very interesting. She'd assumed Gregory's London friends would be tedious and selfish, just like him, but maybe they wouldn't be. Maybe they'd all be just like Mr. Ralston, which was delightful to consider.

She dawdled as a footman came out to tend Mr. Ralston's horse, then Gregory escorted him in. The door was shut behind them, and she continued on at a much slower pace.

Mr. Ralston was staying for a whole week. Fancy that!

She smiled and headed for the servants' entrance at the rear. She had chores to complete and a staff to supervise. She didn't have time to moon over an intriguing Londoner.

No, she'd save her drooling for later on, when she was in her bed-chamber and had a quiet interval to figure out what had transpired.

Chapter

2

"WE'RE HOSTING A PARTY every night until the wedding. But it will always be different guests, so you won't grow bored with the company."

Caleb Ralston stared at Gregory and smirked with annoyance. "I won't grow bored."

"We're the premier family in the area," Gregory boasted. "We have to keep up appearances by inviting the appropriate people. These rural folks can be so prickly if they're not given suitable attention. We can't have anyone feeling slighted."

"Doesn't everyone hate to feel slighted? It's not just rural folks."

"True, Ralston, true," Gregory quickly agreed.

Gregory was an irksome sycophant who was desperate to be liked. He struggled to be fascinating, but he never succeeded. He'd fallen in with a wicked crowd in London who reveled in the very worst habits, and he was proving he could be as dissolute as the rest of them.

He fancied himself a rich dandy, and he certainly carried on as if he was incredibly wealthy. His grandfather had been a miser who'd lived like a pauper, but once he'd died, Gregory and his father had begun spending like fiends.

Gregory was working hard to empty his bank accounts, and Caleb was happy to help him destroy himself. If he'd liked Gregory at all, he might have been suffering a bit of guilt over how he was behaving, but he didn't like Gregory, so he wasn't ruing a single act he'd undertaken.

Supper was over, and several dozen guests were milling and chatting in the front parlor. Dancing would start shortly, and there was a card room where neighborhood gentlemen could play for pennies if they were inclined to have a spot of fun.

After the party ended, and family members went to bed, Gregory's London guests would wager as if they were in town.

Caleb was delighted to have Gregory arranging more games. Gregory was an unlucky and reckless gambler, and Caleb was an excellent and lucky one. He probably should have stopped Gregory from digging such a deep hole, but he wasn't Gregory's nanny.

Was it Caleb's fault that Gregory was a negligent idiot? He didn't think so.

"We missed you at the theater."

The comment was directed at Caleb by Gregory's special *friend*, Lucretia Starling. She and Gregory had been a couple for years, and they lived openly and in sin in Gregory's town house. He wondered if pretty, sweet Caroline Grey had heard any of those rumors.

Since Lucretia was standing by Gregory's side as a wedding guest, Caleb was betting not.

"I had a problem arise at the last minute," Caleb claimed. "I couldn't make it."

"It took us forever to get the tickets. We saved a seat for you, but if we'd known you weren't coming, we could have brought someone else."

"Sorry," Caleb said, even though he wasn't sorry.

"Lucretia, don't nag," Gregory said. "It was a Friday. You're aware of how busy Fridays can be for him."

Caleb owned a gambling club, and his old friend and substitute mother, Sybil Jones, ran a faro parlor in it that earned them small fortunes every evening. He hadn't ever planned to engage in such dubious commerce, but he'd stumbled into it after he'd been kicked out of the navy.

With his having few skills other than manning the sails on a sailing ship, he hadn't had many choices. After his career had been yanked away, he hadn't wanted to generate money in such a duplicitous fashion—or even to stay in England for that matter—but as Sybil constantly advised, he didn't force their customers to gamble.

"I'm not nagging," Lucretia said to Gregory. "I simply can't believe he passed up the chance to see Libby Carstairs."

Caleb calmly sipped his drink, pretending scant interest. "Was she as amazing as the gossips contend?"

"Oh, it's impossible to describe her," Lucretia gushed. "She's celebrated for being stunningly beautiful, but she's stunningly talented too."

Gregory scowled. "I thought it was stuff and nonsense. She's likely a charlatan who wasn't even on that accursed island. She's deluded people into listening to her sob stories."

"You did not think it was nonsense." Lucretia's tone was scolding. "Her tale of woe had you sniffling in your kerchief—along with the whole audience."

Caleb snorted at that and asked Gregory, "Were you sniffling?"

"Perhaps a little," Gregory said, "but she was extraordinary. I'm embarrassed to confess it, but her performance was extremely moving."

"Next time you can manage to obtain tickets," Caleb said, "be sure to apprise me. It sounds as if I shouldn't miss her."

The statement was a total lie. He had no intention of ever seeing Miss Libby Carstairs on the stage.

He'd always known who she was: Libby Carstairs, Mystery Girl of the Caribbean! She was one of the three waifs rescued by British navy sailors when she was five. She'd made a career for herself by repeating various accounts of the shipwreck that had left them stranded on a deserted island.

Previously, she'd traveled around the country, spinning yarns about her ordeal in tiny villages and at rural fairs. She'd only recently arrived in town to dazzle all of London.

She'd taken the city by storm, and even though the event had occurred two decades earlier, Londoners couldn't get enough of her sad, mystifying narrative. They couldn't talk about anything else.

He had his own connection to the *Lost* Girls through his despicable, deceased father, Captain Miles Ralston. Caleb never mentioned it—Miles was a sore spot for him and his brother, Blake—but his father was the captain who'd found them, and Caleb had no desire to dwell on any of those memories.

He glanced over Lucretia's shoulder, and Caroline Grey was behind her and gaping at Lucretia as if she'd just heard shocking news. For a moment, his gaze locked on hers, then she vanished into the crowd.

She was a petite female and nimble as a fairy, so she'd been hiding from him, and he couldn't blame her for being so determined to avoid him. He'd uttered several rude insults about her nuptials, and no doubt, she was affronted and annoyed. It served him right for being such an ass.

He couldn't imagine leaving her alone though. She was gorgeously pretty, and she appeared young and vulnerable too. It was obvious she needed a strong, stable man by her side, but Gregory wasn't that man. He wasn't the man *any* woman needed.

Plus, he was amorously attached to Lucretia Starling. Apparently, he was so devoted to her that he'd brought her to his wedding, as if he couldn't bear to be apart from her for even a few days.

Did Miss Grey realize what was happening? Was she curious as to why Lucretia was there? Then again, Gregory had invited numerous acquaintances from London, so Miss Grey probably figured Lucretia was merely another friend.

Should Caleb disabuse her of that notion? Should he tell her truths she desperately ought to discover? He'd blurted out the fact that Gregory gambled, and she'd insisted that he didn't, which proved Gregory had concealed his habit from her.

Should she be informed of the quagmire that was approaching?

He swallowed down a scoff of disgust. He was *not* Caroline Grey's savior, and if she was foolish enough to bind herself to Gregory Grey, it wasn't any of Caleb's business.

It was just that their encounter out on the lane had been so strange. He'd felt the oddest attraction to her, as if the universe approved of their meeting. As Caleb had strolled with her, he'd caught himself leaning in, as if he should lay a hand on her waist and pull her close so their bodies would touch.

He was handsome, dashing, and rich, so he'd had his share of lovers, but he'd never experienced a sensation similar to what Miss Grey had stirred. He was keen to deduce what was causing it, and until he did, he couldn't ignore her.

She snuck onto the verandah, and he grabbed a glass of wine from a passing waiter and slipped away from Gregory and Lucretia to chase after her.

It took him a minute to find her. She was in the garden, walking down a lighted path. She halted under a hanging lantern, and when she turned to study the house, he studied her. She was slender and willowy, but curved in the right places. England was a world of blond girls, and with her black hair and striking blue eyes, she was refreshingly different.

She emitted an alluring mix of beauty and innocence, and she'd have many interesting layers. He would be delighted to peel them all away.

She saw him on the verandah, and for a charged interval, they froze, a peculiar excitement swirling, as if something wild and uncontrollable was about to transpire. What would it be?

He toasted her, downed the wine, then set the glass on the balustrade. He marched to the stairs and started toward her. She didn't scurry off into the dark to escape. She stood her ground, watching warily, as if she wasn't sure what he intended. He wasn't certain himself. Any bizarre conduct was likely.

He continued until they were toe to toe, and instantly, so many sparks ignited that he felt, should he point his finger, fire might shoot from the tip.

"Are you following me, Mr. Ralston?" she asked.

"Yes," he blatantly admitted.

"Why?"

"You fascinate me."

She scoffed. "I do not. Don't be absurd."

"You've dodged me all evening so we haven't had a chance to chat."

He thought she'd deny her ploy, but instead, she confessed, "Yes, I've been dodging you."

"Are you frightened of me? Have my awful manners scared you? Please tell me you're not that silly."

"I'm not afraid of you."

"Then why have you been hiding?"

"We shouldn't be cordial. It's not a good idea."

"Are we to be enemies then? Is that your plan?"

"No, we won't be enemies. We won't be anything."

"Why not? I'm an amiable person and you are too."

She frowned. "Must I provide an explanation?"

"I guess it's not necessary." Besides, he knew the answer: She perceived their heightened connection, and she was about to marry Gregory. It seemed illicit for them to simply be talking. "Why have you tiptoed away from your party?"

She shrugged. "I'm often claustrophobic. The fresh air helps."

"Are you a nervous Nelly? If you claim you are, I won't believe it."

"I have occasional...issues that render me breathless. It's always been a problem for me. Let's just leave it at that."

"Let's just," he murmured.

He wondered what those issues were. Had she been neglected by her family? Had she been abused? The stories about her grandfather were horrific. What must it have been like to grow up under his cruel thumb?

She exuded an aura of vulnerability that would have emboldened a bully like her grandfather. He'd been dead for years though, so how was she treated by Gregory's father, Samson Grey? How was she treated by Gregory?

Not very well, Caleb suspected, and he was being pelted by the most powerful impression that she needed protecting from her Grey relatives, and that he, Caleb, should be the man to supply that protection.

The concept was unfathomable, and he'd already reminded himself that he could never be her savior. He wasn't *anyone's* savior. He'd learned that lesson from guiding his brother, Blake, through his debacle with the navy.

All Caleb had gotten for his efforts was a black stain on his character and a quick trip to being a civilian. He'd been roiling with fury ever since, so while Miss Grey generated many odd impulses, he wouldn't act on any of them.

"May I still call you Caro?" he asked.

"I suppose—when we're alone—but I'd appreciate it if you wouldn't attempt it when we're in my front parlor."

He grinned. "Why shouldn't I?"

"Because I am about to be married, and you are a pompous roué. I can't have my guests thinking you're flirting with me."

"Is that why you decided we shouldn't be cordial? Your guests might think we're flirting?"

"Among other reasons. I've been pondering our earlier meeting."

"Ooh, I love it when a beautiful female ponders me."

"Don't compliment me and don't be smart." She sounded like a grumpy schoolteacher.

"You are so strange. How can you not like compliments?"

"When they're delivered by a cad like you, I'm sure you don't mean them."

"I might mean them, and you are *very* beautiful. It's not a lie."

"You're too much *man* for me to handle."

"I'm too much man for every woman."

"I'm certain that's true, so I'll avoid you at all costs. It's how I cope with dicey situations."

"I'm not a *situation* you can escape by ignoring me."

"It's always worked for me in the past, so I'm positive it will work with you too."

She peered at the house, clearly trying to devise a pithy parting remark, then abandon him in the garden like a spurned suitor, but he couldn't bear to have her go inside just yet. If she did, he'd have to go in too, then he'd have to pretend he didn't know her.

So far, she was the only person in the manor who intrigued him at all. He was bored and simply waiting for the high-stakes gambling to start later on. It was her party, and she was the hostess. Didn't she have a duty to keep him entertained?

"How is your claustrophobia?" he asked. "Has it waned? Or should we walk until it's completely vanquished?"

She inhaled a deep breath. "I'm fine now, but thank you for worrying about my condition."

"We should walk anyway. You can tell me about yourself."

"I never talk about myself."

"Why not?"

"There's not much to say. I live in the country with my relatives. I'm about to wed my cousin. That's the sum total of my biography."

"You're a veritable bump on a log, aren't you? We can talk about me then. I'll wax on about how marvelous I am."

The comment dragged a laugh out of her. "You're so accursedly vain."

"Yes, I am." He extended his arm, urging her to grab hold. She didn't move, and he goaded, "Are you a coward, Caro?"

"I'm not a coward, but you just might be a bully."

"I might be."

"We can walk for a bit, but I'll turn back if you attempt any mischief."

"Such as what?"

"I'll let you know if you cross any lines with me."

"I shall be on my very best behavior."

"I doubt that very much. It's clear you are a wastrel, and I'd better be careful around you."

"Yes, you'd better be."

They strolled away, the lights and noise from the manor quickly fading. Up ahead, he saw a lake and a gazebo.

"Would you like to sit in the gazebo?" she asked.

"I would."

They sauntered over to the structure and climbed into it. She went to the side facing the lake and clambered onto the cushioned bench. She balanced on her knees and stared out at the water. The moon was up, so it was a pretty night, and its silver glow reflected in a magical way.

He plopped down next to her, and he dawdled in the silence, aware that his lack of conversation would spur her to ease the tension by chattering away. He'd learn all sorts of useful details.

As for himself, he perceived everything about her on a level that was nearly frightening in its intensity.

He could smell the soap with which she'd washed, could feel her bodily heat emanating from under her clothes. There was an air about her that called to his masculine drives, making him want to throw her down and engage in wicked conduct she should never allow.

It was peculiar and thrilling, and he was transfixed, struggling to figure out what it indicated.

"Can I ask you a question?" she said.

"You can ask me a thousand questions." He braced, hoping it wasn't a request for devastating information about Gregory.

"When we were in the manor," she said, "Gregory and Mrs. Starling were discussing the London theater. They mentioned a Miss Libby Carstairs and that she performed on the stage there."

"Yes, she's famous in the city."

"Libby Carstairs? You're certain that's her name?"

"Yes. She was one of those *Lost* Girls. From twenty years ago? Do you remember them? They were traveling to Jamaica with their parents, but their ship sank in a storm in the Caribbean."

"Yes, I remember. They were rescued on an island by British sailors."

"The whole country has always been riveted by the tragedy."

"The whole country has been?" She appeared flummoxed by the notion.

"Yes. People still talk about it all the time."

"My goodness," she murmured. "I had no idea. Why is Miss Carstairs on the stage? Is she an...an...actress?"

"I guess you could describe her as an actress. She tells stories and sings songs about her ordeal. I've never seen her, but I'm told she's extraordinary. She's a celebrity now."

"Libby Carstairs is a celebrity?"

"Yes."

"I suppose it makes sense, doesn't it?"

"What makes sense about it? I've never understood the fascination with those girls or that tragedy, and it's been two decades since it happened. I can't believe Miss Carstairs earns money from it."

"I absolutely can," she said dreamily, as if Miss Carstairs was her idol.

He shifted so he could study her, and he was struck again by how beautiful she was. The moon circled her in a silver halo so she seemed to shimmer as if she were an apparition and not a real woman.

He kept staring, his focus potent, demanding she look back at him, but she didn't. Perhaps she was stronger and more stubborn than he'd assumed.

"How long were you in the navy?" she ultimately inquired.

"Ten years."

"Why are you retired? I've always heard it's a difficult existence that's suitable for younger men. Was that it? Was your anatomy failing you?"

He huffed with feigned offense. "I'm hardly decrepit. I'm only thirty, so no, I wasn't failing—as you so delicately put it. And how old are you? Twenty-four?"

"Yes."

"Whew!" he teased. "It's a good thing you're about to marry. You just avoided being a spinster."

"I've been betrothed since I was seventeen, so I was never destined to be a spinster, and you haven't answered me. Why did you leave the navy?"

"I was kicked out."

Her jaw dropped. "What? No! That's not true. You have to be joking."

"I'm not joking, although it's more accurate to say that I was *asked* to quit, and I received a very firm shove as I was marching out the door."

"Are you pulling my leg? Why would you be kicked out? To me, you're precisely the type of person that I, as a British citizen, would want serving our country."

"Thank you."

"Tell me a credible story about your departure—if you can. Don't lie and don't invent one merely to placate me."

"My brother, Blake, landed himself in some trouble, and I took the blame."

"Was he worth the sacrifice?"

"I'm quite sure not."

She chuckled at that. "I forgot you have a brother. It means you must not have been raised by wolves in the forest."

"I definitely had two parents."

He prayed she wouldn't inquire about them, for he never mentioned imperious, depraved, Captain Miles Ralston, who'd been his father. The man was a classic example of how foolish and complex a human could be.

Luckily, she moved on to a new topic. "How do you keep busy now that you're not a sailor anymore? Are you a rich, indolent dandy, living off your fortune?"

"Gad, no. There are no fortunes in my family. I'm a gambler."

"You are not." She scrutinized him, then added, "Are you?"

"Yes, I own a notorious club in London."

"Gambling is immoral, Mr. Ralston. Why would you involve yourself in such a corrupt enterprise?"

"I have to earn an income somehow, and in my own defense, I don't force any scoundrels to wager. They're adults, and they're responsible for their bad choices."

"That sounds like a very tidy method of excusing your complicity in their downfalls."

He shrugged, not inclined to debate the matter. "Probably."

"You gamble too?"

"Occasionally. I'm not reckless about it though. I only play when there's a good reason."

"What would you define as a *good* reason? Name one."

"To pass the time? To make money? To prove a point? To put a cretin in his place when he deserves it?"

"Would you stop if I begged you to?"

He laughed. "No. First off, we're practically strangers, so I would consider it to be incredibly brash of you to suggest it. And second, I like winning and growing wealthy because of it. Why would I stop?"

She slid off her knees and sank down next to him, so they were sitting very close. Their arms were touching, their thighs too. It was dark, and they were alone, so there were a hundred improprieties swirling, but she didn't notice, and he wasn't about to bring them to her attention.

"Is this how you know Gregory?" she asked. "From your gambling club? Out on the lane, you claimed it was the root of your acquaintance, but I didn't believe you."

He contemplated his reply, and he didn't imagine he had a duty to protect Gregory or to hide his secrets from her. "Yes, he's a member at my club."

She looked aghast. "There are memberships?"

"Well, yes. We don't admit just anybody. It's quite posh, so the standards are very high."

"Has Gregory been there very often?"

"Every night."

"He *gambles* every night?"

"I realize it's hard for you to fathom, but it's a regular mode of entertainment among a certain fast crowd."

"But... but... Gregory is so normal when he's at home."

"He's very normal. He simply amuses himself as all his friends amuse themselves."

"Perhaps he should find some new friends."

"Perhaps," Caleb agreed.

"Is he in debt?"

"They all are. It comes with the territory."

"To whom does he owe money? And how much is owed?"

They'd arrived at a thorny juncture that would take them down a road he didn't intend to travel with her.

Gregory owed money to everyone, but mostly, he owed it to Caleb. They continued playing, with Gregory anxious to win back what he'd lost, but he never could. Caleb was too skilled, and he had great luck. He was clever with numbers and at calculating the odds. Gregory never had any luck at all.

In fact, Caleb was positive the rash oaf would eventually wager away Grey's Corner. It had to be why Gregory had invited him to the wedding. He wanted Caleb to view the property, to understand its value. Or maybe he wanted Caleb to see that Gregory had a fine home and Caleb should cancel the debt and let him keep it.

It would have been a viable ploy—if they'd been the least bit cordial—but they weren't cordial. Gregory was desperate to be able to gamble at Caleb's club with his chums. If Caleb finally cut him off, he'd be ostracized by the very fellows he'd worked relentlessly to glom onto.

"If you'd like information about Gregory's finances," he carefully said, "you should speak to him directly."

"Oh, I will, but it would be nice if you could provide me with some ammunition before I go into battle."

"I can't aid you in that quest."

"I was afraid that would be your position."

"How old were you when you became engaged to Gregory?" he asked. "Seventeen? Why did you consent?"

"Why wouldn't I have? My uncle suggested it, and I've known Gregory all my life. He's always been kind to me."

"Is that what you're searching for in a husband? Someone who's kind?"

"In my book, kindness is a worthy trait."

"I suppose, although I've never had a chance to discover if that's true or not, and you haven't exactly explained why you're marrying Gregory. Nor have you clarified what took you so long."

She tsked with exasperation. "You can be so irritating."

"If I'm keen to learn something, I don't beat around the bush. I delve right to the heart of any matter that's vexing me."

She glared like a fussy nanny. "Will this satisfy your curiosity? I never expected to wed. When my uncle raised the prospect, I was delighted—and a tad astonished."

He scowled. "Why would you have thought you'd never wed? You're beautiful, educated, and interesting. Any man would be glad to have you."

"I have no dowry, so who would want me?"

"Just Gregory apparently, but if you don't have any money, why is he so eager? Is he more altruistic than another beau might have been?"

She grinned an impish grin. "Perhaps he simply likes me more than any other woman."

"If he likes you so much, why the seven-year delay?"

He stared into her pretty blue eyes until he was drowning in them.

He yearned to mention Lucretia Starling. He yearned to talk about Gregory's problems with alcohol, how he drank to excess, then wagered what he couldn't afford to lose. He yearned to point out how unhinged Gregory could be, how self-centered and spoiled.

Yet he wouldn't climb out on that limb. Her uncle had arranged a match for her—to her cousin. It would give her a permanent home, unless of course Gregory frittered it away. Caleb would have to reflect on that situation.

He liked her very much, and he felt sorry for her. But then, he felt sorry for all the wives who visited him and wept over their husbands' negligent habits. He was regularly begged to forgive debts, but he was never swayed by sentiment. He couldn't save his stupid, careless club members, and he wouldn't presume to try.

Caro might wind up crushed by the weight of Gregory's calamity. Should he warn her to beware of what was approaching? Or should he mind his own business and butt out?

"Gregory is a dedicated bachelor, Mr. Ralston," she said, "but he's turned thirty. It's time for him to move forward with his life."

"He's a bachelor, so he waited seven years?" Caleb's tone was incredulous.

"My uncle asked me to wed him. We're a family, and you have a brother who landed you in an ocean of hot water with the navy, so you comprehend why I'd be loyal and behave as is expected of me by my relatives."

"You don't have to proceed you know," he said as he had out on the lane.

"I realize I don't *have* to. I want to."

"Do you?"

The question hung in the air between them, and ultimately, she said, "Why are you so compelled to keep offering that inappropriate comment?"

"I'm merely stating the facts."

"Will you use insomnia again as your excuse for being rude?"

"No, I'll confess to being a rude person in general."

"You're determined to make me distrust my decision, but I can't figure out why."

"Maybe I'm simply worried about you."

"I doubt that very much." She slid away and stood. "I have to get back. I've been gone for ages, and I'm sure I've been missed."

"Don't depart just yet. Tarry with me a bit longer."

"I shouldn't have come with you in the first place, but I allowed you to drag me away. I must be growing deranged."

"You like me more than you should," he cockily said. "It's a common dilemma that females suffer with regard to me."

She rolled her eyes. "You are the vainest creature I've ever met."

At the thought of her fleeing, he was actually a tad morose, and he asked, "Would you call me Caleb?"

"No, but I'm flattered that you suggested it."

Without thinking, he clasped hold of her hand. She froze, and he froze too, those pesky sparks flying again.

"Stay," he murmured.

"To do what?"

"Sit down, and I'll show you."

"I'll just bet you would."

She yanked away and hurried off. As she reached the stairs, he said, "Caro?"

"What?"

"Let's sneak out to the gazebo every evening that I'm in residence."

She gasped with offense. "You and I? Sneak off together? You are mad. I'm convinced of it, and *I* am about to marry."

Then she vanished.

He dawdled in the dark, listening as her strides faded. When it was completely silent again, he rose to his knees, his elbows balanced on the rail so he could stare out at the lake.

"What am I doing here?" he asked the quiet night, but the night had no answer.

His doldrums would improve the next day, once his brother, Blake, arrived. He felt better when Blake was around to guard his back. With Blake present, he wouldn't be so adrift, and Blake would tell him that Gregory deserved his dire fate. Blake would tell him not to waffle, not to second-guess.

Blake was a great judge of human nature, so he would be right.

Chapter

3

CAROLINE STROLLED DOWN THE empty hall. It was very late, the party over, everyone in bed. Mr. Ralston wasn't the only one plagued by occasional insomnia. With so many guests in the house, the energy in the air was all wrong, and she couldn't sleep.

She'd given up and had snuck down to wander and snoop. It was a habit she'd commenced when she'd first returned from the Caribbean. She'd been whisked away from Libby and Joanna without having the chance to say goodbye. It was a cruel act that still haunted her.

She'd been sent to live with her Grandfather Walter. He'd been vicious and unpleasant, and so were the servants. They'd gaped at her as if she were an alien creature, so she'd had no allies in the manor. Gregory and Janet had resided with their father, Samson, at his property several miles away. They'd rarely visited, so there had been no children with whom she could play.

The place had been lonely and frightening. She'd mostly hidden in the nursery, tended by various grouchy nannies, then a succession of lazy, incompetent governesses.

The nights had been the worst. The ancient mansion creaked and groaned, and she'd been terrified that ghosts were stalking her. She'd begun meandering through the downstairs parlors, and it was odd to admit, but she took great solace from sitting in the chilly rooms when there was no one to spy and tattle.

Her conduct felt illicit and dangerous, and the joy she received from her petty insubordination always had her wondering what sort of person she was deep down. If left to her own devices, what mischief might she pursue? It was a liberating question.

She tiptoed into a deserted salon and walked over to the window to gaze at the moon shining over the park. Her mind was awhirl with problems.

She had to speak with Gregory about his gambling. She had to press him for answers about their finances, as well as how he expected them to carry on once they were married. She thought he should sell his bachelor's lodging in town and come home. As his wife, she had the right to make that demand, didn't she?

She had to chat with Uncle Samson too. After she was wed, she'd be the *official* lady of the house. Would she have full authority? Would he agree to cede any?

And what about her cousin, Janet? Janet viewed herself as a liberal blue-stocking, so she was refusing to ever wed. Should Caroline interfere in that situation? Should she persuade her uncle to choose a husband for Janet anyway? Or should she ignore it?

What about Libby Carstairs? Evidently, Libby was performing on the stage in London. She was a celebrity who'd grown famous from sharing stories about their tribulations in the Caribbean, which was such a shocking revelation.

Though she'd always deemed it to be peculiar, Caroline's family treated her experience as a shameful secret. They'd warned her to never discuss her past, to never tell people who she was. For the most part, she didn't. The older neighbors knew her history, but it was never mentioned, so she felt as if the tragedy had been her fault.

She never went to London, but should she ask to go? Gregory had a residence there, and she was about to be his bride. Why shouldn't a trip be permitted?

She wanted to be with Libby so badly that it was like an ache in her heart. If Libby was singing songs about their ordeal, she couldn't have forgotten any of it. Surely she'd remember Caroline. They could become friends again, and Libby would commiserate over what Caroline's life had been like after they'd been brought home.

She laid her palm on the cool glass of the window, and she sent a quiet wish out to the universe that she'd find a way to connect with Libby. If she insisted on going to London, her uncle and Gregory would be stunned, but she wasn't a prisoner at Grey's Corner.

Who was there to stop her from contacting Libby? Perhaps Janet would like to accompany her to town. Janet's presence would calm any reservations her uncle or Gregory might voice.

Excitement flooded through her, and she murmured, "I'll come to London. I swear I'll figure out how!"

From behind her, a man said, "Who are you talking to?"

She jumped a foot and whipped around. Caleb Ralston was seated on the sofa and staring at the hearth where no fire burned.

"Why are you lurking in here all by yourself?" she asked. "It's horrendously rude of you not to have spoken up immediately. You scared me to death!"

"I see that, and you haven't explained yourself. Who were you talking to?"

"No one."

"Liar."

He pushed himself to his feet and sauntered over to stand next to her. Their proximity instantly generated a powerful surge of energy.

If she'd had any sense—and recently, she appeared to have very little—she'd have shoved by him and returned to her bedchamber, but
he claimed to be fascinated by her, and she'd never previously been
declared fascinating.

His words had stoked her hidden vanity, and it made her eager to
linger by his side to hear what other thrilling compliments he might
bestow. Her burgeoning interest in him was very, very wrong, but she
couldn't force herself away. He simply tantalized her in a manner she
shouldn't have allowed, but couldn't seem to prevent.

"You vowed to visit someone," he said. "Who was it?"

Brashly, she admitted, "Miss Libby Carstairs. I want to see her on
the stage."

He chuckled and shook his head. "You are so strange. Of all the
names I might have predicted you'd utter, hers was the very last one."

"You told me she's very famous and audiences love her. Why
shouldn't I have a chance to see her too? I never travel to the city. Why
shouldn't I be permitted a small adventure?"

"Why indeed?"

She wasn't about to clarify her fixation with Libby Carstairs, so she
changed the subject. "Why are you sitting in here?"

"I couldn't sleep. When I confessed that I suffer from insomnia, I
wasn't joking."

"What keeps you awake at night?" she asked.

He countered with, "What keeps *you* awake? I'll tell if you will."

She scoffed with amusement. "A recitation of my worries would
sound incredibly dull to you."

"You should list them for me then. If they're as tedious as you imagine, it might be the tonic I need to doze off. I'll be slumbering in two
seconds flat."

She smiled. He really was charming, but he was hazardous to her
equilibrium too. His arrival had lit a fire under her discontentment.

Suddenly, she was questioning her choices and her path. She was wondering if she should wed Gregory after all, if it was a wise decision.

They shifted toward each other, their shoulders leaned against the window. They were alone, and the most delicious intimacy flared. She felt she could confide any woe, and he would empathize and understand.

"What time do you suppose it is?" he asked.

"The clock chimed four a bit ago, so dawn is about to break. How long have you been loafing on that sofa?"

"Not long. I was gambling, but I got weary of the company, so I quit."

She scowled. "Who is gambling?"

"Gregory and his friends from town. There is quite a game in progress in a rear salon."

At the news, she was astonished. Grey's Corner was her home, was Janet's home, was her Uncle Samson's home. They had a house full of impressionable footmen and housemaids. How dare Gregory bring his dissolute habits into their midst!

She suffered a rare burst of fury that was potent in its intensity, but she tamped it down. Usually, her rage rippled just below the surface, and she never unleashed it. She was terrified it might incinerate the whole world.

"Gambling is regrettable," she tepidly said. "I can't say I'm glad you told me about it."

"Gregory is addicted to wagering. It's obvious you weren't aware of it, so I'm sorry to have apprised you."

"I guess it's better than wallowing in the dark and not knowing."

"I wouldn't agree to that. Some secrets should remain buried."

"Now that you've informed me of Gregory's situation, will you tell me how to deal with it?"

"I'm not smart enough to counsel you on the topic. There are so many men in London who labor under the same failing. It's an impossible dilemma, and there doesn't appear to be a cure—except for the fellow involved to simply give it up. It's the only remedy that seems to work."

"Does anyone ever stop?" she asked.

"Not that I've witnessed."

She sighed with resignation. There would have to be a stern discussion with her uncle and with Gregory, and she couldn't picture it. Her life cruised down a smooth road where she never complained or rocked any boats. She'd learned as a girl, through her grandfather's vicious chastisements, to keep her mouth shut and remember her place.

But she managed the manor for Uncle Samson, and she was about to wed Gregory. Clearly, she had to assume more control, but the notion exhausted her.

At the moment, she didn't want to fret about Gregory though. She'd stumbled into a private encounter with Mr. Ralston, and she wouldn't waste it. He'd be gone shortly, and she'd be a wife and bogged down by the domesticity that drove her cousin, Janet, to rail about the unfairness of women's lives. Caroline would never see him again, but she'd fondly recollect their conversations. For years, she'd mull every word.

"What was your brother's trouble that got you kicked out of the navy?" she asked.

"If I confess it, will you promise not to call me an idiot?"

"It depends on how idiotically you acted. I will be extremely blunt in my assessment of the debacle, and I shall give you my valid opinion."

"I was afraid you'd say that. Maybe I can't bear to hear your *valid* opinion. Maybe I'd like you to lie and say I conducted myself brilliantly."

"It's probably not in the cards."

"No, probably not."

"You mentioned that you were protecting your brother. What did he do?"

"It wasn't him so much as his friends. He was cordial with some aristocrats' sons, and *they* were pilfering supplies and pocketing the money."

"Aristocrats' sons! Stealing from the navy?"

"A lot of those boys are pinching pennies. They're all waiting for their noble fathers to cock up their toes so they can inherit the bank accounts. Until then, they often don't have much in the way of funds. My brother was helping them, but he was young and stupid and didn't realize the danger."

"And the two of you are not aristocrats' sons."

"No. We're very, very common."

"Your brother would have been charged with the theft. The others, who had titled, important fathers, would have waltzed away with no penalty imposed."

"You've pegged the predicament exactly."

"So *you*—being the loyal sibling you are—stepped forward and took the blame."

If there had been a lamp lit, his cheeks would have been flushed with chagrin. "Yes. Was I an idiot?"

"Absolutely. What became of your brother?"

"He's still in the navy, but I beat him bloody for being so gullible and running with a bad crowd. He mostly behaves himself now."

"You beat him bloody?"

"He's incredibly stubborn. It requires quite a bit of persuasion to make him listen."

She chuckled. "I can't ever decide if you're being truthful or not."

"He'll be here tomorrow. Or I suppose it's today, isn't it? You'll see what he's like, and you can ask him how I handled it. He'll tell you."

"Do you miss the navy?"

"Every minute that ticks by."

"I'm sorry to hear it. I really am."

"I used to imagine I'd draw my last breath on a navy ship. I was that devoted, so it was hard to walk away. I think I'm bitter."

"Of course you are."

She sensed it was a stunning admission for him and that he was a proud man. She wondered if he'd ever shared the details about the fiasco with anyone but her. She told herself he hadn't, that the room and the dark and the quiet were fostering confidences.

Without pondering whether she should or not, she reached out and patted his wrist, anxious to comfort him in some small way, and he surprised her by linking their fingers as if they were adolescents who were courting.

"Was it difficult growing up here?" he asked.

"It was very difficult. My grandfather raised me, and he wasn't the kindest person."

"What happened to your parents?"

"They died when I was little." She didn't explain *how* they died: during a violent storm in the Caribbean. It spurred too many questions she'd learned not to answer. "He had to take custody of me, but he didn't want custody. He wasn't a father figure by any means, but I get along with my uncle. It's been much easier since he became head of the family."

"And he found you a husband. Let's not forget that grand gesture."

"That he did, and don't you dare denigrate either my uncle or my future spouse. I'm fortunate to be marrying, and I won't have you making me second-guess."

"Are you second-guessing? Am I having that much of an effect on you?"

"No!" she hastily said. "You're a contrarian who likes to stir mischief. I won't allow you to stir any with me."

"Well, then, I won't even try."

He gazed down at her, his blue eyes studying her with an intensity that was astonishing. How had she survived for twenty-four years without being stared at like that? How would she live without it after he left?

Of a certainty, Gregory never looked at her so fondly. He barely noticed her, and when he deigned to pay her some attention, he treated her just as he treated his sister, Janet.

Caroline had always believed she didn't mind his lack of strong regard, but should she have searched for a husband who adored her? Should she have demanded a spouse who might have delivered a love match?

She'd presumed those sorts of relationships only occurred in stage plays and romantic sonnets. Was amour real? Could a girl marry the perfect man?

The notion that she was contemplating such an unusual conclusion was alarming, and it underscored how reckless she was being by tarrying with him. What good could come from his fomenting so much yearning? It would simply lead to frustration in the end.

Yet even as she reflected on those issues, he was still holding her hand, and she hadn't pulled away.

"Do you ever wish you had a different life?" he asked. "Do you ever wish you could pack a bag and head out into the world?"

"I wish it all the time."

"If you could leave and go anywhere, where would it be?"

"I'd pick a tropical island in the Caribbean." She frequently dreamed about her deserted island. Was there a way to discover its location? If she had a ship to command, could she sail it into that pretty bay?

"A tropical island?" he said. "How exotic of you."

"I read a book once, where the author described the beautiful turquoise color of the water. I'd like to see it for myself."

"I have seen it, and it's spectacular."

"You've been there?" Her voice dripped with envy.

"I was in the navy, remember? I was stationed in the Caribbean for years."

"You men are so lucky. You can travel around the globe and have adventures. We women have to sit at home and knit by the fire."

"Are you filled with wanderlust?"

"I am, and what about you? Are you still brimming with wander-lust or did it vanish after you were forced out of the navy?"

"It never completely vanishes."

"If *you* could go anywhere, where would it be?"

"I'd probably return to the Caribbean. I was born in Jamaica."

"You were not!"

"I was."

The news made them seem even closer. She felt such a connection to Jamaica and the Caribbean. It was a spot that haunted her, and he was born there! Fate must have brought them together.

"I lived there until I was ten," he said.

"What happened then?" she asked.

"My mother died, and my father had already passed away. Our vicar sent us to our British relatives."

"Then at the first opportunity, you joined the navy and went back."

"Yes, but I'm trapped in London now, and I can't escape. I'm earning so much money all of a sudden, and my brother, Blake, has been stationed here. I couldn't abandon him. Plus, my dear friend, Sybil, is here too. She helps me run my business."

Caroline suffered an odd spurt of jealousy. "Who is Sybil? Is she a sweetheart?"

"No, she was my mother's maid when Blake and I were boys. She accompanied us to England to ensure we arrived safe and sound, then she stayed on and acted as our champion."

"Why did you need a champion?"

"We weren't exactly welcomed by my father's kin." She must have looked as if she'd pry into topics best left alone because he quickly said, "It's a long story. I'll tell you about it someday."

She let the matter rest. She understood about skeletons in closets, so she changed the subject. "If you weren't stranded in England, would you reside in Jamaica?"

"I would." He grinned a devastating grin. "Would you come with me?"

"Oh, yes," she teasingly replied, for she would *never* board a ship again. "I would flee my marriage and my husband, just so I could sinfully traipse off to the Caribbean with you."

"It's a lovely fantasy, isn't it?"

"It is."

They were quiet for a bit and staring outside. Out on the horizon, a hint of dawn appeared. And he was still holding her hand.

"What are your plans once the sun is up?" he eventually inquired.

"I'll be busy with chores. We have more guests showing up this afternoon."

"My brother is one of them."

"I can't wait to meet him, so I can ask him about the thrashing you administered after he got you kicked out of the navy. Was he ever sorry?"

He snorted at that. "Sorry enough, I suppose."

"Has his behavior improved? Is he choosing better friends?"

"No and no. He's simply learned to be more furtive."

"If you had to save him again, would you?"

"Of course. He's my brother. If he's not worth saving, who would be?"

"You just might be a very good man."

"Not really. I'm merely pretending to be gallant, so you'll assume I'm amazing."

"You're much too vain, and I wouldn't want to stroke your ego."

"It is very inflated. I admit it."

"Will I like your brother more than you?"

"Everyone does."

She chuckled and finally tried to pull away. She'd been very reckless, and there was no excuse for her conduct except to note that no one had ever held her hand before. Not since she'd been on the island with Libby and Joanna. If there was an adult who had after that, she couldn't recall.

The sense of well-being he generated was too powerful to ignore, and she couldn't bear to have the encounter conclude. But she was betrothed, and he was a guest who'd been invited to her wedding. It was scandalous to be loafing in the dark with him.

Unfortunately—or fortunately, depending on one's point of view—he wouldn't release her.

"Are you leaving?" he asked.

"I have to."

"Why?"

"I've sequestered myself with you again, and I can't figure out why. I keep telling myself to stay away from you, but I can't manage it."

"You shouldn't stay away from me. I'm the most interesting thing that's ever happened to you."

She smirked. "That is definitely not true."

"What has ever happened to you that was more interesting than meeting me?"

A thousand words flooded to the tip of her tongue, but they were words she would never voice aloud: *I'm one of the three Mystery Girls of the Caribbean. I was on that ship with Libby Carstairs when it sank all those years ago. I survived with her and was rescued by navy sailors too, but my family deems it a shocking story, so I never talk about it.*

What event could ever occur in a female's life that would be more astonishing than that?

"I stand corrected," she said. "You are, by far and away, the most interesting thing that has ever happened to me."

"That's more like it."

"You are also an incredible bully."

"Yes, and you are such a milksop. It's easy to push you around. After sufficient acquaintance, what do you imagine I'll be able to coerce you into doing?"

The answer to that question was too frightening to consider, for she was certain he could spur her to all sorts of activity she shouldn't contemplate.

Each time she stumbled on him, she wound up tarrying longer than was wise. Where would it lead? Where would it end?

Before she realized what he intended, he dipped down and kissed her. The move was sudden and unexpected, and for the briefest instant, she dawdled like a statue and let him proceed.

She'd been kissed in the past, at the harvest fair and other places, when she was much younger. Once her betrothal to Gregory had been announced, she'd never walked with any boys again, so it had been ages since anyone had dared.

She was stunned and aghast and happier than she could ever remember being, but she was also blatantly aware that she was participating in a very wicked, very immoral deed. She was *engaged*! When her wedding was so close, why would she allow such mischief? More importantly, why would she enjoy it so much?

Her heart was pounding so hard she feared it might burst out of her chest. She lingered for a second, then a second more, then she physically yanked herself away, but it took such ferocious effort that she staggered and had to latch onto a nearby chair to keep herself upright.

"What are you thinking!" she wailed with dismay.

"I was *thinking* that you look like a woman who desperately needed to be kissed."

"I'm about to be married!"

"Poor you," he murmured.

His comment brought on a surge of bizarre emotion. She wanted to throw herself back into his arms, to kiss him and kiss him and never stop. She wanted to risk everything—her security, her respected position as a wife—simply to have him hold her for a few more minutes.

What was wrong with her? Why did he have such a potent effect?

He was very handsome, very different from other men, and she was so lonely. Was that the problem? Had she been a spinster for too many years?

"Goodnight, Mr. Ralston," she said.

"Call me Caleb."

"I doubt I ever will."

She jerked away and ran from the room, recognizing—if she didn't hurry—she'd never escape.

She yearned to grab the lapels of his coat, to beg him to take her away from quiet, stifling Grey's Corner. She wanted him to help her, to save her, to rescue her from the conclusion that was winging toward her on her wedding day.

But she'd been rescued once by navy sailors, and she'd learned from the experience that a person could completely change her circumstances, but that nothing changed at all.

She raced to the stairs and headed to her bedchamber, and all the while, she scolded herself. She had to buck up and be satisfied with her lot. Caleb Ralston was like a sparkly object that Fate was dangling in front of her to tempt her in ways she shouldn't be tempted.

He was excitement and fun and thrilling kisses in the dark, but Gregory was real life. Gregory was home and family and the world she'd been given by her grandfather. She'd taught herself to be content with that. She always had been and always would be.

Chapter

4

"I HAVE A QUESTION for both of you, and I'd like your opinion about it."

"Yes, Caroline, what is it?"

Samson Grey peered at his son, Gregory, and they exchanged a patronizing smile. Caroline was a peculiar female, and it was always humorous to discover how her convoluted brain was churning away.

They were in the dining parlor, just the three of them with no guests stumbling in yet to eat breakfast. Three footmen hovered, ready to be helpful, and he bit down a smug nod of satisfaction. His father, Walter, had been a grouchy, unlikeable miser who had had his fingers in several very large pots of money, but he'd deemed the funds too ungodly to spend.

He'd forced them to stagger about like paupers, dressed in black as if they were Puritans in perpetual mourning. They'd had to sit through nightly Bible readings and listen to Walter's constant admonitions to walk the straight and narrow. Heaven forbid that any of them exhibit a whiff of independence as Caroline's father—his brother, Winston—had done.

Winston's antics had driven the tightfisted penny-pincher to paroxysms of outrage, and it was such a relief to have the irksome codger dead. As to Samson, he wasn't pious, wasn't devout, and in his view, money wasn't godly or ungodly. It was just money, and he had no qualms about using it to make his life pleasurable.

"I learned the most intriguing information yesterday," Caroline said, "and I'm bewildered by it. Apparently, my old shipmate, Libby Carstairs, is in London and performing on the stage there. She's very famous."

"Oh, yes," Gregory said. "She's taken the city by storm."

"I'm told that her notoriety is due to her telling stories about our ordeal."

"Who told you that?" Samson asked.

"Gregory's London friend, Mr. Ralston. He claims the tale has always riveted the country and that people never get tired of talking about it."

"What a ridiculous assertion," Samson said. "I have no idea why Mr. Ralston would have developed such a bizarre notion, but trust me, no one is tittering about your scandal."

"It wasn't a scandal, Uncle," she mulishly said. "I wish you'd quit calling it that. I was simply a little girl who survived in mysterious circumstances and against all odds. I would appreciate it if you wouldn't be so flippant about it."

Samson never argued with her. She was a woman and not worth the wasted breath. He turned to Gregory and asked, "Son, are people fixated on Caroline's ancient ordeal?"

"Gad, no. I can't imagine Ralston believing such nonsense *or* feeling the need to convince Caroline of it."

"I want to go to London," Caroline blatantly announced.

"Whatever for?" Gregory inquired.

"I'd like to visit Libby. I'd like to find out how she's fared over the years."

Gregory peeked over at Samson, then said, "I don't see why we can't arrange a trip for you."

Samson hid a grin and dug into his food. Gregory would never take Caroline to town. He would never arrange a trip. He had a life there and a life at Grey's Corner, and they would never intersect. Caroline didn't understand that reality though, so it was easy to distract her and have her assume they'd agreed.

They would never draw attention to the fact that she was a *Lost Girl* from that stupid shipwreck. They'd worked hard to ensure there were no reminders of it.

His father, Walter, had tamped them down because he'd viewed her parents as sinners whom the Good Lord had killed as punishment. Samson and Gregory had a more selfish interpretation of it. They couldn't have anyone looking too closely at Caroline and wondering what sort of estate or Last Will her father might have left behind.

"I'm very anxious about London," she said, "so I'd like to go right away. Could we manage it the week after the ceremony?"

"That would be fine," Gregory said. "Perhaps we could ride to London together once I head back."

"I'd like that very much. Thank you." Caroline nodded, evidently deeming the topic resolved. He and Gregory might have relaxed, but she added, "There's another matter too."

Gregory chuckled. "Will it give me indigestion?"

They got along like fond siblings, which a more romantic person might have declared to be an awful basis for a marriage. Not Samson though. He was a happy widower who, on his father's advice, had shackled himself to a vicious termagant, and he thought fondness was a terrific foundation for a couple.

"It might upset your stomach," she said and, without pausing, she asked, "Have you been gambling?"

For an instant, Gregory froze, then he shook off his stupor. "No. Where did you hear that?"

"From Mr. Ralston again."

Samson jumped in. "If that's even remotely true, then you're spending too much time gossiping with him."

Caroline was undeterred, and she glared at Gregory. "After everyone went to bed, were you wagering for high stakes in a rear parlor?"

"It was just for pennies, Caroline," Gregory claimed. "You needn't fret over it."

"I am fretting. I won't have a husband who's a gambler." She shifted her cool gaze to Samson and said, "You can't be excited about this. Please tell me you're on my side."

"I'm absolutely on your side." He glared at Gregory too. "You haven't been gambling, have you, Gregory?"

"No more than anybody else."

"There can't be *any* gambling," Samson said. "I'm sorry, but Caroline is correct to worry about this. It's not like you to be so foolish, and I have to put my foot down."

"Your wish is my command," Gregory blithely retorted, then he grinned at her. "I'll stop—immediately—and your severe tone informs me that you'll learn how to be a wife with scarcely any effort at all. You've always known how to scold me, and with our nuptials so close, you're being even more adept than usual."

She scoffed. "It doesn't take much learning or effort to demand you behave yourself."

"I apologize that Ralston distressed you," Gregory told her. "I'll talk to him."

"You don't have to talk to him," Caroline huffed. "I'm not a child, and I can listen to a man's words and deduce if they seem credible or not. I don't need you to sift through them for me. I'm perfectly capable of making up my own mind."

"Of course you are," Gregory hastily said. "*I* didn't mean to distress you either."

"You haven't, but could I have a few minutes alone with you today? Just you and me, without any of your London friends butting in? I'd like to discuss numerous issues."

"What issues?"

"Well, where you'll be living after the wedding and how *we* will live after it. I'd like you home in the country rather than in town. I'd also like to have some notion of our finances so I have a better idea about our household budget and expenses."

"Yes, we can definitely chat about all of it. How about this afternoon?"

"I'll find you around three o'clock."

"I'm looking forward to it."

With Gregory consenting to a private conversation, she appeared placated. She was finished with her meal, and she tossed down her napkin and left. Samson waved the footmen out so he and Gregory were sequestered by themselves.

As the door was shut behind them, Gregory scowled and inquired, "What bee has gotten into her bonnet?"

Caroline never spoke up for herself or chastised others, and Samson shrugged. "She's about to be a bride, so her life will be dramatically altered. She's probably suffering from a bad case of jitters."

"I hope that's all it is. I would hate to suppose matrimony will change her into a shrew."

"It won't," Samson said. "This is Caroline. There are never any surprises with her."

"It happens to husbands constantly. A fellow assumes he's found a sweet, biddable girl, and next thing he knows... *poof!* She's morphed into a harpy."

"I don't like Mr. Ralston being so cozy with her. We can't have a handsome Londoner filling her head with drivel. You should tell him to stay away from her."

"Believe me, I will."

Years earlier, they'd decided Caroline would wed Gregory. They were so near the end, and they couldn't have any wrenches thrown into the mix.

Gregory went over to the sideboard and retrieved the bottle of brandy that was discreetly hidden there. He returned to the table and added a huge dollop to his tea. He swallowed it down, shuddered with a sort of obscene relief, then muttered, "Ah...hair of the dog."

Gregory's disgusting habits were beginning to take a toll on his condition. He was balding and fat, his face lined from vice and dissipation, so he seemed much older than thirty. Samson, on the other hand, was aging magnificently. At fifty, he was thin and dapper, his blue eyes alert and calculating, his blond hair having faded to silver, but it was still all there.

Gregory—poor boy—took after his unattractive, deceased mother, and Samson's physical differences from Gregory were so stark it was difficult to imagine they were father and son.

"I see your drinking hasn't lessened," Samson said.

"Don't nag, Father."

"Your gambling is out of control too. You're at such a low point that even Caroline has noticed. How many times will you force me to mention it?"

"I never force you to mention it," Gregory snidely replied. "*You* are the one who's determined to complain about every paltry detail."

"Maybe Caroline's suggestion is best. Maybe you should move home. It might diminish your need for extravagance."

"I'm not extravagant. As you're fully aware, I have costs in the city that would never accrue in the country. I spend only what is required as a man of Quality."

"We were never rich before. Is that your problem? You can't moderate your conduct. You're like a toddler who's suddenly been given an entire bowl of candy and gobbles it down all at once."

"I merely enjoy the finer things in life, but so do you. Don't pretend you're turning into a Puritan like Grandfather Walter. We both agreed on this path, and it's a little late now for you to grow sanctimonious."

"I realize that fact, but you've just requested another quarterly advance from the trust. It's the fifth time this year. I can't in good conscience keep funding such luxury. You must live within your means."

"I'll start when you do."

"It would help matters along if you would rid yourself of Mrs. Starling. She's too avaricious, and you indulge her whims to a ridiculous level."

"Leave Lucretia out of it," Gregory said. "I've repeatedly warned you to mind your own business about her. Why won't you listen?"

"Don't be smart with me. She'll be your ruin someday. Mark my words."

Gregory laughed condescendingly. "Let's simply get through the wedding, shall we? Let's get the money secured. Then we can quarrel over it."

He stood and stomped out, and as his strides faded, Samson slumped in his chair.

For the past decade—ever since his father had died—he'd felt as if he was perched on the edge of a cliff. He could have fallen off in either direction: to fiscal affluence and ease or to fiscal destruction and the unraveling of all his plans.

He'd pushed for the betrothal, but Gregory was so reckless, so anxious to frolic in London, that he'd refused to proceed. He believed Caroline would never renege and sever their engagement.

He stupidly assumed that no other man would ever want her, that no other man could entice her, then persuade her to back out. And of course, underlying it all, there was always the possibility that she might discover the genuine source of their prosperity.

Everyone presumed his father, Walter, had been rich but miserly, and it was why they'd carried on like paupers. But Walter hadn't been wealthy. Far from it. The estate accounts had been empty because of his substantial donations to the Church. He'd been convinced that he could buy his way into Heaven.

No, the money they were gleefully spending was Caroline's money, inherited from her deceased father, Winston. It was held in trust for her, with Walter, then Samson being the trustee.

When Winston was young, he'd been wild and free, and he'd regularly gone adventuring. Once, he'd even journeyed to Africa with the famed explorer, Sir Sidney Sinclair. In a stroke of astounding luck, he'd returned to England as owner of a diamond mine. Of all things!

After he'd perished in the shipwreck, Walter had declared it a gift from the Devil, generated in a heathen land and showered on a wicked son. He wouldn't touch a farthing of it.

Well, after he'd passed on to his Great Reward, Samson had had no qualms about using it. Because it had sat quietly unexploited by Walter, it had grown to a fantastical amount, so Caroline was an incredible heiress. Samson's most monumental fear was that she'd learn about it and demand to be involved in deciding how it was distributed.

That could never happen. *He* controlled her fortune. She was a woman after all, which automatically indicated she could never understand her finances. It was appropriate that she have male guidance in managing them. Her marriage to Gregory would simply guarantee that naught went wrong.

If she realized the truth later on and was angry about it, she'd be Gregory's wife, so there would be no remedy available for her to fix what had occurred.

Her final trust fund would vest on her twenty-fifth birthday. If she wasn't a bride by then, thousands of pounds would be squandered. The potential loss was what it had taken to goad Gregory into matrimony. His son was that irresponsible.

The wedding was in six days. It would all be over shortly, and Caroline would be bound to them forever. No other beau could swoop in and charm her. No other man could lure her—and her fortune—away from them.

It would be wrapped up nice and tight, and due to their shrewd manipulation, *she* would never be the wiser. Yet, if by chance, the situation was revealed, she would be Gregory's wife and never get to voice an opinion about it.

In that, he and Gregory had never disagreed at all.

⁓

"Have you talked to them?"

"Yes."

"And...?"

Janet gazed at Caroline, and she couldn't completely conceal her exasperation. She had no doubt as to how her father and brother would have treated Caroline. They'd have patted her on the head like a pet dog, then sent her on her way, with her feeling she'd accomplished her goal.

The two men were like slippery eels, but then, all men were. They said one thing, but meant another. They promised one thing, but did another. Early on, she'd figured out how duplicitous they could be, and it had formed the foundation of her feelings about the male gender. That—and a hefty dose of radical reading.

Women were waking up to the arduous burdens placed on them, and they were being very vocal about their grievances. In the past year, Janet had devoured a dozen books written by the most intelligent, aggrieved women in the kingdom. They insisted that it was time to yank men from their pedestals of power.

Men had ensured that society's benefits were showered on them alone. Women couldn't travel or live on their own or handle their own money. They were expected to wed the oafs their fathers picked for them, and if they refused an arranged match, they could be deemed hysterical and locked in an insane asylum.

She didn't intend to ever marry. Her father had selected Gregory for Caroline, but Gregory was lazy, spoiled, and negligent. Samson recognized all those bad traits in his son, but he'd selected Gregory anyway. If he would make such a horrendous choice for Caroline, Janet could only imagine the dolt he'd find for *her*. She wasn't about to risk it.

Ever since she'd finished her schooling, she'd strenuously asserted her aversion to marriage. Her father laughed and humored her, and with her being just twenty, he assumed she was going through a phase, but she was deadly serious.

She wouldn't wed some cretin simply because her father ordered it. No, her dream was to move to London—as Gregory had—to rent an apartment and lead her own life. She'd surround herself with artists, poets, and philosophers.

She was anxious too to meet some of the brilliant women who were hoping to improve the dreary lot of females. She wanted to apply for a job and work as a secretary for one of them.

Why shouldn't a woman be permitted to divorce a violent husband? Why shouldn't she be able to vote? To manage her own money? Why not?

"Did you pester Gregory about his gambling?" she asked Caroline.

"He claims it's all in good fun, and he's merely amusing himself by playing for pennies."

"He would say that. We'll likely be beggared before he's done with us. The estate isn't entailed to a fancy title. He could wager away the whole property, and we'd wind up residing in a ditch."

"He'd never be that reckless."

Caroline had always been much too naïve. Janet didn't trust or believe Gregory. She was pragmatic in a manner Caroline would never be.

"What about Miss Carstairs and London?" Janet asked. "What was their opinion about that?"

"Gregory said he'd take me after the wedding."

Janet sighed with frustration. "You know he didn't mean it, right?"

"Yes, I know." Caroline grinned. "Which is why you and I shall go by ourselves."

Janet's jaw dropped. "You'd never be that brazen."

"Who could stop us? Gregory and I are chatting this afternoon. I have the allowance your father provides, and I plan to demand one from Gregory too. I won't quit nagging until he consents to it, so we'll pay our own way. It won't be any of his business—or your father's."

Janet grinned too. "Perhaps matrimony will agree with you."

"I've been the *lady* of this house for ages, but I've never had any real authority. After I'm a wife, many things have to change. Most particularly, Uncle Samson and my husband have to start listening to me."

"I can't wait to watch it occur, and I will cheer you on at every turn."

It would give her great pleasure to see her father and brother brought down a peg. They thought they were so important, and they definitely thought they were smarter than Janet and Caroline. The level of power they wielded was all out of proportion to the amount of effort Caroline expended on their behalves.

She and her cousin were in the front foyer, with Caroline having paused to report on her discussion with Samson and Gregory. She continued on to the rear of the manor to confer with their housekeeper, Mrs. Scruggs. Janet went in the other direction, up to her bedchamber, where she would hide for hours.

There were guests loafing in all the parlors, but they were Gregory's London friends, and she couldn't abide any of them. They were as smug and arrogant as he was, and they talked to her as if she was deaf or dimwitted. The entire group was obnoxious.

She reached the landing and was about to walk down the hall when a man bounded down the stairs from the floor above. She halted and, to her disgust, caught herself gaping up at him like a smitten ninny.

With his blond hair and blue eyes, he was annoyingly handsome, and it was obvious he was in the navy. He was wearing his blue coat and white trousers, and his chest was adorned with medals as if he'd bravely fought in numerous battles.

Though she'd never admit it, she loved seeing a man in uniform. It called to her feminine sensibilities, the ones she constantly struggled to ignore.

He was a few years older than she was, twenty-four or twenty-five, and she couldn't help but notice he had no wedding ring. So...he was a bachelor! Gregory occasionally dragged home unattached chums, but none of them ever looked like this divine god. She was embarrassingly aflutter, but working hard to pretend she wasn't paying attention.

"Hello there," he said.

"Hello to you too."

"I just arrived, and I'm starving. Can you point me to a dining room? Might I still be able to be fed? Or will I have to wither away until a formal meal is served?"

"I'm sure the kitchen can stir up a plate for you."

"Marvelous."

He was tall and willowy, and he moved with the grace of a dancer, being light on his feet and at ease in his body as she never was. His shoulders were wide, his waist narrow, his legs long, and she simply couldn't fathom how dull, insufferable Gregory would be friends with him.

"I'm Miss Grey," she said.

"Which Miss Grey?" he asked. "Are you Gregory's sister, Janet, or have I met Miss Caroline, the bride-to-be?"

"I'm Janet."

"You poor dear. I shall pity you forever." He bowed with a dramatic flourish that had her laughing. "I am Ensign Blake Ralston, the most dashing sailor the Royal Navy ever produced."

"You have quite a resumé."

"When you're as splendid as I am, there's no reason to practice humility."

"No, there's not."

"My brother is here," he said, switching topics like a whirlwind. "Mr. Caleb Ralston?"

"Now that you mention it, the resemblance is clear."

"He's an imposing rogue, isn't he?" He leaned in, so close that his boots slipped under the hem of her skirt. "Tell me the truth. What do you think of him?"

"We were only just introduced. I've spoken to him exactly twice, so I've barely had opportunity to make his acquaintance."

He smiled a smile that nearly knocked her off her feet. "You'll like me more than you like him. I promise you that."

"That's a bold statement."

"I'm a bold fellow." He gestured to the stairs. "Will you escort me to the dining room? This mansion is so large that I'm lost. I have no sense of direction."

"How could you have no sense of direction? You're a sailor—the best the navy ever produced, remember?"

"Yes, but we have sextants and other tools to inform us of where we are. It's when I'm staggering down these narrow hallways that I have so much trouble."

It was on the tip of her tongue to announce that she would be delighted to escort him. A fleeting vision flitted through her head: the two of them ensconced at the table where they'd chat intimately, and she would ogle him like a blushing debutante.

The speed with which she was willing to succumb to that sort of blatant entanglement was dumbfounding. What was wrong with her? She wasn't interested in romance, and she deemed all men to be fools.

"I'm sorry," she said, "but at the moment, I'm too busy."

"You can't force me to wander about on my own."

"You are a flirt."

"You accuse me as if it's a bad thing."

"In my book, it is." She pulled herself up to her full height and, next to him, it wasn't very tall at all. "If you follow these stairs to the bottom, you'll find a footman in the front foyer who will assist you."

"You wound me, Miss Grey." He placed a teasing hand over his heart. "How could you decline to dawdle in my charming company?"

"I'll try to bear up."

"I shall absolutely die a little until I see you again."

"Liar."

"Maybe I'm lying," he said, "but maybe I'm not."

He winked at her—he winked!—then he sauntered off, and she almost ran after him and told him she wasn't *that* busy, that she would love to sit with him while he ate. But that's what a silly girl would do, and she was a modern and independent young lady who was much too mature to be tantalized by a scoundrel.

He stopped and called up to her. "Janet?"

At wondering what his comment would be, she was practically breathless with anticipation, so she forgot to be annoyed that he'd used her Christian name.

"What?" she asked.

"Where would I be most likely to locate my brother? I haven't stumbled on him yet."

Her disappointment at the mundane question was exasperating. "Just stroll through the parlors. There are guests seated on every sofa. You'll cross paths with him."

"Will you be there eventually too?"

"I'll let it be a surprise."

He grinned a grin that indicated he was aware of the effect he had on her, that she'd come down as soon as she could. Then he whipped away and continued on. She shook her head and proceeded to her room, but somehow, the thought of spending the afternoon reading and writing in her journal had lost its appeal.

She was actually pondering what gown she should wear to supper, and she decided to see if her maid could style her hair in a more flattering fashion.

⌇

LUCRETIA STARLING STUDIED HERSELF in the mirror in her bedchamber, eager to be certain she looked perfect. Gullible Gregory was thirty, and he believed she was twenty-four, but she was really thirty-two. It was a fact she would fight to the death to conceal, so she worked hard to appear gorgeous and glamorous—and young!

Although Caroline Grey was the bride-to-be, Lucretia was the important woman in Gregory's life.

With her lush blond hair and big blue eyes, her curvaceous figure and statuesque height, she was stunning. Men drooled over her and women loathed her, always fretting when their men noticed her, and their worries were valid. She'd stolen a few beaux and spouses in her day. It was humorous to take what belonged to someone else. She was greedy and had no conscience. Moral qualms never vexed her.

She'd initially met Gregory when she'd been twenty, and he'd been eighteen and reveling in town for the first time. Even back then, he'd been a drunken sot, *and* he'd been poor, so he hadn't intrigued her in the slightest. But eight years later, when she'd bumped into him again, he'd been wildly wealthy.

She was no fool, so she'd grabbed hold and hadn't let go. They were so thoroughly attached that they might have been an old married couple.

In her new red gown, the bodice cut low to reveal plenty of bosom, there was no doubt she looked fabulous, and she spun away and exited the room. She went to the floor below and knocked on Gregory's door. She was furious that they hadn't been able to share quarters, that she was being treated as simply an ordinary guest, but then, he was about to wed, and his fiancée was right down the hall.

Lucretia probably couldn't expect any favors.

She didn't tarry until he bid her enter, but brazenly marched into his suite. She found him in the dressing room where he was fussing with his cravat. He'd never been a particularly handsome man, and he wasn't the type who would improve with age.

He was blond and blue-eyed too, but his face showed clear evidence of dissipation. Previously, he'd been thin and dapper, and he'd had all his hair. Now though, he was balding, and he'd developed a paunch around his belly. At five-foot-nine, he was an inch shorter than she was, so he didn't carry the extra weight very well, but as her deceased mother had counseled, beggars couldn't be choosers.

"Where is my valet?" he asked, his mood dour. "Didn't we bring him along?"

"No, darling," she said. "You gave him the week off—with all the other servants."

"You should have stopped me."

She walked over and kissed him on the mouth. "Yes, I should have, and I'm sorry to have been so negligent. Aren't there any footmen in the manor who could handle the job for you?"

"None that I'd trust."

She turned him toward her, then she clasped the lace and began tying an intricate knot. She was nothing if not functional. She'd dressed—and undressed—many men in her life. She could certainly tie a bloody cravat.

"What is on the schedule for today?" he asked her.

"I heard it's lawn games out in the garden. I peeked out my window, and I could see tents and tables arranged in the grass."

"Lawn games!" He was incredulous. "Why would I play lawn games? I had planned to get Ralston into the card room again. I can feel a lucky streak coming on."

"I'm sure you can, but you have to oblige Caroline, don't you? She's gone to so much trouble to entertain your company. You can't hide yourself in a parlor with Caleb Ralston."

"No, I don't suppose I can." He sighed as if he had heavy burdens that were a great trial. "I'll have to wait until tonight. That's likely better anyway. Caroline was nagging about it this morning at breakfast."

"Nagging about what?"

"About my gambling."

"She's a sheltered country mouse, darling. She could never comprehend the sorts of amusements we enjoy in town."

"I know." She finished with his cravat, and he whirled away and assessed himself in the mirror. "I'm doing the right thing, aren't I? Have I made the correct decision?"

"About what? About marrying your cousin?"

"Yes. I like her very much, and she's possessed of all the traits a fellow seeks in a bride. She's beautiful, educated, kind, loyal—"

Lucretia couldn't bear to have him extolling his cousin's attributes, and she cut him off. "Yes, she's quite a catch. You were a genius to snatch her up when you had the chance."

"I'm forging ahead merely to please my father, and I hate how he's been pressuring me."

She could barely contain her exasperation. "Gregory! You had her twiddling her thumbs for seven years! A girl shouldn't have to delay until she's an old maid."

"Yes, yes, and I'm securing the money. I have to keep reminding myself of that."

She bit down on all the aggrieved words that were begging to spill out.

They'd officially been a couple for four years, and in the beginning, she'd foolishly persuaded herself that he would wed *her*, but he'd conveniently neglected to mention that he was already engaged.

When he'd deigned to confide the situation, they'd had such a spat that she hadn't thought their relationship would survive it. She'd actually packed her bags and had nearly left him, but she'd calmed down quickly enough.

He was filthy rich, and he spoiled her rotten—without nitpicking over her expenditures. He provided her with a generous allowance too, and as any wise mistress would do, she was quietly squirreling away various amounts. Should the day ever arrive when he tired of her, she'd have a hefty nest egg to tide her over.

He never noticed what she stole from him. Most of the time, he was too intoxicated to focus on any detail. She should have felt guilty over how she was protecting herself, but she would never forgive him for choosing his cousin over her. Each farthing she pilfered was a salve to her wounded feelings.

She understood about Caroline's fortune, about the trust fund that would vest when she turned twenty-five. She understood that her ostentatious style of living was wholly dependent on his shackling himself to Caroline.

She understood it, but she didn't have to like it.

She was a selfish female who didn't like to share, and—if Gregory had been a real *man*—he'd have confessed about Lucretia to Caroline. He'd have explained that Caroline would be his wife, but Lucretia was his partner.

He was too much of a coward to confess it though, and he expected Lucretia to cower in the background and pretend to have no heightened claim on him. Well, she'd never been good at cowering or pretending, and if the truth leaked out to Caroline, Lucretia would be delighted to clarify a few facts.

Once Gregory was wed, Caroline would have to swallow her pride and permit him to gambol in the city with his favorite person in the world. And that person was Lucretia. Caroline Grey couldn't interfere in Lucretia's happiness. It simply wasn't in the realm of possibilities.

"Let's go down to the party, shall we?" she said. "Your guests are waiting."

"I imagine I have to."

"Buck up and cease your complaints. It will be an interesting after-noon. I promise."

"What if it's not? What if the games Caroline has devised are stupid and tedious?"

"Then we shall hover in the corner of a tent and snicker about her failings. It would be lovely to admit that she has some."

For just an instant, her smile slipped, but she shoved it back into place. She clasped his arm and led him away, being determined that everyone see them stroll outside together.

Chapter 5

CAROLINE HOVERED ON THE verandah, staring down at the garden party and studying the guests who were reveling in the grass. There were dozens of people present, the majority of them Gregory's friends from town. The rest were younger neighbors from the area who'd visited to join in the fun.

She'd had the cook prepare buffet tables of food, and the beverage offered was supposed to be a fruity punch. But from the animation of the London crowd, she suspected a stronger ingredient had been added, and she tamped down a sigh of frustration.

She tried to never be a prude, but was it necessary to imbibe of hard spirits in the middle of the afternoon? It seemed illicit, as if they were on a bad track.

Since the worst offenders appeared to be Gregory's chums, what was she to make of their conduct? He had an exciting life in town that didn't include her. Had she the right to complain about his choices and habits? Or should she keep her criticisms to herself?

Ooh, how she wished there was a wise matron with whom to discuss various issues before she walked down the aisle. It would have been nice to receive some useful guidance on numerous weighty topics.

It was three o'clock, the hour when Gregory had told her they could have a private chat. He was standing in the center of a boisterous group and had obviously forgotten about it. Lucretia Starling was hovered by his side, and she was clutching his arm as if they were more closely attached than they should be.

A hint of unease slithered down her spine. What was the actual situation between the pair? What did she really know about Mrs. Starling? Should she nag at Gregory until he supplied some firm answers?

An archery target had been set up, and male guests were shooting at it, but none of them were very good. Most of the arrows had flown off into the shrubbery. After significant ribbing, Mr. Ralston had agreed to participate, and she observed from her higher vantage point.

He was next to Gregory, so it provided an exhausting chance to assess them in a manner that was wrong and unfair. In any comparison, Mr. Ralston would win hands down. He was tall and handsome, slender and fit, sophisticated and elegant. His expensive coat showed off his healthy physique in an arresting way.

Gregory, in contrast, was shorter, plumper, his hair balding, his face lined from dissipation. He and Mr. Ralston were both thirty, but Gregory might have been twenty years older. His suit looked cheap and poorly sewn, and he'd gained so much weight that his shirt and trousers were stretched to the limit.

She realized how avidly she was tabulating Mr. Ralston's stellar attributes, and Gregory's lack of them, and she scoffed with disgust. She had no business drooling over Mr. Ralston, but she couldn't stop. She pushed away from the balustrade and headed down into the grass.

As she approached the group, Gregory was crowing, "A hundred pounds says you can't."

Someone in the crowd hollered, "Gregory, have you a hundred pounds to throw away?"

People snickered as if it was common knowledge that Gregory had no money.

Mr. Ralston replied with, "A hundred pounds would be fine. How many arrows shall I shoot?"

"Everyone else shot three," Gregory said.

"Must I hit the bullseye with all of them?" Mr. Ralston asked.

Gregory inquired of Mrs. Starling, "What is your opinion, Lucretia?"

"The other contestants had to hit the target once, but it's such a large bet. He should be required to hit it three times."

"You heard her, Ralston," Gregory said. "It must be all three."

They were gambling! Right in the yard! The guests surrounding them were whispering animatedly, as if side wagers were being placed on Mr. Ralston's prowess. She gaped in horror. To all of them, the huge bet was a perfectly ordinary occurrence. Yet it was an obscene amount of money.

Her temper soared, and she took several deep breaths to calm herself. She would never create a scene, and she had no idea how to bluster up and scold them. She would never behave like a shrew and embarrass Gregory.

Mr. Ralston went over to a table where there were bows arranged for the contestants to utilize. He picked up one and fussed with it, testing the tension of the string. Then, with his barely glancing at the target, he fired off the trio of arrows in quick succession. They landed directly in the center.

Spectators cheered or groaned, depending on their wagers, and Gregory's shoulders slumped with defeat. Then he glared at Mr. Ralston in a way that had others nervously shifting in their shoes. Clearly, there was more transpiring between them than she understood.

Mrs. Starling jumped in with, "Don't worry, Gregory. You'll best him tonight. I'm sure you will."

She grinned and swept her gaze around the group, wearing everyone down until they grinned too. Swiftly, the bystanders were chortling wildly, chattering over Mr. Ralston's remarkable ability, over the size of the wager. Men hurried out to the target, and they were gesturing and measuring, obviously awed by his skill.

Mr. Ralston laid the bow on the table, and when he straightened, he saw her lurking in the back. He stared intensely, as if imparting a secret message she needed to decode, but she couldn't fret about him. At the moment, he was the last of her concerns.

She felt aggrieved and very, very angry. She wanted to throttle Gregory, but with the party in progress, how could she make him listen? He never did. Not even her Uncle Samson could get through to him.

Earlier, Janet had wondered if he'd beggar them in the end, and Caroline had sworn he'd never be that reckless. What was she to think now?

She wedged herself into the crowd until she reached Gregory, but it was Mrs. Starling who noticed her.

"Gregory," she said, "look who's arrived."

"Caroline!" Gregory spun toward her. "Were you here when Ralston was shooting? Isn't he something?"

"Yes, he definitely is." She leaned nearer. "It's three o'clock."

Gregory frowned. "So it is."

"We had an appointment."

"Oh..." He sipped his beverage, then toasted her with his glass. "It's not convenient for me. The fun has just begun, and we're the hosts. It wouldn't be sporting for me to sneak off."

"Please?" She hated the beseeching tone in her voice.

"I'll find you later—after the competition is over. There are a few more men who want to have a chance." He laughed too eagerly.

"Although after the show Ralston gave us, I don't know why anyone would humiliate himself. Who could match him?"

There was a strong odor of alcohol emanating from his person, and she bit her tongue so hard she was surprised it wasn't gnawed bloody.

He smiled a condescending smile, the one that warned her she was simply being placated, and he murmured, "In the meantime, could you talk to the kitchen for me? This punch is awful. It's supposed to be lemony, but it tastes like dishwater."

"I will speak to someone. I'm sorry that it's not to your liking."

Mrs. Starling flashed a derisive smirk, then snuggled closer to Gregory, leaving Caroline with the distinct impression that *they* were a couple and Caroline an interloper. Another contestant had picked up a bow, and they turned away from her as the wagers commenced again.

She'd been dismissed, as if she was Gregory's servant, and she was trying not to be furious. After all, she ran the manor and managed the staff. It was only natural—if he had a complaint—that he would expect her to deal with it.

But *she* should have been the female standing with him. The fact that she wasn't, that he was enjoying an afternoon of debauchery that didn't appeal to her in the slightest, underscored that she was marching down a road she shouldn't be on.

How could she get off it?

She whirled away, but not before she saw Mr. Ralston still gazing at her from across the crowd. That was the worst piece of it for her. She couldn't bear that he'd watched her being humiliated by her betrothed.

She walked to the verandah, and as she climbed the stairs, Janet emerged from the house. With her blond hair, blue eyes, and curvaceous figure, she was very pretty, but she usually dressed like a grumpy governess. She had declared beauty and fashion to be a wily scheme pushed by men to keep women oppressed.

Yet suddenly, she appeared to be the rich, winsome girl she was. Her hair had been curled and braided, and she was attired in a fetching blue gown. The sight was so odd that Caroline was stunned.

"My, my," Caroline said, "don't you look smart."

"Thank you."

"What brought this on?"

"I decided to join in the festivities." She studied the revelers. "Is Mr. Ralston's brother here. Blake Ralston? Have you met him?"

"No."

"Then I don't imagine you can tell me where he is."

"No, but Mr. Ralston is in the thick of it. He might know."

"Perfect."

Janet sauntered off, a lovely, determined young lady on a mission. Apparently, Blake Ralston had intrigued her, and Caroline should have been humored by the prospect. She should have dawdled and smiled fondly as Janet searched for Blake and found him, but she simply couldn't tarry another second.

She was distressed and feeling completely adrift. She wished she had magical powers, that she was a bird and could fly away to a better place, to a happier place.

With a vehemence that almost knocked her over, it dawned on her that she didn't want to wed Gregory. She couldn't abide the idea, and the whole charade left her nauseous.

She went inside, and she raced to the stairs, not caring if she was observed. She couldn't breathe, and she yearned to break down and start sobbing. She dashed up to her bedchamber, not slowing until she was safely sequestered inside it.

She didn't have a posh suite like Gregory, Janet, or her Uncle Samson. She had a tidy bedroom that was just a single room, with no fancy sitting or dressing room. What would she have used them for anyway? She had a few gowns and undergarments, a few shawls and other accoutrements. They fit in the wardrobe and dresser.

It was the room she'd been given when she'd returned from the Caribbean, and after she'd become an adult, she could have requested more spacious quarters, but she hadn't been interested. The spot, located down a deserted hall, was her sanctuary where she could hide from the craziness in the rest of the manor.

As a child, she'd spent untold hours loafing in it, peering out the window and wondering where Libby and Joanna had gone. When times had gotten particularly bad, when she'd been scolded or even whipped for sassing, she'd fantasized about running away to find them.

In her juvenile mind, she'd envisioned them being a family, with no adults to hurt or chastise them.

The years had passed though and that dream had faded. She acclimated to her quiet, untenable existence. She'd learned how to avoid her grandfather, how to keep from enraging him. He'd died when she was fourteen, and he hadn't been mourned, most especially by her. Her Uncle Samson had moved home, and he'd brought Janet and Gregory with him. Matters had improved significantly after that.

He wasn't the kindest person, but he was never deliberately cruel. He never whipped her or shouted at her. He never sent her to bed without supper. Why, his initial act had been to buy her some clothes! She'd outgrown the items she'd had, but no one had noticed.

She'd been glad for the changes her uncle had wrought, and when he'd suggested she wed Gregory, she'd agreed without reflecting. She'd been seventeen! What did she know about marriage? What did she know about anything?

She lurched to her bed and eased down, her hips balanced on the edge of the mattress. Usually, the solitude was very comforting, but she was too angry to be soothed.

In a moment of irksome clarity, it occurred to her that she possessed so few things she could truly call her very own. Why was that exactly?

Her uncle and Gregory were carrying on in a very grand style. Why wasn't she? She wasn't a stranger who'd wandered in off the street.

She was one of Walter Grey's three grandchildren. Her father, Winston, had been the oldest son when he'd perished in the Caribbean. Why had she been given so little by her uncle and grandfather? Why hadn't she demanded more for herself?

She was fuming in a manner that was rare for her. Her life had been hard and miserable, and it had played out in such an unfair way—due to her male kin.

Maybe Janet was correct in her attitude. Maybe the two of them should cast off the yokes imposed by Gregory and Samson and head to the city. They could live together without the drama and irritation men caused. It was such a pleasant notion that tears flooded her eyes.

What should she do? It was painfully obvious she couldn't continue on as she was. There had to be some massive concessions on Gregory's part or she couldn't proceed with the wedding. How could she produce that sort of conclusion though? How could she simply announce—six days before the ceremony—that she was backing out?

The door opened, and she braced, not able to fathom who might have followed her up the stairs. When she realized who'd arrived, she was thrilled, but alarmed too, and the first words out of her mouth were, "You can't be in here."

"Too late, Caro," Mr. Ralston said. "I already am."

"What if someone saw you?"

"I was cautious, but if I was observed, I don't care."

"Well, I care! Have you any idea of the trouble I'd be in if you were discovered in my bedchamber?"

"I can vividly imagine it, but your relatives are a bunch of buffoons. Why let their opinions matter?"

"They're the only family I have."

"Yes, poor you."

He spun the key in the lock, sealing them in, then he leaned against the dresser and stared at her.

She stared back, a thousand comments clogging her throat. She had so many grievances to air, and she was feeling so maligned. She'd never had a confidante, and she was desperate to have someone listen and offer advice she could trust, but she was afraid—should she ever begin to unburden herself—she might ignite a whirlwind that would sweep the whole world off its axis.

Yet for once, she couldn't remain silent.

"Is Gregory a drunkard?" she asked, figuring it was a good place to start.

"He has a terrible problem with liquor."

"And with gambling too?"

"Yes."

"I badgered him about it this morning, and he claimed it's merely fun and games."

"It's not fun and games," he quietly said.

"How much debt has he accrued?"

"Just to me, do you mean?"

She gasped. "How many people are owed money by him?"

"I couldn't guess, but the amount he owes me is staggering."

Her jaw dropped with astonishment. "How did that happen?"

He shrugged. "As it usually happens, I suppose. He's a lousy gambler, and his drinking doesn't help. He grows inebriated, and he can't track the cards or the dice. Once he's dug a hole, he keeps digging, assuming he can wager himself out of it."

"That's insane."

"I've always thought so."

"Would you cancel his debt? If I begged, would you?"

"No," he callously replied. "I don't like Gregory, and I have no duty to him. It's not my business if he can't control himself."

"It's *my* business though. It's my home and my family's money. Please?"

"No." He bristled. "I wish I had a farthing for every woman who ever prostrated herself to me over some wastrel man."

"You and I are friends, aren't we?"

"I don't think so."

"Well, we're... something." She was unable to clarify their relationship. "Why won't you oblige me?"

"I'm not Gregory's nanny, and it's not up to me to make him behave."

"Will we lose the estate over this? Is that where we are with him?" He frowned at her for so long that her heart pounded with dread. "Tell me. How dire is it?"

"It's dire."

"But he continues on with you."

"He hopes he'll eventually get lucky."

She scoffed at that. "I've known Gregory for twenty years. He's not exactly a *lucky* fellow."

"No, he's not."

"How can I change your mind?" she asked. "I'll do anything."

He winced. "You shouldn't utter a remark like that to a man like me. I might take you up on it, and since you're still a maiden, you can't grasp the boons I'd demand."

She tsked with offense. "Don't pretend to be horrid. You'd never hurt me."

"You haven't a clue what I'm capable of perpetrating."

As he voiced the warning, there was a steeliness in his tone that was unnerving. It forced her to realize he could be dangerous if pushed to a steep ledge. Though it wounded her to admit it, he could harm her without batting an eye.

It occurred to her that she was being very stupid. They were practically strangers, and she'd imbued him with traits he obviously didn't possess.

"I can't marry him," she blurted out, letting the perilous words fly into the air.

He didn't jump to agree that it was the right decision. He merely raised a brow. "Can you back out? At this late date, is it even a possibility?"

"I don't know. I'd have to go to my uncle and insist we end it, but I can't imagine having that conversation with him."

"If it's any consolation, I feel very sorry for you."

She batted her lashes in a mocking way. "Aren't I fortunate to have your sympathy!"

"I have naught to give you but sympathy."

"You could give me Gregory's promissory notes."

"That won't ever happen."

She stood and went to the window. From her room, she couldn't see the party, and she was glad she couldn't. She had no desire to watch what was transpiring.

He was behind her, and she could sense him studying her, his presence brash and overwhelming. He simply took up too much space, and she yearned to whip around, to shout at him to stop tormenting her, but she'd never been the type of person who shouted.

After a bit, she asked, "Why are you at Grey's Corner, Mr. Ralston? You and Gregory aren't friends. Why did he invite you to the wedding? Why did you accept?"

"He's anxious to stay on my good side. He owes me so much money, and if I cut him off and he couldn't play at my club anymore, he'd be devastated. It would make him a pariah. All his acquaintances revel there. If he couldn't revel with them, his social world would collapse."

"Maybe it should collapse. Maybe it would save him."

He didn't respond to her comment, and she glanced over her shoulder. He was still studying her, his gaze potent and thrilling. She'd never had anyone look at her as he looked, as if he could delve down to the tiniest pore, as if she had no secrets from him.

"Why follow me to my room?" She was terrified to hear his answer. Would she be delighted? Or would it leave her even more conflicted?

"I didn't like how you were treated out in the garden."

"I can't say I was overly keen about it either."

"I thought about punching him and ordering him to quit being such an ass. Should I have?"

She smirked with irritation. "No, you shouldn't have punched him."

"I didn't think you'd like me to. It's the only reason I didn't."

"Are you here because you're simply being kind? Is that it? You noticed I was upset, and you had to check on me?"

"I wouldn't admit to that."

"What is it then?"

He came over to her, crossing the floor in three quick strides. Before she could move, before she could blink, he pulled her into his arms. Then he was kissing her and kissing her.

It was wild and unrestrained and bizarre. She might have been out of her body, assessing another woman as she behaved precisely as she shouldn't. She'd decided she couldn't marry Gregory, but she was still officially betrothed, so her conduct was sinful and wrong. She'd probably wind up in Hell for it, but at the moment, she couldn't worry about her immortal soul.

She was perplexed and aggrieved, and Mr. Ralston was the sole person who'd recognized she was hurting and shouldn't be alone. He'd had to find out if she was all right. He'd been eager to comfort her, and she was elated to let him.

His hands were in her hair, his tongue in her mouth. His curious fingers roamed over her torso, touching her everywhere, as if imprinting her shape into his memory.

The embrace grew more unruly. They scratched, clawed, and wrestled, going at it like two cats trapped in a sack. Who kissed like this? Who carried on as if they were the last people on earth who would ever kiss?

She felt as if they'd tumbled off a cliff together, that they were falling down and down and down, and she wondered where she'd be when they landed at the bottom. Would it be a soft and cushioned place? Or would she hit the ground hard and never recover?

Gradually, they ran out of steam. They slowed, their lips parting, and he rested his forehead on her own. For a long while, they hovered just there, both of them seemingly stunned by the powerful emotions generated.

Eventually, he eased away. He smiled down at her, appearing wicked and fabulous and even a tad bewildered. She had no idea what he was thinking, what he might say, but when she heard what it was, she chuckled.

"I'm afraid I like you more than I should," he told her.

"That might be an understatement."

"I can't figure out what's driving me. There's nothing about you to indicate you're my *type* of female. You too short and too skinny, and you're not blond."

"You certainly know how to make a girl feel special."

"It's one of my great skills."

"Can't you shower me with flattery so I'll believe I'm too marvelous to resist?"

"I'm much too manly to shower you with flattery."

"Perhaps you could spew some poetry. Can you recite any sonnets?"

"I'm fresh out of sonnets."

She sighed, and he sighed too, and she leaned into him, their bodies pressed tight from chest to toe.

"What now?" she asked.

He linked their fingers. "Have you calmed down? Will you come back down to the party?"

"I will in a bit. I need some time by myself to consider my options."

"Don't dawdle by yourself, fretting and moping. Gregory isn't worth it."

"That's recently become very clear to me, so there are some massive changes approaching. I'll have to devise a means of implementing them without being buried in the rubble of the chaos I'll cause."

"You know what the changes have to be. You don't have to dither and reflect. Deep in your heart, you *know*."

"Yes, I suppose I do."

She peered out the window, worried over how long they'd tarried. She was so completely enchanted by him that, if the sun had set without her noticing, she wouldn't have been surprised. It was still afternoon though, but much later than it had been.

"I should probably get out of here," he said.

"I never thought you should have arrived in the first place."

"Of course you didn't, but aren't you glad I risked it?"

"I might be glad."

"Promise you'll come downstairs. I'd like to introduce you to my brother."

"I'd like that too."

"Why don't you rearrange the seating chart at supper? Sit next to me."

"I wouldn't dare."

"Why not?"

"I might like you more than I should too," she admitted. "I wouldn't be able to hide my heightened fondness."

"No one pays any attention to you, Caro. Trust me on this. You could gaze at me until your eyes fell out of your head, and there isn't a single person who would note what was amiss."

"Truer words were never spoken," she murmured.

"Don't be sad."

"I'm not. I'm...exhausted, I guess."

"Don't be exhausted either. Be relieved that you're about to walk a new path."

"I'll tell myself that's what is happening."

"And be happy that you met me."

"I don't believe I should be happy about it. In fact, I'm predicting you'll bring me nothing but trouble in the end."

"You could be right."

He gave her fingers a tight squeeze, kissed her a quick, final time, then went to the door. He unlocked it, peeked out, and slipped away. But not before glancing back, his expression so full of longing that she was bowled over by it.

"Don't marry your cousin," he said. "If you never follow another piece of advice, follow that one. If you marry him, you'll always be sorry."

Then he was gone.

She was frozen in her spot, trying to hear his footsteps retreating down the hall, but he vanished like smoke.

She sank down on her chair, her elbows on her knees, her chin in her hand, listening as the silence settled around her.

"What to do? What to do?" she asked the empty room, but the room had no answer, and she was all alone.

Chapter

6

"WON'T YOU ASK ME how my career is going?"

"No."

Blake Ralston grinned at his brother, but Caleb didn't grin back. The navy—and Blake's career in it—was a sore spot between them. He shouldn't have mentioned it, but he felt weighted down by guilt for the mess he'd caused, and he wished Caleb would forgive him.

It had happened four years earlier. Why couldn't they move beyond it?

The navy had been Caleb's whole life, and Blake believed, if they talked about it occasionally, it might stop being such a jagged wound. Yet maybe it wasn't possible to repair the damage. Maybe Caleb would always suffer from the catastrophe Blake had stirred.

At least they were friends again. For a lengthy interval, they hadn't spoken, and Blake had been terrified that Caleb meant for their rift to last forever. But as Sybil had counseled—Sybil being their substitute mother—Caleb would calm down, and he had.

He and Blake were all alone in the world. Well, if he didn't include their half-brother, Jacob Ralston, and his two sisters. Caleb might get angry at Blake, but their firm bond would survive.

It was the tenor of his relationship with his brother. When they'd been growing up, Blake had been a constant trial. They would fight over his mischief, and Caleb would declare that he was washing his hands of Blake, but Caleb was too loyal. He'd never leave Blake behind.

They'd gradually fallen back into the rhythm that set the tone for their lives. He loved his brother, but Caleb wasn't the cheeriest fellow. In that, they were complete opposites. Caleb was older—thirty to Blake's twenty-five—so he worried and planned and remained alert for bumps in their road.

Blake, in contrast, was happy, lucky, and content to follow wherever Caleb led him. In his view, problems resolved themselves, and there was never a reason to fret.

"Shall we discuss *your* career then?" Blake asked.

"What career would that be? My ownership of a prosperous gambling house?"

"Yes, that one."

"You should be glad I've been so successful. When you're elderly and crippled, with your joints swollen from your decades at sea, I'll be able to support you."

"Will you hire beautiful nurses to tend me 'round the clock?"

"No, I'll hire aged crones."

"You're a cruel, heartless sibling."

"If I am, you deserve it."

They were chatting in the main parlor at Grey's Corner. A festive dance was in progress, with couples promenading down the center of the room. There were plenty of female guests, so he'd been dragged onto the floor over and over. He was taking a break and catching his breath.

With Blake still in the navy, and Caleb having resigned and residing in London, they didn't see each other very often. He hardly knew Gregory Grey, but he'd used the nuptials as an excuse to obtain a furlough. He wasn't interested in the celebration, but Caleb needed him to guard his back, a request Blake deemed odd for a wedding.

What sort of man needed his *back* guarded at a wedding?

But then, Caleb and Gregory Grey were gambling, and Mr. Grey was pushing the stakes higher and higher. The negligent sot would ultimately wager away the estate, and that type of tragic apex could always generate trouble.

"Will you play with Gregory again tonight?" he asked.

Caleb sighed. "I suppose I will."

"You don't have to. Why don't you chuck it in and return to London? You and I can spend some time together and revel like bachelors."

"We *are* bachelors," Caleb said. "We don't require an excuse to act like it."

"Mr. Grey is an obnoxious prick. I don't understand why you're fussing with him."

"I keep trying to stop, but he won't let me."

Blake tsked with disgust. "That's a nonsense reply. You've kept on because you enjoy tormenting him."

"Maybe."

Caleb detested lazy, slothful idiots. He liked taking their money, jewels, and properties. The fact that many of them had fathers in the navy, that those fathers were the kind of men their own father had been, was a motivating influence. He relished having the chance to inflict himself on them.

"What did you think of Caroline Grey?" Caleb asked.

Caleb had introduced Blake to the gorgeous woman. She'd been pert and funny, and she'd had an intriguing manner of interacting with Caleb. She'd talked to him as if he didn't impress her, which was incredibly humorous. His brother had never crossed paths with a female who didn't immediately throw herself at his feet.

"I can't believe she's Gregory's fiancée," Blake said.

"Neither can I. I feel sorry for her."

Blake scoffed. "No, you don't. You don't feel sorry for anyone."

"I feel sorry for myself—for being related to you. I feel sorry that Sybil had to watch over us for so many years. I feel sorry for all the people in the world who aren't as wealthy as I am now. *And* I feel sorry for Caroline Grey."

"I stand corrected. You are a teeming ball of empathy."

"I'm concerned about what will happen to her if Gregory continues marching down the road he's on."

Blake gaped at Caleb and shook his head. "Are you sure you're Caleb Ralston? If you've told me once, you've told me a thousand times: You don't care about the women who are harmed by the reckless men in their lives."

"I'm concerned about *her*." Caleb shrugged. "She might cry off from the wedding."

"Don't you dare tell me you encouraged her."

"I didn't, but she'd be smart to run from Gregory Grey."

"If you've been discussing such a dangerous idea with her, it's clear you're getting involved with her when you shouldn't." Blake frowned. "What's wrong with you? Are you all right?"

"I'm fine, and don't mind me. I'm in a strange mood."

"You certainly are."

Caleb waved toward the dancers. "Why don't you dance again? Leave me alone. My thoughts are bouncing around at such a furious rate that I can't carry on a civil conversation."

"It's absolutely typical that I would travel all this way to socialize with you, only to be told you'd rather mope in the corner by yourself."

"I'm good at moping, so please go charm the ladies. If you keep them busy, perhaps they'll ignore me."

"Dear brother, just for you, I will give it my all."

Blake sauntered off, thinking that no amount of distraction would prevent the females in the crowd from seeking Caleb's attention. Or his own.

He and his brother were amazingly handsome, as well as suave and sophisticated. Caleb was rich too, so that made Blake rich. It would be pointless to pretend they didn't cut dashing figures, and Blake was wearing his uniform. There wasn't a woman in the kingdom who could resist him.

He was still overheated, so he slipped out to the verandah and strolled down into the garden. He walked until he was quite a distance from the house, then he turned to study it. The windows were lit, the doors open so it might have been a fairy palace.

He loved fancy houses, and there had been plenty of occasions as a boy where he'd had to tarry outside and wonder what it would be like to be welcomed inside. Now, with his career providing esteem, and his brother being powerful and important, Blake could bluster into any bloody mansion he chose, and people would be glad to see him.

Behind him, a woman sneezed, and she tried to be furtive so he wouldn't hear her. He glanced over his shoulder to where there was a bench off in the grass. She was sitting on it, and with her attired in a black gown, the night swallowed her up.

He went over to discover who it was, being surprised to find Janet Grey. He'd met her on the stairs when he'd first arrived, but he hadn't stumbled on her since.

"Well, well, if it isn't Miss Grey," he said. "Why are you hiding out here all by yourself?"

"If I'd wanted to be found, Ensign Ralston, I would have made my presence known."

"You did make it known. You sneezed."

Without invitation, he plopped down next to her, and she glowered like a fussy schoolteacher.

"I didn't ask you to join me," she said.

"No, but you look like you could use some company."

It wasn't completely dark. There was a lantern hanging from a post a few feet away, and the moon was up, so he could clearly assess her. She was younger than he was, probably twenty or so. With her blond hair and blue eyes, she was very pretty, but she concealed her feminine attributes, almost as if she couldn't bear to have them noticed.

When he'd bumped into her earlier, she'd been dressed like a governess, and she still was. Her hair was pulled back in a tight, unflattering chignon, and while the other women at the party were decked out in their most stylish clothes, her dreary garment had a high neck, long sleeves, and grey trim on the collar and cuffs.

"Your face is so scrunched up," he said, "you could be a prune. Why are you scowling? And you shouldn't be scowling at *me*. I couldn't have vexed you. Not yet anyway. You should be happy to see me, for I can guarantee—whatever is ailing you—I shall cure it before I'm through.

"I doubt that very much."

She shifted, so he shifted too, but the bench was narrow, so there wasn't much space to maneuver. Their arms and legs were crushed together all the way down.

"I hate parties," she said.

"Who hates a party? That's a ridiculous comment."

"I especially hate this one."

"Why?"

"I don't like my brother, and I can't abide his London friends."

He pondered his reply, debating whether he should be polite or if he should be candid. Candor won out. "I can't abide any of them either. I'm here because my brother dragged me along. I'm often away in the navy, so I don't spend as much time with him as I'd like."

"You get on with him?"

"We're best chums."

"You're lucky then. Gregory is my only sibling, and I don't have the luxury of a close bond. I like my cousin, Caroline, though. She's always been like a sister to me."

"I like her too," Blake said, "and I'm sad that she's marrying Gregory. She seems very sweet. It's too bad she couldn't wind up with a husband who deserves her."

"My father arranged the match ages ago. She's twiddled her thumbs for seven years, but Gregory wouldn't proceed. Have you ever heard of anything so rude?"

"Seven years? Your brother must have been convinced of her affection. How could he be sure no other fellow would swoop in and steal her away when he wasn't paying attention?"

"He's fortunate no one ever did, but we don't have many handsome bachelors stopping by. She's never been doted on by a beau, so she waited for Gregory."

Fleetingly, Blake wondered if Caleb might have decided to *dote* on her. His brother was surrounded by women. With his being notorious, every doxy in the demimonde tried to curry his favor, but he was persnickety and rarely interested.

Their father, and his licentious habits, had made Caleb wary of romantic entanglements. A man could orchestrate enormous folly if he wasn't careful where he sired his children.

Miss Grey yanked his focus back to her. "I wish I could stuff Caroline in a traveling trunk and take her to London. I'd like to save her from her dire fate. I have some money of my own. I ought to beg her to run away with me. We could rent an apartment and live alone—a pair of contented spinsters."

"You'd run away to save her from matrimony? What a bizarre statement. Isn't marriage the goal all women seek?"

"Not *every* woman. Some of us realize the trap a man can present."

"Men and marriage are a trap?" He cocked his head and studied her. "You have to be the strangest female I've ever encountered."

"There are more women like me than you can imagine," she snottily said. "And just so you know, I'm not impressed by you, so don't flirt with me."

"Oh, I definitely won't flirt."

The remark was a lie. He was fascinating and enchanting, and women couldn't resist him. His impulses couldn't be tamped down or controlled.

"Charm practically oozes out of you," she scathingly said.

"I can't hold it in. I've never been able to. Should I apologize for being marvelous?"

"No! I don't care if you're marvelous."

"Well, you certainly told me, didn't you?"

"For a few minutes this afternoon, I allowed myself to be swept away by the notion of engaging in a dalliance with you, but I came to my senses quickly enough."

"What was it, pray tell, that jerked you to reality?"

"After we chatted on the stairs, I actually went to my room and changed my clothes so I'd look more fetching for you. I had my hair curled and my slippers brushed, then I rushed down to find you. I was hoping to... to... entice you, but you were nowhere to be found, which was a great relief. I didn't make a fool of myself."

She'd spewed so many odd comments that he felt dizzy with trying to sift through them all. He settled on the one least likely to provoke her. "I would love to have seen you in a pretty gown."

"But don't you understand? I don't want to look fetching!"

She was so aggrieved that he laughed out loud; he couldn't help it. "I repeat: You are incredibly strange. What's wrong with being fetching? To me, it seems a normal feminine instinct. Are you determined to be completely abnormal?"

"There are more important things than flirtation and romance."

"I've never stumbled on any."

"I have no desire to tempt men with my looks. I intend to be respected for my intellect and my stimulating personality. I'm smart and driven to succeed. I should be able to accomplish any goal I pursue. I shouldn't have to demean myself into believing matrimony is my only option."

"Yes, but the sole avenue society permits is for you to be a wife and mother. What alternative is there?"

"I most particularly don't want to be a wife and mother!" She glared at him as if the unfairness of her lot was all his fault.

"What will become of you then?"

"I haven't figured it out yet, but I will. There has to be a road that will lead me to the life I crave."

"What life would that be? Are you planning to be a dictatorial spinster who constantly complains about men?"

"We should complain. My brother is the prime example of why! I'd say it's time for women to speak up."

Since his own father, the grand and glorious Captain Miles Ralston, had been a philandering roué, Blake couldn't argue the point. Then there were the irresponsible wastrels who ruined themselves at Caleb's club. They would blithely imperil their wives and children by wagering until their pockets were empty.

Maybe if women ran the kingdom, it wouldn't be in such a dire condition.

The instant the peculiar thought slithered by, he tossed it away. As if women should run the world! As if things would be better if they did!

"Do you actually assume that you're different?" he asked. "Would you ignore the chance to enjoy an amour if it came winging in your direction?"

"I have big dreams, and they don't include a tedious marriage to a country dolt."

Blake gave a mock shudder. "Yes, that sounds like a fate worse than death."

"I shall move to London and have my own apartment. I'll be acclaimed as a gracious hostess, and every night, I'll have supper parties that will be attended by the most interesting people in the land."

It was a sweet idea, but he supposed—before too many more months had passed—her father would announce that he'd selected a fiancé for her. She wouldn't have a choice in the matter, and the prospect made him sad.

He was glad he wasn't a female.

She gestured to the manor. "Why don't you head back? I'm sitting out here because I'm thinking and plotting, and I can't have you distracting me."

"Am I distracting you?"

"You know you are. Don't pretend."

"I hate your gown and the severe way you've pinned your hair."

"Why would I care about that? Haven't you been listening? I'm not trying to entice you. If you notice a single one of my stellar traits, I should like it to be my brilliant mind."

"I've never liked smart women—they're too bossy—so I don't view feminine intellect as much of a benefit. You're a beautiful girl. It's such a waste that you're working so hard to be plain and ordinary."

"Real beauty is found on the inside."

He scowled at her. "Did you read that in a book somewhere?"

"What if I did? The fact that I *read* it doesn't make it any less true."

"I especially hate women who read. When a female constantly sticks her nose in a book, she grows too domineering. A man like me can end up totally emasculated."

She rolled her eyes. "You are positively deranged, and I can't fathom why I'm talking to you. You have nothing to say that's worth hearing. Would you please go away?"

He knew more about women than he probably should. They chased him relentlessly, hoping he'd catch them, and Miss Grey looked absolutely miserable. She was brimming with odd notions, and he couldn't imagine why her father had allowed her to develop such radical leanings.

If Blake had had a daughter, he'd have been a little more cautious about the reading material brought into the house.

He wondered how much of her diatribe she believed deep down. If a handsome swain swept her off her feet, wouldn't she succumb? Should he test that theory? She claimed to be modern and independent, but he figured—if push came to shove—she'd jump in with both feet.

Should he give her the opportunity? If he could tantalize her, wouldn't he be doing her a favor? She needed to be shown that a passionate relationship could be very satisfying. Shouldn't he prevent her from making idiotic choices that couldn't be reversed?

"You're not serious," he said. "You wax on exhaustively, but I predict—if the right fellow seduced you—you wouldn't be able to resist. You've let a bunch of aged old crones indoctrinate you with nonsense."

"For your information, the authors I idolize have all been wed, so they're experts at what they're writing about. They're wives, not spinsters, but so what if they were spinsters? It's not a crime."

He shifted nearer, using his male body to ease her into the bench. She really was pretty, and it was too bad she was so silly. If he dallied with her, she'd likely talk him to death.

"Let's bet, Miss Grey."

"I'm not my brother. I don't gamble."

"May I call you Janet?" She frowned, as if it was a trick question, and he said, "You can call me Blake. We'll be on familiar terms."

"I'd rather not be."

"Call me Blake. You know you want to."

"You're such a bully."

"I definitely can be. Now about that bet..."

"We're not wagering!"

He rested a hand on her waist, and he couldn't help but note that she didn't pull away and order him to stop being so forward.

"If I begin flirting with you in a dedicated manner," he told her, "you'll be delighted by my attention. You'll revel in it."

"I would never capitulate in my convictions. I'm too adamant, so you could never persuade me. It wouldn't be a fair fight."

He leaned even nearer, his lips a hairsbreadth from her own. "What shall we declare to be the prize? If I win, what will you give me?"

She tsked with annoyance. "You're being absurd."

"Am I?"

He closed the distance between them and kissed her. It was a quick brush of his mouth to hers. Then he drew away.

They stared, both a tad startled. She—because she hadn't expected him to be so brazen. He—because it had been much more delicious than he'd anticipated.

Perhaps Miss Janet Grey had a few hidden depths!

She regrouped, her tone scolding. "You can't just bluster up and kiss me!"

"It's how adults behave, Janet. Didn't you know that? If you didn't, maybe you shouldn't have developed such strong opinions about men and romance."

"I didn't like it!" she claimed.

He laughed. "You little liar. You're all aflutter, wondering if I might do it again, and I *will* do it again. I promise. I'll wait until you're not looking, so it can be a surprise."

He stood and gazed down at her, and she appeared young and a bit lost.

"How old are you, Janet?" he asked.

"Twenty. Why?"

"Was that your first kiss?"

There was enough light to see that her cheeks heated. "No! I've been kissed dozens of times."

"Well, then. . . good. It means you've learned how."

He bent down, and he hovered an inch away. There was gladness in her expression, but excitement and nerves too, which was humorous to observe. She was completely off balance.

"Goodnight, Janet," he whispered, then he straightened and walked away.

He headed toward the manor, and he counted the steps he took—four—until she couldn't stand it and called to him.

"Ensign Ralston! Why did you do it? Why did you kiss me?"

He halted and glanced at her. "I did it because I knew you'd like it, and we have a bet running, remember?"

"We don't have a bet!"

"We do," he said, "and it's obvious I'm already winning."

He kept on to the house and went inside. He could feel her watching him the whole way, her eyes like daggers in his back. The next day, he had no doubt she'd be wearing a more fetching gown and her hair wouldn't be pinned in such a severe style.

When Caleb had invited him to the wedding, he'd thought it would be a dull bore, that he'd simply sit in a corner while Caleb gambled with Gregory Grey. But the sojourn might provide some entertainment. He always like to trifle with a pretty girl, and Janet Grey needed his help like nobody's business. Once he was through with her, who could guess what kind of person he'd leave behind?

He couldn't wait to find out.

Chapter
7

"WHAT DO YOU THINK of my bride-to-be?"

"I like her," Caleb said to Gregory, "and she's much too good for you. You're lucky she agreed to a betrothal."

Gregory smirked. "Everyone tells me that."

"Everyone is correct."

They were in the front parlor, enjoying a final glass of wine as the party wound down for the night. Gregory wasn't exactly rushing guests out the door, but he couldn't completely hide his impatience. He was anxious to get Caleb and his other London friends off by themselves so the *real* party could begin.

Caleb couldn't deduce why he was still at Grey's Corner. He'd visited in order to evaluate the property and determine—should Gregory risk it in a wager—whether it was worth having. It definitely was, but now that he'd met Caro, the notion of taking it from Gregory wasn't as amusing as it had previously been.

If he let Gregory continue until he was beggared, what would happen to her?

Why didn't he pack his bags and leave? He and Blake could return to town and spend the remainder of Blake's furlough together. Sybil would love to have Blake at home for a bit. Why didn't Caleb oblige her? Why tarry where the situation was so untenable?

The verve required to keep on with Gregory had vanished, but if he departed, he'd never see Caro again, which was a strange problem to have. Why would it matter if he never saw her again? He barely knew her and didn't intend to develop a bond. Why worry about separating himself from her?

He *was* worrying though, and he couldn't stop.

She was prepared to cry off from her engagement, and he hoped she'd have the fortitude to forge ahead, but he felt deep in his bones that it would never come to fruition. If he stayed on though, it might help to imbue her with the courage she needed to follow through.

If his presence was necessary for her to stand up to her uncle, it was a small price for Caleb to pay.

He had another important concern with regard to her. If he quit gambling with Gregory, and locked Gregory out of his club, Gregory would simply start racking up new debts at other clubs.

If he didn't lose the estate to Caleb, he'd lose it to someone else. Was it better for Caleb to seize it from him? Would Caro be safer that way? He couldn't decide, and he had no idea why he was dithering over such a ludicrous issue.

"Have I told you Caroline's secret?" Gregory asked, yanking Caleb out of his reverie.

Gregory was intoxicated to the point of slurring his words, and Caleb couldn't imagine what he might confide. He sighed with aggravation. "What is her secret? If it's horrid, please keep it to yourself. I meant it when I said I like her, and I'd rather not hear any awful rumors."

"It's not awful," Gregory claimed. "It's just incredibly peculiar."

"What is it?"

"Caroline is one of the Lost Girls."

"What are you babbling about?"

"You know the ones. They were found on that deserted island in the Caribbean. It's been twenty years ago, but you can't have forgotten. Gad, that siren, Libby Carstairs, has the whole city buzzing about it again."

Nothing surprised Caleb anymore, but this did. He scowled. "Your fiancée is not one of those girls. You're spewing nonsense."

Gregory's sister, Janet, was walking by, and he motioned to her. "Janet, tell Mr. Ralston."

"Tell him what, Gregory? You're drunk, and I don't like to talk to you when you are."

"He doesn't believe me about Caroline being a Lost Girl."

Miss Grey glowered at her brother. "We don't mention it to strangers, Gregory. You're aware of that fact, so be silent."

Caleb frowned at her. "Is it true?"

Miss Grey peered around, as if to be certain there were no eavesdroppers. "We don't like to remind people about it, Mr. Ralston. It was a terrible ordeal that she suffered as a tiny child. We've tried to let it fade into the background, but yes, she's one of them."

Gregory puffed himself up. "Told you."

Caleb was stunned. He ignored Gregory and inquired of Miss Grey, "Are you sure about this?"

"Yes, Mr. Ralston, I'm very, very sure. It was a defining event in my family's life. My uncle and his wife drowned at sea, and my cousin, Caroline—who was only four—somehow survived against all odds. It's not exactly an incident about which I would be confused."

"I'm not doubting your veracity. I'm just...astonished, I guess."

"As I said, we don't mention it, and I'd appreciate it if you wouldn't raise the topic with her. And don't gossip about it with the other guests either. If they're apprised, they'll pepper her with questions, and the subject is very distressing for her."

"I understand," he murmured.

Miss Grey continued on, and Gregory said, "You *like* my fiancée, but what do you think of her now? She's a deep dish, Ralston. She has layers you couldn't fathom in a thousand years."

"You're right about that," he muttered. "Would you excuse me?"

"Where are you going? We're about to head to the card room."

"I have to speak to my brother. I'll join you there in a bit."

"Don't dawdle. I'm feeling lucky, and I want to get started."

Caleb didn't respond, but hurried off. He was desperate to find Caro, and he searched through the various parlors that were mostly empty. She was probably already in bed, and he knew where her bed-chamber was located. Dare he risk seeking her out in it again? He couldn't avoid it. This discussion couldn't be delayed.

He went to the front foyer, and as he reached it, Blake was there too. He grabbed his brother's arm and pulled him aside.

"You look as if you've seen a ghost," Blake said. "What's wrong?"

"You won't believe what that fool, Gregory Grey, told me."

"Yes, I will. He's an ass, so it might have been any horrendous thing."

"His fiancée, Caroline, is one of the Mystery Girls of the Caribbean."

Blake blanched. "Could he have been lying?"

"I figured he was, so I asked his sister, Janet. She insisted it was true, but she begged me not to tell anyone. Apparently, it's very upsetting to Caroline."

"A shiver just worked its way down my spine," Blake said. "What are the odds that we'd finally stumble on one of those girls? What are the odds that it would be here at Grey's Corner? I don't like this. Is Fate toying with us for some reason?"

He and Blake had incessantly debated whether to track down the Lost Girls. Especially when Libby Carstairs had begun performing in London. They'd wondered if they shouldn't arrange an introduction to her.

But would she want to confer with them? Would she recall that it was Caleb's father who'd rescued her? Would she be delighted to learn about their connection? Or would it have been an embarrassing encounter?

In the end, they hadn't pursued a meeting, but now, Caroline Grey had been pushed into the middle of their lives. What were they to make of it?

"Have you spoken to her?" Blake asked.

"No. I just heard about it."

"It's so late; she's likely in bed."

"I'll look for her for a few minutes," Caleb said, "in case she's still up. Would you go to the card room and keep Gregory occupied? I'll be there shortly."

"I won't be able to concentrate. I'm too excited over what her comments might be."

"We'll corner her tomorrow and spend hours chatting. I'd like to pry out every detail."

"If she recollects any."

"I'm sure she does. Libby Carstairs has a successful career from telling stories about it. I'm betting Miss Grey has some interesting tales to tell too."

Caleb walked off, needing to get away from Blake before his brother realized he could have accompanied Caleb on his hunt for Caro. This was a conversation Caleb intended to have with her in private.

He climbed the stairs and headed for the other wing of the manor where the smaller rooms and unimportant guests were lodged. He hadn't asked Caro why *she* was lodged there. Why didn't she have a bigger suite overlooking the park?

She ran the house and was in charge of the staff, so she had plenty of authority. The servants appeared to like her, and they exhibited the appropriate deference, so he hoped *she* had chosen the spot and not that her uncle was treating her poorly.

He knocked once, then slipped inside, not pausing to ponder what he'd do if she had a maid tending her. Luckily, she was alone. She'd dressed for bed, so she was wearing a nightgown and naught else. Her glorious black hair was down and brushed out, her arms and toes bare.

The nightgown was white, with purple flowers embroidered along the bodice. It should have appeared virginal and innocent, but it was sewn from a thin fabric that had grown thinner from much laundering. There were two narrow straps across her shoulders, so she was displaying lots of bosom.

He was viewing much more of her than was proper or that should ever have been allowed to a rogue such as himself.

"Mr. Ralston!" she scolded in a whisper. "This is becoming a very bad habit."

"I had to talk to you about a significant topic."

"It couldn't wait until morning?"

"No, it definitely couldn't wait."

She grabbed a robe off the chair, and she yanked it on, tying the belt with an angry flourish. Her nerves had flared, and she clutched at the lapels, trying to pull them closer.

He stepped away from the door, and in three quick strides, he was standing next to her. He pressed her against the dresser, their bodies crushed together from chests to shins. She glared up at him like a grouchy governess, but she didn't draw away.

Apparently, she was as thrilled by their proximity as he was. Their nearness generated such extreme sensations. Why ignore them?

"Your cousins, Janet and Gregory, shared the most shocking information about you, and I'm bowled over by it."

"There is not a single piece of my personal history that I would describe as shocking, so I can't imagine to what you refer."

"You can't? Really?"

"Yes, really, and you're being obnoxious. I wish you'd sneak out before you get me in trouble."

"I can't leave yet. For you see, Miss Grey, I have discovered that you are a dreadful liar, and I must be apprised as to why you've kept this pesky secret from me."

"I have no secrets, sir. What could I possibly have kept from you?"

"I have it on credible authority that you are one of the Mystery Girls of the Caribbean."

She stared at him forever as she picked what her reply should be. She settled on, "I'm not supposed to talk about it, so I probably shouldn't."

He frowned. "Meaning what?"

"My uncle and Gregory don't like me to remind people of what transpired. They insist it's left me too peculiar, and they act as if the whole thing was my fault somehow."

"You were four!"

"I know. Their attitude has always been very unfair, but I've accepted their position, and it happened twenty years ago. It's ancient history, and I fail to comprehend why it would be of any interest to you at all."

She pushed away from him and went to huddle by the bed. She was struggling to project an air of nonchalance, as if the incident had been of no consequence, but he was so attuned to her that he could practically feel her pulse pounding through her veins. She was trembling slightly and very anxious, but why would she be anxious?

Janet had explained how it had been a traumatic experience for her, so it was difficult to discuss. He completely concurred. He didn't like to discuss his father either, but the man's rescue of the Lost Girls was his most notorious feat.

"Caro," he said, "could we please review my surname?"

"It's Ralston. So?" She paused, then blanched. "Ralston? By any chance, are you related to Captain Miles Ralston?"

"He was my father."

"You are joking!"

"No, I'm not joking."

"I asked if you knew him, and you claimed you didn't! Why lie about it?"

"It's a long story," he said, which was his typical response concerning his father.

"When I first heard you were coming, I wondered if you might be kin to him. I've met a few Ralstons in my life, and I've always been curious if there was a connection, but as I mentioned, my own relatives don't like me to announce my link to the tragedy, and I learned the hard way that it was best to remain silent."

The remark sounded ominous, and he speculated over what she'd *learned* from the men in her family. Rumor had it that her grandfather had been a monster. It couldn't have been easy for her to have been thrust into his home. After what she'd suffered in the Caribbean, she'd likely needed some love and care, but old Walter Grey wouldn't have provided it.

"Do you remember my father?" he asked.

"Oh, absolutely! When he marched onto our island, we'd been stranded for ages. He'd seemed big and important and scary, and he was so...so...official, I guess. He was all decked out in his uniform with his medals glowing in the sun. We'd been living like abandoned wolf pups, and it was such a relief to have him in charge." She smiled and sighed. "I have such fond memories of him."

"I'm so glad. I was afraid you might not recollect."

"I recollect every tiny detail." Her smile slipped, and she scowled. "You said that he *was* your father. Has he passed on?"

"Yes, when I was ten. It was shortly after he stumbled on you girls."

"I'm so sorry that I won't be able to thank him."

"For what?"

"For being kind to me when I desperately needed him to be. I've dreamed about him so often. I hope you won't deem me to be terribly silly, but I was so bewildered when I arrived back in England. I'd never previously met my grandfather, and to describe him as awful and frightening would be an understatement."

"There has been gossip about him to that effect."

"I was confused and unhappy, and I used to fantasize that Captain Ralston was my father. I'd pretend he was searching for me, and he'd find me and whisk me away. I'd pray at night that he and I would return to our pretty island and that we would reside there with Libby and Joanna."

"Joanna was the third girl?"

"Yes. Joanna and Libby. Once we were in London and family members showed up to take us home, we were yanked apart without our being allowed to say goodbye to each other. After what we'd suffered, it was an incredibly traumatic conclusion." She started to shake. "I'm still haunted by that separation."

"Of course you are," he murmured in response. "You were just little children."

"And the authorities here in England were so mean and abrupt. They wouldn't tell us what was occurring or what they were arranging. It's impossible to explain what we went through. Your father made us feel safe. It's what I liked best about him, but we were only with him a few days. We sailed to Jamaica, and he handed us over to the navy. After we left his ship, we never felt safe again." She gazed down at the floor, her shaking more pronounced. "I believe that just might be the most words I've ever spoken about any of it."

"I'm delighted you shared them with me. I've been eager to talk to one of you Lost Girls, but when you asked me about him, I couldn't bear to admit I was his son. If you'd told me you didn't remember him, I'd have been too disappointed."

"Not remember him! Are you mad? I haven't forgotten a single aspect about that period. Occasionally, it seems as if it just happened yesterday."

He hated to witness her trembling, to realize how distraught she'd grown. He stepped over and drew her into his arms. She didn't scold him or scoot away. She snuggled herself to his chest, and it was a good sign of things to come.

She was wearing just her robe and nightgown, no corset or petticoats to furnish a barrier, so every delicious inch of her torso was pressed to his. Though she was very slender, she was curved in the appropriate spots.

"Don't fret about the past," he said. "As you mentioned, it happened such a long time ago. Don't let it vex you."

"I'm not fretting. I'm ecstatic! I've finally discussed it with someone who didn't shout and order me to be silent. I never saw Libby or Joanna again, and I've been anxious to hunt for them, but I couldn't imagine how. Even if I'd succeeded in locating them, I wouldn't have been permitted to contact them, and now, I discover Libby is performing on the stage in London. The first minute I have the chance, I'm going to town to visit her."

"When you inquired about her, you truly had no idea how famous she's become?"

"No. I was floored by the news."

"I think it would be terrific—maybe even cathartic—for you to visit her."

"I have to find out if she's ever heard from Joanna. I viewed them as my sisters, and Joanna was younger than we were—and very traumatized. I've been tormented to not know her fate."

"I'll help you with your search," he said, wondering if he was serious.

As far as he was aware, she was engaged to her cousin, and there had been no whispers about the wedding being called off. He had no right to be in her bedchamber, no right to assist her in resolving a personal situation.

Still though, it felt fitting to extend the offer. It generated a perception that their relationship was headed in a positive direction, that they wouldn't part forever once he fled Grey's Corner.

Did he want that? Did he want to continue on with her? If urged to voice an opinion, he'd have said *no,* he didn't want a relationship with her—or any woman—but he was being pelted by the overwhelming sensation that he was exactly where he was supposed to be.

She peered up at him and asked, "Was your father a good father? I don't remember my own, so I used yours as a substitute. I pictured him as being perfect. Was he? If he wasn't, please lie to me, so you don't spoil my fantasy."

Her expression was so sincere that he wouldn't have dared burst any of her bubbles.

His father—the exalted Captain Miles Ralston—had been a complicated fellow whom Caleb loved and loathed in equal measure. The man had been a decorated navy sailor, renowned for his bravery and wild exploits, the most notorious one being his stumbling on the Lost Girls.

But he'd also had two wives and two families, which had come as quite a surprise to Caleb and Blake when they'd learned about it as orphaned boys. They'd assumed they were his only sons, but they hadn't been.

Over the years, they'd debated endlessly as to whether their mother had been apprised of Miles's bigamy. Caleb and Blake certainly hadn't been.

They'd been five and ten when they'd been confronted by the humiliating quagmire, and by then, their parents had been deceased. A vicar had sent them to their English kin, and their mother's maid, Sybil Jones, had traveled with them to get them settled.

Once they'd arrived, they'd been greeted by Miles's stunned *other* family. It had included the woman, Esther Ralston, he'd married before their own mother—as well as several of his children. The oldest, their half-brother, Jacob, had recently been trying to become friendly with Caleb. Caleb kept putting him off, not able to decide how he felt about Jacob's overtures.

Sybil had intervened with Esther, had taken charge of the situation and fought on their behalf. She'd shamed Esther into providing assistance—by pestering the navy. She'd threatened to publicly disseminate the lurid story unless Caleb and Blake were supported as was commensurate with their position as Miles's sons. Naval authorities had prevailed on Esther, the first and *real* Mrs. Ralston, to help them.

They'd been enrolled in boarding school, then they'd had commissions purchased for them after they'd finished their educations. But it hadn't been easy, and it definitely hadn't been any fun. If Sybil hadn't acted as their champion, he couldn't guess what would have occurred.

They'd likely have starved on the streets of London.

As with Caro never talking about her ordeal, he and Blake never talked about theirs. Part of the agreement the navy had brokered with Esther Ralston was that Blake and Caleb would never mention their father or his secret, scandalous life.

They hadn't, and they didn't. Who would reveal such a hideous parentage?

He wouldn't confess any of it to Caro either. She appeared to idolize Miles, and Caleb couldn't bear to tarnish the halo she'd placed on Miles's head.

"Will it hurt you if I confide that I hardly knew my father?" he asked.

"Why didn't you know him?"

"Well, he was in the navy, so he was never home."

"When he *was* there, was it grand? Were you happy and contented? Did he adore your mother? Did he dote on you and your brother?"

"Yes, he adored my mother, but I wouldn't claim he doted on Blake and me. He was a gruff sailor, so he wasn't exactly warm and cuddly."

"He must have raised you to be manly men. Is that why you and your brother are so dashing?"

He grinned. "I'm dashing? Really?"

"I'll only admit it in this room. I won't stroke your vanity outside it. Now then, would you go? You had an imperative need to speak with me immediately, but you can't dawdle."

She tried to wiggle away, but he wasn't about to let her. Her bed was a few feet away, and without giving her a hint as to his intentions, he lifted her and tossed her onto the mattress. She was light as a feather, so it was simple to manhandle her. Before she could escape, he followed her down and stretched out atop her.

They were touching from chin to toes, and his entire body rejoiced, but she yanked him to his senses swiftly enough.

"What are you thinking?" she asked, looking startled and aghast.

"I'm thinking I'd like to kiss you again, and I'm not about to do it standing up."

"I have been much too polite with you, and you have to leave. At once! If you don't, I'll scream. I mean it. I will!"

"You will not scream. People might come running. Imagine the trouble you'd be in."

She frowned ferociously. "I might scream."

He wasn't about to argue the point, not when he finally had them both where they were destined to be. He dipped down and kissed her, as he'd been dying to do since he'd kissed her previously.

For some reason, he couldn't stay away from her. He wanted to spend every minute in her charming company. He wanted to do things to her he didn't dare do. He wanted her to give him things she should never relinquish.

It was insane, but he was attracted beyond any rational level. Where would it lead? Where would it end?

Nowhere good, he was sure of that.

She struggled not to join in, but it wasn't possible to ignore the fire that ignited between them. She was very moralistic though, and she was betrothed. He hadn't heard that she'd cried off, so she'd be fretting over their behavior.

Yet it didn't feel as if she belonged to Gregory anymore. By any standard he could identify, she seemed to belong to *him*.

How had that happened? He had no idea.

Quite quickly, she abandoned her restraint, and she participated in a gleeful way that rattled him. They kept on until he caught himself loosening the belt on her robe. He was an inch away from removing clothing, from taking steps he shouldn't take.

Gradually, he slowed, then drew away. He smiled at her, and though it was very strange, his heart was aching, as if it didn't fit under his ribs just right. He was awash with the oddest feelings of poignant affection. The most frightening words had surged to the tip of his tongue.

He yearned to have her by his side forever. He yearned to make promises and commitments he would be foolish to extend—because he wouldn't be serious about any of them.

She was smiling too, but she looked exasperated, as if she couldn't figure out how she'd come to be lying beneath him on her bed.

"We have to stop doing this, Caleb."

He smirked. "You called me Caleb."

"I'm still engaged to Gregory."

"I intended to ask you about that. You can't proceed with him."

"I haven't had two seconds to speak with Uncle Samson, so nothing's occurred to change my situation."

"You and I are so attuned. It's proof that you're in no position to marry him."

"I understand that now, and you're putting me in such a horrendous predicament."

"How?"

"You know how. Don't pretend."

He did know. He constantly showed up where he shouldn't be, then pushed her into conduct she shouldn't attempt. He wasn't sorry though, and he didn't suppose he'd desist.

"I've been dithering over how to approach my uncle," she said.

"Would you like me to talk to him for you? I could explain how reckless Gregory is in town."

"It's a sweet offer, but I don't need your help. I can handle it on my own."

He didn't believe that was true at all. She'd regularly been coerced by her male relatives. They wouldn't heed her. Her uncle would probably laugh, and Caleb couldn't envision how Gregory might respond.

There had never been rumors about him being violent, but he was very proud. If she backed out, would he lash out at her? And how might he lash out? Was it any of Caleb's business?

Her current problems were caused in part by the fact that Caleb let Gregory wager at his gambling club. Caleb had butted his nose into her dilemma, had encouraged her to run from her marriage. If she suffered difficulties later on, had he any duty toward her?

At the moment, he couldn't answer that question. He would have to watch and ponder, would have to see how events unfolded.

"Will you leave now?" she said. "Please?"

"I guess I should."

"And for pity's sake, be more furtive when you tiptoe away. I've sinned and disgraced myself with you, and I—"

He laid a finger on her lips. "Everything about our being together seems exactly right."

"Since I am betrothed, and you are not, you're not the person to give me advice on the morality of my behavior."

"You're likely correct, but I'll give you some anyway: Don't you dare feel bad or guilty. I certainly don't."

"Of course you don't. You have naught to lose by trifling with me. I, on the other hand, have a whole life and family to squander."

"We'll chat in the morning. We'll devise a viable path for you."

"What path? You can't fix this—unless you're prepared to wed me yourself. Is that it, you bachelor, you? Are you about to propose and save me from Gregory?"

She'd uttered her comment in a teasing way, but it had the oddest effect. For a brief instant, they froze, and the notion of his marrying her brought such a giddy swell of elation that he was practically dizzy with excitement.

He nearly blurted out, *Yes, yes! Marry me instead of Gregory!*

But that was a bizarre idea. Had she bewitched him?

He shook his head, chasing away the deranged thought, then he scoffed with amusement. "No, I'm not about to propose. I hardly know you."

"And *I* hardly know you, so what is our plan?"

"We'll figure it out."

"I'm glad one of us is so confident."

"Will you do me a favor tomorrow?" he asked.

"That depends on what it is."

"I would like to sit down with you and my brother and have you share every single detail you remember about our father. Would you be interested in that?"

She sighed with what sounded like gladness. "I would be delighted to tell you what I remember, but will you tell me what *you* remember?"

"I'll tell you what I can."

He slid away and stood, and he brushed his fingers through his hair and over his clothes so he wasn't too disheveled. She remained stretched out on the bed, like a seductive harem girl who'd just serviced her master.

"Will you end your engagement?" he asked her. "Promise you will."

"I'll *try* to end it, but I can't imagine the chaos I'll stir."

"If you need my assistance, I'd be happy to provide it. I can deliver a scathing recitation of Gregory's malignant habits to your uncle."

"I'll be fine on my own."

He doubted she would be, but he wouldn't admit it. He gestured to the door. "Will you glance out for me to make sure the hall is empty?"

She climbed to the floor, and as she walked by him, he pulled her close for a final, desperate kiss.

She huffed with aggravation. "What am I going to do with you?"

"What am *I* going to do with you?" he replied.

"We're mad," she said. "We're both mad. You realize that, don't you?"

"Oh, yes, I realize it."

She peeked out, then whispered, "The coast is clear."

"I'll find you tomorrow. We'll talk about my father."

"I can't wait."

He stepped by her and hurried away. He had an appointment with her fiancé, and he was suddenly more eager than ever to help Gregory dig a very deep hole.

Chapter

8

"How much did you lose?"

"I have no idea."

Lucretia glared at Gregory, but he was such a vain ass, he couldn't be shamed. He'd gambled all night, but she hadn't stayed to watch. It was too nerve-wracking.

He and his friends loved to hover over the table, eager to see which card would appear or which dice would land. That level of frantic energy didn't appeal to her in the slightest.

Gregory was an awful gambler too, and he was perfectly capable of disgracing himself without her as a witness. And was it really any of her business how much money he frittered away? So long as they were able to maintain their affluent style of living, why should she be concerned?

It was just that he constantly complained about being short of funds, and then, he'd have to beg his father for a quarterly disbursement from the trust fund. The request would precipitate a huge quarrel and threats by his father to cut off Gregory's allowance. Lucretia wound up having to expend enormous effort calming Gregory and pushing him back to an acceptable condition.

It was exhausting, and on occasion, she thought—if she could meet someone richer—she'd leave him in a quick minute. Then again, every man in her social circle was addicted to wagering. Who would be any better?

"How does Caleb Ralston always beat you?" she asked, climbing out onto a ledge she shouldn't have pursued. Gregory never liked to have his chums denigrated, although why he viewed Ralston as a *chum* was a mystery.

"He's simply lucky, and I'm not."

"You don't suppose he cheats, do you?"

Gregory blanched and glanced around, anxious to ensure the perilous comment hadn't been overheard. A man accused of cheating would take it very personally. The insult would be settled with pistols at dawn.

There were no eavesdroppers though. They were out on the verandah by themselves, the noon hour fast approaching, so few guests had risen to face the day. Their London friends had gambled all night too.

Gregory hadn't had the luxury of dawdling in bed with the rest of them. The vicar was visiting to chat about the wedding service, and Gregory was expected to sit through it—and to look like a devoted fiancé. To him, the wedding was a necessary evil, and if he could have managed it, he'd have arrived as the ceremony was starting, spoken the vows, then headed back to town.

He was that disinterested in what was occurring.

The entire debacle was a tedious bore, and he'd been so grouchy that Lucretia had dragged him outside to adjust his attitude.

"Ralston doesn't cheat!" he insisted, exhibiting great umbrage at the notion. "He's a navy veteran. He wouldn't stoop that low."

"Why did he resign his commission in the navy? There was that rumor about how he got caught in a swindle, and he had to quit or be court marshalled. A fellow who would jeopardize his position like that might do anything to you. A little cheating at cards is probably the least of his crimes."

"I'm not about to salivate over old gossip with you."

"Why is he so wealthy anyway? He went from being a simple sailor to being a rich cretin in a matter of years. It seems terribly fishy to me."

"He owns a gambling club, Lucretia. It's a lucrative business."

"Why must you play with him? Can't he find another victim to fleece?"

"*I* ask him to continue playing. You're aware of that fact. I owe him a bloody fortune, and I have to win some of it back before my father discovers the depth of my situation."

She thought he should tell his father to sod off. The man was a blowhard and busybody who treated Gregory like a child, but that was an argument for a different morning.

He groaned and rubbed his temples. "Ooh, my head is pounding. Would you stop nagging at me?"

If they'd been at home, she might have voiced a vicious reply to his whiny remark. As it was, she could only cluck and coo and pretend to be worried about him.

"You poor dear," she murmured. "I keep forgetting you're hungover. Has your stomach calmed down? Let's go have some breakfast. We'll see if the housekeeper has a remedy that can ease your suffering."

Without thinking, she rose on tiptoe and kissed him on the mouth. They were a firmly established couple after all, and they were alone on the patio. For her, it was the most normal conduct in the world. Except as she drew away, she peered toward the manor, and to her consternation, Caroline was watching them out a window.

Gregory didn't notice her. He was facing the garden, but Lucretia's mind was awhirl as she tried to figure out the best path. Should she notify Gregory? Should she remain silent? Should she do something? Should she do nothing?

On the spur of the moment, she couldn't decide, but she hated Caroline Grey, and she grinned a smug, contemptuous grin. Then she laid a possessive palm on Gregory's chest and stroked it in a slow circle.

Caroline yanked away and fled like a frightened rabbit, with Gregory none the wiser as to what had happened.

CAROLINE HAD NO IDEA what made her look outside. She was at loose ends and conflicted about numerous issues.

She had a meeting with the vicar and his wife to talk about the church service, but how would she endure it? Through the whole charade, she'd be on the edge of her seat, ready to jump up and say, *This marriage is a grotesque mistake. I'm calling it off.*

She couldn't imagine doing it though. Nor could she imagine the ramifications once she spoke up. Her uncle would likely think she'd gone mad, and she couldn't predict how he'd react.

Another problem involved Caleb Ralston. She was gravely sinning with him, and if she could misbehave in such an egregious way, what did it indicate about her moral character? She viewed herself as an honorable person. Evidently, she wasn't. Evidently, when push came to shove, she was no better than she had to be.

She was fascinated by the news that his father was *her* Captain Ralston. His son had waltzed into Grey's Corner, which was shocking and disturbing. She felt as if Fate had brought him or perhaps that his father had led Caleb to her.

If that was her assessment, then it was obvious there was destiny at work. With that being the case, how could she proceed with the wedding to Gregory?

The house was quiet, no guests up even though it was almost noon, so she'd been curious when she noted a couple out on the verandah. She looked closer and realized it was Gregory and Mrs. Starling.

They were always together, and Caroline had observed them as they'd socialized. She'd been left with the impression that they had a connection that wasn't exactly illicit, but that wasn't exactly acceptable either. Mrs. Starling was polite to Caroline, but there was always an undercurrent of tension, as if Mrs. Starling was secretly enjoying a joke at Caroline's expense.

She and Gregory were having an animated conversation, when suddenly, Mrs. Starling kissed Gregory right on the mouth. It was such an unexpected sight that Caroline was amazed she didn't fall to the floor in a stunned heap.

As Mrs. Starling pulled away, she saw Caroline spying on them. The horrid shrew smiled an arrogant, condescending smile, appearing gleeful that Caroline had witnessed the intimate exchange.

She laid a hand on Gregory's chest, and she rubbed in a slow circle that sent a stern message to Caroline: Gregory belonged to Mrs. Starling, and even if Caroline wound up with a ring on her finger, Mrs. Starling wasn't about to let Caroline have him.

Caroline had never been more astonished. She stumbled away and ran, simply yearning to find a secluded spot and hide while she pondered the disaster.

She was desperate to discuss the situation with someone, but who? Gregory would deny any indiscretion. Her uncle would scoff at her concerns. Janet would say, *My brother is a dog. Why are you surprised by this?*

Mr. Ralston would probably have all sorts of gossip to share about the disgusting pair, but Caroline couldn't bear to hear it.

As usual, as it had been since she was returned to England at age five, she was on her own with no one to guide her, no one to care.

CALEB HAD BEEN SEARCHING everywhere for Caroline, being eager to sit down with her and reminisce about his father.

It was mid-afternoon, and guests had begun to stagger down for a very late breakfast, but Caroline had been conspicuously absent.

He'd been up until dawn, helping Gregory grow even more indebted. Everyone was hungover, but he was fit as a fiddle, his mental faculties alert and functioning. When he was gambling, he didn't imbibe, and with him being regularly plagued by insomnia, he was accustomed to staying up all night. He wasn't tired.

He was walking down a deserted hall, wondering if Caroline might be ill, if he shouldn't sneak to her bedchamber and check on her, when a parlor door opened, and she emerged from the empty room.

"Caro! There you are! I was starting to worry about you."

"Hello."

Her greeting was morose and subdued, and he studied her, thinking she was sad and despondent, as if she'd received a terrible blow.

"What's wrong?" he asked.

"Nothing."

"You're an awful liar, and you're devastated. What's happened?"

She didn't reply, but gazed up at him with those poignant blue eyes of hers. They killed him, those eyes. He peeked both ways down the hall, then urged her back into the room. He shut the door behind them.

He would have pulled her into his arms, but she scooted around a small sofa, using it as a barrier to keep him away.

He wanted to complain and call her a nervous ninny, but he understood her qualms about their burgeoning relationship. She was engaged, and she hadn't reneged on her commitment to her cousin, so her flirtation with Caleb—if that's what it was—was foolish and reckless.

"I just saw...something I shouldn't have," she said, "and it upset me. I'm glad I saw it though. It showed me an important problem I failed to notice on my own."

"From how forlorn you are, it must have been crushing."

"I haven't decided if it is or not. I've been trying to figure out what it indicates."

"I hate to have you so distraught," he said. "Describe what you witnessed. Let me give you my opinion about it."

"How much do you know about Gregory's life in town?"

He could have guessed Gregory would be the topic, and he sighed. "I know a lot."

"Then tell me about Mrs. Starling. What do you know about her?"

He paused, choosing his words carefully. "She's an interesting character."

"How is she interesting? Why would you pick that term? In my view, she's smug, unlikable, and a tad patronizing."

"She definitely comes across that way."

"Is she a doxy?"

"She has that reputation in various circles."

"She's a guest in my home. She was invited to my wedding."

"What are you really asking me, Caro? Just spit it out."

"Are she and Gregory romantically involved?"

He didn't hesitate. "Yes."

"How long have they been together?"

"It's been four or five years."

"Years!" She looked as if she might faint.

"Men lead decadent lives in town. It's common for them to have affairs and mistresses."

"But he's about to be married!"

"I realize that."

"How closely attached are they? Have you any idea?"

"They share lodging, which seems very *close* to me."

"They cohabitate?"

"Yes. She's his hostess, and she manages his household as if she's his wife."

She was so stunned that she lurched over to a chair and plopped down. "If I'd married him, what was I supposed to be? Where would I have fit in that seedy scenario?"

"I can't clarify his thinking. He's as much a mystery to me as he is to you."

"Might it have occurred to you that I'd like to be apprised about this? If I hadn't stumbled on it myself, would you ever have mentioned it to me?"

He debated lying, but didn't. "Probably not. I have plenty of issues of my own with regard to your cousin, mostly concerning the fact that I'm not his nanny. It's not up to me to force him to behave, and it's certainly not up to me to blab his secrets."

It was exactly the wrong comment. Her eyes flashed with a spark of temper. "How could you keep this from me?"

"That's not fair. You're angry about Mrs. Starling, so you're blaming me for Gregory's conduct with her."

"I don't blame you for his conduct. I blame you because you would have let me march blindly to the altar without giving me a hint as to the morass that was about to envelop me."

"That's not fair either. I warned you about Gregory from the very first minute."

"Well, you didn't bother to point out the very worst part of it. What on earth am I to do?"

"I've provided my opinion over and over: You shouldn't marry him."

"It's easy for you to say, but quite a bit harder for me to accomplish."

"As I've previously stated, I'm happy to talk to your uncle for you, although I can't guess if he'd listen to me." She rounded the sofa and started for the door, and he asked, "Where are you going?"

She stopped beside him, so he was able to clasp her hand and link their fingers.

"I have to speak to my uncle. I can't keep putting it off, but he's been out of the house since this morning. I have to find out if he's home so I can get this over with."

"Shall I come with you?"

"No. This is a conversation I have to have on my own."

He dipped down and kissed her. "Be a warrior, Caro. He'll try to humor you. Or he'll treat you like a child. Don't let him."

"He'll *try* to humor and distract me, but for once, he won't succeed." She swept out and vanished.

He couldn't predict what was about to happen, but the party would probably be ending shortly. If the wedding was called off, the party would be too. He'd head to London and wouldn't have a reason to see her again. The dismal prospect was much more disheartening than it should have been, and as he reflected on it, he scoffed.

As if her Uncle Samson would allow her to back out. As if Gregory would agree. Of course he'd see her again.

He was positive, when he next bumped into her, naught would have changed.

⌒⌒

HOWARD PERIWINKLE PULLED A slip of paper from his coat and checked the directions the clerk in the village had jotted down for him. He thought he was in the correct spot. It wasn't as if there were any other cottages in the vicinity, but then, he was a Londoner and every tree in the forest looked exactly alike to him.

He opened the rickety gate and strolled up the walk. It was a cozy cottage, set deep in the woods, with a brook babbling in the distance. There were rose bushes blooming along the front, green shutters framing the windows. The thatched roof appeared thick and dry, as if the dwelling was well-tended.

It was the sort of place a bewitched princess might have resided. Or maybe it was an abode for fairies. Or, more likely, a witch lived in it and the charming façade was simply a ploy to lure in unsuspecting travelers.

He tamped down a shiver and knocked several times, but there was no answer. He stepped over and peeked in a window, but no one was home.

The afternoon sun was barely visible through the dense foliage, so he returned to the lane. A more potent shiver bubbled up, and it made its way to the surface. He'd heard too many stories as a boy about wolves and goblins, so he wasn't a fellow to lurk in the countryside.

He hurried off, anxious to get to the village before evening was any nearer. He'd try again the following day. Or better yet, he'd leave a letter at the inn and request that it be delivered. The locals wouldn't have any qualms about venturing into such an isolated location, but he didn't care for it overly much.

As he reached the road, a young woman was approaching. He watched her come, and he was swamped by the certainty that he'd found the person he'd been seeking. She was the right age, twenty-four or so, and she was very pretty as the man at the inn had said she was: auburn hair, big green eyes.

She was slender and petite, as if her ordeal as a child had altered her physique so she would never garner the height or weight another adult female might have.

"Miss James?" he called. "Joanna James?"

She halted and studied him, her magnificent eyes calculating whether he was friend or foe, and he couldn't blame her. They were in the middle of nowhere, and she was a tiny thing. He was harmless though, and she realized it.

"Yes, I'm Miss James."

He went over to her, removed his cap, and bowed. "I am Mr. Howard Periwinkle. I'm a newspaper reporter for the London Times."

"My goodness, what a thrilling remark. I always thought it would be so exciting to write for a living. You love your work, don't you? I can see that you do."

"Well, yes. Yes, I do love it."

"You're quite a distance from the city, but you're not lost. What brings you to my neighborhood?"

"I was looking for you."

"For me! My goodness again. I'm flattered. What is it you need from me?"

"I've been searching for you," he told her. "Aren't you a Mystery Girl of the Caribbean? You were in a shipwreck when you were little. You survived with your two companions, Libby and Caroline."

She smiled a weary smile, and he couldn't determine if he'd jogged a sad memory or a dear one.

"Yes, I was a Mystery Girl. You sought me out over that? How very odd."

"The three of you are famous."

She chuckled, her voice sweet and enchanting, and he was reminded again of princesses and fairies. "*We* are famous? I find that very hard to believe."

"No one has ever stopped talking about you."

She scowled. "You're pulling my leg. I'm convinced of it."

"No, no, it's true! Why, Libby is in London right now, appearing on the stage to gushing audiences. She regales them with stories about the tragedy."

Her jaw dropped with surprise. "You're joking."

"No. People were agog when you were returned to England years ago, and they still are."

"I had no idea."

"It's the reason I'm here—because it's the twentieth anniversary."

"So it is," she murmured. "The time has passed so quickly."

"My newspaper would like to print a retrospective about the three of you."

"What kind of retrospective?"

"We'd like to draft a few articles about how your lives unfolded after you were claimed by your relatives."

"Who would be interested in that?"

"Everyone?"

"I doubt that very much."

"I guess I've failed to explain how popular you've been."

"Mr... Periwinkle, is it? I can't think that *popular* is a word I would use to describe my life."

"How was it then? Was it scary? Was it horrid? Were your relatives cruel? Did they mistreat you? Our readers are eager to know how you've fared."

"Again, sir, I doubt that very much."

She was about to walk on, so he hastily added, "We'd like to arrange a reunion too." He hadn't posited the possibility to his boss or received permission, but it sounded grand. "For you, Libby, and Caroline. Would you like that? Would you like to see them?"

Her weary smile became radiant. "I would like that, and if you could arrange it, I would be happy to participate. I've missed them so much."

"I've heard that you were closer than sisters."

"Yes, I suppose that's true."

"And that you were ripped apart, without having a chance to say goodbye."

"It was a trying situation. The authorities weren't sure of what was best for us. They had difficult decisions to make, and I shouldn't judge them."

"Would you like to confide in me about those terrible days? How was it difficult?"

She sighed. "That, Mr. Periwinkle, is none of your business at all."

She circled around him and kept on toward her quaint, isolated cottage, where she lived alone and probably communicated with elves and had only fairies for friends.

"I'll write you," he called to her. "As soon as I've conferred with Libby and Caroline, I'll contact you about the plans for the reunion."

"I shall be waiting on pins and needles until then," she called back.

He blinked, and in that brief instant, she vanished. Or was it a trick of the light? It had to be. A woman couldn't vanish before a man's eyes. Yet she'd seemed to be part of the forest, a sprite with magical powers who could appear and disappear at will.

He stood very still, struggling to hear her footsteps retreating, but the sole noises were the beating of his heart and the air whooshing through his lungs as he inhaled and exhaled.

He spun and dashed off, being in a frightful hurry to get out of the dark, eerie woods. Once the trees thinned, and the road widened, he saw the village's church steeple up ahead. He slowed and laughed at his foolishness, suddenly feeling like a dunce.

He should be celebrating. His journey had been a success! He'd tracked down a Mystery Girl! He'd done his research and had found her! She'd agreed to a reunion!

It was an idea Howard would present to his boss at the newspaper. Initially, he'd scoff and declare it silly, but then, Libby Carstairs had arrived in London, and the whole city was drooling over her performances. She'd tantalized everyone anew with their fascinating tale of survival. People couldn't talk about anything else, and they were anxious for more stories to be shared.

And he, Howard Periwinkle, would be the man to tell them to the world.

"Caroline, wait!"

Gregory called to Caroline, but she didn't halt. He was in the front foyer, and she was climbing the stairs and headed for her bedchamber.

He'd just escorted the vicar and his wife out to their carriage. They'd driven away, clearly bewildered and a tad aggrieved. The dreary pair had obviously been dying to ask what was wrong with Caroline, but hadn't known how to inquire.

The meeting with them had been incredibly awkward. The vicar had bloviated about the wedding service, and his wife had waxed on about the type and placement of decorations that were allowed in the church.

It had been a perfectly ordinary nuptial appointment, one Caroline had reminded him about a dozen times so he wouldn't miss it. But once it had begun, she'd acted so strangely that he couldn't figure out what had happened to her.

Caroline was a very pleasant person. She was never unhappy or discourteous. She exuded a composure and contentment that was constantly praised by others, but she'd sat like a bump on a log. A *rude, disinterested* bump on a log.

She hadn't replied to any comments or suggestions. She hadn't had any questions. Mostly, she'd stared at the floor, with them having to speak her name over and over in order to get her attention.

Every so often, she would glance up and gape at Gregory as if she couldn't remember who he was. Was she sick? Or maybe she was weary from having a house full of company. Or maybe she was exhausted by the wedding preparations. Perhaps it was a combination of all three.

She had to have heard him summon her, but she didn't pause, didn't ask what he wanted, didn't stop so he could catch up to her. She was in a sort of trance, and she blindly continued on.

For a moment, it dawned on him that she might be suffering an episode of madness. Their grandfather had claimed her father, Winston, was mad as a hatter, and lunacy was an inherited trait.

An appalling notion occurred to him: If she was growing deranged, she'd have to be committed to an asylum. It was a common fate for women. They had a habit of being disobedient and incorrigible, and the laws were written so male family members could keep them in line.

If she was locked away, he and his father wouldn't have to worry about the trust fund. She would be judged incompetent to manage her own affairs, and she'd never be able to gain her release unless they decided she'd improved, which few women could ever demonstrate. She would never learn about her money.

But that was an awful, awful thought, and he was disgusted with himself for letting it take root. Shame on him!

He dashed up the stairs, reaching her in the hall.

"Caroline!" he said.

She braced her shoulders and staggered on, so he grabbed her arm and pulled her around to face him. They froze, both of them realizing how odd it was for him to manhandle her. He drew away at the same instant she jerked back.

"What's the matter with you?" he asked. "Didn't you hear me?"

"Yes, I heard."

She looked young and vulnerable, like a mongrel puppy that had been kicked to the curb, and he wondered what was ailing her. It was likely one of those mysterious female problems they never discussed with men, so he supposed he should find Janet and have her deal with it.

"Would you like to explain yourself?" he said. "You were horrid to the vicar and his wife, and they were extremely perplexed by your behavior."

"Were they?" she vaguely responded, as if she didn't care about their pique.

"You've been nagging about the appointment ever since I arrived from town, and I feel you were hardly present. You were lost in the clouds. Are you all right?"

She studied him as if he were a peculiar insect. Then she asked the most outlandish question. "Why are you marrying me?"

He hadn't expected the unusual query, and he'd never mentally debated the issue. It just *was*, so he had no answer for her. "Well, I guess...ah...because we're engaged? We have been for years, and it's time we get on with it."

"That's it?"

"What more could there be? We're kin. We're cousins. It's what families do."

"What if we didn't marry?"

A wave of fear clutched at his innards. "What a ridiculous comment."

"I only mean that you've resided in London for over a decade. Haven't you crossed paths with any women who tickle your fancy? You're bound to me, but what if there are better choices out there? Haven't you been curious?"

"I stumble on all kinds of women in the city, but none of them are *you*." He forced a laugh. "You're Caroline, my dearest cousin, and you've always been the one for me."

"Have I?"

She assessed him so meticulously that he had to tamp down a shudder. Had she listened to gossip she shouldn't have? Was she about to unleash another diatribe about his gambling? His hangover hadn't completely vanished, and he was still angry over the money Ralston had won from him the prior night. He really, really wasn't in the mood to be scolded.

"What's come over you?" he asked. "Should I send for Janet?"

"Why would I need Janet?"

"You're acting so strangely. I'm not sure you're well."

Footsteps sounded behind them, and when they glanced over, Lucretia was approaching.

"Oh, look." Caroline's tone was a tad snotty. "It's Mrs. Starling."

"Gregory," Lucretia said, "there are lawn games starting out in the garden. Would you like to join in the fun?"

Caroline glared at Lucretia, and Lucretia glared back, and there was a vicious undercurrent swirling, one he didn't understand at all.

Then Caroline yanked her furious gaze to Gregory and said, "Is there something you'd like to tell me?"

"No, except that I think you ought to lie down for awhile."

"I will do that—right after I talk to Uncle Samson. Is he here yet?"

"Not that I know of. He's been out all day."

"I can see the road from my room. I'll wait for him there."

"Aren't you coming down to the party?" Gregory asked. "Shouldn't you supervise the staff and put in an appearance for our guests?"

"I'd rather watch for Uncle Samson. It seems like a more productive use of my time."

She whipped away and stomped off, then Lucretia slipped her arm into his.

"She's a bit out of sorts," Lucretia said. "What's wrong with her?"

"I have no bloody idea," Gregory replied, "but she's behaving so oddly."

"Don't concern yourself. Whatever it is, I'm certain she'll get over it shortly. Let's go down to the garden."

"Is there brandy on any of the tables? I need a little hair of the dog."

"There's plenty. I already checked for you."

Lucretia smirked toward the corner around which Caroline had fled, then she led him off in the other direction.

Chapter
9

"I HAVE TO TALK to you."

"About what?"

Caroline had finally tracked down her uncle. They were in his library, and he was seated behind the desk, while she hovered in the doorway like a supplicant. He waved her over, and she slid into the chair across from him, trying to ignore his impatient glare.

He didn't like to be bothered when he was in the ostentatious room. It was his private enclave, where he could escape the chaos of the manor. The interruption aggravated him, and he couldn't completely conceal his irritation.

He was having a brandy, which was one of his secret vices. When her grandfather had been alive, no drinking had been permitted, but after he'd died, her uncle had made up for lost time. Gregory too. They both imbibed to excess, although Gregory was the worst of the two.

"I can see you wish I'd have delayed," she said, "but this can't wait. I'm sorry."

"You don't look sorry."

"I'd have cornered you earlier, but you weren't home."

He harrumphed in a way that might have meant anything. "Well, you've barged in, even though you understand you shouldn't have, so your mission must be dire. What is it? And before you start, let me beg you not to raise a horrid issue. It's too late in the afternoon to deal with a calamity."

"I'll get right to the point. I've been engaged to Gregory for seven years, but I don't really know him."

"Don't be ridiculous. Of course you know him. He's your cousin."

"He left when he was sixteen and I was ten. Initially, he attended university, then he abandoned his studies and moved to town. He stayed there. Please don't tell me I *know* him. I really, really don't."

He blew out a heavy breath, as if she was being a nuisance. "From your dour expression, it's clear you're about to launch into a diatribe about his faults. You don't seem to realize that marriages are a mystery. A wife can live with a husband for decades, and he'll still be a stranger to her. If you're feeling anxious, it's only natural. Every bride suffers qualms before her big day."

"They're not mere qualms," she said with uncharacteristic vehemence, "and I would appreciate it if you would actually listen to me for once."

"I constantly listen to you, Caroline, but you're young and you're a female. You're not always the best judge of a situation."

"Don't patronize me. I'm not stupid, and I'm not a fool. I most especially am not blind or deaf."

"No, you are not blind or deaf, so what precisely are you so eager to confide? I'm sure, whatever your comment, I'm already aware of the problem."

"Gregory is here so rarely that we just catch glimpses of his bad habits. Yet each occasion he's back, they've grown more entrenched."

"I guess that's an accurate assessment."

"He's a drunkard."

"That accusation is a little harsh. Every man drinks." He lifted his glass and snidely toasted her with it. "It's an enjoyable hobby."

"He gambles to excess."

"Again, Caroline, all gentlemen gamble."

"It's more than that, Uncle Samson. He's holding parties in a rear parlor, with his London friends, after you and I go to bed. He can't bear for a night to pass where he's not wagering. He's that addicted."

"I'll speak to him about it."

"He's heavily in debt, to an amount that could imperil our ownership of Grey's Corner. He could fritter it away with a roll of the dice or a fall of the cards! Who could stop him?"

Samson scoffed. "He wouldn't jeopardize the property. He can be frivolous, but he's never reckless. I must inquire as to where you heard this rumor about his debts. I hate to think you're gossiping about our private family business."

"It doesn't matter where I heard it," she said.

"It matters to me. Who was it? Who would spread such a foul lie?"

"It was Mr. Ralston. Gregory is a member at his club. I assume he would have a valid idea of how much money Gregory has lost—since it sounds as if he's lost most of it to Mr. Ralston."

"First off, you shouldn't be so cordial with Mr. Ralston. I have it on good authority that he was kicked out of the navy for being a thief."

"He was not."

"Second of all, if he's told you this sort of privileged information, you're spending entirely too much time with him. He's a handsome, dashing scoundrel, and you've been very sheltered in your life, Caroline. You shouldn't be socializing with a fiend of his status and low repute."

She bristled with annoyance. "Don't change the subject by placing the blame on Mr. Ralston. We're discussing Gregory and his conduct. Mr. Ralston is an innocent bystander."

"There's nothing innocent about him, and if you imagine there is, you are greatly deluded." Her uncle snickered in a nasty way. "Will that be all? Have we covered your list of grievances?"

"I haven't raised the worst one."

"What is it? What could possibly be worse than his being a drunkard and gambler?"

She braced herself, recognizing—once she uttered the words aloud—she would be walking down a new path. "He has a mistress to whom he is incredibly devoted."

He froze, then frowned. "He does not."

"It's Mrs. Starling. Lucretia Starling? She's a guest. Apparently, he's so attached to her that he couldn't leave her home for a week. He brought her to his wedding, and at every activity I have arranged as hostess, *she* has stood by his side while I ran about managing the servants as if I were a servant too."

"Why would you believe such a shocking tale?"

"I saw them kissing, right out on the verandah in broad daylight. I saw them with my own two eyes."

"Are you certain you're not mistaken about what you observed? I mean, the sun may have been—"

She slapped a palm on the desktop to cut him off. "They are a dedicated couple! I asked Mr. Ralston about them, and he apprises me that they've been together for years. They live together openly in town!"

"They cohabitate?" He smirked dismissively. "That can't be true. It would be a grave sin, as well as a public insult to you and me."

"Mr. Ralston offered to speak directly to you about them, but I insisted I could do it myself."

"You're being very clear, very blunt, but it's difficult for me to accept these wild allegations."

"She is his wife in all but name, which definitely has me curious as to why he's marrying me instead of her. If she's pretending to be his wife, what am I supposed to be?"

A lethal silence descended as they stared, their minds whirring. Samson rose and went to the sideboard to fill his glass with more brandy, then he returned and sat down. He sipped it slowly, studying her over the rim.

Eventually, he said, "I have to explain a delicate issue for you, and after you hear what it is, you must promise you won't fly off the handle."

"I can't promise you that. My reaction will depend on what you are about to tell me."

"You won't like it, but I'm going to share it with you anyway."

"Fine. What is it?"

"Men have affairs, Caroline. They have mistresses and sire bastards. They revel in disgusting amusements that offend the conscience of decent people like you and me."

"Is that your answer? Men have *affairs?*"

"Gregory has resided in town for twelve years. He has friends and hobbies you and I would never countenance. But you have to remember this: Whatever his relationship with Mrs. Starling—and I'm not admitting there is one—their liaison has nothing to do with you. If they're involved, she is a trollop who's degraded herself by entering into an illicit amour that any Christian person would condemn."

"And...?" she asked.

"It has *nothing* to do with you. He's not engaged to her. He's not marrying her. He's marrying *you*. You will be his bride and bear him his lawful children. You will have the respect and esteem that comes from being Mrs. Gregory Grey. Mrs. Starling will never receive any boons from Gregory that matter in the slightest."

Caroline gaped at him, wondering if she'd stumbled into a strange world where up was down and bad was good. "Gregory has committed a hideous indiscretion and moral lapse. Are you claiming I should ignore it? Is that it?"

"Yes. It's how wives deal with this type of situation, Caroline. They look the other way. They ignore the hurtful wounds that husbands regularly inflict."

"So... I should let him philander with a strumpet and convince myself it's not happening? What is wrong with you?"

"I'm clarifying how a clever girl thrives in trying circumstances. You're not the first woman in history who's faced this dilemma. The trick is to move beyond it, to not allow it to impede your happiness."

"That just might be the most ridiculous comment you've ever uttered in my presence."

"What option is there for you, Caroline? Your wedding is in four days, and our home is full of guests who've traveled here to watch you tie the knot. Honestly, you're carrying on as if we should call it off!"

"Yes, it's what I've decided. I'm calling off the wedding. You encouraged me to betroth myself when I was much too young to understand the ramifications. I consented to have Gregory as my husband when I shouldn't have, and now, when I'm almost at the end of this road, I find out he's not the man I assumed him to be."

"He's exactly who he's always been. You simply weren't paying attention."

"He's in love with someone else!"

She actually shouted the accusation, and they were both stunned by her volume.

In every instance, she was unfailingly polite and mild-mannered, especially to him. From the moment Samson had become head of the family, she'd been grateful to him, but gratitude could only take them so far.

He glared at her as if he'd never previously witnessed such a peculiar creature, then a hardness came into his expression.

"He is not in love with Mrs. Starling. She is a passing fancy, a bit of... of... *fluff* to keep him entertained. If he is pursuing this affair you've described, I've explained your position with regard to it."

"I will not be shamed like this," she seethed. "I want her out of this house! Immediately!"

"I'll see if Gregory can arrange for her to pack her bags and return to the city."

She threw up her hands. "And then what? She leaves for London, then Gregory and I will blithely march down the aisle—as if she doesn't exist?"

"Yes, I expect that you and Gregory will walk down the aisle. You will have a poignant ceremony, followed by a delicious breakfast, then two days of celebration afterward. The whole family will rejoice."

Her fury boiled over. It was the tenor of their relationship that he placated her. He humored her. He would pretend to listen, then ignore her. He was a man, so he thought he was smarter and more important than she was.

To him, she was merely the orphaned daughter of an unruly, unlikable brother. None of her kin had ever had a kind remark to offer about her father, and she was heartily sick of it.

Suddenly, a wave of umbrage bubbled up, and it was so powerful that it scared her. If she opened her mouth, she might flood the world with her rage. She'd swallowed down twenty years of snubs, slights, and affronts to her dignity, and she was finished being so meek and compliant.

How dare he discount the situation! How dare he belittle her objections! How dare he think he could coerce her into the union.

She wouldn't be pressured! It wasn't the Middle Ages, and he couldn't force her. No one could.

In their prior interactions, he'd been able to mollify her with lies and half-truths. He'd coddle and calm her, would talk and talk and talk until he'd begin to sound reasonable, and she'd wind up capitulating to his point of view.

Not this time. Not ever again.

"I won't do it, Uncle Samson," she quietly stated. "I won't marry Gregory."

"Yes, you will. If I have to drag you to the church bound and gagged, that is what will transpire."

"No. We're changing course—today—so I suggest you get used to the idea." She stood and stared him down like a judge decreeing a sentence. "Will you tell Gregory or shall I?"

"We are not telling Gregory this ludicrous news. We are not calling off the wedding."

"I'll be delighted to inform him myself, but *you* will have to confer with Mrs. Starling for me. I don't believe I should have to converse with that doxy ever again. I demand that she vacate the premises first thing in the morning."

She whipped away and stormed out.

"Caroline!" he bellowed. "Stop right there!"

She kept on without pausing or glancing back.

CALEB WAS IN HIS dressing room, debating over what clothes to wear down to supper, when the door in the outer sitting room opened and closed. He was attired in only his trousers. He'd just washed, so his hair was damp, and he had a towel draped over his shoulders.

He was a tad anxious over who'd blundered in. It wasn't a servant; a servant would have knocked. It wasn't his brother; Blake would have hollered to announce himself.

Whoever had entered, the person was standing very still, and the stealth had him suspecting it was a female who shouldn't have snuck in. Gad, but he hoped it wasn't another guest. He couldn't bear to endure the awkwardness of rejecting a romantic overture.

He tiptoed out and, somewhat nervously, peeked into the sitting room.

"Caro...?" he said when he saw who'd arrived.

"Are you alone?"

"Yes."

"Thank goodness."

With no more words voiced, she flew over to him and practically jumped into his arms. He was thrilled to catch her. In an instant, he was kissing her like a deranged lunatic, twirling them in circles as, gradually, they staggered over to the bed and tumbled onto the mattress.

The embrace heated rapidly, growing so wild they couldn't continue. As their lips parted, they were giggling like naughty children who'd misbehaved and had gotten away with it.

"I must point out, Miss Grey," he teasingly said, "that you are in my bedchamber and lying on my bed. What's come over you?"

"I had to talk to you; it couldn't wait. If you hadn't been here, I might have torn the manor down brick by brick until I located you."

He slid onto his side, and she slid too so they were nose to nose. He rested a hand on her waist and asked, "What happened?"

"I discussed Gregory with my uncle."

"How did it go? In light of your agitated condition, I'm predicting it was difficult."

"It was, and it wasn't. He made excuses and tried to sweep Gregory's conduct under the rug. He actually explained that it's very common for men to have affairs. That was his exact comment! Men have affairs, and if Gregory was having one, I should learn to live with it."

Caleb's jaw dropped in shock. "You're joking."

"No, and he also warned me that *you* are a very shady character, and if it was you who had claimed Gregory was out of control, I shouldn't believe you."

"I *am* a shady character; he's right about that. And men have affairs; he's right about that too. If you ever spent time in London, you'd be stunned by the antics you'd witness."

"Well, there may be mischief occurring in town, and Gregory may be one of the worst offenders, but I don't have to put up with it. Uncle

Samson told me I should ignore Gregory's flaws, so guess what *I* told him?"

"Considering the wicked gleam in your eye, I'm almost afraid to ask."

"I told him I'm not marrying Gregory. I insisted the wedding is off, and I won't pretend about it. I informed him too that Mrs. Starling must depart the premises and that he could have the dubious honor of apprising her that she'd been kicked out at my specific command."

"I don't suppose that decision will be greeted with much enthusiasm by Mrs. Starling."

"I don't care. I shouldn't have to consort with a tart like her, and now that I've discovered her base nature, I won't tolerate her presence in my home."

He grinned with amusement, but with amazement too. He was surprised by her fit of pique, but by her willingness to give it free rein too. Women weren't permitted to quarrel and hurl ultimatums at men. He was astounded that she'd have the fortitude to stand up for herself.

"I'm proud of you," he said. "You resemble a warrior goddess in an ancient fable. If you don't watch out, you might start smiting people with your blazing sword."

"A warrior goddess, hm? I like the sound of that. I haven't felt this good in...ever? If you had any idea of how often I've had to bite my tongue in this blasted house!" She smirked, appearing impish and full of mischief. "He was so bewildered by my attitude. I hope he didn't suffer an apoplexy."

"Maybe he did."

"When I left the room, he was shouting. He's probably worried that a fairy changeling has swooped in and taken over my body."

Caleb laughed, enjoying her spurt of temper. She was so pretty, and with her cheeks flushed with rage, she was even more fetching. She reminded him of Sybil and how she'd fought on his behalf when he was a boy. For years, she'd gone toe to toe with his Ralston kin, with officials in the navy, with headmasters at his boarding school. She'd refused to let him be mistreated simply because his father had been a bigamist and liar.

Usually, he presumed he didn't like feisty women, but on occasion, he was thrilled to observe such brazenness. Especially when the men in question deserved to be put in their places.

As if to emphasize her new confidence, she initiated a kiss of her own. It was hot and sultry and even a tad dangerous. It had him wishing again that he could unbutton buttons and untie laces, but he wasn't ready to walk down that road, so he was relieved when she pulled away.

"I just realized you're not dressed," she said.

"I was bathing when you came in."

"I've caught you in a complete state of dishabille, and I'm not even sorry."

"You're turning into a wench."

"Since I met you, I've become shameless. Is that possible? Or do you imagine I had shameless proclivities buried deep down and you've lured them to the fore?"

"I'm sure you were shameless deep down, but I never thought a smidgen of immorality was a bad trait in a female."

"You're a man, so you would say that."

She slipped off the bed and stood. He sat up, his hips balanced on the edge of the mattress, his feet on the floor. He relished the sight of her as she adjusted the combs in her chignon and fussed with her clothes so she'd be more presentable.

"I have to get downstairs," she said, "to check on the supper preparations. The servants will be frantically searching for me."

"Let them search. Let's stay in here all night and act precisely as we shouldn't."

"To my great delight—and horror—that notion excites me." She leaned in and took another quick, desperate kiss. "Have you noticed there's something different about me all of a sudden? You don't seem to have."

"You're quite a bit wilder than I ever pictured you being, but that's probably not what you mean."

"No. I *mean* that I'm not engaged anymore, so I can flirt without feeling guilty."

"I'm tickled to hear it."

"I'm also free to encourage the attentions of other gentlemen—if I find myself in the mood." She scrutinized him saucily, then raised a brow. "Aren't you a bachelor, Mr. Ralston? I'm being greedy for once, and I think *you* should be the first fellow in line."

She whipped away and sauntered out, and he listened to her sneaking away. Then he sighed with pleasure.

From the minute they'd crossed paths, he'd liked her more than he should, and he'd delayed his return to London so he could continue to socialize with her. It was foolish conduct, but he'd tarried anyway.

She assumed she'd severed her betrothal, but he doubted she had. Her uncle wouldn't merrily accept her decision. Nor would Gregory. They were determined to force the match, even though Caleb couldn't figure out why. It wasn't as if Caroline was an heiress with a fortune.

The Grey family was rich and landed, and Samson Grey didn't have to shackle his only son to a poverty-stricken cousin. Why would he? It made no sense, but then, in Caleb's view, families never made sense. Just look at his own father and the mess he'd created by having two wives.

Samson Grey had arranged the union when Caroline was a girl, but she'd grown up and now had a mind of her own. It left her at odds with her relatives, so the next hours and days would be filled with drama and intrigue—and even some intense sparring.

Caro was already moving on, and she wanted a new man in her life. She hadn't paused to wonder if *he* wanted to be that man. Did he?

He could see himself trifling with her, sharing torrid kisses when no one was watching. But...

He couldn't fathom why he'd become more involved with her than that. If that was his opinion, what was he planning?

He had no idea, so he'd lurk in the shadows, and if he could help her deal with her male kin, he would. Other than that dubious assistance, he couldn't predict what he might or might not do with regard to her.

In the meantime, he had to get down to supper. He rose and went to the dressing room to pick out a shirt.

Chapter

10

JANET ROUNDED A CORNER on the way to the stairs and physically bumped into Blake Ralston. She staggered, nearly fell, and he grabbed her arm to help her regain her balance.

"Why are you lurking in this hall?" she demanded.

"I was looking for you."

"Why? Are you stalking me? Are you spying on me?"

"Yes, to both. You've been avoiding me, so I accuse you of cheating."

"Your comment indicates you deem us to be involved in some sort of game."

"It's not a game. It's a bet. I'm trying to prove you're not as averse to romance as you pretend to be. If you constantly hide and surround yourself with people so I can't get close to you, how are we to stumble on the answer?"

"I haven't been hiding. That would mean I was afraid I'd be susceptible to your dubious charms."

He scoffed. "You are so full of yourself."

"I am not. I'm discerning and pragmatic."

"No, you're pompous and ridiculous, and you're a coward too."

"I'm not a coward!"

"You're scared to find out if I'm right. It sounds cowardly to me."

She gazed up at him, and her heart actually palpitated, as if she was a blushing debutante, which was so annoying.

She'd spent years, figuring out what kind of adult she yearned to be. She'd read, studied, and listened to wiser women talk about female roles, and she liked what she'd learned. She'd groomed herself to be an independent thinker, to have modern attitudes about everything from matrimony to child-bearing.

It was galling to admit that, deep down, she was no different from any other girl. Blake Ralston had recognized it too—before she had.

He was standing in front of her, attired in his uniform, and he created such a vision of manly strength and beauty that she was completely bowled over. It wasn't fair for him to be so striking. It wasn't fair for him to cause such turmoil.

From the minute he'd kissed her in the garden, she'd struggled to keep him at bay. He'd immediately deduced her ploy, and he'd been taunting her ever since. Suddenly, she was questioning what she believed about society and herself.

He'd merely showered her with a bit of attention, and she wanted to throw herself at him and engage in conduct she couldn't describe. Her body was on fire as it had never been in the past, and she had no idea how to quell the peculiar cravings he stirred. But why should she quell them?

What if she succumbed to passion? Would the world end if she did? The female authors she idolized all claimed that women should be able to make the same amorous choices as men—and they shouldn't be shunned for it. Was she a modern woman or not?

Was she ready to practice what she preached? Was she brave enough to seize the day? Or was she simply dull, provincial, Janet Grey, who was frightened of her own shadow?

She should probably test a few of her theories. She didn't have to moon over him and exhaust herself with wondering if he was about to propose. She could view their relationship as a man would. They could have a brief dalliance. Why not? Men pursued them all the time. Why couldn't she?

She would trifle with him while he was at Grey's Corner for the wedding, then, once he departed, she'd never think of him again. It's how a man would behave, and she tamped down a smirk. When they were finished, she'd let him down gently. They'd part on good terms. Perhaps she'd even give him a gift to remember her by.

She glanced down the hall, but saw no one. People were in their bedchambers, dressing for supper, and soon, they'd head downstairs to mingle and chat prior to the meal being served. She'd intended to go down too, having heard from a housemaid that there was trouble brewing between Caroline and Janet's father.

Janet had to discover what was happening, but Blake had accosted her before she could. He was much more interesting than Caroline and the problem plaguing her. Her cousin would just have to wait.

She gestured to him, then went back to her room, and as she stepped inside, he followed like a puppet on a string. He shut the door and spun the key in the lock.

"What's your plan, Miss Grey?" he asked. "You've lured me to your boudoir like the naughtiest courtesan. Are you hoping to have your wicked way with me?"

"Maybe."

"Why would I oblige you? I'm simply an innocent young sailor."

"You liar. You're a rutting dog, and you've been lusting after me from the moment we met."

"You could be right about that."

"It's a common fact that men can't control their desires. It's physically impossible, and I would hate to have you injure yourself by panting after me, so I've decided to have mercy on you."

"Are we about to engage in a flirtation?"

"Yes, we are."

He grinned a grin she felt clear down to her toes, then he pulled her into his arms—as she'd been wishing he would—and she was dreadfully glad he'd thought to lock the door.

⌒⌒⌒

"Sɪᴛ ᴅᴏᴡɴ."

Samson glared at Gregory, watching as his son slunk to the nearest chair. It was early evening, the house quiet, with guests dressing for supper.

Samson, himself, had been trying to get ready, but he was so irate that he couldn't focus on the elemental task. Finally, he'd given up and had summoned Gregory to his bedchamber.

He could smell a strong odor of alcohol emanating from Gregory's person, and his beleaguered condition highlighted the urgency of Caroline's complaints.

"What is it, Father?" Gregory asked. "From your dour expression, it appears I'm about to be scolded for another infraction, but I'm not in the mood for any of your nagging."

"Don't be insolent."

"I'm thirty years old and about to become a husband. I can't abide your incessant lectures. What reason is there to visit Grey's Corner? I should stay in town and not bother making these futile trips to the country."

"Have you seen Caroline today?" he asked.

"Yes. She and I had that idiotic appointment with the vicar and his wife, so I spent two hours with her."

"How did she seem to you?"

"She was peculiar as a bird with a broken wing. She'd badgered me about the meeting, so I dragged myself to it, but it was the most awkward encounter ever. She was sullen and morose, almost as if she was in a trance."

"Was she rude to them?"

"Not rude precisely. She simply acted as if she was a stranger who had no connection to the discussion." Gregory bristled with annoyance. "Just to warn you, they were bewildered by her behavior and even a tad insulted. You'll likely have to mend that fence."

"We have bigger fish to fry than the vicar's hurt feelings."

"What could be bigger than that? Those religious types can be a massive pain in the ass when they've been slighted."

"Tell me about you and Mrs. Starling," Samson said, deftly switching to the only subject that mattered. "I realize you're involved with her, but are you openly cohabitating?"

Gregory's cheeks heated. "Have I mentioned that I'm thirty? Have I mentioned that these lectures have to stop?"

Samson's temper flared. "As you conveyed her to Grey's Corner, had it occurred to you that there might be people in the manor who would find that invitation to be very shocking?"

"Who would find it shocking?" Gregory inquired like a dunce.

"Your fiancée, for starters."

"Oh."

"Yes, oh! Your liaison with Mrs. Starling has been exposed, and Caroline is incredibly enraged."

"My life in London doesn't have anything to do with my life at Grey's Corner. It's really none of Caroline's business, is it?"

"That's exactly what I told her, but unfortunately for you, she would beg to disagree."

Gregory scowled. "Meaning what?"

"First off, she is demanding Mrs. Starling vacate the premises."

"Don't be ridiculous. I enjoy having Lucretia here."

"*I* am demanding it too," Samson added. "I recognize that you're entitled to pick your friends, and I'm to have no opinion about them, but this is the limit of what I can tolerate. She'll depart in the morning—the minute she's eaten her breakfast."

"I don't believe she'll go quietly." Gregory smirked. "Would you like to be the one to order her out?"

"I would be glad to speak to her the instant this conversation is over."

Gregory sighed as if Samson was a great burden. "I'll handle it, but I must point out that you're being absurd. Caroline too."

"Is that what you imagine? She and I are being absurd?"

"Yes. She isn't even my wife yet, and she's whining like a shrew."

"She's called off the wedding," Samson bluntly announced.

Gregory blanched with astonishment. "What?"

"She doesn't want to marry you!" Samson uttered each word slowly, as if clarifying for an imbecile. "She's changed her mind!"

"Why would she? It's deranged thinking."

"It's recently dawned on her that you are a foul choice for a spouse. You're a gambler and drunkard, and you have a doxy to whom you are devoted. Evidently, you're very stupid too. You brought that trollop home with you, and someone tattled."

"Caroline is such a little mouse," Gregory said, "and she and I have always been cordial. At this late date, why would she be chafing over any of my failings?"

"That scoundrel, Caleb Ralston, has been gossiping with her."

"Ralston is a chum. He wouldn't have betrayed me."

"Caleb Ralston wouldn't have?" Samson shook his head, feeling disgusted and even a bit afraid. "How much money do you owe him? How many promissory notes have you signed?"

"The amount is a pittance. Don't worry about it. I'm certainly not concerned."

"He has to go in the morning too," Samson said. "You can tell him after you've finished informing Mrs. Starling."

"Could we forget about Ralston and focus on Caroline. I hope you told her she couldn't cry off."

"I told her I won't permit it, and she told *me* to stuff it."

"You're her guardian, and you contracted the match. It's not up to her who she weds. It's up to you. Her opinion is irrelevant."

Samson laughed a nasty laugh. "I'll let you explain that to her. I'm sure she'll be happy to listen."

"She can't walk away. We have to secure the trust fund."

"You think I don't understand that fact? I'm the one who's pushed you to cease your delays. I'm the one who harangued and begged while you loafed and claimed you were having too much fun as a bachelor and weren't ready to tie the knot."

"I wasn't ready," Gregory insisted. "We can't allow her to defy us like this."

"Then I suggest you rein in your pompous attitude and haul your ass up to her bedchamber where you will tender a thousand apologies. You will swear to her that you're parting with Mrs. Starling, that you'll curb your drinking, and that your gambling days are behind you. You'd better sound sincere or you'll never convince her."

"You know, Father, if she refuses to proceed, any court in the land would deem it a symptom of female hysteria. We could have her declared insane, and we could lock her in an asylum and never release her. If we committed her to Bedlam, we could do whatever we like with the money. We wouldn't have to fret about it."

Samson gaped at him as if he were a lunatic himself. "Lock Caroline in an asylum?"

"Why not consider it? It would solve so many problems."

Samson studied his son, wondering how he could have sired such an idiot. What kind of fiend would behave so egregiously toward his betrothed and cousin?

"Get out of here," he muttered. Gregory didn't move, and Samson shouted, "Get out!"

"I didn't mean to anger you. I was just throwing out ideas."

"When I next stumble on you, I expect to hear that Mrs. Starling and Mr. Ralston are departing and that you've fixed matters with Caroline."

"I'll begin working on both situations right away, but you're an optimist if you suppose I'll have much success with Caroline. She can really climb on a high-horse sometimes."

"Then you had best yank her off it, hadn't you?"

Gregory still hadn't moved, and Samson grabbed him by his coat, pulled him from his chair, and dragged him across the floor to the door. He jerked it open and flung the oaf into the hall, startling a footman who was strolling by and was nearly knocked down.

"Pardon me," Gregory said to the footman, as he straightened and tried to look as if he hadn't been tossed out bodily.

Samson glared at them, then slammed the door as hard as he could.

⌒⌒

"The thing of it is... is..."

Gregory's cheeks flushed such a bright shade of red that Lucretia was surprised he didn't ignite. They were in her bedroom, and he'd blustered in just as she'd finished dressing to head down to supper. He was disheveled and distraught.

"Spit it out, darling," she said. "It can't be all that bad."

She had wine on the dresser. He poured himself a glass, then spun toward her.

"It appears Caroline has learned of our affair."

Lucretia's mind whirred as to what her reply should be. She settled on, "We aren't having an *affair*, Gregory. Our bond runs much deeper than that. Don't debase it by using feathery terminology."

"This is not the moment to play semantic games with me, Lucretia. Caroline knows we're involved, and she's furious. She's... ah... demanding you vacate the premises."

"What? When? Right this very minute? After we dine, it will be dark. Am I to scurry away when night is falling?"

"No, no, you may leave in the morning."

"May I hope you told her to sod off?"

"I haven't talked to her, but my father is demanding this too."

"Why?"

"She's insisting she'll call off the wedding due to my having a paramour." He chuckled, as if a bit of levity would lighten the discussion. "If it's any consolation, Ralston has to leave too. Caroline has been gossiping with him, and my father is incensed about it. Perhaps the two of you can ride to town together."

"If that was your attempt to make a joke, it wasn't funny."

She stomped over to him, took the glass, and downed the contents. Then she smacked the goblet down on the dresser so forcefully that he flinched.

"Will you allow her to command you?" she said. "She's not even your wife yet, and she's issuing orders she expects you to obey. If you submit to her in this, what else will she expect? You have to stand up to her."

"I won't fight with her. I just want to get the wedding behind me. It's easier for all concerned if you'd oblige me without any quarreling."

"You asked me not to raise a fuss about your marriage, and I haven't. In exchange, you promised I could come as a guest."

"It was probably a stupid idea."

She was amazed she didn't slap him. "Having me here was stupid?"

"I simply mean that we've thrown our liaison in her face, and it's blown up into a huge dilemma. I need a few days to calm her down."

"Without *me* by your side."

"Yes, without you. Please don't be difficult."

"I can't believe you'd treat me this way."

"I'm not disrespecting you. I'm giving you a chance to help me save my marriage, which will protect my income. If you wish to retain our elevated style of living, you have to agree."

She seized the lapels of his coat and shook him. "Swear to me that you will return to London when this is over. Swear that we'll continue on as we always have and you're not about to toss me over."

He gaped at her as if she were deranged. "Toss you over? What a ludicrous comment. I've asked you to assist me with a vital task. I haven't uttered a word about separating from you."

"Yes, well, Caroline snapped her fingers, and you instantly jumped to comply. How can I be sure she won't hurl other demands after I've walked out the door?"

He rested his palms on her shoulders. "I swear to you, Lucretia, that nothing has changed and nothing will. Now tell me you'll aid me as I've requested. The entire afternoon has been dreadful, what with my father nagging and Caroline proving herself to be stark raving mad. I can't bear to fight with you too."

"Fine," she said, reining in her temper. "I shall trust you, but I vow—if you've lied and you try to cut me loose later on—I will track you down and castrate you in your sleep."

He smiled. "That's my Lucretia. Let's go down to supper, shall we? Are you ready?"

"Not quite. I'll have to join you shortly."

"I should find Caroline and beg her pardon," he said.

"Should you accost her before the meal?"

"I can hardly wait until after it. She'd be glowering at me while people were eating. They'd notice her fit of pique, and I would hate to have to explain it."

"We should convene prior to our dining. I'll be anxious to hear that you've resolved it with her to our satisfaction."

"It will be resolved," he said. "I have the perfect method for dealing with her."

"What is it?"

"Her signature on the marriage license, of course. If she thinks she can refuse, I have another trick up my sleeve that will persuade her."

He winked, as if he had numerous schemes fomenting, then he strolled out. Lucretia listened as his strides faded, then she studied her reflection in the mirror. She looked rich, glamorous, and sophisticated, and it was the image she always projected.

She was seething over Caroline's audacity. Gregory had blithely consented to send Lucretia away without even arguing over it. While currently, Gregory was acting very tough, Lucretia doubted he'd remain firm. If she wasn't vigilant, she might suddenly be set aside, but that wasn't about to happen.

Caroline Grey assumed she held all the cards. She assumed she could command Lucretia and get away with it. How did Lucretia feel about that fact? She never let anyone boss her. Would she meekly acquiesce to Caroline's edicts?

She snorted with derision. She'd leave in the morning, but before she departed, she would clarify a few pertinent issues for Miss Caroline Grey. Caroline had inflicted her opinions on Lucretia, and Lucretia was happy to return the favor.

⌁

CAROLINE WAS WALKING DOWN the hall toward her bedchamber, wondering if she should visit the kitchen to check on how the supper preparations were progressing. It was her usual sort of chore, and she should have seen to it, but she couldn't force herself down the stairs.

She hadn't yet spoken to Gregory, and she had no desire to bump into him. She simply wished he'd corral his London friends, load them into a carriage, and head for town. Then she'd like him to stay there forever.

She supposed she should locate a servant and deliver a message that she was indisposed, but she couldn't be bothered.

She was in a peculiar condition, excited, sad, and scared about the future. She'd been miserable for so long, without really knowing that she was. With her abrupt decision to break off her engagement, she felt lighter, as if she'd been carrying a heavy burden and it had been lifted away.

At the whimsical thought, she smiled, and there was practically a spring in her step as she neared her door.

She wasn't paying much attention to her surroundings, so she jumped a foot when a very angry woman said, "There you are, Miss Grey. It's about time you arrived."

Mrs. Starling emerged from the shadows, and she exuded such a sense of menace that Caroline was a tad frightened. She glanced over her shoulder, pondering whether she should run in the other direction, but she didn't move.

Grey's Corner was her home, and Mrs. Starling was an unwanted guest. Caroline wasn't afraid of her.

Still though, Mrs. Starling was taller, bigger, and wider. She towered over Caroline, looming up in a threatening manner, and Caroline warned herself to hide any unease. Mrs. Starling would be emboldened by an attack of nerves.

"May I help you?" Caroline asked. "You're quite a distance from the main section of the house. Are you lost? Shall I guide you to the front foyer?"

"I'm not lost, Miss Grey. I figured we should have a little chat."

"On what topic?"

"You have been spreading lies about me. You have maligned my character and gossiped about me with Samson Grey—to my great detriment."

"It's the truth Mrs. Starling, so you can't accuse me of gossiping."

"I am not involved in an illicit relationship with Gregory. He and I are just friends, and I cannot ignore the slurs you've spewed about either of us."

"You don't live with him? You don't openly cohabitate? If I traveled to London and searched his closets, I wouldn't see your clothes hanging there?"

Mrs. Starling's cheeks heated. "No, you would not!"

"I don't believe you."

She circled around Mrs. Starling, eager to slip into her room so the ghastly scene would conclude, but the insane shrew grabbed her arm and yanked her to a stop.

"I've agreed to leave," Mrs. Starling said, "but only because I won't cause any trouble."

"It's too late to pretend you haven't caused trouble."

"Don't you dare tell anyone that you ordered me to depart. I better not hear that you've been disseminating false stories. I will not allow you to harm my reputation any further. Keep your mouth shut."

"Or what?"

"Cross me, and you'll learn how I can lash out. I guarantee you won't like it."

"Mrs. Starling, I declare that you are too ridiculous for words, and I can't wait until we're shed of you."

Caroline jerked away and continued on. Thankfully, the witch didn't try to stop her again. Nor did she hurl any other insults.

Caroline scooted into her room and closed the door. She didn't slam it as she was yearning to do, merely because she wouldn't let Mrs. Starling realize how furious she was.

Very quietly, she spun the key in the lock. She pressed her ear to the wood and listened until the vicious harpy stomped away. Then she staggered to the bed and sank down.

"What next?" she asked aloud, then she shuddered with distaste and flopped down onto the mattress.

Chapter

11

CAROLINE SLIPPED OUT A rear door and onto the verandah. She'd avoided supper and had hovered in her room, not terrified by Mrs. Starling's visit precisely, but not keen to wander any deserted halls where she might bump into the deranged woman again.

She'd thought, when she didn't stagger down for the meal, that Caleb might knock to learn why she hadn't arrived, but he hadn't visited. Or she'd expected Gregory to show up and inquire about her crying off from their engagement.

Why hadn't he sought her out? Didn't he care that she'd changed her mind? The more likely scenario was that he assumed she hadn't been serious, that she'd simply been having a female tantrum and it would pass.

Unfortunately for him, she was already so far down the road from the notion of marrying him that she could scarcely remember it had once been a reality.

She wanted a different ending for herself. Might Caleb Ralston become part of her new and exciting path? She certainly hoped so.

The servants were competent, and while she liked to imagine she was indispensable, the house was running just fine without her. In the windows, she could see guests chatting, drinking, and playing cards. Dancing was about to start.

She might have been invisible, with her absence proving her presence to be unnecessary for any reason.

Out in the garden, a couple was furtively hovered in the shadows, as if they were trying to conceal the fact that they were together. She peered closer and realized that it was Janet and Blake Ralston. Caroline had been introduced to the younger Ralston, but she hadn't shared more than a dozen words with him.

He was as handsome as his brother, and with him wearing his uniform, he looked extremely dashing. When he walked through a parlor, the ladies sighed with pleasure.

As Caroline spied on them, Blake dipped down and kissed Janet on the lips. He drew away and whispered a comment in her ear, and Janet giggled as if she were a blushing debutante.

Caroline froze in her spot, struggling to decide what her opinion should be about what she'd witnessed. Janet was twenty, and she should have been betrothed and marching toward her own nuptials, but she insisted she wouldn't ever wed.

Blake Ralston was a sailor, and it was common knowledge that sailors had the very lowest morals. They traveled the globe, where they were exposed to foreign women and cultures and the rules about propriety were very relaxed.

Except for the year Janet had spent at boarding school, she'd lived at their small, rural estate. Blake had been born in Jamaica, then he'd journeyed to England for school and had eventually joined the navy. He was sophisticated and mature in a way Janet would never be.

There was danger percolating for her cousin. Janet would have no idea how to deal with a man like Blake Ralston, and there was no chance he was considering matrimony. It meant he had no business sneaking off with Janet.

What should Caroline's position be? She wasn't Janet's chaperone or nanny, and she definitely wasn't her mother. If she had to describe their relationship, it was one of a fond, older sister.

Should she talk to Janet? From how happy her cousin appeared to be, Caroline doubted Janet would heed any warnings. Should she talk to Blake Ralston? Or maybe to his brother? She hadn't heard when Blake was returning to the navy, but perhaps that situation could be hurried along.

She figured it would be prudent to interrupt them before they wandered farther into the dark garden. She went over to the stairs and skipped down them, calling, "Janet! There you are! I've been searching for you."

The amorous pair leapt apart, and their reaction underscored that Caroline was correct to fret over what was occurring.

Janet had been holding Blake's hand, and she stealthily dropped it. She spun to Caroline, saying, "I've been searching for you too."

"I was hiding."

"When you didn't come to supper, I was afraid my father might have locked you in a closet."

"I've been in my room, pondering a few issues. I didn't think I'd be good company, so I stayed away."

She focused her scolding gaze on Blake, but it was hard to shame the wastrel. He wasn't disturbed in the slightest by her caustic expression.

"Hello, Miss Grey," he said. "It's grand to see you up and about. We were all worried you might be ill."

"No, I was just tired."

"We were so busy today," he added, "that my brother and I didn't have our chat with you."

"What chat?" Janet asked him.

"Didn't I mention it?" Blake said. "With your cousin being one of the Mystery Girls of the Caribbean, we have an interesting connection to her. We were supposed to meet to discuss it."

Janet scowled. "Who told you about her being a Mystery Girl? Your brother? I warned him to be silent about it." Janet turned to Caroline. "I'm sorry, Caroline. Gregory was drunk and blabbing your secrets."

"It's all right," Caroline said. "I'm glad the Ralston men learned about it. It's fine that they were informed."

She always thought it was *fine* when her tragic history was revealed. It was her kin who were uncomfortable with the story.

She glared at Blake, giving him the direct hint that his presence in the garden was no longer required. In response, the cheeky devil grinned and said, "I should get back to the party."

"Must you go in so soon?" Janet asked, and she had an aggravating amount of yearning in her voice.

Caroline shot another caustic glare at him, and he nodded that he understood her message. "The dancing is about to begin, and the ladies will be dying to have me as a partner. I hate to disappoint them."

He clicked his heels and bowed over Janet's hand. Then he sauntered away. They watched until he vanished into the house, and Janet was beaming with delight, as if he hung the moon.

Once the quiet settled, Caroline said, "You two are awfully friendly."

"I like him."

"I think you *more* than like him. What's happening between you?"

"Nothing is happening, so don't glower at me. He's here for the wedding, and he'll leave when it's over. We're simply flirting."

"It looks like more than flirting to me."

"It's not."

Janet's tone was steely and firm, advising Caroline to butt out, but she couldn't. Not yet.

"He's older than you are."

"Not that much older. I'm twenty, and he's twenty-five."

"He's sailed the globe and seen the world. Are you expecting a proposal? For I feel compelled to suggest that *he* won't be hoping for that. I'm predicting, after he departs Grey's Corner, you'll never hear from him again."

"You're probably correct."

"Please be careful." Caroline sounded as if she was begging.

"I'm always careful."

"He might be out of your league."

"Or maybe *he* is out of mine. Maybe I'm trifling with him, and his heart will be broken when I'm through."

"You don't really believe that. If anyone's heart is broken, it will be yours."

"It's how men behave. They dally with no strings attached. Why can't a woman behave the same way?"

"Our problem is that we grow more ardently devoted than men."

Janet smirked, then changed the subject, indicating the topic was closed. "The strangest rumors are swirling. The wedding is off. The wedding isn't off. You quarreled with Father. You didn't quarrel. What is the truth?"

"Promise you won't faint when I confide this, but I found out Gregory is intimately involved with Mrs. Starling. They've been a dedicated couple for years, to the point where they live in sin in London."

"The shrew is Gregory's mistress?"

"It's shocking, isn't it? She's a guest in our home because, apparently, he couldn't bear to be away from her for even the few days it would take to marry me."

"I often wonder if Gregory isn't the most disgusting man in the kingdom, then you tell me this foul tale, and I'm convinced of it."

"I've demanded she leave for London in the morning."

"Will she? She seems terribly impressed with herself. I can't imagine she'll like being kicked out."

Considering Mrs. Starling's fit of pique outside Caroline's bedroom, it was a gross understatement. "She's not happy about it, but she's agreed to depart."

"What about Gregory?" Janet asked. "What about the wedding?"

"I told your father I won't go through with it."

Janet gasped with astonishment. "What was his response? Was he incredibly angry?"

"He insisted he wouldn't allow me to cry off, but it doesn't matter what he thinks. I never should have engaged myself to Gregory. The only part I regret is that I waited so long to come to my senses."

"Have you talked to Gregory?"

"Not yet. I haven't been able to find him, and he certainly hasn't tried to find *me*. I can't decide if he hasn't been searching very hard or if he's avoiding me."

"When you finally confront him, can I sit in the corner and listen?"

"Don't be flippant about this," Caroline said. "I'm stirring a morass, and it will get worse before it gets better. I'll need your support to remain strong."

"Are you sure you can sever the betrothal?"

"It's not the Middle Ages, Janet. No one can force me."

"No, but men have such power over us. There are all sorts of tricks Father can use to coerce you. He's likely in his library right now, writing lists of the hideous methods he could utilize to make you obey."

"It won't do him any good. I'm quite resolved."

"I'm proud of you." Janet stepped forward and gave Caroline a tight hug. Then she said, "I want to walk a new path too. We should both march off in different directions."

Caroline raised a fist, as if she was a radical troublemaker. "The women of the Grey family seize the day!"

Janet chuckled. "If we assert a bit of independence, it might send the Earth spinning off its axis."

"I will pray the conclusion is not that dramatic."

They sighed, then Janet scrutinized Caroline in an odd way, her expression becoming calculating and a tad devious.

"You're positive you're not marrying him?" she asked.

"Yes. Your father and brother can harangue at me until they're blue in the face, but they'll never persuade me to proceed."

"I would hate to jump out of bed on Saturday, only to discover you're curling your hair and putting on your wedding gown so we can get to the church on time."

"There will be no wedding. I guarantee it."

"So...if I wasn't here on Saturday, I wouldn't miss an important occasion."

"If you weren't *here*? Where else would you be?"

Janet waved away her comment. "I have no idea why I said that. Don't pay any attention to me. I'm being ridiculous." She studied Caroline, then the manor, then Caroline. "Would you excuse me? I forgot to tell Blake something."

"This flirtation can't end well for either of you, but I suppose it's futile to warn you away from him."

"You worry too much." Janet flashed a tepid smile. "We'll chat later. You have to fill me in on the details after you've spoken to Gregory. I predict he'll be an absolute prig to you."

"I agree."

"I like this new and improved you!"

"I like me a lot better too."

Janet paused forever, as if she might whisper a secret, but she didn't. She smiled again and dashed away.

Caroline watched until she was safely inside, then she headed back to her room. She wasn't about to stroll through the downstairs parlors where she'd bump into Gregory. If she stumbled on him cooing with Mrs. Starling, she couldn't imagine how she might react.

He could seek her out whenever he was ready. In the meantime, she had to confer with their housekeeper, Mrs. Scruggs, so they could figure out how to announce that the party was over and the guests should depart for home.

Like a thief in the night, she snuck in the rear of the house. A significant event was about to happen. She could sense it in the air. What would it be? How would she weather it? Where would she be when it was over?

Oh, how she yearned for that significant *event* to involve Caleb! Why couldn't it? She was an optimist and would hope for the best.

As she rounded the last corner that would take her to her door, she was delighted to see him standing in the hall, as if he'd been waiting for her.

His sweet regard washed over her so intensely that she must have been glowing. He made her feel as if she was too precious for words, and she hurried over to him and clasped his hands. He dipped down to steal a quick kiss.

"You missed supper," he said, "and I was afraid you might have experienced some difficulties with Gregory or your uncle."

"My cousin, Janet, thought they might have locked me in a closet."

He was aghast. "Would they have?"

She laughed. "No. They like to boss and coerce me, but they've never been cruel."

"I shall pray that stays true."

"I'm definitely stirring a pot that has everyone boiling. Lucretia Starling stopped by a bit ago."

"What did she want?"

"Mostly to scare me, I think. And to insist I was completely wrong about her and Gregory, and I shouldn't spread gossip that might ruin her reputation."

"What gall." He snorted with amusement. "She has no reputation to protect."

"That's what I told her."

"I don't suppose your insult was enthusiastically received."

"No, but she's leaving in the morning, so I'm shed of her."

She went by him and into her room. He didn't enter, but stood in the doorway, observing as she lit a candle on the dresser.

As she whirled to face him, he said, "I never asked you why your bedchamber is in this modest spot in this deserted hallway. Why aren't you lodged with the rest of your family? Please don't tell me they forced you to use this one."

"Oh, no, it's nothing like that. This is where my grandfather put me when I first arrived as a little girl. Initially, it was lonely and frightening, but back then, every minute of my life was frightening. After Uncle Samson took charge of the manor, I could have moved over to a bigger, prettier suite, but I like this one. It fits me."

"You have small wishes."

"I don't require much to be happy."

"Is the wedding still off?"

"Yes. I haven't talked to Gregory though. I've been hiding from him, so we haven't hashed it out, but I won't be able to avoid him forever."

He chuckled, his fondness even more apparent, and she was perched on tenterhooks, wondering what he was thinking. Had he, by chance, suffered any of the excitement she'd been suffering? Might he be pondering a closer acquaintance too?

She wasn't very adept at flirtation, but they seemed to be at a point where a remarkable conclusion could present itself. Though it was probably silly, she wouldn't discount her connection to his father. She felt as if Captain Ralston had brought Caleb to her, and she wouldn't let him walk away without a fight.

She realized she was holding her breath, expecting him to offer a comment that would be an overture to their discussing the important matters churning below the surface. But suddenly, he straightened and smoothed his expression, his affection vanishing in an instant.

She heard footsteps, then Gregory said, "Hello, Ralston. Fancy meeting you here."

Caleb didn't respond to Gregory's greeting. He flicked a commiserating glance at Caroline, and he was acting nonchalant, as if he'd strolled past by accident. She allowed herself a moment of self-pity over the conversation that had just been lost, then she braced for the pending confrontation.

❦

GREGORY STOMPED TOWARD CAROLINE'S door. It was peculiar to find Ralston lurking, but he was too irked to be curious about it.

He'd known Caroline since she was five, when she'd been dumped on their Grandfather Walter by the navy. The story of the three Lost Girls had riveted the kingdom, and she'd been an oddity, like an exotic specimen in the freak show at the circus.

Neighbors had visited to gawk at her. She'd been tiny and quiet, and she'd stared at people with those huge blue eyes of hers. Because she'd rarely spoken, there had been speculation that she was deaf or dim-witted, but it had turned out she was simply traumatized.

A doctor had examined her, and he'd claimed she was merely plagued by lingering shock, which would gradually fade, and it had. Once Walter had died and Samson had taken over, she'd quickly improved, growing so ordinary that it was hard to recollect how eccentric she'd seemed in the beginning.

If Gregory had been prone to much reflection, he'd have wondered how she'd managed to be such a sweet, pleasant adult. She'd finished her schooling and had commenced running the house for Samson. She was a fair, firm, and sociable young lady whom the servants and neighbors adored.

She'd always minded her manners and did as she was told. She'd obeyed the men in her life who were placed above her as the Good Lord intended, the two main ones being Gregory and his father.

What had happened to her? In recent days, she'd become a shrew he didn't recognize. How was he to view such a metamorphosis? And how could he change her back into the polite, compliant person she'd been previously?

"Would you excuse us, Ralston?" he said. "I have to confer privately with my cousin."

Ralston didn't move though, but asked Caroline, who was inside the room, "What is your opinion, Miss Grey? Would you like to be alone with him?"

Gregory heard Caroline's heavy sigh. "I suppose I should get this over with."

"Shall I tarry and listen in on the discussion?" Ralston asked her.

"No, no," Caroline replied. "I'll be fine."

"Of course she'll be fine," Gregory said. "Why wouldn't she be?"

Still, Ralston ignored Gregory and addressed Caroline. "Are you sure?"

"Yes, I'm sure. You go on. I can handle this."

Ralston tipped his head to her, as if he was perfectly happy to do her bidding. Then he whipped his caustic focus to Gregory.

"I'll see you downstairs in a bit," Ralston said like a threat. "You and I have business to conduct, so I'd appreciate it if you didn't waste too much time with her."

"This won't take long." Gregory truly expected it wouldn't. "I'll be down shortly."

Ralston shared a final glance with Caroline that Gregory didn't understand, then he continued on. Gregory watched until he vanished, then he spun to Caroline. She was blandly peering out at him, as if he was a great trial to her, as if she couldn't figure out why he'd arrived.

He'd hunted for her all evening, but in a half-hearted way. He hadn't been that eager to locate her. He never liked to quarrel, and he'd assumed he could bluster in, tease her, make a few points, then leave her to ponder his comments.

He'd been certain she'd come to her senses, so scant persuasion would be necessary. But now that they were face to face, he couldn't start.

He hadn't rehearsed any remarks, for it hadn't occurred to him that she had such adamant tendencies. As he glared at her through the open door, it dawned on him that he was a tad afraid of her. In light of how bizarrely she was behaving, who could predict how she might act?

"What did you need, Gregory?" she asked.

She stepped into the hall and pulled the door shut behind her, as if she didn't like him looking into her bedchamber. Well, wasn't that a snooty attitude for her to have! He was her fiancé, and Grey's Corner was his home. He could *look* into any bloody room he chose.

"I thought we should talk," he said like an idiot.

"What is there to say? I've called off the wedding."

"Father told me that was your plan, but I didn't believe him."

"We don't suit, Gregory. You can't honestly tell me you think so."

"We're cousins! We grew up together, and we've always been fond. You're being ridiculous."

"Uncle Samson convinced me to betroth myself to you, but I shouldn't have. You shouldn't have agreed either. You *know* that, Gregory. Deep down, you know I'm right."

"I don't know that. What's come over you? I feel as if you've turned into a stranger."

"I've been questioning our engagement for months—for years!—and I've realized I can't proceed."

"The ceremony is Saturday!"

"It *was* Saturday, but it's been cancelled. Could you send a message to the vicar for me? Or will you make me do it?"

"Caroline Grey! Stop it this instant."

"Fine then. I'll pen a note to him in the morning."

"What is wrong with you?"

"I want a different life. I want to walk a different path. I'm sorry, but that path doesn't include having you as my husband."

He huffed with offense. "What could be better than having *me* as your husband? Name one thing."

She smiled oddly, as if there were dozens of candidates who would be better than him, but she hadn't seemed to notice there was no line of suitors begging to marry her instead. He was the only fellow who'd ever been willing.

"Could we not bicker?" she said. "It's late, and I'm weary."

"We'll stand here all night if that's what it takes for me to get you to listen."

"I'm listening to you, Gregory, but *you* are not listening to me—as usual—so goodnight for now. We'll chat again tomorrow. I'm sure we can settle this amicably without having to brawl over a single issue."

With that, she slipped into her room and closed the door. She spun the key in the lock, and he dawdled like an imbecile who had been completely emasculated.

He thought about pounding on the door and demanding to be admitted. He thought about shouting at her, informing her that she was being absurd. He thought about reminding her that he was about to be her spouse, and he didn't have to put up with such insolence, but he couldn't imagine behaving that way.

Obviously, she was fixated on some weird ideas he couldn't chase away. But his father could. That was probably what the situation required. Samson was her guardian, and he would decide who her husband should be. It wasn't up to her.

She had to realize there could be consequences to force her compliance. Gregory had already explained them to his father: Female hysteria was a dangerous condition in a woman, and male relatives didn't have to tolerate it.

There were laws and asylums to deal with the illness. Gregory was incredibly fond of her and always had been, but he liked the money in her trust fund much more than he liked her. When it was a question between having her or her money, he would always pick the money.

She couldn't be allowed to imperil Gregory's livelihood. It simply couldn't be permitted, and he needed to have another frank talk with his father. Immediately.

Chapter

12

"DAMMIT, RALSTON. HOW DO you keep winning?"

"I'm lucky and you're not."

Caleb stared at Gregory, and he was struggling to hide his loathing, but he wasn't succeeding.

There were bizarre, unspoken rules attached to gambling, the main one being that when a man incurred extensive losses, the winner had to provide him with a chance to get even. Caleb had wound up furnishing Gregory with dozens of chances, but it always ended badly—for Gregory.

They were in a rear parlor at Grey's Corner, engaged in another pointless session of cards. Gregory was too proud to quit and too drunk to realize he should stop. The other London guests had given up and gone to bed. A footman had been serving them their alcoholic beverages, but he had to be up at dawn to work at his usual chores, so he'd departed too.

Even Lucretia Starling had left. Thank goodness.

Caleb and Gregory were the only two still seated at the table. Blake hovered by the sideboard, pretending not to be interested in the proceedings, but Blake was a sly character. If Gregory grew disruptive, his brother would jump in and yank him to his senses.

"Lucretia thinks you cheat," Gregory blurted out.

Caleb and Blake stiffened. It was a dangerous comment, and Blake said, "Be careful, Mr. Grey. You haven't ever seen my brother when he's angry, and I can guarantee you wouldn't like him when he's in a temper."

Gregory harrumphed. "I didn't mean anything by it. I was simply repeating what Lucretia mentioned."

Blake warned, "Perhaps your mistress should learn to be more circumspect. I would hate to have her unfortunate words land you in trouble."

Gregory downed the whiskey in his glass, then Blake—delighted to make matters worse—filled it again. Gregory sipped it more slowly, rubbing his forehead as if it was aching.

"I don't understand why I can't beat you," Gregory said.

"You never beat anyone," Caleb replied. "It's not just me."

"Yes, but with others, I win every so often. With you, it never happens."

"You're a lousy gambler, Gregory, and I'm a skilled one. It's easily explained. You really ought to find a new hobby."

Caleb wasn't about to continue discussing the topic, for he feared Gregory would walk out onto a limb that Caleb would have to chop off. He would never shoot Gregory in a duel, but the stupid oaf had to shut his mouth. Caleb owned a gambling club, and he couldn't have the idiot waltzing around and claiming he was a cheat. That sort of rumor wasn't conducive to running a profitable business.

"I'm weary," Caleb said. "How about if we call it a night?"

"I have to recover from these latest losses. You have to let me."

"We'll have to draft another promissory note. It's the only route open to you."

Blake chimed in with, "Unless you'd like to sign over Grey's Corner. My brother would probably be willing to take it off your hands."

Caleb had been marching toward this conclusion for weeks, and he'd arranged for Blake to propose the option. A transfer of title had become the sole viable ending, but it hadn't seemed to occur to Gregory. He couldn't square his debt otherwise. Not if he'd had a hundred years of trying.

"I can't sign over the estate," Gregory said.

"Why not?" Caleb asked.

"It doesn't belong to me. It's my father's. It will be mine after he cocks up his toes, but he's in disgustingly good health. He may live forever merely to spite me."

Gregory laughed a weak laugh, and he glanced at Caleb, hoping Caleb would laugh too, but he didn't. He held himself very still, his mind awhirl over how he should react.

Gregory had repeatedly bragged that he owned Grey's Corner, but from the start, Caleb had recognized Gregory was a blowhard.

Why hadn't he researched the property? Why hadn't he posed a few pertinent questions? Of course it belonged to Gregory's father! When had Caleb grown so oblivious that he wouldn't have realized that fact?

Blake broke the awkward silence. "How about your trust fund? There has to be a way to glom onto the balance."

"It's not mine either."

"Whose is it?" Blake asked.

"It's just... ah... not mine. I'm permitted quarterly disbursements, but that's it."

"Who gives you the disbursements?"

"My father."

"Is it *his* money?"

"No, it's...it's...family money. He's the trustee."

"I guess you'd best confer with him about this little problem we're having."

Gregory looked aghast. "I couldn't!"

"Why not?"

"He's...ah...not aware of the extent of my arrears."

"Then you're in a definite pickle, aren't you?"

Through their parley, Caleb had let Blake do the talking. He'd simply relaxed in his chair, watching Gregory squirm and dissemble, while he kicked himself for being such a dunce.

He finally spoke up. "I've noticed, Gregory, that you like to boast and crow about how wealthy you are, but you're naught more than an irresponsible boy who receives a quarterly allowance from his father."

Blake warmed to Caleb's steely tone, and he said to Gregory, "You'll never be able to fix this. My brother's murdered men for much less."

Gregory gulped with dismay. "There's no need to resort to violence. It would be completely unnecessary."

Blake scoffed. "I suppose that depends on where you're sitting. From my point of view, you have one foot in the grave."

Gregory began to sweat and tremble. He was such a wretched dolt, and Caleb thought—if he saved Caroline from having the fiend as her husband—it would be such a good deed that it would buy him a ticket into Heaven after he passed on.

"We'll have to work out an arrangement," Gregory said. "For repayment."

"Yes, we will," Caleb told him, "and just so we're clear, this is our last game. Don't pester me again. I won't oblige you."

"A gentleman has to provide a fellow with the chance to recoup his losses," Gregory whined.

"A gentleman does," Caleb said, "but I've never been one."

"He's a scoundrel," Blake added, "and you've gambled with him at your peril."

Gregory blanched, as he struggled to deduce a method by which he could smooth over the situation. Caleb hadn't declared that Gregory would be banned from his club, but they both knew it was coming. The drastic move would render him a pariah. His dubious chums could forgive many sins, but fiscal disgrace was not one of them.

He owed money everywhere, and once word spread that Caleb had stopped obliging him, his other creditors would be out for blood. It was a crime for a scofflaw to not pay his bills, and he wouldn't be able to walk down the street without facing arrest.

"There is one thing I could offer you," Gregory said.

"What could it possibly be?" Caleb asked. "You've admitted you don't own the estate. The trust isn't yours. What could be left?"

Blake stepped to the table. "Shall I take him out into the woods, Caleb? I could kill him and—"

"Kill me!" Gregory shrieked. "Are you deranged? This is England. There are laws against homicide."

Blake snickered. "They only apply if a man is caught. If he's not caught, he gets away with it. I'm willing to risk it."

Gregory was gaping like a fish tossed on a riverbank. "You're in the King's navy. You serve the Crown! How can you utter such felonious comments when you're wearing your uniform?"

"It's easy," Blake casually said. "Some people are too stupid to live, and I think you're in that group." Blake turned to Caleb. "I can slit his throat and have him buried before dawn. No one will miss him or care that he vanished."

Gregory winced with dismay. "Your brother is a maniac, Ralston. Don't listen to him."

"I won't—for the moment—but you'd better tell me something interesting that will distract me."

"You've met my fiancée, and you have to agree she's beautiful and graceful."

"From the rumors circulating, the wedding is off, so she's not your fiancée anymore."

Gregory waved a hand, as if Caroline's decision was of no consequence. "Her opinion is irrelevant. My father is her guardian, and *he* will never let her back out."

"Fine." Caleb shrugged, his patience exhausted. "She's still your fiancée. What of it?"

"She's a pristine virgin, Ralston. Pristine!"

The personal remark made Caleb so angry he nearly reached over and whacked Gregory alongside the head. Blake sidled closer, as if he'd deliver a clout himself.

"I'm not in the mood to discuss her chastity," Caleb coldly said. "Let's finish this."

"No, no, hear me out!" Gregory hurried to insist. "What if...if...you could have my wedding night?"

"What are you talking about?"

"You could spend my wedding night with her. In fact...ah...how about this? You could have her for an entire month. Her virginity can be yours—if the price is right."

A calculating gleam entered Gregory's eye, and Caleb was suddenly reconsidering Blake's suggestion to murder the idiotic swine. He peeked at his brother, and Blake shot back a look that said, *I'll end this however you want. What's your preference?*

"I can have her," Caleb said, "in exchange for what?"

"How about...to cover...all the losses I've incurred from the very beginning?"

"She's not worth that much. It wouldn't be a fair trade."

"Then how about a month for a month? You can do whatever you like with her for thirty days, and *I* shall receive thirty days of cancelled arrears."

"No."

"Ralston! Don't be a fool. You know you'd love to fornicate with her. Any fellow would."

Blake muttered, "Any fellow but *you* apparently."

"I'll have the rest of my life to climb into her bed," Gregory said.

Caleb studied the prick, wondering how long he'd pondered the foul idea. And who would have put the notion into his sick head? Lucretia Starling perhaps?

It was common for gamblers to barter over their wives and sisters. A man who was addicted to wagering, a man who had nothing left to lose, would flail as if drowning, as if searching for a rope. Sometimes, a female family member was all he could find.

Caleb didn't allow these sorts of stakes in his club, so this was his first experience with such sordid thinking. If Caleb didn't accept, who might Gregory bargain with next?

Despite how Gregory negotiated over her, Caroline would never consent to such a wicked scheme, but a corrupt rogue wouldn't give her a choice. He'd kidnap her out on the lane and force her to supply what Gregory had pledged.

Should Caleb agree to be the one instead? He'd never follow through, but it would be a way to protect her. Should he?

Clearly, he had to have Gregory swept up as a debtor. If he was in debtor's prison, he couldn't harm her. Not for awhile anyway, so she'd have a bit of breathing room.

Caleb glanced at Blake again, seeking his brother's opinion, but Blake simply wanted to kill Gregory and be done with it. Blake shrugged, advising Caleb to handle it as he saw fit.

"I'll obtain her virginity from you," he told Gregory, "but these are the terms."

"It's to be a month for a month," Gregory said. "That's what I offered. You get to use her for a month—and I get a month of debts cancelled."

"No," Caleb said. "I get her for a month, starting on your wedding night. She'll stay with me in town and please me in any fashion I require. For that dubious privilege, we'll wipe away the amounts that have accrued since I arrived at Grey's Corner. It's a substantial sum, and you should be glad I'm willing to go that far merely for the chance to fornicate with your insipid cousin."

He voiced the insult blandly, his expression bored, but inside, he was raging. He had to save Caro from the negligent wretch, and he'd need to contemplate the appropriate conclusion. Caleb understood Gregory was reckless, but he hadn't realized he was incredibly dangerous too.

Gregory fumed, downed his liquor, fumed some more. "I intended it to be thirty days for thirty days."

"Take it or leave it. It doesn't matter to me. My world is chock full of beautiful women. I can dally with your cousin or not. It's up to you."

"There has to be more in it for me," Gregory complained.

"How about this? I won't call in your markers for a year, so you'll have twelve months to figure out how to square yourself with me." Caleb smiled a grim smile. "And I won't beat you to a pulp tonight for being such a horse's ass. Nor will I have Blake murder you—even though he's dying to. It's the limit of what I'll consider."

Caleb finally poured his own whiskey, relishing how it slid down and burned in his belly. The clock seemed to slow, Time dragging as if it had halted.

Ultimately, Gregory said, "It's a deal."

He extended his hand, as if they'd shake on it, but Caleb simply glared at the dangling limb, and Gregory withdrew it.

"Will you tell her about this," Caleb asked, "or will it be a surprise?"

"I'll tell her, but not until after the wedding. I won't give her an excuse to delay the inevitable."

Gregory looked at Caleb as if he expected them to continue chatting, but Caleb sat like a statue.

Gregory picked up the deck of cards and shuffled them. "Let's play," he urged. "What do you say?"

"Get out of here," was Caleb's reply.

"I just shed a ton of debt. There's no reason we can't begin again."

"There's every reason," Caleb said.

"Name one."

"I can't abide you. I never could."

Gregory huffed with offense. "There's no need to be rude."

"I'm not being rude. I'm being brutally honest for a change. Now slither away so I can enjoy my drink in the peace and quiet."

Gregory didn't move, so Blake grabbed him and yanked him to his feet.

"Goodnight, Mr. Grey. We've had enough of you for one evening."

Gregory shrugged him away. "It's my own damn house. You have some gall to order me about in it."

"It's not your house," Blake said. "It's your father's house, and I suggest you skedaddle or I might wake him up and blab some of your secrets."

Gregory paled and rushed for the door. When he reached it though, he stopped and peered back. "Ah... Ralston?"

Caleb didn't bother to turn around. "What?"

"I hate to mention this, but you have to leave tomorrow. My father has requested it. He thinks you're a bad influence."

"You just wagered away your fiancée's virginity, but *I* am the bad influence?"

"No hard feelings, hm?"

"Get out of my sight!" Caleb seethed, and Blake lunged toward Gregory as if he'd attack him.

Gregory dashed away like a frightened rabbit. Caleb and Blake listened as he vanished down the hall, then Blake refilled their glasses and eased into the chair Gregory had vacated. They sipped their liquor, being a tad startled by what had occurred.

"What a weasely little prick," Blake said.

"That's the nicest description that can be used on him."

"I can't believe he'd imperil Miss Grey like that. Will you tell her about it? She probably ought to be apprised."

"I can't imagine having that discussion with her. I'd likely die of embarrassment. I'll warn her to be careful with him, but she's already figured that out."

"She's not safe with him. Neither is his sister Janet. Should you talk to his father? He might be able to put his foot down."

"It's another discussion I can't imagine having. The better route might be to demand payment on my promissory notes and have him arrested. If he was in jail, he couldn't harm them."

"Until he was released."

"He should be ruined forever. I have several options that will accomplish it, and I need to settle on the quickest, most ruthless one."

"My dearest brother, Caleb," Blake facetiously said, "you told him you'd give him a year to come up with the money."

"I lied."

"Like the sinner you are!"

"We didn't write down the terms, and you were the only witness."

"And I've suddenly grown deaf." Blake snorted with amusement. "You've been escalating your games with him, hoping you'd wind up owning Grey's Corner, and the property doesn't even belong to him. The trust fund either."

"It serves me right for being so greedy," Caleb said.

"Will you depart as Samson Grey has requested?"

"I can hardly stay when I've been kicked out, and *we* are departing. We'll return to London and let Sybil pamper us. It's how we should have spent your furlough anyway."

"You've been kicked out, but that doesn't necessarily mean I have been too. I think I'll tarry for a bit."

"I *don't* think you will. Why would you consider it?"

"I've been flirting with Janet Grey."

"Well, stop it."

Caleb glowered at his brother, but Blake smirked. "I don't want to stop. I'm having too much fun."

"Why would Janet Grey participate in a dalliance with you? Doesn't she hate all men?"

"I'm changing her mind."

"You are not. You're working to lift her skirt. At least be honest about it."

"It might end up being a benefit."

Caleb was aggravated and alarmed by Blake's flippant attitude. "I could have sworn—after I saved your sorry hide from a swift court martial—that you promised you were finished being reckless."

"I've been innocent as a choirboy."

"If you keep telling such whopping falsehoods, you'll be struck by lightning."

"Besides," Blake said, "that nonsense with the navy involved commerce to help my chums. This is romance. It's entirely different."

"Oh, Lord, spare me..."

Caleb glared at his brother, but his stern expression had no effect. Blake would act however he pleased. They were lucky some angry father hadn't already dragged him to the altar.

"I can't have you stirring a pot with Janet Grey," Caleb said. "After we leave in the morning, we shouldn't have any further dealings with any of them."

"What about Caroline Grey's wedding night? If I remember correctly, she has to supply you with thirty nights of unending debauchery."

Caleb's blood boiled. "If you ever mention that ridiculous wager again, I will gut you like a fish."

"I notice you jumped at the bet plenty quick when Gregory offered her."

"I did it to protect her from him. I was afraid—if I didn't accept—he'd rush to town and hand her over to some other cretin."

"If she ever learns about your grand gesture, do you suppose she'll be grateful?"

"We're never telling her." Caleb's tone was scolding. "It may take some shrewd plotting, but I'll yank Gregory out of her life."

"We could sell him into the Merchant Marines. A dissolute ship's captain could make off with him, and he'd never be seen in England again."

"It's definitely a thought."

"I could still kill him," Blake said.

"No." Caleb chuckled. "You'd like it too much."

"You could be right."

Caleb stood, and he motioned for Blake to stand too, but he didn't.

"It's late," Caleb said, "and we should get some sleep. I want to be riding down the road by nine."

"May we eat breakfast first? Since Samson Grey has evicted us, I'd like to gorge on some of his food before we slink away."

"We can have breakfast, but we're not dawdling."

"I have to say goodbye to Janet."

"Where would this goodbye occur? In her bedchamber?"

Blake grinned a cocky grin. "Maybe."

"Absolutely not! You are not to sneak in there. I'm serious about this. Stay away from her."

"I will—immediately after I bid her farewell."

"If you provoke a scandal with her, Gregory Grey won't be the only man facing death in this house."

"You would never murder me," Blake said. "If I passed away, you'd be all alone in the world, and I'm your favorite person."

"Your luster is fading."

Blake finally stood too. They headed out together, went to the front foyer, and climbed the stairs, but when Caleb wasn't paying attention,

Blake vanished down a dark hall. Caleb wasn't about to call out or chase after him. Everyone was in bed, and he wouldn't cause a ruckus.

He loafed on the landing, listening as the silence settled in. Suddenly, he realized he was very lonely. He couldn't imagine fleeing Grey's Corner without talking to Caro one last time. He wouldn't ever confide about the bet, but he'd like her to have some idea of how much he'd enjoyed meeting her.

If he'd been a different sort of man—a *marrying* sort of man—he'd have carried her away when he left, but he wasn't Prince Charming. He wasn't a knight in shining armor, and he wouldn't pretend to be.

Might she still be awake? Might she be glad to see him? He'd warned Blake to keep away from Janet, but Blake had ignored him. Apparently, Caleb wouldn't behave any better than his wastrel brother. They were both Miles Ralston's sons and that tainted blood made them reckless and ridiculous.

He went up to the next floor and wound down the deserted halls until he came to her room. He paused for a moment and inhaled a deep breath, needing to calm himself, needing to be sure he should proceed.

Why not?

Why not sneak in? Why not have a poignant parting?

His way clear, he reached for the knob, spun it as quietly as he could, and...?

The door was locked.

He gaped at it for an eternity, wondering if he dared knock, if he dared murmur her name, but the manor was filled with guests. The rooms surrounding hers were occupied by people who might peek out to discover who was there.

Was this a sign that their relationship wasn't meant to be? Was it a sign that they'd been destined to cross paths, but that Fate had no plan beyond that? It hadn't occurred to him that he wouldn't be able to slip in. He'd thought she'd be up and staring out at the stars, an insomniac waiting for a visitor.

He smirked with regret. He was an idiot, and the lock had saved him from doing something stupid. For he had no doubt, had he entered, he would have engaged in conduct he shouldn't have.

He crept away and returned to his own bedchamber. He pulled a chair over to the window, and he gazed out at the sky, watching the moon glide toward the horizon, counting the minutes until morning arrived and he could leave Grey's Corner forever.

Chapter

13

JANET WOKE WITH A start. She'd been fast asleep and a noise had roused her. Her heart was pounding, and she stared into the dark, overwhelmed by the strongest sense that she wasn't alone.

"Who's there?" she whispered.

"It's me," Blake whispered back.

She blew out a heavy sigh. "You scared the life out of me."

He came over and rested a hip on the edge of the mattress, then he leaned down and kissed her.

"What are you thinking?" she asked, feeling a tad irked at his brazenly entering her bedchamber. "What if someone saw you?"

"The halls are empty, and everyone is in bed but me."

She yawned and sat up, and with her wearing just her nightgown, the air was chilly. She shivered and pulled the blankets up to cover her bosom. She didn't want to seem too prim and proper to him, but she *was* prim and proper.

"Why are you still up?" she inquired.

"Your brother and mine were gambling. I was there to guarantee there wouldn't be any trouble."

"What kind of trouble might there have been?"

"I could tell you stories that would make you faint."

"Did Gregory lose again?"

"He lost plenty, but then, he's awful at wagering."

"I wish I had the power to stop him, but he'd never listen to me."

"Have you ever wondered if you're safe around him?"

She scowled. "Safe? What do you mean?"

"He's so reckless. He owes Caleb a fortune, and Caleb is tired of fussing with him, so he plans to call in Gregory's markers. Gregory could never pay even a small portion of what's due, so he'll probably end up in debtor's prison."

She snorted out a laugh. "Will I sound like a horrid sister if I say I don't care if he's arrested? It would serve him right for being so stupid." Blake had a strange look on his face, and she asked, "Why are you warning me about him? Why are you so worried?"

"A man like your brother—one who's trapped and has nothing left—can be very dangerous."

"Other than frittering away all our money, how could he imperil me?"

Blake pondered what to reveal and finally settled on, "I'd rather not provide any details. Just watch yourself with him. Don't trust him and don't believe him."

She scoffed. "I figured that out on my own."

"I'm glad to hear it."

Their conversation dwindled, and she smiled at him, riveted by how handsome he was. There was a hint of moonlight shining in the window, casting him in a silver halo. He was like an angel sent down to Earth to tempt mortal women.

She was definitely tempted, and he was spurring her to consider conduct she shouldn't be considering. She hadn't thought she would ever wed, but when she gazed at him, her modern ideas flew out the window. She caught herself contemplating how marriage to him would be perfectly lovely.

"There's a reason I snuck in to talk to you" he said. "It couldn't wait until morning."

"Why not?"

"Your father kicked my brother out."

Her jaw dropped with astonishment. "Will you obey him and slither away?"

"It's pointless for us to stay. Caleb is here to attend the wedding, but the wedding is off."

"But...but...why do *you* have to go? No one's kicked you out, have they?"

"Not yet." He grinned a wicked grin.

"Why don't you tarry then?"

"I better not. Your father would eventually notice me lurking and demand I go too. Besides, I'm on furlough from the navy, and I'd like to spend the rest of my holiday with my brother."

"Will you ever come to Grey's Corner again?"

"I can't imagine why I would."

Her heart literally skipped a beat. "Are you sure? I could have sworn you were enjoying yourself."

"I always like to dawdle in a fancy house, but I detest your brother. I'm not in the mood to ever bump into him in the future."

"What about me? Would you ever be keen to bump into me?"

"I'll always hope we cross paths."

Her mind whirred frantically as she struggled to deduce how she could keep him in her life for awhile longer. A few minutes earlier, she'd been thinking it would be delightful to wed him, but *he* had stopped by to tell her he was leaving.

It was a brutal indication that men and women were such different creatures. With their thought processes so divergent, how could she have assumed they could genuinely bond?

She understood all of that, but she was desperately anxious to remain connected to him anyway. He was the only thrilling thing that had ever happened to her. If he departed, she'd be too bereft to carry on.

"I hate to suppose we'll part forever," she said. "I was expecting we'd be. . . ah. . . friends."

"I guess it's not in the cards."

He was so blasé about it, as if meeting her hadn't meant very much to him, so she had to be nonchalant too. "Could we correspond? Would you like that?"

"I'm not much of a letter writer. You'd work your fingers to the bone, penning lengthy diatribes to me, but I'd never reply."

Her mind clipped on at an even faster pace. There had to be a way for them to be together. "What if I came to London?"

"For a visit?"

"Well, no. I'd like to live there. Gregory was allowed to move to town when he was eighteen. It's not fair that he was given the chance, but I wasn't."

"I can't picture your father letting you."

"I wouldn't exactly request his permission."

"You'd run away?"

"Yes."

"You scamp, you. When would you go?"

She tossed the dice to discover where they would land. "How about now? What if I went with you tomorrow?"

He blanched. "My brother would never agree to that. He can be a stickler for the proprieties."

"Your brother owns a gambling club. How much of a stickler could he be about anything?"

"He had to start it because of me. I got him drummed out of the navy."

"What did you do?"

"I was swept up in a scandal, and he took the blame. Otherwise, I'd have been court marshalled. He saved me, but the end result was that I kept my career and he lost his."

"Has he forgiven you?"

"Of course. I'm his only kin, so he couldn't stay angry. What would be the point?"

"If you'd harmed me like that, I doubt I'd have been so magnanimous. I'd have punished you for years so I could be certain you'd learned your lesson."

"I'm very hard-headed. If he has to teach me a lesson, he pummels me. That sort of firm message is necessary to get my attention."

"Your admission doesn't make you sound like much of a catch for a young lady such as myself."

"I'm a great catch," he said, "if the young lady in question is looking for fun and excitement." He scrutinized her meticulously. "But if she's looking for commitment and marriage, I'm not the fellow for the job."

"Well, *I* am looking for fun and excitement, and I'm not looking for marriage or commitment, so I might be the precise female you're seeking."

"You constantly claim you loathe matrimony, but I've never met a woman who believed that insane idea deep down."

"I believe it," she said in a huff. "I want to be free and independent."

"Your father might have an opinion about that notion. I can't figure out why he hasn't already engaged you to some tedious dolt."

"It's my biggest fear."

"If he proceeded, you couldn't stop him."

"Yes, and the prospect gives me even more incentive to run away."

"Is it your plan to flit off to London and pretend to be a rich spinster?"

"I have a small trust fund, so I have my own money. I could do exactly that."

"A female living alone is generally viewed as a trollop."

"So I'll hire a companion, but secretly, maybe I'll be a bit of a trollop too."

She pulled him close and kissed him, being eager to impress on him that she wasn't like the other girls he'd known. He'd likely broken hearts all over the kingdom, and if she hoped to hold onto him, she'd have to prove she was different from the tarts who'd tantalized him in the past.

She suffered a stirring vision of what was approaching. She'd rent a pretty apartment, and she'd have tons of smart, interesting friends. They'd be actors, authors, and other notorious types, all of whom were pursuing her sort of unusual existence.

She'd become an intellectual and write books about women and their need to be liberated from societal constraints. She'd practice what she preached by shunning matrimony. She'd be a vivacious, spirited girl who could make a man like Blake Ralston happy.

Gregory carried on that way. Why couldn't she? Gregory had a town house and a paramour. Why couldn't she? Gregory spent money with a reckless abandon. Why couldn't she? She could barely breathe from yearning for it to transpire.

As their lips parted, she was overcome by the image that had flared. She had to alter herself into the person she'd pictured. She wouldn't accept any other future.

"Will you help me move to London?" she asked. "My father will try to prevent me, so I'll have to sneak away. Then I'll require some assistance after I arrive."

"You definitely will. A female in the city can't even rent lodging on her own."

"Precisely. Some *man* will have to do it for me."

"I suppose I can aid you," he said, "but there can't be any strings attached."

"No strings," she vowed.

"You say that now, but I see how you're gazing at me. You're keen to snare me into marriage, but you can't."

"I want your *help*. I don't want your ring on my finger."

"I can't betroth myself anyway. I'm heading back to the navy as soon as my furlough ends. Depending where my ship is stationed, there's no telling when I'll be in England again."

Her pulse raced at the possibility of his departure, but she ignored it. "You'll be around long enough to get me settled, won't you?"

"I shouldn't agree to this."

"But will you? Please?"

He assessed her forever, then he said. "Fine, Janet Grey. I will help you settle in the city, and there will be no strings attached. If my name is ever linked to yours, you have to insist you barely know me."

She chuckled. "I *do* barely know you."

"That's true, isn't it?"

"But I think I should know you quite a bit better."

He raised a brow. "How might we accomplish it?"

She felt as if she was running toward a cliff and about to jump over. "It's awfully chilly in here. Aren't you freezing?"

"Now that you mention it, I am cold."

"Would you like me to warm you? We could snuggle for awhile."

She lifted the blankets and patted the spot next to her on the bed. He studied her, studied the blankets, then said, "Why the hell not? I have a lengthy ride tomorrow. I might as well have some fun tonight."

⌒⌒

CAROLINE WOKE WITH A start. She'd been fast asleep and a noise had roused her. She stared into the dark, overwhelmed by the strongest sense that someone was out in the hall.

She glared at the wood, wishing she had magical eyes so she could see who was on the other side. Her first thought was that it had to be Caleb, and she nearly tossed off the covers and rushed over to peek out, but what if it was Mrs. Starling? What if it was Gregory?

It was late and, no doubt, people had been drinking. If it was either of them, they'd be intoxicated and much more disagreeable than normal. She wouldn't risk an encounter.

Yet she could practically feel the person reaching out, pondering whether to knock. Then, whoever it had been, he tiptoed away, and she was sure it had been Caleb.

He must have needed to talk to her, and the topic must have been vitally important. What might it have been? Marriage perhaps? It seemed to be their unfinished business.

She threw off the blankets and dashed to the door. She fumbled with the key and yanked it open, but the hall was empty, and she wondered if she'd imagined the whole thing. She listened intently, but she couldn't hear anyone retreating.

She staggered to the bed and nestled under the covers. She focused her mind, sending a frantic message to him, apprising him to come back. He didn't though, and eventually, she fell into a fitful slumber.

When morning finally arrived, she was grouchy and peevish, and clearly, it would be a very long day.

⌇

"I'VE GIVEN THE ISSUE significant thought."

"Good. So have I."

Samson frowned at Caroline, and she looked miserable. Her reduced condition proved she was conflicted about her decision to cry off, so he had to decide for her. He had to keep her on the appropriate path, that *path* being marriage to Gregory.

They were in the dining room and having breakfast. Gregory was nowhere to be found, but for some reason, Janet was up and eating too. She appeared annoyingly perky.

Samson had ordered Lucretia Starling and Caleb Ralston to vacate the premises, but it was already nine o'clock and—unless they'd left early—he hadn't noticed them preparing to depart.

If they didn't slither away shortly, he would begin knocking on bedchamber doors to hurry them along. He was determined to get the nuptials back on track, and he was certain, once the infuriating duo vanished—so they weren't shoved in Caroline's face every second—matters would calm and she would return to being the malleable young lady she'd been in the past.

"I command you to proceed with the wedding," he said.

"I'm sorry, but I can't."

She sipped her tea, staring blandly, as if she hadn't just brazenly defied him. He rarely lost his temper. He'd observed too much of that kind of behavior from his horrid father, but she was being so recalcitrant. Would a sound whipping bring her around?

"You can marry Gregory and you will," he firmly stated.

Janet chimed in with, "Stop badgering her, Father. I'm delighted that she called it off. You should be too. Gregory has so many problems, and we need to address them. It's cruel to pressure her."

"Stay out of this, Janet. Caroline is my ward, and I am her guardian. I'm standing in for her father, and her welfare is my primary concern. I'm only trying to do what's best for her."

Janet chuckled snidely. "You think Gregory is *best?*"

He slammed his fork down on his plate. "This is between Caroline and me. Your comments are neither wanted nor necessary. Be silent or leave."

"No. You're hoping to browbeat her, and you're a bully who manipulates her to your own benefit. I am her staunchest ally, and I shall be a bulwark to ensure she thwarts you for a change."

For years, Janet had been snippy and rude. She read radical books and cherished the theories contained in them. He'd humored her, assuming it was a phase and she'd grow out of it. But it was obvious she'd adopted the peculiar teachings to where she presumed she could disrespect her father without consequence.

Her impertinence had him realizing it was time she had a husband. She was twenty, and she was entirely too bold in her attitudes and ideas. A stern husband would tamp them down quickly enough.

He sat in his chair, studying the two women as they continued with their meal. They were chatting quietly, ignoring him as if he were invisible, and their insolence had him fuming.

He absolutely would not lose control of Caroline's fortune. If he had to drag her to the altar in chains and speak the vows for her, he would seriously consider doing that. He couldn't imagine their local vicar would participate though, but there were ways for a father or uncle to garner what he desired from an intractable daughter or niece.

There had to be a corrupt preacher in the country who could be bribed to host a ceremony that would bind her to Gregory. Samson was in charge of her, so he could probably accomplish it without her even being present. And of course, there was the option Gregory had suggested: They could declare she was suffering from hysteria and have her committed to an asylum.

With the stroke of a judge's pen, she could be ruled incompetent to handle her own affairs. The money would be safely his forever, but he didn't want to treat her badly. He'd loved her father—his only brother—and he was very fond of her. He merely wanted her to obey him as was proper and fitting.

Janet interrupted his furious reverie. "Father, would you ever permit me to move to London?"

"No, never."

"Why? You've let Gregory stay there all these years."

"Gregory is a man and you're not. Your situation is completely different."

"I have the trust fund I inherited from my grandmother, so I'm not a pauper. I could pay my own expenses. I could just go—whether I have your permission or not."

"I manage your trust, Janet. Currently, I give you an allowance from it, but I don't have to do that. I could cut it off. You wouldn't get very far without it."

"I could hire a lawyer and replace you as trustee."

It was such a brash remark that he was amazed he didn't slap her. "Am I to endure a full-blown insurrection from you two?"

"I simply think it would be fun to reside in town," Janet said. "I don't understand why you find the prospect so threatening."

"Only trollops with loose morals live alone. I'd lock you in a convent before you were able to disgrace yourself like that."

Janet rolled her eyes, then muttered under her breath, "And you wonder why I'd like to move away."

"Don't harass Uncle Samson," Caroline said to her. "I've irritated him to a very high level with my decision about the wedding. It's unkind of you to nit and pick when he's in such a foul mood."

"Caroline is correct about my mood," he said. "You can't fathom how angry I am. You shouldn't push your luck."

"You never listen to me," Janet said. "You refuse to see my point of view on any topic."

"I've watched you throw your life away over radical ideas, and I'm sick of it. It's time you were yanked to your senses. If you had a husband and a few children to keep you busy, you'd be too exhausted to engage in such folderol."

"You needn't search for a candidate. For I can guarantee—whoever you might select—I would hate him."

"Is it your position—both you and Caroline—that I have no authority over you? That I can't force you into matrimony?"

His tone was very sharp, and Caroline—always the peacemaker—reached over and patted Janet's hand. "Please cease your taunts. Your father is out of sorts today."

Janet scoffed and glared at him. "No, Father, I don't believe you can force us, so quit being so annoying. It's not the Middle Ages."

"You'd be surprised by the power I can wield. You cross me at your peril."

Caroline tried to placate him. "I'm not *crossing* you, Uncle. I've simply realized I can't behave as you were expecting."

"Gregory is a disgusting drunkard," Janet added, "with a horrendous gambling habit. We'll likely be camping in a ditch after he beggars us. You have to take off your blinders, Father."

"He is a gentleman reveling in town," Samson claimed.

He was worried about the same issues with regard to Gregory, but he wouldn't admit it to them. It would simply supply Caroline with more ammunition to bolster her rebellion.

"He's so deranged," Janet said, "that he brought his paramour home with him. Are we to have no opinion about that? He's shamed Caroline in every conceivable way, yet still—still!—you demand she shackle herself. What is wrong with you?"

He whacked a palm on the table. "I will not debate the subject with you."

Janet turned to Caroline. "Did you know he kicked out Caleb and Blake Ralston? He was so rude about it that he ordered them to leave immediately."

Caroline whipped her gaze to him. "You didn't, Uncle. Really? Why would you?"

His cheeks heated, but he wasn't about to be scolded over the decision. "Due to your sudden announcement that you won't marry Gregory, it's clear that you've grown entirely too cordial with Mr. Ralston. He's filled your head with lies to where you're acting like a lunatic."

"They weren't lies," Caroline had the temerity to insist.

"I've had enough of your sass and disobedience," he warned her. "I've had enough of Mr. Ralston and his interference. He's departing shortly. In fact, he may already be gone. I fervidly hope—once we're shed of him—that familial matters will revert to normal."

She tossed down her napkin and leapt to her feet. Without a word, she marched to the door, and Samson asked, "Where are you going?"

"To see if Mr. Ralston has left."

"I forbid you to speak with him," Samson said.

"And I am ignoring you."

"Caroline!" he shouted. "Let him be away without a fuss."

"I intend to tell him goodbye, and just so you're aware, I will be instructing Mrs. Scruggs to inform our guests that the wedding is off and they can begin packing their bags."

"Then *I* shall countermand your edict."

"It will be a waste of breath."

She hurried out, and Janet smirked with amusement. "I think you might be done bossing her."

"If you mouth off to me one more time, I swear I'll take a belt to you."

"Sticks and stones, Father. Sticks and stones." She stood too. "Is it still your position that I can't move to London?"

"Of course it's my position. Why aggravate me by raising the issue again?"

"I was merely giving you a chance to change your mind."

"I will never change my mind about it."

She walked out, and he slumped in his chair, wondering how he'd fostered such insurgents in his own home. How dare they defy him! How dare they assume he had no authority.

Well, he wasn't without options, as both of them were about to discover.

Chapter

14

CAROLINE HURRIED DOWN THE halls, trying not to run, but she had to find Caleb. How could he ride away without apprising her? If he'd already departed, she'd be crushed.

In his bedchamber, the wardrobe and dresser were empty. She stood in the quiet, listening to her heart beating and wondering if it might not break into tiny pieces.

She dashed out and down to the foyer, and as she reached the bottom of the stairs, the front door was open. Caleb was standing in the driveway with his brother. Their horses were saddled, and they were chatting amicably—as if nothing was wrong.

Her relief at stumbling on him was so intense she was surprised she didn't collapse. She slowed her pace, then walked outside, not wanting to appear as if she'd been chasing him through the manor.

"Caleb!" she called as she marched toward him. "I heard you were leaving, but I refused to believe it."

He spun to her, smiling affectionately. "Caro! There you are. I had an early breakfast, and I was hoping I'd see you. When you didn't come down, I couldn't wait. We have a long day ahead of us, and we should be off."

"I'm embarrassed that my uncle kicked you out."

"You needn't be embarrassed."

"I wish you'd spoken to me before you agreed to oblige him."

"I didn't think I should argue about it."

"I hate that he treated you so rudely."

Caleb shrugged. "It probably couldn't be helped. In light of my relationship with Gregory, I shouldn't have visited Grey's Corner in the first place."

Their conversation dwindled, and an awkward silence ensued. There were a thousand issues she yearned to address, but would he care about any of them?

If she'd awakened a bit later, if Janet hadn't warned her that he'd been evicted, he'd have vanished without her realizing what had happened. How many hours would have passed before she'd figured out he was gone?

"Could I talk to you for a minute?" She sounded as if she was begging.

He delayed forever, giving her every indication that he felt it was a bad idea. He glared up at the house, then finally, he said, "I guess we can talk."

His brother raised a brow. "Don't dither, Caleb. I'm eager to get to town. If we dawdle, we'll have to spend the night on the road."

"This won't take long," Caleb said to his brother.

He extended his arm so she could grab hold. She glanced about, searching for a private spot where they could be alone and away from any prying eyes. Ultimately, she led him back into the manor. They went down a hall and entered a deserted parlor.

They turned to each other, and she studied his handsome face, cataloguing every detail so she'd never forget. Yet she couldn't accept that it was the *last* time they'd ever be together.

In she had her way, she'd see him again—and soon. She wasn't about to let him trot away without extracting a promise that, whatever was escalating between them, it wasn't ending simply because her Uncle Samson was being an ass.

What thoughts were racing through his head? He was such an enigmatic fellow. How was he assessing the situation? She doubted they shared similar views on what the conclusion should be.

She started the discussion. "You were leaving without a goodbye."

"When I missed you at breakfast, I told myself it was a sign."

"A sign of what? That I didn't deserve an explanation? If you'd left without my knowing, I'd have been devastated."

He winced. "Don't tell me that. I recognize that your life here has been hard, and I'm afraid my brief association with you has made it even harder. I'm sorry."

"Why are you sorry?"

"I've been flirting with you when I shouldn't have been, and it's skewed your impression of me. You're gazing at me as if we've pledged ourselves."

"It seems as if we have."

Thankfully, he didn't disparage her for voicing the comment. "Yes, it seems as if we're very close, and in a sane world, we'd act on our attraction. We'd become engaged and marry."

He halted, and when his pause grew too excruciating, she said, "But...?"

"I'm not interested in matrimony."

He proclaimed it with such certainty, but it wasn't true. He was rich and charismatic. Women would throw themselves at his feet, and eventually, he'd break down and catch one of them.

Yes, he would wed someday, but it wouldn't be to her. A vision pummeled her—of the type of gorgeous creature it would be—and she suffered such a wave of jealousy that she was dizzy with dismay.

"Will you be a permanent bachelor?" she asked. "Is that your plan? You'll be all alone."

"I'm not alone," he said. "I have Blake and our old guardian, Sybil Jones. She's like our mother. The three of us have had many difficult experiences, and we're tightly bonded."

"And that's enough for you? Blake and your old guardian?"

"It always has been."

She peered down at the floor, her mood at its lowest ebb. She'd endured many distressing moments, but this one was the worst of all.

She'd cried off from her betrothal to Gregory, and as she'd reached that decision, Caleb had appeared—as if by magic. He'd given her something to dream about, and it had been so long since she'd dreamed about anything. It was inordinately cruel for him to snatch it away.

"Don't be sad, Caro. Please?"

He clasped her hand and linked their fingers, and he pulled her to him so they were snuggled together.

"I can't help it," she said. "I was counting on you, although I have no idea why. We're barely acquainted, but it seems as if we're connected in a thrilling way."

"I agree, but I'll never be anyone's husband. I have too much of my father's blood flowing in my veins. I wouldn't inflict myself on any female."

"Don't disparage him to me. I have such fond memories of him, and he has a special place in my affection. He saved my life, Caleb."

"I know that."

"This will sound silly, but I feel as if he brought you to me."

Caleb stared at her for an eternity, and she could practically read his mind. He sensed it too, but he was too stubborn to admit it. And maybe that was for the best. If he was determined to traipse off without a commitment, she shouldn't hope and pine away.

"My father wouldn't have brought me to you," he said. "He didn't have a romantic bone in his body. He seldom watched over me while he was alive and walking around on Earth. I can't picture him watching over me from Heaven."

"From your dour tone, are you positive he's in Heaven?"

"No, I'm not positive at all."

She'd asked the question teasingly, but he'd responded seriously, providing a clear indication that Captain Ralston hadn't been the man she'd fantasized about. She'd frequently envisioned him galloping up on a white horse, that he'd hug her and say, *Caroline, I've finally found you!*

He'd have told her grandfather to stuff it, would have cantered away with her. They'd have gone to a happy spot, one where she was wanted and loved.

She'd imagined it a thousand times, and it was typical that his son—who stood there killing her with his disregard—would smash that image to pieces.

"So...I guess this is goodbye." She was so despondent she was surprised she didn't fall to the floor and weep.

"Yes, I guess it is."

"Can you really ride away? Can you bear to never see me again?"

Her pleading was a waste of breath. "We should have a clean break. It's better this way."

"Could we correspond?"

"We shouldn't."

Her shoulders slumped with defeat. "I suppose you're right."

If she corresponded with him, she'd be able to keep track of his antics, and they would ultimately include the news that he was betrothed. She refused to put herself in a position where she'd ever hear that information.

"Take care of yourself," he said.

"I always do."

He chuckled. "That's not true. Aren't you the girl who survived a shipwreck in the Caribbean?"

"Well, except for that little mishap, I'm incredibly cautious."

"Be wary of Gregory. Promise me you will be."

"Gregory is rarely home, so I'm not concerned about him."

"You're not safe with him."

"He's annoying, but harmless."

At the comment, he studied her intently, as if debating whether to share a vital secret. He settled on, "I will pray you're correct."

"I'll be fine. Don't worry about me."

"Your uncle will pressure you about the wedding. Swear to me you won't relent."

"I won't relent. I swear."

"I'll miss you," he said.

"That's some consolation."

He grinned a delicious grin. "Will you miss me too?"

"Every minute of every day."

"I like the sound of that."

He dipped down and kissed her. She shouldn't have let him. She *never* should have let him, but she wrapped her arms around his waist and held on as if he were a rope tethering her to the ground.

He deepened the kiss, his passion proving he was more conflicted than he claimed to be. In the ensuing weeks and months, it would be her balm. She'd remember that he'd been a tad distressed too.

She had no notion of how long they continued, but they only stopped when there was a knock on the door, and Blake said, "Caleb, are you in there? What's delaying you? We need to get going."

They drew apart, and he smiled at her with such affection that she nearly exploded with grief. A terrifying sob bubbled up, but she swallowed it down, not eager for him to realize the depth of her woe.

"My brother has always had the worst timing," he murmured.

"If you ever change your mind about me," she said, murmuring too, "you know where I am. I'll be waiting for you. I'll never give up hope."

"I won't change my mind, Caro." His tone was firm, but fond. "Don't wait for me. If the man of your dreams strolls by, I would hate to have you ignore him simply because you're expecting me to magically appear."

She snorted with a very sad amusement. "I'm an optimist. I will yearn for you to come to your senses."

"It won't alter our situation."

"I'll think of you in town. I'll imagine you happy and content."

"I'll think of you here in the country. I'll imagine the same."

Blake knocked again. "Caleb! It's late!"

"If you ever need anything," Caleb said, "my club in London is called *Ralston's*. You can find me there. Or write. If you're ever in trouble, contact me."

Fleetingly, she struggled to envision the sorts of incidents that might arise where she would urgently seek his assistance. It would be thrilling to have him rush to aid her, but she was a very proud woman. She would never ask him for help. She would never contact him. If he could blithely saunter away, she would never lower herself by begging.

"I won't ever need you," she told him.

"You never know what might happen." Tears flooded her eyes, and he said, "Don't you dare cry. I don't want there to be tears in my last glimpse of you."

"I will save my anguish for the hours when I'm alone, and I can ponder how bereft I am without you."

"You won't be bereft, Caro. You'll be grand. In fact, I'll bet in a few weeks, after you've had occasion to reflect, you'll figure you dodged a bullet when I left."

"From your lips to God's ear," she whispered.

His brother was too impatient, and he opened the door. He flashed a look at Caroline that she couldn't decipher. Was it pity? Was it irritation? Was it disgust?

Then he said to Caleb, "Let's go! I'm tired of cooling my heels."

Caleb squeezed her hand. "Goodbye, Caro."

"Goodbye, Caleb."

"Will you walk me out? Will you wave to me as I ride down the driveway?"

Could she stand to see him vanish down the lane? No. His request was far beyond what she could tolerate.

"Will you forgive me if I stay right where I am?"

"I already have."

He winked, eased away from her, then marched off without a backward glance. He and Blake hurried down the hall, but she didn't peek out to watch them depart. She would focus instead on that final smile, that final wink.

His brother said, "You didn't tell me you were engaged in a flirtation with her."

"I wasn't flirting," Caleb replied.

The remark should have crushed her, but it was so accursedly true. They hadn't enjoyed a flirtation. They'd simply reveled in some torrid kisses she couldn't mention aloud.

Despite how fervidly she listened, she heard no more than that. She staggered over to a nearby sofa and sank down. She stared blankly at the wall. The morning ticked by, the afternoon too, but she didn't notice.

She understood that time would pass, and she'd get over him. She understood that he was correct, that she'd eventually accept she'd dodged a bullet when he'd declined to bind himself. After all, he owned a gambling club where he ruined men financially merely so he could grow obscenely rich.

What kind of person pursued such a wicked career? What kind of morals—or lack of them—did it take to be so cold-blooded?

Yes, she'd gradually heal and be glad he'd gone. But just that moment, when her wound was new and raw, she wondered if her heart might simply quit beating.

"You're the most audacious oaf I've ever met."

Caleb didn't bother to peer over at Blake as he asked, "Why would you think so?"

"You traveled to Grey's Corner for an acquaintance's wedding, then you seduced his fiancée. I don't imagine it helped spur the union to its logical conclusion."

"I didn't seduce her," Caleb felt compelled to insist.

"I must point out that she's severed her betrothal."

"She'd been waffling long before I arrived," Caleb firmly stated. "Our relationship simply galvanized her opinion."

They were trotting away from Grey's Corner, their horses clopping side by side. He was struggling to appear nonchalant, but he wasn't having much luck.

"You didn't seduce her?" Blake snorted with annoyance. "I could swear I just caught you kissing her senseless."

"It's not your business, little brother."

"Was she expecting a commitment from you? It definitely looked as if she was."

"We're friends. Nothing more, nothing less."

"A man like you can never be *friends* with a woman like her."

"I realize that."

"Does she though?"

"No."

"Should I ride back and share a few facts about the type of cad you are? She probably assumes you'll change your mind and return for her someday. I hate to have her pining away. You're not worth the despair she'll suffer as she waits and waits, but you never show up to claim her."

He sighed with regret. "I wish I could be the man she needs."

"Don't tell me you'll suffer as well. I'll never believe it."

Caleb shook his head, as if he'd been in a stupor. "I'm being ridiculous. Don't pay any attention to me."

"I never do." Blake cast a sly glance in Caleb's direction. "If you leave her there, she'll end up shackled to Gregory. She won't be able to deflect the pressure her uncle will apply, and how old is she?"

"Almost twenty-five."

"A spinster by any measure," Blake said. "Gregory is likely her one and only chance to have a husband. Considering what you've learned about him, can you bow out and let her marry him?"

"It's none of my affair. I'm nobody's savior, and I most especially can't be hers."

"So if you discover that she's his bride, you'll be fine with that?"

"Shut up, Blake."

Blake chuckled. "I want to be sure you recognize the consequences you'll set in motion by abandoning her."

"I have no illusions as to her fate."

"Have you ever wondered if you could be happily married?"

"No, I've never wondered."

"Neither have I. I'm certain it's beyond our ability."

"I'm certain it is too."

They reached the trees that would swallow them up, which meant the manor was about to vanish from view. He couldn't stand it. He reined in and gazed back, studying the house, searching for Caroline.

She'd been too sad to escort him out, but he'd been positive she'd be watching from a window. He stared forever, but she wasn't there.

Blake smirked. "Maybe she's already over you."

"I wasn't looking for her."

"You can deceive yourself but not me."

"I feel sorry for her."

"As well you should. She's not safe with those people."

"No, probably not," Caleb agreed.

"Doesn't that incense you?"

"Yes, but how can I aid her? The only viable solution would be to wed her myself, and I won't do that."

"No, definitely not," Blake said. "The sons of Captain Miles Ralston should never inflict themselves on any female."

"She deserves to find someone much better than me."

"By slinking away, you're behaving honorably?"

"I hope I am," Caleb said.

"We never chatted with her about Father. With our stumbling on her like this, it seems as if we were destined to meet her."

"She has very fond memories of him."

Blake barked out a laugh. "Then he obviously fooled her—as he fooled everyone."

"She was four when he found her on that island. Over the past two decades, he's grown to mythical proportions in her mind."

"We shouldn't shatter any of her pretty recollections then. It would be cruel to tell her the truth." Blake gestured down the road. "Are we going or what?"

"Yes, we're going."

Caleb couldn't spur his horse to move though. He would never admit it, but he was incredibly distraught at the notion of parting from her. He didn't understand why he was so dismayed. He barely knew her, and it was silly to have become so attached, but he couldn't help it.

He couldn't ignore the perception that Fate—or perhaps his dastardly father—had guided him to her, so how could he ride off without her? He'd convinced himself that he never wanted to be a husband, but what if that was a stupid idea?

He could rush to the manor and beg her to depart with him. He was vain enough to suppose she wouldn't even pause to pack a bag. She realized that they belonged together. The impression of connection was so powerful. How could he disregard it?

What if he continued on with her, and it turned out he was ecstatically content? Shouldn't he discover if that ending was possible?

His anxiety was spiraling, which was hilarious. He wasn't a fellow who dithered and debated. He picked a path and marched down it. In his own defense though, he'd never been so conflicted.

He viewed himself as a confirmed bachelor. Caroline Grey had nibbled away at the foundation of his attitudes about his future, but they were both better off with fond memories. It was better for her to wonder what might have been. As to himself, he wouldn't wonder at all. He was too tough to mourn and lament, too tough to pine away.

"For pity's sake," Blake scolded. "Make a decision about her. Either go and fetch her away or forget about her and we'll keep on. What's it to be?"

Caleb allowed a lovely vision to unfold, of his racing to the house, then running through the halls until he located her. They would jump on his horse and gallop into the sunset—as if they were characters in a romantic novel. But this wasn't a fictional story. This wasn't a fantasy. This was real life.

He was Caleb Ralston, a man who owned a gambling business in town, and he needed to get to it.

"Let's keep on," he said.

He yanked on the reins, kicked his horse into a canter, and loped away without glancing back again.

Chapter

15

CAROLINE SAT IN HER bedchamber, staring out the window and trying to muster the energy to get on with her morning.

It was Saturday, which would have been her wedding day, but now, it was no different from any other day. She was greatly relieved by that fact, but suffering incredible guilt too. She always hated to upset others, and her uncle was furious.

The only way she could soothe his temper was to proceed with the ceremony, but she kept refusing, so he'd resorted to shouts and threats. His behavior was so disheartening that she'd begun hiding in her room to avoid him.

The guests had departed, so the manor seemed inordinately somber, as if someone had died. It felt as if *she* had died. Caleb Ralston had burst into her life and forced her to look at her circumstances. The end result was that she couldn't continue down the path she'd been traveling. She'd finally taken charge and had focused on what she really wanted for herself, that being Caleb Ralston.

Wasn't that the most foolish dream ever?

How could he ride off without her? She'd perceived their powerful bond. How could he not have perceived it with the same intensity?

Since he'd fled, she hadn't stopped pondering him for a single second, and she wondered if he ever thought of her. In her more gullible moments, she'd persuade herself he hadn't meant to go, so he'd return for her. Then she'd come to her senses.

He was a rich, handsome bachelor. He had a thriving business in the city where he was surrounded by glamorous, sophisticated women. Why would she—provincial, boring Caroline Grey—have tantalized him?

He'd made no promises, had declared no heightened affection. They'd shared numerous torrid kisses, but that was it.

A knock sounded on the door, and she called, "Yes, who is it?"

A housemaid peeked in. "Are you all right, Miss Caroline? Mrs. Scruggs sent me to check on you. You didn't come down to breakfast, and she was worried."

"I wasn't hungry."

"It's almost eleven," the maid said. "Would you like me to bring you a tray?"

"No. I'll be down soon. If I decide to eat, I'll head directly to the kitchen."

"It's clear you're not your usual self today, so I can't bear to distress you further, but there's something you should know. Mrs. Scruggs ordered me to leave you be, but I couldn't. This is too important."

"What's wrong?"

"Miss Janet didn't sleep in her bed last night. When I went in to light the fire this morning, she wasn't there. The covers hadn't even been mussed."

"She wasn't...there?"

"No, and it appeared she'd packed some of her clothes. I'm afraid to speculate over what it indicates."

"Oh, no," Caroline murmured, and she recollected Janet's odd remark where she'd had to be sure the Saturday wedding was cancelled, that her presence wouldn't be required.

"She left a note for you on her pillow," the maid said. "We've been debating whether to show it to you. As I mentioned, we're loathe to bother you when your mood is so low."

She held it out, and Caroline walked over to retrieve it. She flicked the seal, blanching with alarm when she saw what Janet had penned.

I've moved to London to make my way there. I will provide you with my address once I know what it is. I hope you'll join me in town after I'm settled. You'll always be welcome...

Caroline gaped at the words, reading and re-reading them as if they were written in a foreign language she didn't comprehend. What was Janet thinking?

Janet had argued with her father about the prospect of living in the city, but Caroline had assumed Janet was simply needling Uncle Samson. It had never occurred to her that Janet would actually pick up and go.

She sighed with regret, and the maid asked, "Is it bad news?"

"Yes, it's bad. You were correct about Janet. She's run away to London."

"By herself?" The maid was aghast. "I don't imagine her father will be too happy about it."

Caroline chuckled miserably. "That's a gross understatement."

"Will you come down and inform him, Miss Caroline?"

"I suppose I'd better."

Footsteps echoed in the hall, and Caroline's pulse raced. Whenever someone approached, her immediate thought was that it would be Caleb. But it was a footman.

"Miss Caroline, your uncle requested I fetch you down to the library. He has to speak with you right away."

"I was just about to attend him," she said. "Tell him I'll be there shortly."

She eased away and shut the door, trying to ignore their concerned expressions. She was pale and sickly, and the staff had to be gossiping about her. She'd like to proclaim that she wasn't ill. She'd merely had her heart broken, and there was no cure for her terrible affliction.

She'd fallen madly in love with Caleb Ralston, and she couldn't cope with the sentiment rocking her. She had to privately mourn the loss of him, and eventually, her despondency would wane. At least she expected it would wane. A person couldn't be this dejected forever. Could she be?

She checked her reduced condition in the mirror, and she pinched her cheeks and straightened a comb to hold her chignon more firmly in place. Then she headed down to confer with her uncle. She was rehearsing various comments, being anxious to devise a suitable explanation for Janet's conduct, so he wouldn't explode with rage.

As she marched toward the library, the butler and housekeeper, Mrs. Scruggs, were there. They were whispering animatedly, and when they saw her, they braced as if with dismay.

The butler said, "Miss Caroline has arrived, sir."

"Marvelous," her uncle replied. "Send her in."

They weren't a fancy family, and there was no need to announce her, so it was very odd. She swept by the pair and entered without pausing to wonder what was happening. But the instant she was inside, she staggered to a halt.

The vicar was there, and he was over by the hearth and gripping his prayer book. Gregory was there too, dressed in his best suit, and his presence definitely flummoxed her. Mrs. Starling had slithered away a few days earlier, and he'd left with her. Caroline hadn't realized he was home.

"What's going on?" she asked Gregory.

He shot a furtive glance at her uncle, then he bustled forward and clasped her hands. He pulled her over to the vicar, and she was so bewildered that she lurched after him like a puppet on a string.

"You're here, and the vicar's here," Gregory said. "Why not proceed with the ceremony?"

"With the wedding ceremony?" she inquired like a dunce.

"Yes. It's our wedding day after all, and it hasn't been officially cancelled, so Father and I thought, *why not*? The vicar was kind enough to oblige us."

Her uncle came over, and he stood on one side of her, Gregory on the other. They boxed her in, as if trapping her so she couldn't dash out.

"You've been upset," Uncle Samson told her, "but we were sure you didn't mean to cry off. Gregory and I are sorry to have quarreled with you, and we'd like to put this bickering behind us."

Caroline bristled, recognizing it to be the most awkward moment she'd ever suffered. She was fuming, but she wouldn't lash out at them in front of the vicar.

"The wedding has been called off—by me," she tightly stated. "I've been very clear. I can't and won't marry Gregory. We don't suit, and there are too many... *issues* between us."

She didn't cite them: Gregory's mistress, drinking, gambling, and dissolute existence in town.

As she should have anticipated, her uncle disregarded her remark and waved to the vicar. "Don't listen to her. Open your prayer book. Read the vows."

"Mr. Grey!" The vicar's tone was scolding. "I have two functioning ears, and she spoke in plain English, so I understood her with no difficulty. She has refused."

Uncle Samson scoffed. "She doesn't know what she wants."

Gregory chimed in with, "My father is her guardian. Her choice of spouse is up to him. Not her. He and I are both committed to the union. Please begin."

The vicar glowered at them, then spun to Caroline. "What is your preference, Miss Caroline? Will you continue—as your uncle is demanding?"

"No!" she insisted. "I've been very firm about it. I sent you a note to inform you that the service was cancelled. Didn't you receive it?"

"Yes, I received it."

"Then I apologize for your being dragged here on false pretenses."

"Once I grasped what you had penned," he said, "I wasn't certain what to think, but your uncle claimed you were confused. I stopped by because this is a big decision, and I must be convinced that you've weighed the consequences. I ask you again: Do you—or do you not—wish to wed Gregory Grey?"

"No, I don't wish it. I will *never* marry him. I just can't."

Caroline whipped away and stomped out. Behind her, the vicar said to her uncle, "You have wasted my time, sir!"

"She's not serious!" Samson said. "Let me talk to her. Stay where you are. I'll be right back."

"I won't stay," the vicar replied. "I will not perform a ceremony when the bride is so vehemently opposed."

She didn't hear the rest of their conversation. She hurried to the foyer and up the stairs to her room. She went inside and slammed the door.

Typically, she viewed herself as being very calm. She never liked to rock a boat or cause a scene. But buried deep down, she had a terrible temper. She'd spent too many years tamping it down, and when it exploded, it was hard to control. She never liked to have it flare, but it was flaring now.

How dare they put her in such a hideous position!

She'd never been more embarrassed, and her mind was awhirl with trying to figure out what her next moves should be. Gregory and Uncle Samson were so determined she wed Gregory. Why? Their resolve made no sense.

Gregory was a rich bachelor from a landed family. He could marry practically any girl he liked. Why not search for her? Why harangue at Caroline when she was so reluctant? Why torment her like this?

She couldn't remember ever being so angry, but she had to relax and focus on what was important. The two idiots had to be reined in, but she wouldn't confront them when her fury was sparking. Nor would she chastise them while the vicar was still present.

She started to pace across her bedchamber, and she walked back and forth, back and forth, until she might have traveled for miles. She was actually tired and out of breath.

She wandered to the window and stared out, and it dawned on her that she hadn't told Uncle Samson about Janet. Well, Janet's problems would just have to wait. Caroline had other fish to fry.

After a bit, as she'd quieted sufficiently to head downstairs, there were footsteps in the hall. It was a male from the sound of it, and she braced, curious if it would be Gregory or Samson.

He halted, and she expected him to knock. There was a lengthy pause, then, to her stunned surprise, a key was stuck in the lock. It was turned! Then, whoever it had been, he continued on.

She gaped with dismay, then tiptoed over and tried the knob.

They'd locked her in! From the outside! Was she to be their prisoner? Was that it?

She began to pound on the wood, to shout for help. She kept on until her knuckles were bloody and her voice hoarse, but no one heard her. Or if they did, no one came to find out what was wrong.

"WHAT ARE YOU LOOKING at?"

"It's an old drawing that was in the newspaper when I was little."

Libby Carstairs peered over at her friend and companion, Edwina Fishburn, who was called Fish by everyone. They were in the house they were renting in London, in Libby's bedchamber, and Libby was modeling a gown Fish had finished sewing.

Libby was famous as the Mystery Girl of the Caribbean, and Fish was her seamstress and costumer.

Libby had spent her life journeying across the kingdom, performing at fairs and in small playhouses. With her duplicitous Uncle Harry guiding her way, she'd regaled rural audiences with monologues and ballads about her ordeal at age five when she, Caro, and Joanna, had survived their shipwreck.

In recent months, after Harry's untimely demise—he'd been shot dead by a jealous husband after he'd seduced the fellow's wife—she'd come to London and had taken the city by storm. She appeared nightly at London's most prestigious theater where she brought even the most hardened cynics to tears.

Two decades had passed since they'd been found by Captain Miles Ralston, but people still couldn't get enough of her. It was the twentieth anniversary of the rescue, and she remained more fascinating than ever.

Harry had hired Fish when Libby was sixteen and had needed to be dressing like an adult rather than the orphaned waif she'd pretended to be. She and Fish were thick as thieves. They existed beyond the bounds of civilized society and pretty much carried on however they pleased.

She held up the tattered page from the newspaper and asked Fish, "Haven't I ever showed this to you?"

"No. Let me see."

"When Caro, Joanna, and I first returned to England, there was a desperate push to figure out who we were. The authorities had an artist sketch a picture of us, and it was distributed everywhere. I kept this copy."

Fish took it from Libby. The paper was thin from Libby caressing it over the years. Fish studied the three cherubic faces, tracing her finger over them. "You were so tiny. I forget how young you were when it happened."

"I'm a walking miracle. I still can't explain how or why I lived through it."

Fish pointed to Libby's likeness, and she smirked. "Even when you were five, you were too precocious for words."

"From the very start, I was amazing. Harry always said so."

As the navy had advertised for family members to claim them, Harry had blustered in and insisted he was a relative. He hadn't been though. He'd merely been an acquaintance of her mother's, but no one had realized it, and he'd been allowed to saunter off with her.

He'd been a lazy, shrewd schemer, so it could have been a dicey situation, but with her obvious flair so prevalent, he'd provided a perfect conclusion.

He'd recognized her many talents, and he'd groomed her for a life on the stage. He'd written hundreds of vignettes and songs about the shipwreck. Most of them were invented. She had scant recollection of the dreadful event, but Harry had had a vivid imagination, and she made the stories genuine during her stellar performances.

All in all, she was naught more than a very gifted fraud. Except that she really had been on a ship that sunk. She really had been stuck on a deserted island with Caro and Joanna. It really was a miracle that they'd survived.

She had no idea how long they were stranded. Captain Ralston had tried to get her to describe the length of the period when they'd been marooned, and supposedly, she'd told him that it had been *a very, very long time.* She hadn't been able to quantify it any better than that.

The drawing was a priceless memento, and she slid it from Fish's hand, folded it, and put it back in the dresser. It was like a secret amulet she liked to hold whenever she was feeling low. It soothed her to gaze at Caro and Joanna, to recollect how fond she'd been of them.

Her separation from them was a wound that hadn't healed. She'd been yanked away from them without their even having a chance to say goodbye.

One minute they'd been huddled in a hotel room, wondering what would transpire, and the next, she'd been given to Harry—a stranger she didn't know—and whisked away from them. The so-called *experts* had counselled that a quick, clean break was for the best, so that was the ending that had been implemented.

Over the years, she'd occasionally asked Harry if he could tell her where Caro and Joanna had gone. He'd maintained that he had no idea where they were, and he couldn't find out.

Once, when she'd been older and particularly adamant that she wanted to search for them, he'd claimed he'd contacted the navy for her, and they'd lost the records.

Libby had believed him. He'd been her world, her family, and she'd relied on him for everything, so whatever lies he'd concocted, she'd swallowed them. She'd trusted him, being terrified he might vanish when she wasn't looking. Her fear of being abandoned by him had shaped her existence.

She'd never completely recovered from her ordeal, and she had many problems that relentlessly plagued her. She hated the dark and bodies of water, and she grew incredibly anxious in tight spaces. After the voyage to England, she'd definitely never climbed onto a ship again! She'd learned the hard way that they could sink, and she wasn't willing to tempt Fate ever again.

"Did I tell you," she said to Fish, "about that newspaper reporter, Howard Periwinkle?"

"Isn't he the one who's been harassing you?"

"He insists he knows where Caro and Joanna are living. He's talked to them."

"Didn't Harry check with the navy and they had no information?"

"Yes, but I wouldn't necessarily assume it was the truth."

"How about this Periwinkle fellow?" Fish asked. "Might he be lying?"

"He doesn't seem to be. He'd like to arrange a reunion for the three of us so he can write an article about it."

"How would you feel about that?"

"I would like to meet with them, but not with him watching my every move. It would have to be quiet and private."

"You're a wealthy young lady these days. If Mr. Periwinkle can locate them, you could probably hire an investigator to locate them too."

Libby scowled. "Should I?"

"Why not? Your parting from them has haunted you for twenty years. Maybe they could fill in some missing pieces of your memory. Maybe you'd finally garner some resolution about what occurred."

"Isn't that a pretty notion?"

She stared out the window, trying to envision what a reunion would be like. She was renowned for being flamboyant and charismatic, but still, she could be nervous and shy. Any discussion about the shipwreck always left her breathless with apprehension. It was an odd twist that she publicly performed tales describing the tragedy, but she never talked about it otherwise.

The stage persona of Libby Carstairs was separate from the flesh and blood woman.

"Do you think Caro and Joanna would like me?" she asked.

Fish scoffed with derision. "Is that a real question?"

"Yes. What if we got together, and they wound up wishing we hadn't?"

"You can be such a dunce. You're Libby Carstairs, Mystery Girl of the Caribbean, and the whole kingdom loves you. Caro and Joanna will love you too. I guarantee it."

"Then perhaps I will hire someone," Libby said. "I'll have him begin working on it right away."

Chapter
16

"STOP SCOWLING SO FEROCIOUSLY. You're scaring away our customers."

Caleb smirked at his partner and sort-of mother, Sybil Jones. When he and Blake had been boys and their mother still alive, Sybil had been their maid. Their mother had passed away suddenly, and soon after, they'd learned that their father had died at sea.

In the blink of an eye, they'd become orphans.

Their vicar had sent them to their relatives in England, but unfortunately, no one in Jamaica had realized that Miles Ralston had a wife and children in England. They were his family, his *real* family, and Blake and Caleb were simply a pair of unwanted bastards.

At the time, they'd been just five and ten years old, so Sybil had been sent too, to watch over them and deliver them safely to their destination. If she hadn't accompanied them, Caleb couldn't guess what might have happened. He and Blake might have wound up on the streets.

She was a decade older than he was, so she'd been twenty when their troubles had commenced. She'd taken her role as their guardian very seriously, and she'd been a fierce warrior on their behalf. Due to her incessant nagging, the navy had negotiated with Miles's wife, Esther, for Caleb and Blake to attend boarding school. Then, once they'd turned sixteen and their educations were complete, she'd paid for navy commissions.

Blake was in the navy and pursuing the career they'd loved. Caleb was sitting in his posh gambling club and raking in money hand over fist, but when he was feeling peevish, he thought Blake had ended up with the better conclusion.

The main benefit of his current situation was that he'd never have to go begging ever again. And he'd always be able to care for Blake and Sybil. He'd never have to depend on the pricks from the Ralston family to buy them food or clothes.

"Blake tells me you fell in love at Grey's Corner," Sybil said.

"Blake is an idiot. You know that."

"He claims the woman is gorgeous, and you were absolutely besotted."

"I wasn't," he lied.

"You can admit it. I'd be thrilled to have you married and happy."

"Since when do you believe matrimony makes a man happy?"

Sybil was a confirmed spinster who'd never been interested in having a husband. She was forty and aging well. At five-feet-five in her slippers, she was plump and curvaceous, her brown eyes merry, her brown hair showing just a few strands of gray.

She'd wasted her good years, arguing with various adults to behave themselves, demanding he receive financial support from his father's estate. She was a fighter, a winner, and she was loyal to a fault.

She'd expended her energy ensuring he and Blake were treated as was appropriate to their station as Miles Ralston's sons. In exchange, he would spend his life protecting her.

Because she'd exhaustively bickered and pleaded for him and Blake, she'd seen the very worst side of men. Their owning a gambling club hadn't helped matters. She deemed men to be reckless fools, and he could hardly insist they weren't.

"I think Blake has a new paramour," she said. "Have you heard any rumors?"

"He hasn't mentioned it to me."

"Apparently, it's very hush-hush. He might even be *keeping* her."

Caleb scoffed. "He is not keeping a mistress. If he considered it, he'd have to request a bigger allowance, and I wouldn't give it to him for such a frivolous reason."

Blake had his sailor's salary, but Caleb furnished him with a hefty stipend every quarter too. He was frugal with it and never liked it to seem as if he was taking advantage of Caleb's wealth. After all, Blake's antics were the catalyst for Caleb growing so rich.

"The young lady in question is hiding from her father," Sybil said. "Blake is assisting her, and evidently, she has some of her own money. He might not have had to seek any extra from you."

"Is she an innocent miss who's run away from home? If Blake has involved himself in that kind of dicey predicament, he'll wind up dragged to the altar by her male kin."

Sybil chuckled. "Should I start planning a wedding?"

"I'll ask him about her. Luckily, his furlough will be over shortly, so if he's engaged in mischief, it can't last long."

"A fellow doesn't need much time to plant a babe in a girl's belly. I'm quite sure it can occur after a single romp under the covers."

Caleb winced. "Don't even say it. I'm not ready to be an uncle, and he's definitely not ready to be a father."

It was a Saturday night, and the club was packed. He and Sybil were up on the stairs and staring down into the gaming room, watching all the negligent dunces throw their fortunes away.

He never permitted anyone to quarrel, imbibe to excess, or be too obnoxious. A man who resorted to fisticuffs was banned forever. For the moment, his establishment was novel enough that no one wanted to be exiled from it.

A kerfuffle erupted by the door, and they glanced over to find that it was Gregory Grey, presuming he could simply stroll inside. Caleb had footmen working as guards, and they dressed as befitted the ostentatious surroundings, but they were ruffians, mostly ex-soldiers. They'd been notified to block Gregory.

"There must be some mistake," Gregory said, his words drifting up. "I'm a member. You ought to check your records rather than annoy me."

"Sorry, sir," his footman answered, "but you should come in during morning business hours. You can discuss the problem with Miss Jones. She's in charge of the clientele list."

Gregory had arrived with a group of acquaintances, and they bustled by him and hurried out to the tables. Nary a one peeked back to worry about Gregory.

He had a heated argument with the footman, and when he made no headway, he peered into the room, frantically searching for an ally. He saw Caleb up on the stairs, and he hollered, "Ralston! This dolt won't let me in!"

It was all the complaint he could manage. The footman grabbed him by his collar and yanked him out—as if he were a mongrel dog. A few members noticed Gregory's shout, and they frowned, curious as to what had transpired, but the din of noise concealed any signs of a scuffle. Their attention quickly reverted to their cards and dice.

After the commotion settled, Sybil said, "What a hideous little man. I'm so glad we're shed of him. I never understood why you played with him in the first place."

"Temporary insanity?"

She laughed. "It's as good an excuse as any."

"I thought he owned that bloody estate of his. He bragged about it constantly. And that trust fund! He constantly boasted about it too. I have no idea how I'll ever recoup even a fraction of what he owes us."

"You're calling in your markers, aren't you? You have to ruin him once and for all. Tell me you haven't changed your mind about that."

"I haven't changed my mind."

"Then I guess Mr. Grey's life is about to grow quite a bit more unpleasant."

Caleb started down the stairs, Sybil walking with him.

"I'll be in the office," he told her, "but I won't be busy. Fetch me if you need me."

"You can head home if you like. You've been in a bad mood since you returned from the country. Maybe if you got some sleep, you wouldn't be so grouchy."

"I doubt it would cure what's ailing me. Besides, I never sleep, remember?"

"What's ailing you? Has your heart been broken? Is that what's wrong?"

"If it had been, I'd never confide in you. You're too nosy, and I'd never hear the end of it."

"Will I ever meet the gorgeous woman who tempted you?"

"No," he said. "You'll never meet her."

"What's her name?"

"If you must know, it's Caroline Grey. She was Gregory Grey's fiancée."

Sybil's jaw dropped. "You wicked boy! You interfered with their engagement?"

Caleb shrugged. "It was over before I appeared on the scene. Caroline had already had her fill of him."

"I don't blame her, but why leave her there? Why not bring her to London? Wouldn't you like that?"

"I'll never bring her here. She believes gambling is a terrible sin, and I would hate to have her see how I carry on."

"It may be a sin, but it pays well."

They reached the floor, and she sauntered away. It was a gentleman's club, but she managed it for him. The men who were members had to accept her presence or they could wager somewhere else. There were plenty of spots in London where a fellow could destroy himself, and it was all the same to Caleb.

He went down the hall, the sounds of merriment fading, and he entered the office. Technically, it was Sybil's office, so she'd decorated it more comfortably than he would have. It was cozy, with plush chairs, warm rugs, and pretty paintings on the walls. It looked like a library in a country cottage.

She had numerous vices, one of them being a penchant for hard spirits, so she kept a stocked liquor tray. He poured himself a whiskey and sat behind the desk. He sipped his drink and pondered the recent past.

His trip to Grey's Corner seemed like an event in a dream. Had he really crossed paths with Caroline Grey? Had he really led her on to where she'd assumed they might have had a future?

It was horrid of him to have behaved that way. He never should have trifled with her, but for inexplicable reasons, he hadn't been able to resist her. She was beautiful, smart, sweet, and interesting, and she exuded a vulnerability that made a man anxious to take care of her.

He had certainly been riveted by that notion, and he shouldn't have abandoned her to her awful relatives. On that final day, she'd told him she'd always watch for him, that he could come back and she'd be waiting. Why didn't he do that? Why didn't he ride to Grey's Corner and abscond with her?

His problem was that he was so stubborn. He'd convinced himself that they couldn't be together, and he couldn't persuade himself to crawl off that ledge. He had to stop pining away and questioning his every action with regard to her. Otherwise, his low mood would never wane.

He had to buck up and recollect who he was. He didn't bond with females, and he wouldn't ever attach himself to her. After a few more weeks had passed, he'd likely be wondering why he'd been so smitten. After a few months, he likely wouldn't remember her at all.

Sybil knocked and poked her nose in. "You have a visitor."

He grimaced. "It better not be Gregory Grey. If the guards let him in, I'll have to murder somebody, and I'd rather not commit a homicide this evening."

"It's not Mr. Grey, but when you discover who it is, you might murder *me*. Promise you won't."

"That depends on who it is."

"I think this is a good idea or I wouldn't have pushed it on you." She stepped into the hall and spoke to whoever had accompanied her. "It's nice to see you again. Feel free to call on us whenever you like."

"I will," a man replied, and Caleb sighed, figuring he knew who it was.

She glanced in at Caleb and said, "No fighting! You're not children, so I would appreciate it if you didn't act as if you were."

Then she strolled off, and his guest entered the room. They glared, not shooting visual daggers, but not exhibiting any fondness either.

"Jacob," Caleb said to his half-brother, "this is a surprise. What brings you by?"

"I was in the neighborhood, and I simply walked through your door."

"Aren't I lucky?" Caleb muttered, and he gestured to the liquor tray in the corner. "Help yourself or must I summon a footman to serve you?"

"Don't be an ass. I'm tired, and I don't want to quarrel."

Caleb reined in his snotty attitude, silently fuming as Jacob poured himself a whiskey. He refilled Caleb's glass too, then set the bottle between them. Apparently, this was a conversation that would require copious amounts of alcohol.

He pulled up a chair, and they sipped their beverages, studying one another as if they were strangers or enemies, but those two words failed to describe their connection. Caleb wasn't sure what they were, but they definitely weren't friends.

Jacob was dressed for a night on the town, wearing a formal black suit, the velvet jacket expensive and perfectly tailored, his white cravat stitched from the finest Belgian lace, so he'd wisely left his navy uniform at home. Thank goodness.

It was bad enough for Blake to strut around in his naval garb, but to witness Jacob in it too, to be reminded that he was captain of his own bloody ship...

Well, that was a bit more aggravation than Caleb should have to swallow while sitting in his own office.

Disgusting as it was to admit, he never stopped being curious about his half-brother. They looked exactly alike: same height and weight, same striking blue eyes, same brawny shoulders and healthy physique. The genuine difference was that Caleb's hair was blond and Jacob's was black.

They were the same age of thirty, their birthdays a few months apart, providing stark evidence that their father had been an immoral dog.

Caleb and Blake told themselves that Miles had married his first wife—Jacob's mother, Esther—out of duty to his family, but that he'd married their mother, Pearl, because he'd loved her and couldn't live without her. Yet they couldn't guess if that view was accurate or not.

By the time they'd realized Miles was a bigamist, their parents had been dead, so they couldn't inquire as to his reasoning.

Miles's fellow officers had claimed they were unaware of his sinful existence, and Caleb suspected they'd probably known about it, but had ignored the situation. The burden of it, the shame of it, had fallen on Blake and Caleb when they'd been much too young to carry the load.

Caleb had initially learned about Jacob when he was ten and newly arrived in England, but they hadn't met until they were twenty. Even then, they'd bumped into each other by accident, at a party for a senior officer who'd been retiring.

Since then, they'd been forced into each other's company on a handful of awkward occasions, and they couldn't deduce how to socialize. They weren't responsible for their father's conduct, but they'd suffered for it. Caleb and Blake were a stain on the Ralston family name, and Jacob's mother in particular had been very cruel about it.

Miles's behavior was a stain on Jacob and his siblings too. He had two sisters, and they'd assumed themselves to be his only children. Caleb and Blake had shattered any illusions they'd harbored about Miles.

It was a horrendous quagmire, and Caleb didn't begrudge his half-siblings their anger or disdain. He was angry too and had been raging for two decades, and he couldn't imagine why Jacob had waltzed in. There was no point in chatting, and Caleb had no desire to be cordial.

He was very rich now, as Jacob would have heard, and he hoped Jacob wasn't about to ask for a loan! He wasn't privy to the condition of the Ralston finances. What had been accumulated over the years? After Miles's death, how much remained?

Jacob had inherited their father's estate, which included a manor house that could have been a castle fit for a king. That kind of property cost a fortune to maintain. Was Jacob broke? Was he seeking fiscal assistance?

Maybe he was about to demand repayment of the monies his mother had forked over for Caleb and Blake's schooling and commissions. If that was the case, Caleb couldn't predict how he'd react.

One thing was certain: He wouldn't give Jacob Ralston a single farthing. Any money Esther Ralston had shelled out to get Blake and Caleb situated in life was money that was fully warranted.

"What can I do for you, Jacob?" he asked. "What is it you need?"

"I don't need anything. I was being truthful when I told you I was simply walking by. I had to say hello."

"Fine. Hello to you too."

"It looks as if you're doing really well."

"I'm doing well enough," Caleb said.

"I'm glad. After you left the navy, I was worried about what would happen to you."

Caleb tsked with offense. "I'm sure you were a veritable boiling pot of concern."

"I *was* worried. I'm delighted to find that you've landed on your feet."

Jacob toasted him with his glass, and Caleb accepted it as an olive branch of sorts.

"It's nice to have some money for a change," Caleb said. "I can't deny it." More caustically, he added, "In the future, I won't ever have to beg anyone for help."

Jacob winced. "In light of our history, I suppose I deserved that."

"Your mother deserved it anyway. Not you. I just mean that I can take care of Blake and Sybil. It's always been my biggest fear: that disaster would arise and I wouldn't be able to protect them."

"What was your issue with the navy? Why did you resign? There was a rumor you were swept up in an embezzlement scheme, but I didn't believe it."

Caleb yearned to confide Blake's mischief, how Blake had always been a great trial, how he'd been a burden to Caleb from the moment they'd been orphaned. They'd staggered to England only to discover there was no family waiting to greet them, no inheritance to smooth their path, and Blake had been wild and negligent ever since.

Caleb was very loyal though, and Blake was still in the navy. Caleb had quit so his brother could *stay* in the navy. Blake needed the structure it provided. Jacob was in the navy too, and his connections ran high and deep. Any admission about Blake's debacle would drift into the wrong ears, and Blake would be in trouble again.

Caleb would never risk it. Instead, he said, "Do you have many memories of our father?"

"Not many, no. He was always at sea, and he and my mother didn't get along. When he was in England, he rarely spent time with us. He and Mother quarreled too viciously. How about your mother? Did he get along with her? Did they spend much time together?"

"He was rarely home with us either, but when he was there, he and my mother seemed happy. I was a boy though, so I might have misread their relationship."

"He must have been madly in love with her. Why else would he have married her?"

Caleb wouldn't wander down that road. He wasn't about to debate the topic of which *wife* their father had liked more. There was no way to win that comparison.

"You're a tad nostalgic tonight," Caleb said.

Jacob shrugged. "Perhaps I am."

"I can't discuss these subjects with you."

"I think we should though. Don't you? The involved parties are deceased—"

"Your mother passed away?"

"Yes."

"I wasn't informed. My condolences."

"It's just me and my sisters now. That's it—unless I start to consider you and Blake to be part of the family."

Caleb chuckled. "If Blake and I are suddenly *family*, your mother will be spinning in her grave."

"It's not as if I'll mention it to her in my prayers. She doesn't have to be apprised of every little detail."

"I can't imagine us being friends," Caleb said. "Isn't there too much water under the bridge?"

"The water was between our mothers, wasn't it?"

"I guess it was," Caleb grudgingly agreed.

"There's no reason you and I should fight, and I've always been fascinated by you and Blake. I'd hoped to have some brothers, but I wound up with a pair of bossy, annoying sisters."

"Trust me. Blake and I aren't fascinating."

"I beg to differ. Look at what you've made of yourself." Jacob gestured around the room, indicating Caleb's expensive building and thriving business. "In this accursed country where lineage is the sole thing that matters, you've shocked everyone. Have you listened to any of the gossip as to how you've grown so wealthy? Do your dealers cheat? Do you use black magic? Were spells cast by a sorcerer? No one can fathom you being successful due to intellect and hard work."

"People are idiots."

"I've always thought so."

They grinned identical Ralston grins, and Jacob leaned across the desk so they could clink their glasses. He sat back, and Caleb refilled their liquor. They sipped companionably, then Jacob said, "Have you heard about that actress, Libby Carstairs? She's one of the Mystery Girls of the Caribbean. She's performing here in town."

"I've heard of her, but I haven't seen her on the stage. I can't bear to."

"I've been reticent as well, but apparently, she talks about Father constantly during her shows. I'm curious as to what she might tell me in private."

"I stumbled on a Mystery Girl recently. Not Miss Carstairs, but Caroline Grey? Remember her?"

"Vaguely. Miss Carstairs garnered all the attention, but then, she sought it out."

"Miss Grey told me she has very fond recollections of him. Over the years, he's reached near-mythical proportions."

"He saved their lives, so I can understand why she'd worship him. He received such praise for rescuing them. Isn't it odd how a man can have such diverse sides to his personality? Father was a great hero, but also quite a dastardly fiend. Have you ever pondered that about him?"

"I ponder it relentlessly. When he was married to our mothers, would he have tossed and turned at night, wondering if his bigamy was about to be exposed? He must have been terrified every minute."

"Or the bloody oaf had nerves of steel."

They smirked in unison, then Jacob downed his drink and put the glass on the desk. "I shouldn't overstay my welcome."

"You haven't—yet."

"If I keep this visit short and sweet, can I stop by in the future?"

Caleb found himself thinking he might enjoy subsequent encounters. "You can stop by as often as you like."

"I'll be in England for the next three months. I'm having a house party in September before I ship out, and I'd like you to come. Would you consider it? You can bring Sybil too. And Blake—if he's not at sea by then."

"It might be a step farther than I can go at the moment."

The last time Caleb had been at the Ralston estate, he'd been ten. He'd staggered in with Sybil and Blake, after their lengthy voyage from Jamaica. They'd been introduced to Jacob's mother, then promptly escorted off the property. The gate had been barred behind them, and several footmen had been posted as guards to ensure they didn't slither back in.

The memory was still humiliating, and he'd sworn he'd never set foot there ever again.

"Reflect on it for me," Jacob said, "and I'll invite Sybil. I'll suggest she nag at you. As I recall, she's very effective at getting what she wants." He stood and gave a mock salute. "I'll be in town this whole week."

"I'm here every evening."

"I'll catch Miss Carstairs's performance at the theater. I might even ask to meet her afterward."

"She's a siren who lures sailors to their doom. Be careful around her. She might suck you into a vortex you didn't intend."

"I won't let her doom me, but I would like to chat with her about Father."

"If she provides any interesting details, I can't wait to hear them."

They stared for ages, then Jacob said, "I've decided we should be friends. I'm planning on it."

"Maybe." Caleb was more tentative. "We'll see how it plays out."

Jacob walked out the door, and Caleb relaxed in his seat, listening as his booted strides faded down the hall. The silence enveloped him, then a few minutes later, Sybil rushed in.

"You didn't fight with him!"

"We were tediously polite."

"We have to attend his house party. You realize that, don't you?"

"We'll talk about it."

"Yes, we will," she said like a threat.

She spun and dashed out. He loafed in his chair, drinking his whiskey, and mulling life in general.

He should be friendly with Jacob, shouldn't he? The man had made the first move. Why not be cordial? When all the guilty people were dead, why bicker?

He felt his father's ghost swirling, his father's hand shifting them into the correct positions so they would cross paths. Jacob Ralston. Jacob's sisters. Caroline Grey. Perhaps Libby Carstairs too. Where would it lead?

If Miles was truly guiding them, what was his purpose? Caleb supposed, if he didn't at least try to answer that question, his father would haunt him forever.

CAROLINE WAS IN HER bedchamber and gazing out at the garden. It was very quiet, and the situation was eerily similar to the years when she'd lived with her grandfather.

She'd frequently been punished for small infractions—tearing her dress, scuffing her shoe—and she'd been locked in her room for days on end, with the rare servant visiting to check on her.

She'd learned to be content on her own, to relish the solitude.

She was locked in now too. Her uncle had come by occasionally to confer with her, and though she'd demanded he let her out, he'd refused. She probably could have physically wrestled with him to escape, but she wasn't a brawler, so she hadn't.

It was like being trapped in a peculiar dream, one where she'd been thrust back to her childhood: imprisoned in her room, without a friend in the manor to worry about her. The only difference was that her uncle didn't shout and lash out as her grandfather used to do.

He simply droned on in his cold, incessant way about how much she *owed* him. She would cock her head and study him, anxious to figure out how it would conclude. She sensed that her fate was about to be sealed, and it would be in a manner she wouldn't like.

She'd grown so introspective that she hadn't told him about Janet. Had the servants informed him she'd fled? Had he noticed she'd vanished? Or was he so fixated on Caroline that he wasn't concerned about his daughter?

What was his goal in treating her like this? How long would she be confined? He likely assumed his conduct would force her to relent and change her mind, but it wouldn't, so how would they resolve it?

If he ever deigned to release her, their amicable relationship had been shattered. How would they reside in the same house? She'd be afraid every second that she'd be punished again for the slightest gaffe.

Footsteps sounded in the hall, but they were soft and furtive, as if someone was tiptoeing toward her. She braced, unnerved over what was about to transpire. The key was inserted and turned, then the door was opened. The housekeeper, Mrs. Scruggs, peeked in.

"Mrs. Scruggs?" Caroline said. "It's lovely to finally see you. I was wondering if you'd been apprised of where I was."

"I'm sorry I didn't come sooner," the older woman replied, "but your uncle has been watching us like a hawk."

"You're here now."

Mrs. Scruggs flitted inside and closed the door. She was carrying a portmanteau. She put it on the floor, then hurried over to Caroline and clasped her hands. "We don't have much time, so I have to be blunt. I've arranged for you to sneak away."

"From... my room? Good. I'm weary of being a prisoner."

"Not your room, Miss Caroline. You need to leave Grey's Corner. A footman eavesdropped on your uncle and Mr. Gregory. They're planning to have you committed to an insane asylum."

Caroline gasped. "On what grounds?"

"They claim you're suffering from hysteria. Their proof is that you won't marry Gregory. To them, it's bizarre behavior, so they feel you've had a complete mental breakdown. They're positive they can convince a judge."

Caroline shook her head. "I don't understand any of this."

"Neither do I, but you have to depart immediately. I bribed a footman to whisk you away."

"But... but... where would I go?"

"I thought you could catch the mail coach to London. Perhaps you could stay with Miss Janet? I'm sure she would hide you from them."

"I'm sure she would too, but I have no idea where she is."

"You could find out, couldn't you?" Mrs. Scruggs wrung her hands. "You could place an advertisement in the newspaper or... or..." She cut off and patted her flushed cheeks. "I simply know we can't let them succeed. We'd never get you out of there."

"I should speak to my uncle. I'll stop his mischief."

"No, no, you shouldn't! You should be safely away first, then I'll consult with the vicar and some of the neighbors. I'll seek their advice. We have to enlist some help—from people who are more influential than we are. You and I don't have the power to fight them on our own."

"Why is my uncle doing this, Mrs. Scruggs? I am so bewildered."

"I can't guess his motives, but I had a sister once who was committed to an asylum by her husband. He was a spoiled monster who wanted a divorce, but he had no cause to obtain one, so he locked her away, then he was able to gad about as he pleased. We could never free her, and she died in that terrible facility."

"Oh, Mrs. Scruggs! Don't tell me a story like that."

"I'm just so frightened for you! Your uncle has a wicked purpose that I can't deduce, but at the moment, he is out of the house and Mr. Gregory is in London. Let's get you away while they're not looking."

Caroline dithered, pondering what was best. The entire debacle seemed too far-fetched, like a plot in a theatrical play. Her uncle had always been such a rational fellow. What had possessed him to become so malicious?

She was frozen with indecision, and Mrs. Scruggs interrupted her miserable musing.

"What if he returns with a court order? What if he brings attendants from the hospital? They'd drag you away, and we'd never see you again. I'm certain of it."

"This is too strange to be believed," Caroline said. "I can't fathom him acting this way."

"A man can do anything to a woman. You're aware of that."

Mrs. Scruggs wouldn't debate the issue. She went to Caroline's dresser and started yanking out clothes and stuffing them into the portmanteau. Caroline observed in a sort of dazed stupor.

For days, she'd been drifting in an odd languor, as she'd tried to come to grips with her uncle's perfidy. She'd been the perfect niece, the perfect girl, then the perfect young lady. How dare he treat her so badly! How dare he lock her in!

Her temper flared, and she was unusually incensed. Mrs. Scruggs was correct that a man could do anything to a woman, and her uncle had manipulated her her whole life. Gregory too, but she was finished with their running roughshod over her. She was finished with their making her feel guilty because she was different from other people.

As a child, she'd survived a tragedy. That was it. It wasn't a crime, but they carried on as if it was.

An asylum? She'd see about that!

"Have you any money, Miss Caroline?" Mrs. Scruggs asked.

Caroline pulled a small purse out of her wardrobe. She opened it so Mrs. Scruggs could peek into it. "I have a good amount. My uncle gives me an allowance, but I never spend any of it."

Mrs. Scruggs withdrew a wad of money from her own pocket, and she shoved it at Caroline. "Take this too."

"I couldn't."

"London is very expensive. Use it for the necessities."

Caroline gaped at the money, deliberating. It was wrong to prevail on a servant, but in the end, she accepted it. She hugged Mrs. Scruggs, saying, "You have to be the kindest person I've ever known."

"I shouldn't admit it, but I've never liked your uncle. And I like Mr. Gregory even less. You were right to cry off from your betrothal."

"I'll pay you back. I swear."

"I don't doubt you will."

Caroline assisted with the rest of the packing, then they snuck down and out a rear door. A carriage was harnessed and waiting for her, her favorite footman seated in the box.

It was all accomplished in a quick minute. She climbed in and laid on the floor, and they rolled away.

They'd agreed that Mrs. Scruggs would return to Caroline's bed-chamber, tidy up, and relock the door so it would appear as if Caroline had vanished up to Heaven. When her uncle arrived to badger her, he would discover that his prisoner had flown the coop when he wasn't watching.

Caroline smirked with a grim satisfaction. She had no idea why her uncle was plotting against her, but whatever his scheme, she wasn't about to blithely succumb. Perhaps now that she was really, really angry, Samson Grey had finally met his match.

He just didn't realize it yet.

Chapter 17

"MUST YOU GO SO SOON?"

"I'm needed at home for supper. I told Sybil I'd be there."

Janet smiled at Blake and kept her tone light. "Will I ever meet Sybil?"

"Maybe. If you can learn to behave yourself."

"I always behave myself."

He chuckled and swatted her on the rear. "Since you are naked and completely ruined, we both know that's not true."

"I just asked you to help me run away. I didn't ask you to seduce me."

"You didn't have to ask. Your wicked intentions were clear from the start."

"Can a woman have wicked intentions?"

Blake scoffed. "The world is full of trollops, so yes, a woman can be very wicked. In fact, they can be more dissolute than men. Once they tumble off the moral wagon, they're incredibly corrupt."

"Am I a trollop now? Should I think of myself as one?"

"Well, you have a very debauched character, but you hid it when you were residing under your father's roof. Since you came to London, you've let it fly free. So, yes, you might have become a trollop."

They were in the bedchamber of the pretty apartment she'd rented. It was located in the theater district, an area filled with musicians, actors, and other artistic types. The people she encountered had odd careers and schedules, so no one thought twice about her living alone.

He'd had to sign the lease—he'd pretended to be her brother—and the ruse had worked. She'd moved in the next day, but after she had, there was nothing *brotherly* about what had sprung up between them.

They were stretched out on the bed, with him having arrived to surprise her in the middle of the afternoon.

Her fall from grace had been accomplished with very little contemplation or effort. She was no longer a sheltered virgin from a rural estate in the country. She was a modern female in the city who was settling into her new life, while keeping a paramour to amuse her.

It was the exact sort of existence about which she'd fantasized, but her metamorphosis had been too abrupt. She felt dizzy with trying to regain her balance.

She'd wanted to seem very sophisticated to him, and she'd convinced herself that she could bind him with licentious conduct, but with how they'd forged ahead into their carnal affair, she'd been forced to accept that it was a horrendous decision.

She hadn't bound him in the slightest. She'd simply given him what he never should have had without marrying her first. She didn't have any friends yet, and she was too nervous to venture out after dark, so the nights were particularly long. She'd sit by the window, yearning for him to visit, but not ever knowing when he would.

He'd agreed to assist her with her flight to town, but with no strings attached. He deemed them to be intimate companions, climbing under the blankets when the mood suited him, and not stopping by when the mood didn't.

To her great dismay, she wasn't cut out for such a callous liaison, but if she'd walked an ordinary path with him, she'd never have snagged him for her own. Her father would have refused to arrange a betrothal or, more likely, Blake wouldn't have been interested in one.

He was a confirmed bachelor, a navy sailor who relished his freedom and his career, and he had no desire to be tied down. There was no spot for Janet in his world, so apparently, she'd made her bed—quite literally—and now she had to lie in it.

He kissed her, then slid away and stood. He was wearing his trousers and boots, but for their quick coupling, he'd shed his shirt. She had a fine view of his bare chest. His shoulders were broad, his waist narrow, his arms muscled from strenuous endeavor. She never grew tired of looking at him without his clothes.

"What time do you suppose it is?" he asked.

She glanced outside. "I have no idea. Four? Five?"

"Whew! I won't be late. We're eating at seven. Sybil has us dine early so she can get to my brother's club before the crowds are too big."

"She's so lucky he employs her there."

"She's not an employee. She runs the business for him. If he'd started it without her, he wouldn't have been half so successful."

Janet was fascinated by Sybil Jones. Caleb Ralston permitted her to manage his club, and the situation was peculiar and electrifying. She wished she knew a man like Caleb Ralston, one who recognized that a female could handle that kind of responsibility. *She* would love to be offered such a huge post.

As it was, she was hoping to find a job as a writer's assistant. She constantly penned letters to the women whose books she'd read. She begged for introductions, begged for recommendations. She was a pupil of their teachings, and she'd grabbed hold of the independence they'd extolled.

So far though, it didn't feel very fun or liberating. She was alone in the city, with just Blake Ralston as an acquaintance. She hadn't met any of the radical females who'd tantalized her with their philosophies. She hadn't met anyone really. She was isolated and afraid over what she'd set in motion.

She'd like to write to Caroline, but she didn't dare contact her cousin. Her father might intercept the letter, and if he discovered how Janet had ruined herself, she couldn't predict how he might react. She truly feared he might murder her.

She'd burned her bridges at Grey's Corner, so she couldn't go home. Everything about her life had changed, and her new circumstance was so disorienting. After a few months had passed, she was certain she'd be less adrift. But just that moment, when Blake was about to sneak out, and she couldn't guess when he'd stop by again, it was extremely difficult to be perky.

"What are your plans for the evening?" she asked. She posed the question in a teasing way so he wouldn't think she was needy.

"We're having a family supper, by which I mean it's just the three of us: Sybil, me, and my brother. Then I'll probably loaf at Caleb's club."

"Does he let you gamble there?"

"Definitely not, but he supplies his members with delicious wine and food, so I'll stand in the corner and indulge myself."

"I'd like to see the place, but I imagine if a woman ever waltzed in the door, the foundations of the building would collapse."

"No women allowed. Just Sybil."

"Will women ever be able to join clubs like that?"

"Why would they want to? When men are wagering, they're disgusting. Why watch them when they're being idiots?"

He tugged his shirt on. His coat was next, and shortly, he was dressed and prepared to leave.

"Would you toss me my robe?" she asked. She wasn't comfortable with her nudity. She'd spent too many years buttoned up from chin to toe.

He didn't mock her for her modesty, and she appreciated it. He threw her the robe, then he strolled out to the sitting room, giving her a minute of privacy to slip it on. She cinched the belt and went out to tell him goodbye.

Her mind was frantically whirring, trying to devise reasons to delay him. It was always thrilling when he arrived and always depressing when he departed.

He was by the window and staring out. He peered over at her and asked, "Have you had any replies to your letters?"

"Not yet, but it's early. I'm sure someone will want my help."

"I can picture you at a rally. You'll be leading the protesters with cheers and jeers as you deride all men everywhere."

"You men will deserve it."

She came over and snuggled herself to his side, inhaling his luscious scent. He draped an arm over her shoulders and kissed the top of her head. He was such a tall fellow, and when she was with him, she felt pretty and petite.

"What will *you* do this evening?" he inquired.

"I'll write more letters, and I'll read the advertisements in the newspaper. I may stumble on a position that appears interesting."

"You should hire a lawyer too, so you can switch the trustee on your trust fund. You have to have your father removed from the account. I'm worried he'll cut off your money—I'm amazed he hasn't already—then you'll be in big trouble."

"I hadn't thought of that. Can you suggest a viable candidate? He'd have to agree to deal with a female, *and* he'd have to promise to listen to me rather than my father."

"I'll ask my brother about it." He halted, then scowled. "No, actually, I'll ask Sybil. She might have a better notion of who you need."

He kissed her, then walked to the door. She remained where she was, determined not to rush over and glom onto him, determined not to beg him to stay a bit longer.

"Are you still glad you're in London?" he asked.

"I'm still glad."

"It will get easier. You merely have to assimilate."

"I realize that."

"I'm proud of you," he suddenly said.

"Proud? Why would you be?"

"You've engaged in a dramatic adventure. You were desperate to change your life, and you did. I've never met a woman who was so bold. I like it."

She yearned to ask when he'd be back, but she swallowed down the question. She would not demean herself by seeming inordinately fond.

He flashed a wicked grin and sauntered out, the sound of his boots fading on the stairs. She gazed down into the street, anxious to watch him as he mounted his horse and rode away, but even though she stared for an eternity, she didn't see him.

She tarried in the quiet. She could hear her heart beating, could hear a clock ticking in the adjacent apartment, and when she recognized how terribly morose she was being, she shook off her dour mood. This was the existence she'd picked for herself, and she wouldn't rue and regret. There was no point to it.

Blake Ralston was the man of her dreams, the man she adored, and she could have wept over how she'd misplayed her hand with him. She didn't want a cold, detached relationship where he visited for an afternoon romp. She wanted a ring on her finger and a home of her own, with Blake as her husband.

She shouldn't have fallen into the trap she had with him. She grasped that now but, in her own defense, she hadn't understood how intimate a physical affair would be. How could she have known? And once they'd started in, how could she have resisted him?

He was simply too dashing for words.

She wished she was acquainted with an older woman who could advise her as to what she should do—for she had absolutely no idea.

Finally, she yanked away from the window and went to the table in the corner to peruse the newspaper. There were so many intriguing jobs described in it, but they were all for men. She waded through them anyway, forcing herself to be optimistic.

She sat down and began to read when a personal notice caused her to blanch with surprise: *Caroline seeking Janet. I'm in London. Where are you? Please reply as indicated so I can find you.* There was a box listed at the newspaper office where a response could be sent.

Was it Caroline? Should Janet answer the query? But why would Caroline be in town? What if it was Janet's father? What if it was a trick he'd used to locate her? If she was caught by him, he might lock her in a convent for being so reckless. She wouldn't put it past him.

Her pulse pounded with dread—but with excitement too. She couldn't decide what was best, and she laid the page aside. She would show it to Blake to garner his opinion, and she would figure out a path from there.

CAROLINE LEFT THE NEWSPAPER office, and she dawdled on the side-walk, debating how to proceed. She'd been checking every morning for a month, but there had been no message from Janet, and she was out of options. There was no guarantee Janet would ever chance upon her advertisement, but other than publishing her appeal, she couldn't guess how to contact her cousin.

She'd arrived in London with no difficulty. On the mail coach, she'd chatted with a widow who'd offered information about the city and how Caroline should settle in. On her recommendation, Caroline had taken a room at a boarding house that was clean and situated in a safe neighborhood.

But the next month's rent was due, and Caroline had to pay or move out. She was conflicted over her choices. No alternative seemed to be the right one.

She'd been to London on several occasions, so it wasn't completely strange to her. So far, she'd spent her days meandering and sightseeing, and she'd spent her nights fretting and fuming.

She wanted to return to Grey's Corner and confront her uncle. He was intending to inflict grave harm on her for no reason she could discern. She'd always been kind to him, and the only time she'd ever been stubborn was over the wedding. Why had he reacted so cruelly? Why would he be so eager to hurt her?

When she was feeling particularly harassed, she'd wonder about Mrs. Scruggs's belief that he was planning to have her committed to an asylum. What if Mrs. Scruggs had been mistaken about what the footman had overheard? What if Uncle Samson hadn't planned any such outrage? If so, she'd fled for nothing. Should she go home?

The instant she pondered the notion, she'd scold herself. Mrs. Scruggs wasn't prone to fantasy. If she thought Caroline was imperiled, then she was.

She had to find Janet. It was growing ever more imperative. She'd be less anxious once they were reunited. Janet was smart and pragmatic, and she'd provide shrewd counsel as to how Caroline could protect herself.

She started down the block, and at the corner, a crowd had gathered. A newsboy was hawking the latest edition of the paper, and people were rushing up to buy copies. She stood on the edge of the group, curious as to why everyone was so agitated.

One fellow had purchased his copy, and he muttered, "Look what the dirty dog has done to her!"

"What is it?" Caroline asked him. "What's happened?"

"This can't stand, Miss!" he said. "It simply can't stand!"

He shoved the paper under her nose, and the headline practically leapt off the page: *LITTLE HENRIETTA FOUND AT LAST!*

"Oh, my goodness," she murmured.

The *Little Henrietta* scandal had occurred twenty years earlier. Henrietta had been Lord Roland's baby daughter, and his crazed ex-wife had absconded with her. Lord Roland had searched for her relentlessly, but to no avail. Because of the tragedy, he was a sympathetic character for whom the masses possessed a great affection.

She continued to read, and under the large headline, there were others that were smaller, but even more shocking: *Libby Carstairs, Mystery Girl of the Caribbean, Revealed as Little Henrietta!* and *Lord Roland Denies His Long-Lost Daughter!* and *Libby Carstairs Under Arrest! Lord Roland Determined to Hide the Truth!*

Caroline gasped. "Libby Carstairs is Little Henrietta? Let me see that!"

She jerked the paper out of the man's hands, and she raced through the stories. Apparently, Libby was Henrietta, but when she'd announced her identity to Lord Roland, he'd called her a liar and had had her arrested for fraud.

"I know Libby Carstairs," she told him. "She's a friend of mine."

"Why would Lord Roland be so awful to her? You'd think he'd be celebrating."

"Where would they have taken her?" Caroline asked.

He pointed to a paragraph lower in the article. "It says here Newgate Prison."

"Newgate!" Caroline huffed with offense. "What is wrong with Lord Roland? Is he insane? Can you give me directions to the prison?"

"I'm going there myself," he said. "I'll show you where it is. I predict half the city will be there to protest this infamy. Libby Carstairs is England's darling! This barbarity can't be born!"

His opinion was shared by many. A mob marched down the street together, keeping on for quite a distance. As they neared the facility, the walls were visible, and the crowd had swelled to an enormous size. There was loud chanting of, *Let her out! Let her out!*

With all of Caroline's recent troubles, she'd forgotten to seek out Libby. Now Libby was in jail, and Caroline had to talk to her. There had to be a way to aid her.

Caroline wound into the throng and to the gate. There were guards positioned in front of it, and they warily assessed the spectators, as if expecting them to storm the barricades and rescue Libby. They were holding clubs, and they looked as if they'd be delighted to use them.

Despite their angry glowers, she approached the man in the middle and asked to visit Libby.

He laughed snidely. "Allow me to guess. You're her only sibling. Or you're her business partner. Or are you her theater manager? What excuse will you provide?"

"I'm probably her oldest friend. How can I be admitted inside?"

"Several dozen fools have already demanded an audience. They've all told me sob stories."

"Well, *my* story is true. I'm Caroline Grey. I'm one of the Mystery Girls too. Libby is like my very own sister."

"That's a novel one I haven't heard yet, so I'll credit you with having a very vivid imagination."

"I *am* Caroline Grey. I *am* a Mystery Girl. May I see her?"

"No, you may not." He nodded to another guard. "Harry, would you get this woman out of here? She's annoying me." The fellow, Harry, grabbed her, and the first guard said, "She tells me she's a bloody Mystery Girl of the Caribbean, just like Miss Carstairs, so treat her with all the respect she deserves."

Her identity was declared loudly and rudely, and the other guards snickered. Then Harry dragged her away. She struggled to free herself, and he said, "Don't come back, Miss. We have a situation brewing, and there's no time to deal with nonsense like this."

"I have to be sure Libby is all right."

"The entire citizenry wants to be sure about Miss Carstairs," he said, "and schemers like you will never be permitted to bother her."

He tossed her away, and she lost her balance, then fell to the ground. Her bonnet went flying, her shawl too. She scraped her palms and tore her skirt. The area was packed with protesters, and they were wedged shoulder to shoulder. She curled into a ball, terrified she'd be stepped on and trampled.

Suddenly, her reticule was yanked off her wrist.

She shouted and reached for it, but there was too much noise, so her cry of alarm wasn't noted. She glared into a forest of legs and saw a pair of shoes dashing away. Her purse—and all her money—was gone.

She staggered about and climbed to her knees as a man leaned down and lifted her up.

"Are you hurt, Miss?"

"My purse!" she wailed. "Someone stole my purse!"

"Oh, no."

He frowned, as if he'd chase after the interloper, but the crowd was milling, shifting, heaving. They were immediately separated, and she was worried she might be crushed in the melee.

She ducked and moved in the direction of those felonious feet. Eventually, she was spit out onto the edge of the mob. She peered about, expecting to espy a miscreant running down the block with her reticule tucked under his arm.

But there was no sign of the fiend. There were just teeming, livid people bellowing for Libby's release, and no one noticed Caroline at all.

Chapter

18

CAROLINE WAS HOVERED OUTSIDE the prison, yearning to talk to Libby in a manner that was almost manic in its intensity. Over the past few days, she'd visited several times, but she still hadn't been admitted into the facility.

When she'd initially arrived in the city, she'd believed herself lucky and shrewd, but she'd been a fool to think she knew what she was doing. Women constantly moved to London, and the kingdom was rife with horror stories about the disasters that befell them when they behaved so rashly.

Janet hadn't replied to any of her advertisements, and Caroline's money had been stolen. She'd run through her nights of lodging at the boarding house and hadn't been able to pay for more of them. While she'd been visiting the newspaper office, the proprietor had set her portmanteau out on the porch. It had been stolen too, so the possessions she'd brought with her to London were gone.

She was out of options, and she had to return to Grey's Corner. What choice did she have? She simply had to swallow her pride, beg her uncle's forgiveness, then prepare to endure whatever punishment he inflicted. She was feeling that beleaguered and distraught.

The only problem was that she hadn't the funds to buy a ticket on the mail coach. If she went home, she'd have to walk. She'd have to ask teamsters and farmers for rides in their wagons, but there was great risk involved in traveling that way.

There were always stories too about women, usually younger ones, who accepted rides from strangers, then they vanished.

She'd decided to make a last attempt to speak to Libby, then she had to get out of the city. Her situation was too dire, and she couldn't dawdle.

The crowd had grown to an enormous size, and there was a new energy in the air. Rumor had it that Libby was about to be released. Her bail had been posted, and shortly, she would emerge from the front gate.

Caroline was wedging herself toward it, but she was so petite, and many of the protesters were large, angry men. She was jostled and stepped on and once even pushed to the ground again.

She looked a sight. Her palms were scraped and bleeding, her face smudged with dirt. Her hair was drooping down her back.

Finally, she neared the gate. A pink carriage was parked next to it. Suddenly, the gate was flung open. A phalanx of guards marched out, and they were swinging clubs, creating a path to the carriage.

Then the spectators parted and...?

There she was! Dear Libby! Her oldest friend. Libby, the fearless companion who had haunted her dreams for two decades. Libby, the lone female in all the world who could comprehend the challenging life Caroline had led after their terrible ordeal in the Caribbean.

She recollected Libby being very pretty, but she was even more beautiful now. Her adult years had added drama and elegance to her features so she could have been a princess trapped in a tower.

She was being hustled along and wasn't focused on any of the unruly bystanders. She didn't so much as peek at Caroline, and why would she have? Caroline was filthy, and with her hand extended, she might have been a beggar, pleading for alms.

"Libby!" she shouted, but the noise was overwhelming. "Libby! It's me! It's Caroline Grey! Do you remember me? You can't have forgotten!"

Libby was lifted into the vehicle, the horses pulling her away so swiftly she might never have been there at all. Caroline's shoulders slumped with defeat, and she was about to stagger away when she noticed a wealthy gentleman staring at Libby's retreating coach. His desire to be inside it with her was blatantly apparent.

She brazenly said to him, "Pardon me, sir, but you were gazing at Miss Carstairs so fondly. Do you know her?"

"Yes, I know her."

"I know her too."

"Good for you," he muttered, clearly not wanting to be bothered.

"I called to her, but she couldn't hear me."

"Yes, it's been very loud."

He tried to skirt by her, but she clasped his arm. "Can you tell me where she went? Are you going there now?"

"No, I'm not going there."

"Where does she live? How would I find her lodging?"

He assessed her deteriorated condition, and it was obvious he deemed her to be a tad deranged.

"I can't tell you any of that," he said.

"When you talk to her, will you inform her you spoke to Caroline Grey? I've been searching for her."

"Yes, I'll be sure to apprise her for you."

His snooty tone indicated he didn't mean it. He circled by her and kept on, and she said, "It's Caroline Grey! Little Caro! Don't forget! I've missed her desperately!"

She hollered other comments, yearning for him to believe she wasn't a lunatic making up stories, but he was anxious to get away from her. He was swallowed up, and she couldn't see him. She breathed out a heavy sigh.

Could she possibly suffer one more calamity? What *hadn't* happened to her? What other disasters *might* happen before Fate was through with her?

She had to head to Grey's Corner. She had to confess to Mrs. Scruggs that she'd lost her money. Then she had to throw herself on her uncle's mercy and hope he'd let her in the door. If he wouldn't, she supposed she'd end up in the poor house.

She started walking, and ultimately, she was far away from the prison and the commotion that had erupted there. She was hungry, thirty, and miserable, and she wondered if she could be directed to a rescue mission so she could have something to eat.

She began to cry, and people noted her deteriorated state, but no one asked what was wrong. No one asked if she could use some help. They rushed by her, as if—whatever her issue—it might be catching.

She shouldn't have fled Grey's Corner at Mrs. Scruggs's urging. She should have stayed in her small, isolated bedroom and allowed her uncle to implement his scheme. Despite the plot he'd cooked up with Gregory, she doubted he'd have let her starve.

Eventually, she glanced around, finding herself on a busy thoroughfare. Commerce was brisk. Wagons, carriages, and hansom cabs rolled by. Vendors hawked wares from carts. Pedestrians hurried to their destinations.

She gazed up at the building next to her. There was a sign over the door, and as she read it, she gasped with surprise. It couldn't be. Could it?

"Ralston's..." she murmured, and a shiver ran down her spine. What were the odds?

It had to be Caleb Ralston's gambling club, didn't it? Dare she inquire? Dare she request the chance to chat with him?

He'd aid her; she just knew he would. He wouldn't permit Uncle Samson to lock her in an asylum. He simply wouldn't!

Why hadn't she sought him out earlier? As he'd departed Grey's Corner, he'd encouraged her to contact him if she ever needed his help. She'd assumed she'd be too proud to ever consider it, but pride was the main casualty of her current position. She had none remaining.

It hadn't occurred to her to pester him. After all, they were barely acquainted, and it would have seemed presumptuous to have him intervene in her problems, but at the notion that he'd assist her, she was so relieved that her knees buckled. She staggered and had to fight to keep her balance.

There were three steps that led to the entrance. She marched over, climbed them, and briskly knocked.

CALEB WAS SITTING IN Sybil's office. She was conferring with a deliveryman, then they would go home for a few hours. They'd return later, when the crowds arrived.

For a brief moment, his temper flared, and he reveled in it. He'd been born and raised in Jamaica and had spent much of his life out on the water, but now, he was stuck inside. With his business thriving, he'd likely never escape England. It was galling, and the unfairness nibbled away at him, but he tamped it down.

He was an adult who was free to pick his own path. He'd chosen to accept the blame for Blake's mischief in the navy, so he'd had to retire. He'd chosen to tarry in London rather than sail to the Caribbean. He'd chosen to buy a house and settle down. He'd chosen to open a gambling club with Sybil.

No one had held a gun to his head, and his decisions meant he was very rich. What kind of idiot would complain about it?

A footman knocked and peeked in. "A young lady has asked for you. Should I claim you've left? What's your preference?"

He bristled, figuring it would be a wife or sister of a member. She'd beg him for mercy and would perhaps even offer salacious favors so he'd cancel a debt. He never cancelled any of them though, and once a member reached the spot where his female kin were bothering Caleb, the fellow was kicked out.

"Did she mention who her relative is?" he asked. "On whose behalf am I being petitioned?"

"She didn't tell me."

"I don't have the patience for it today. Have her come back tomorrow afternoon—and talk to Sybil."

"I hate to send her away, Mr. Ralston. She looks as if she's experienced some difficulties. She could probably use a hot meal. Could I take her to the kitchen and feed her?"

"That's fine, but escort her out the minute she's finished."

"And...ah...she told me—in case you were reluctant—to remind you that you invited her to contact you if she was ever in trouble. She asked me to add that she hoped you were serious."

Caleb scowled, struggling to remember any woman to whom he might have tendered such a vow. "What's her name?"

"It's Caroline Grey, sir. Miss Caroline Grey? From Grey's Corner?"

Had he heard that correctly? "Caroline is here?"

"Yes, Mr. Ralston, and I'm afraid she's—"

Before the man could complete his sentence, Caleb had leapt up and rushed by him. He ran down the hall to the foyer, and he skidded to a halt, feeling as if he was hallucinating.

There was Caro! Standing in his lobby! She was filthy and bedraggled, her hair hanging down, her skirt ripped, her face smudged, but he'd never observed a more glorious sight.

In the past few weeks, he'd nearly saddled a horse and ridden to Grey's Corner on a hundred different occasions. He hadn't been able to stop thinking about her, and he'd been anxious over her plight, as if she might need him. Apparently, his intuition was working quite well. Since he'd last been with her, she'd definitely suffered a catastrophe.

"Caro," he said tentatively, as if she were a wild animal that might bolt. "Is it really you?"

She spun toward him in a sort of slow motion that was thrilling and peculiar. It seemed as if the entire universe was noting the encounter.

"Oh, Caleb! Am I glad to see you!"

"What happened?"

"I've been having the worst time of it."

She burst into tears, and he hurried over and pulled her into his arms. She wrapped herself around him, holding on as if they were floating in the middle of the ocean and—should he release her—she'd sink to the bottom.

He began kissing her, and instantly, he was in too deep. He'd forgotten how intensely connected they'd been. He'd forgotten the sparks they generated, the joy she induced.

He couldn't guess how long they continued. He was vaguely aware of members gaping and servants staring. It was Sybil who penetrated the fog of elation that had enveloped him.

"Caleb," she said, "I have to point out that you're making a spectacle of yourself."

He drew away from Caro. She hadn't loosened her grip on him, and he wondered if she'd ever calm down enough to let go.

"Everything will be all right now," he murmured to her.

"I know."

"At the first sign of trouble, you should have come to me. Who put you in this condition? Was it Gregory? Was it your uncle?"

Caro might have expounded, but Sybil bustled over, saying, "We shouldn't dither over it here. It's clear she's too distraught to explain."

"You're correct, as always," Caleb said.

Sybil focused her wily gaze on Caro and said, "Will you introduce me, Caleb?"

"This is Miss Caroline Grey. I told you about her."

Sybil snorted with amusement. "You told me about her, but obviously, you didn't *tell* me."

"We met when I was in the country." He smiled at Caro. "Caro, this is my friend and business partner, Sybil Jones."

"Hello, Miss Jones." Caro was trembling slightly, tears still dripping down her cheeks as if there were so many she couldn't keep them at bay.

Sybil wedged herself between them, deftly separating her from Caleb. "I'm sorry for your dilemma, Miss Grey. Will you permit us to tend you for a bit? We'll have you improved in no time at all."

Sybil led her through the gaming room, through the kitchens, and out to the alley, where their carriage was parked. They'd been about to head off, so the horses were harnessed and waiting for them.

Caro seemed to have deflated. Sybil was practically carrying her, as if every ounce of Caro's energy had evaporated.

Several footmen had tagged after them, and they appeared stricken over her plight. The carriage door was opened, and two of them stepped forward and lifted her in. She was limp as a ragdoll, so it was easy for them to manhandle her.

Sybil climbed in, then Caleb followed. Sybil slid onto the seat across from Caro, but Caleb sat next to her and tugged her onto his lap. She nestled herself to his chest and wept quietly all the way home.

⌒⌒

CALEB LURKED IN THE hall outside the guest bedchamber where Sybil had sequestered Caro after they'd arrived at their London house. The minute they'd entered, Sybil had begun shouting orders. Caro had been whisked up the stairs, and Sybil had locked them in, with their female servants mobilized to offer assistance.

He'd been relegated to the status of observer and hadn't been allowed into the room. He'd cooled his heels, trying to keep his impatience in check, as they fussed over her.

It was evening already, the lamps and fires lit. She'd been bathed and fed, her cuts washed and bandaged. The servants had left, but Sybil was still with her. The hum of their voices was audible, but he couldn't discern any words, and he couldn't imagine what they were discussing.

Finally—finally!—Sybil emerged. She walked over to Caleb, and they huddled together.

"Did she tell you what happened?" he asked.

"Yes, but I'll let her tell you herself." Sybil clucked her tongue. "Would you kill Gregory Grey for me? And his father? Would that be an awful favor to request?"

His temper flared. He'd suspected Gregory Grey was the culprit. "I could kill them. I don't have any problem with that conclusion."

Sybil smirked, then raised a brow. "I like her."

"So do I."

"I think she'll be perfect for you."

He shrugged noncommittally. "You might be right."

"You certainly took your time deciding she was the one."

"I haven't decided that," he claimed.

She simply flashed a look that told him he was being ridiculous. "I'm needed at the club, so you'll be alone with her."

He tamped down a wave of delight. "I won't misbehave."

"I didn't insist you act like a saint. If I were a matronly sort of woman, I'd warn you not to go in there, but I'm not your mother, and I'm definitely not *her* chaperone."

"I wouldn't listen to you anyway."

"I recognize that fact, so figure out what you want from her. Don't be stupid about it."

"I'm never stupid about anything."

She scoffed. "You're the stupidest man I know. Except for your brother. He's worse than you are."

"I won't argue the point."

"We'll talk in the morning about what's to be done with her—and her relatives."

"I'm moving against Gregory in the courts, but I can speed up that process."

"Good."

"I'm working to attach their property to secure the debt. It belongs to Gregory's father, but Gregory is the heir, so it will be his someday. My lawyers are pursuing that angle."

"Maybe, before you're through with them, you'll end up owning the estate, and you can present it to her as a gift. It would be damages owed for what she's endured."

"I like that idea."

"You can also murder them."

"Without batting an eye."

"I'll see you tomorrow."

She patted him on the chest and sauntered away, then he spun the knob and tiptoed into Caro's room. He'd expected her to be asleep, but she was awake and waiting for him.

She was in bed and leaned against the pillows, the blankets pulled to her waist. Sybil had produced a robe for her to wear, and she appeared snug and relaxed, her condition a hundred percent improved from when she'd stumbled into his club.

A thousand comments swirled between them, then he asked, "What on earth happened to you? I could have sworn you were safe and sound when I fled Grey's Corner. You've given me the fright of my life. You realize that, don't you?"

"I'm sorry. I'm just so glad I staggered in your door. If I hadn't, I truly can't imagine what might have become of me."

She held out her hand, and he dashed over and clasped it as tightly as he could. He eased a hip onto the mattress and dipped down to kiss her.

"I like Sybil," she said when he drew away.

"She likes you too, which is amazing because she usually doesn't like anybody."

She batted her lashes in a teasing way. "It's my abundant charm. It simply flows out of me."

"Why are you in London? What's wrong? Please inform me in a bland manner so I'm not inclined to rush out and commit a homicide."

"Well, after you departed, I stuck to my guns and called off the wedding, but my uncle refused to consider it. He even had our vicar come over to perform the ceremony, in an attempt to force me into it, but I wouldn't comply. My uncle was so angry that he locked me in my room."

"The bastard," he muttered, then he hastily said, "I apologize. I don't mean to be crude."

"The derogatory term is completely fitting, so I'm not offended. One afternoon when he was out of the house, our housekeeper, Mrs. Scruggs, snuck in. A footman had overheard Gregory conspiring with my uncle. They were secretly planning to put me in an asylum."

"An asylum? Seriously? On what grounds?"

"They intended to claim I was suffering from hysteria. If they'd managed to obtain a court order, Mrs. Scruggs feared I'd never be released. She slipped me some money, and I ran away to London."

"I don't understand any of this."

"Neither do I. It's not as if I'm a great heiress." She sighed, looking young and vulnerable and desperately in need of a strong ally. "My cousin, Janet, is here in the city. She ran away too, and I've been searching for her, but I couldn't find her."

"London is a very big place."

"I know, and I shouldn't have come, but I wasn't thinking clearly. I was so scared, and I've been acting like a dunce."

"If you had money," he asked, "how did you wind up so bedraggled?"

"I was robbed! And all my belongings were stolen!"

"Oh, no."

"When I strolled by your gambling club—quite by accident, I might add—I was at the end of my rope."

"We're lucky you arrived before your calamity grew any worse. You should have sought me out sooner, you silly girl."

"Yes, but as I mentioned, I haven't been thinking clearly. I've made one bad choice after the next. I'd given up and was heading home. I decided I'd be better off in an asylum than wandering the streets with no funds and no friends."

"I missed you," he admitted. "I almost traveled to Grey's Corner a hundred times to fetch you away."

"I missed you too, and I still can't believe you abandoned me there."

"I am very stubborn, but I should have listened to you. It's blatantly obvious that you have no ability to take care of yourself. You're not a woman who should be left to her own devices."

"In light of the disasters I've experienced, I have to agree with you."

"I don't dare let you out of my sight ever again."

He climbed onto the mattress and nestled her to his chest. They were quiet, lost in thought, then she said, "I don't know what to do now."

"You don't have to figure it out immediately."

"I don't have a penny to my name, and I don't have a stitch of clothing. I'm an indigent beggar."

"Sybil dug up a few garments for you. They'll be fine for tomorrow, then we'll buy you what else you require."

"I hate that I've imposed."

"You haven't imposed. I've recently earned an obscene fortune. I can afford to purchase a gown or two for you."

She chuckled at that. "I'm so relieved that I'm here, but I'm afraid of my uncle. What if he finds me? Could he yank me away from you? Could he force you to hand me over?"

"I would never permit it. I swear it to you on my life." He stated the vow firmly, vehemently, and he truly meant it. He'd murder Samson Grey before he'd allow him to move against her. "Don't fret about it. I want you to rest and recuperate. At the moment, that should be your only concern."

"Why is he so adamant that I wed Gregory?" she asked. "It's been vexing me. What is your opinion? His behavior is so bizarre, and I've been driving myself mad, trying to deduce their reasoning."

"I have no idea, and we're not debating it tonight. Stop worrying. That's an order."

"Yes, sir."

She gave a mock salute, and it had him laughing, but also wondering if he was about to marry her. Was that what was approaching? Were his bachelor days over? For once, the prospect didn't sound quite so terrifying.

They were quiet again, and she yawned.

"I feel as if I haven't slept in a year," she said. "I'm exhausted."

"It's the stress you've endured, but with me watching over you, your condition will improve quickly."

"I'd like to chat until dawn, but I can't manage it."

"You don't have to stay awake. Why don't you snuggle under the covers? I'm betting you'll nod off in an instant."

He lifted the blankets so she could scoot farther down, and he tucked her in as if she were a toddler. They stared for an eternity, neither of them ready to part, and finally, she asked, "Would you sit with me? Just until I doze off? I'm so accursedly skittish, and I can't bear to be alone."

Affection rocked him. "Of course I'll sit with you. I can tarry until dawn if you need me to."

There was a candle on the table by the bed, and he blew it out. The moon was shining in the window, so it wasn't completely dark. In the moonlight, she looked small and defenseless, and her vulnerability stoked his male impulses so he yearned to keep her safe from harm, to protect her forever.

He stretched out next to her, and he pulled her into his arms, listening as her breathing slowed.

He thought she was asleep, but she murmured, "Did you hear my old friend, Libby Carstairs, was arrested?"

"The whole kingdom heard."

"I went to the prison as she was being released, but I couldn't get close to her."

"She was released?"

"Yes. Earlier today."

"I almost went myself, to post her bail. I've never met her, but I have such a connection to her—because of my father."

"You couldn't have spoken to her. There were tons of charlatans who tried, and the guards were wary of everyone who inquired."

"Maybe after matters calm for you, we'll seek her out together. We'll introduce ourselves."

"I'd like that." She was silent for a bit, then she mumbled, "I'm happy."

"I'm happy too."

She fit by his side perfectly, as if she'd been created to lie there and no place else in the world. Fate certainly seemed to think she belonged right where she was. His father's ghost too.

He'd walked away from her once. He couldn't do it again.

Chapter

19

CAROLINE SLOWLY DRIFTED AWAKE, and she didn't panic, didn't peer about nervously in order to recall where she was. She knew: She was at Caleb's home in London. She was in a guest bedchamber, and he was snuggled under the blankets with her.

When she'd initially climbed into the bed, she'd been wearing a robe, but the belt had come loose. The lapels were open, her nude torso pressed to his clothes.

She stared at the ceiling, her mind awhirl as she tried to deduce her opinion about her predicament. She should have leapt up and demanded he depart immediately, but she was delighted to remain right where she was.

She wondered what would happen with them. From the moment they'd met, it had seemed as if they belonged together, but the only way a man and woman could truly be joined was by marriage. Yet he was a confirmed bachelor who wasn't interested in matrimony, so what possible ending could they have?

The prior day, he'd been so excited to have her arrive. It was obvious he was still besotted. What might he be prepared to do about it? She was positive about what she wanted—a proposal of marriage—but how could she convince him that he wanted it too?

She studied his handsome face. Even though it was dark out, there was enough light filtering in that she could see him clearly. It wasn't fair for him to be so attractive. He appeared younger and more content when he was sleeping, and she never got tired of looking at him.

He must have perceived her heightened attention, for he woke up too. He laid a palm on her cheek and asked, "How are you feeling?"

"Much better—now that I'm with you."

"What time is it?"

"I suppose dawn is approaching."

"Your expression is so serious. What are you thinking about?"

"I'm worrying about where we're headed."

"I have a few suggestions about that," he said. "I don't believe I can walk away from you again. I have to take steps that guarantee you're glued to my side forever."

She assumed he was referring to marriage, but how was she to be sure? Should she inquire as to what he meant? She had no notion of how to begin that discussion, but she suspected they ought to engage in it before they went any farther.

He closed the distance between them and kissed her, so he removed any opportunity to debate the issue. She jumped into the embrace, and it quickly grew heated and out of control.

Gradually, he guided his hand down her body and slipped it under the fabric of her robe. She was naked underneath, and she should have grabbed his wrist and prevented any exploration, but she didn't.

She was breathless with anticipation, her anatomy alive and on fire in an intensely dramatic manner. He could do many delicious things to her, and she would relish every one of them.

Would she stop him? She doubted it. Their current situation, where they were alone in an isolated bedchamber—and she was undressed—made it seem as if any mischief would be permitted.

He deepened the kiss and started massaging her breast, pinching the nipple, and causing such a ripple of elation to shoot through her limbs that she was bewildered by the raucous sensations being induced.

Much too rapidly, the encounter escalated past any limit she should have allowed. He rolled on top of her and played with both nipples, which was too riveting to describe, and she was anxious to learn where it would lead.

He drew away and nibbled a trail down her neck, to her chest. Before she realized his plan, he sucked a nipple into his mouth and nursed at it. The agitation produced was so shocking that she was afraid she might explode. It felt that debauched.

He kept on for ages, arousing her, tormenting her, as his curious hand wandered down her stomach, then lower. A finger glided through her womanly hair and into her sheath. He stroked it in and out, in and out, as his thumb touched the spot at the vee of her thighs.

Suddenly, she was pitched into a wild, exotic spiral of ecstasy, and she seemed to be flying to the heavens. She raced up and up, reached a peak of sorts, then tumbled down.

As he caught her, he was preening in a completely male fashion that was incredibly annoying.

"What was that?" she sputtered when she could speak again.

"*That* was sexual pleasure," he told her, "and a very fine example of it too."

"Can it occur every time a man and woman are together like this?"

"It can—if the couple is physically compatible. And if the man is adept at performing on a mattress."

"Am I...with child now?"

At her naiveté, he smiled affectionately. "No. You're not with child. There's quite a bit more to it than that."

"How does it happen?"

"It's difficult to explain."

"Was that a ridiculous question? I'm twenty-four. I should probably have some idea of what transpires."

"There are no ridiculous questions, and I find your innocence to be very charming. I spend my nights around so many dissolute scoundrels that I forget there are virtuous people in the world."

She chuckled, figuring she should be embarrassed by how she'd just carried on, but she wasn't. She was simply calculating how quickly she could persuade him to bring on the wave of ecstasy again.

"I didn't know that was possible," she said.

"We don't tell you virginal maidens how fun carnal conduct can be. If you had the slightest clue, you'd never behave yourselves."

"We shouldn't have done this." She halted and grinned. "But I'm not sorry."

He grinned too. "Neither am I."

He slid off her and onto his side, so they were nose to nose. Her robe was open at the front, so her torso was crushed to his.

"I think I have to marry you," he abruptly announced.

He looked so glum that she laughed. "Was that a proposal?"

"I guess it was."

"You could sound a tad more enthusiastic. Men marry every day. It won't kill you."

"I merely thought I'd always be a bachelor."

"And I always thought *I* would be a wife, so if I'm to stay with you, then matrimony is the only path that will satisfy me."

He physically kicked himself under the covers. "I'm being an ass, and I apologize. Let me rephrase my comment. Caro, will you marry me? Will you make me the happiest man in the kingdom and say you'll be mine?"

"I suppose I have to. You've had your wicked way with me, so I'm damaged goods. It's you or no one, so I don't have any choice."

It was his turn to laugh. "Could *you* please sound a tad more eager? If I'm prepared to stop being single, you have to at least pretend to be glad about my horrendous sacrifice."

"I was being a snot," she said, "and I apologize too. I would be honored to be your bride. I can't *wait* to be your bride."

"I'm so terrified to have asked you. I'm worried my heart might burst out of my chest."

"As I mentioned, men wed all the time. You'll survive. I promise."

"I hope so. If I die from it, I'll blame you."

"I shall make your transition from bachelor to husband as easy as I can. I wouldn't want to be a widow so soon after I snagged you for my own."

He was totally overwhelmed, as if he wasn't sure he should have proceeded, but she wasn't about to let him renege. Not when he'd finally offered exactly what she'd craved from him.

As to herself, she was disappointed that no words of love had been voiced. Shouldn't they have been?

She was madly in love with him, and he probably loved her too. Shouldn't a couple contemplating marriage proclaim their heightened fondness? Love wasn't usually a factor in matrimonial decisions, but when it was present, wasn't that a sign of a positive outcome? Shouldn't it be celebrated?

She couldn't fathom how to talk about it though, and when *he* hadn't talked about it, she didn't see how she could either.

Well, they would have many decades together, and their current emotions would blossom as they went forward. He would eventually love her. She was convinced of it.

"When will we do it?" she asked. "Where will we do it? Do you attend a church here in the city?"

"No, I'm a dedicated heathen."

She tsked with exasperation. "We'll have to work on that situation. I'm very devout, so I'll expect you to accompany me to services *and* to act as if you're enjoying yourself."

"For you, I will attempt anything, even church services."

"It may be tricky to figure out where to hold the ceremony. We can't return to the country and beg my vicar to call the banns. I doubt he would. Not when my betrothal to Gregory hasn't been officially terminated, and I would hate to quarrel with my uncle about it."

He smirked. "You naughty girl. Will you notify him after you've become my bride?"

"Yes, definitely. I won't give him a chance to stop me."

"I'm not keen to have the banns called. It would mean we'd have to delay a whole month, and you might come to your senses and change your mind."

"I won't ever change my mind," she firmly stated.

"We could apply for a Special License, but there's likely not a single bishop in the land who would provide me with one."

"We could elope."

"Caroline Grey! In the time we've been apart, you've altered into someone I don't recognize. Elope! What a scandalous proposition! I'm astounded that you would suggest it."

"You're not the only one who's concerned about minds being changed. I'm not about to let you think about this. If anyone will get cold feet, it's *you*. Not me. I'm perfectly content to be your wife, but you will be fretting and quailing and devising reasons to postpone. I intend to attach a leg shackle, and I want it to be so tight that you can never pry it off."

He sighed with gladness. "An elopement it is, Miss Grey."

"I've always yearned to visit Scotland. I guess this will be my opportunity." She cradled his cheek in her palm. "It will be all right, Caleb. I swear."

"I know, and I'm very excited."

"What will Sybil's opinion be? And how about your brother?"

"Sybil will be thrilled about it, but she'll be angry that we're running off to accomplish it away from home. She's the type who'd have liked to make a big fuss."

"We can have her host a reception after we're back."

"She'd like that, and as to my brother, this news will probably kill him."

"He'll be upset to have you wed me?"

"Not *you* precisely. Just that I'm marrying anybody. He and I thought we'd always be bachelors. He'll be stunned, but he likes you. He'll be happy for me."

"I'll be Mrs. Caleb Ralston," she said. "What do you think of that?"

"I think it sounds quite grand."

CALEB CLASPED CARO'S HAND and kissed the center of it. Then he rolled her onto her back again, and he rolled too so he was stretched out atop her.

He couldn't believe he'd proposed, but after he'd spent the night in her bed, it was the only logical conclusion.

When he'd left Grey's Corner, he should have brought her to London with him, but he'd left her there to fend for herself. Why had he? She'd instantly been imperiled by her male relatives, which he could have predicted.

From the minute he'd ridden away, he'd been worried about her. Now she'd walked back into his life, and he wasn't about to ever let her walk out again.

A pertinent benefit to their marrying concerned Gregory and her uncle and their contemplating drastic actions toward her. Once Caleb was her husband, she would belong to him, and *he* would be in charge of her. They wouldn't be able to harm her in the future.

He needed to commence a detailed investigation of them. Why would her uncle be so determined about the union? It was very strange, and Caleb would figure out his motive. He was already on the road to ruining Gregory, and he would dig deeper than he normally would to unravel the secret that was driving both men.

At the moment though, he wasn't about to waste energy pondering them. He had more agreeable topics to consider. Namely that he was snuggled under the blankets with her. He'd proposed, she'd accepted, and they would be wed before the week was over. Why not rush their wedding night just a bit? Why restrain himself?

He had no great qualms about carnal conduct outside of marriage. He wasn't religiously inclined, and he didn't view sexual play to be wrong. Life was short, and a fellow should enjoy himself as much as possible.

He began kissing her again, and she enthusiastically joined in. She was a lush, passionate creature, and he was certain she would grow to relish their bedroom antics. He was eager to teach her some of them. Starting immediately.

He stroked and caressed her, massaged and teased, pushing her up the spiral of desire again. She oohed and aahed, grinned and laughed, being delighted to have him torment her. Cad that he was, he took full advantage of her fervor and naiveté.

As he noticed he was wearing too many clothes, he drew back onto his haunches. He yanked off his shirt and tossed it over his shoulder. She studied his bare chest, then held out her arms, urging him to lie down again. When their skin connected, the sensation was so intense he was surprised they didn't ignite. The pleasure was that riveting.

He toyed with her breasts and touched her between her legs. His lust was escalating, and he couldn't tamp it down. They'd climbed out onto a dangerous erotic ledge, and he couldn't pull them off it.

"I'd like you to do something for me," he said.

"What is it?"

"You know... *what*."

"Will we engage in the... the... marital act?"

"Yes."

"I have no idea what that entails."

"You're a maiden, so you're not supposed to have any idea. I'll be your husband, so it's my duty to tutor you."

"Since we're not wed yet, it would be a sin."

He shrugged. "We'll speak the vows in a few days, so it would just be a little tiny sin."

"You're a man, so you would call it a *little* sin."

"This can be our wedding night. You can't want me to return to my own bedchamber. Don't tell me you want that."

She scrutinized him, and he froze, thinking—if she ordered him out—he would be crushed by disappointment. But she smiled and shook her head.

"No, I definitely couldn't bear to have you leave."

"Good girl." He dipped down and kissed her. "Have you truly never been informed of the details?"

"I've merely heard that it's very physical."

"It is, and the first time is a tad awkward. It can hurt too."

"Hurt!"

He'd panicked her, and he hastily said, "Just for *some* women, then forever after, it's marvelous."

"You better mean it."

"Look at it this way: Once we proceed with this, we can't back out."

She chuckled. "I told you I'm never crying off. You're stuck with me."

"I like the sound of that."

He was being swamped by the most powerful impulses. He wanted to cherish and protect her. He wanted to keep her by his side until his dying day. He wanted her to be the mother of his children. That was the oddest impression pelting him; he hadn't realized he wanted to have children!

With her though, he couldn't wait to sire a house full of them.

Was this love? he wondered. If it wasn't love, what could it be?

"Can you explain what will occur?" she asked.

Usually, he could talk about any subject, and he tried to deduce the verbal account he could provide that wouldn't render him tongue-tied with embarrassment, but he couldn't picture himself describing fornication.

"It's easier if I show you," he said. "It involves more of what we've been doing."

"Will I like it?"

"I promise you will."

Suddenly though, he didn't feel up to the task. He'd had many paramours, so he was hardly a novice. He was anxious for it to be special, but he was certain he could never make it as splendid or romantic as it ought to be.

He started in yet again, kissing her and caressing her most sensitive spots, and she leapt into the fray with a particular eagerness. It seemed as if, with their deciding to wed, any conduct was allowed. She was as excited as he was to secure their bond.

Her desire was rising, and down below, he was unbuttoning his trousers, tugging them down. Then he widened her thighs, his torso dropping between them.

He nursed at her breast, his fingers gliding into her sheath. She was wet and relaxed, her virginal body prepared for what was approaching. He removed his hand and positioned the tip of his cock directly where it was so desperate to be. With a flick of his thumb, he sent her soaring to the heavens again.

As she flew up, he pushed himself into her. With scarcely any effort, his phallus was impaled, and he lay very still as her anatomy acclimated to its new condition.

"What just happened?" she asked.

"I've joined us together," he told her.

"How?"

"Men and women are built differently in our private parts."

"I didn't know that."

"It's for mating. That's what this is called. We've mated."

She gazed up at him, a frown on her pretty face. "It feels strange."

"It's not like anything you've ever tried previously. It's why I couldn't describe it to you."

"Are we finished?"

"Not quite."

"What should I do?"

"Wrap your arms around me and hold me tight."

"Like this?"

"Yes, just like that."

She pulled him close, and he began flexing into her. Initially, he was careful and slow, but he couldn't maintain his measured pace. He was quickly overwhelmed, and he proceeded with a reckless abandon.

To his great delight, she swiftly adapted to the rhythm he'd set, but much before he was ready, his seed surged from his loins. With a final, frantic thrust, he shoved in and spilled himself against her womb. He didn't consider withdrawing. They would wed shortly, so there was no need for caution.

He collapsed onto her, and he remained there until he realized she was likely being crushed by his heavy weight. He slid away and rolled onto his side. She rolled too, so they were nose to nose again.

He probably should have offered a profound comment, but he couldn't think of one. He grinned, then she grinned too and said, "Are we finished now?"

"Yes, that's how it ends. You're mine, Caroline Grey. You'll never escape my dastardly clutches."

"You're mine too. It works both ways. Could I be with child? Could that be the result?"

"You might be. Each time we do this, it's a possibility."

"I will pray for it," she fervidly said. "I can't wait to give you a son."

Tears flooded her eyes, and he was stricken. "Are you sad? You can't be sad."

"I'm not sad, you oaf. I'm glad! And my *gladness* is leaking out. I can't keep it in."

"You are so perfect for me."

He kissed her urgently, desperately, then he flopped onto his back and draped her over his chest. He stared at the ceiling, and his thoughts were practically bouncing off the walls.

"What was your opinion of it?" he asked after awhile. "Tell me the truth."

"It wasn't what I was expecting. I'd heard it was very physical, but I didn't understand just *how* physical."

"Are you sore?"

"No. It didn't hurt at all."

"You tantalize me so completely that I couldn't restrain myself."

"I didn't want you to restrain yourself." She sighed and said, "I'm happy."

"So am I. No regrets, Caro. Promise me you'll never suffer any."

"Me? Regret marrying you? Don't be daft." She reached for his hand and linked their fingers. "Don't you dare fret about this."

"I won't."

"What do we do now?"

"We can doze for a bit, then we can try it again."

"I'd like that," she said.

"But dawn is about to break. If the sky starts to lighten, I'll sneak out."

"Good. I can't have a housemaid find you in here."

"I'll vanish long before that can happen. You sleep in though—as late as you like."

"I'll miss you every second until I see you again."

"Come down to breakfast whenever you're ready. I'll watch for you."

"For the rest of our lives," she said, "we'll be able to snuggle like this all night, then have breakfast in the morning. Aren't we lucky?"

"I never thought I was, but since I met you, my fortunes seem to be improving."

"Mrs. Caleb Ralston..." she murmured, then she drifted off.

He nestled with her, listening to her breathe.

He was drifting off too—had she cured his insomnia?—and he glanced toward the window. The sky was brightening, and a bird chirped, so he had to get going. He eased away from her, and she was so exhausted that she didn't stir.

He stood by the bed, gazing down at her as he tugged on his shirt and straightened his clothes. A wave of pride rushed through him. She was his, and she would be forever.

I love you...

He mouthed the words, then he spun and tiptoed away.

It would be a great day, the best day ever, and he couldn't wait for it to arrive.

Chapter
20

"Where is she?"

"How would I know?"

Gregory glared at his father, wishing the man would cease his nagging. Gregory's hangover was particularly brutal, and the slightest noise sent jolts of pain shooting behind his eyes.

He was back at Grey's Corner, in the dining room and trying to have some breakfast, even though it was one o'clock in the afternoon. He'd had to flee the city, and there had been nowhere to go but to his father's house.

For some reason, creditors were hounding him all over London. He couldn't round a corner without some oaf jamming legal papers into his hand. Numerous humiliations had piled up, the worst being his eviction from Caleb Ralston's gambling club.

After suffering Ralston's perfidy, word had spread that he couldn't pay his bills, that he wasn't nearly as wealthy as he claimed to be. In a pathetic instant, his social standing had plummeted into a void from which it would never recover.

He'd begun to fear he was about to be arrested. It was a felony to defraud a merchant, and he'd received several notices of hearings where he'd been accused of being a flagrant debtor. He wasn't an aristocrat who could thumb his nose at a court order, and there was no judge in the kingdom who would show him any mercy, so he would hide at Grey's Corner until the worst had passed.

"She didn't visit you in town?" Samson asked.

They were talking about Caroline who'd managed to run away. Gregory was actually a tad impressed by her brash escape. No one could explain how she'd accomplished it, and no one had a clue as to where she was. Someone had to be providing shelter, but who could it be?

"I told you I didn't see her," Gregory said. "Give it a rest, Father. Please."

"Dammit. I was hoping she was with you."

"Why would she have been? It's clear she wants nothing to do with me."

"Whose fault is that?" his father sneered.

"Don't blame me for the fiasco. I treated her as I always have. *She* has become a stranger we don't know at all. I can't fathom what's come over her."

"Can't you? You are a drunken, gambling-addicted sot. What sensible girl would agree to have you?"

Lucretia had traveled with him, and she was seated at the table too. At the insult, she bristled and had the temerity to say, "I'm happy to have him by my side, and I consider myself to be eminently sensible."

"Mrs. Starling," Samson said, "I'm discussing a family issue with my son. Your opinion is neither necessary nor required. Depart my presence at once."

"I haven't finished eating."

Samson slapped a palm on the table, the sound echoing off the high ceiling, and he turned to a hovering footman. "Grab Mrs. Starling's plate and teacup and carry them up to her bedchamber. She can enjoy the remainder of her meal in the privacy of her own room."

The footman blanched, peeked from Samson to Lucretia, then to Gregory, seeking guidance, and Gregory said, "Go upstairs, Lucretia. I can't abide this bickering. I'll be up in a few minutes—just as soon as Father has vented his wrath."

She never liked to be bossed, so they'd have a fight later on, but at the moment, he was feeling too poorly to worry about her wounded feelings.

She threw down her napkin and stood so rapidly that her chair tipped over. "I'm trying to remember why I journeyed to the country with you."

"You're here because we're devoted companions."

"Keep telling yourself that's true, Gregory."

She stomped out, and an awkward silence ensued. There were two footmen lurking, and they appeared relieved when Samson shooed them out. They scurried away and shut the door, so he and his father were alone.

"Why are you involved with that obnoxious strumpet?" his father snidely inquired. "It's bad enough that Caroline found out about her, but it's really the limit to expect me to socialize with her."

"We are an... *item*, Father. You understand that. I wasn't about to leave her in town."

Gregory didn't add that he couldn't have left her there.

Creditors had stopped by constantly to demand money he didn't have. The pathetic situation had encouraged their servants to quit, but only after the spoiled group had created a huge scene by insisting their back wages be forked over. When he'd admitted he couldn't pay them, they'd walked out.

Evidently, they'd gossiped about his penury because no other candidates had applied for their vacated positions. It was a predicament that simply couldn't be tolerated, and he had to fix it, the problem being that he had no idea how.

He needed to beg his father for an infusion of funds, but from his dour expression, an advance wasn't in the cards. Gregory didn't dare suggest it.

"I haven't seen Caroline since my failed wedding day," Gregory said. "I thought you'd locked her in her bedchamber. Wasn't that what we decided should happen? I thought you'd gotten control of her."

"She escaped when I was out of the house!"

"A servant must have let her out."

"None of them had a key that fit except for me. They couldn't have helped her."

"Well, she didn't vanish into thin air, so I don't believe their claims of innocence. They likely all conspired to aid her. We should line them up in front of Lucretia. She has a nasty way with intractable employees. She could pry out some answers."

"Don't mention Mrs. Starling to me again. It's a mystery to me how you could be stupid enough to bring her back here. How could you imagine she'd be welcome?"

"Why shouldn't I have brought her? It's not as if Caroline is going to marry me."

"I haven't given up on the prospect."

"I have," Gregory said. "Why would I care if she's angry about Lucretia? It hardly matters now. The wedding is off—permanently. Or have you stumbled on a vicar who's a little less ethical than our local one? Have you dug up some reprobate who will perform the ceremony, despite her being so mortally opposed?"

"I haven't a clue how to find a corrupt minister. I talked to a judge instead. He signed a commitment order, but when I arrived home with it, the bloody girl was missing. I'm sick at heart about the whole debacle. She doesn't deserve to be sent to an asylum, and if she ends up in one, I'll always blame you."

"Don't glower at me as if it's my fault. I was in town the entire time. *You* were supposed to handle her."

"Where could she be?" Samson asked. "Who would she turn to for assistance?"

"Why would I have learned any details about her paltry life? Ask Janet. She'd know Caroline's secrets—if Caroline has any."

"Janet ran away too!"

Gregory's jaw dropped, then he laughed. "You're joking."

"No. I figure she's in London. She was pestering me about moving there. I specifically informed her that she couldn't, but she left without my permission."

"Will you search for her?"

"London is a massive city. How would I?"

"Caroline must be with her. They have to be together, don't you think?"

"I wouldn't doubt it for a single second."

"Perhaps you should hire an investigator. There must be people who saw them hire a carriage or buy a ticket on the mail coach. They can't have flown off like a pair of birds."

His father pondered the comment, then nodded vigorously. "That's a good plan, and I swear to God, when I locate them, I will lock Janet in a convent for the rest of her days."

"The better conclusion would be to shackle her to a farmer. In light of her peculiar views on matrimony, it would be a more suitable punishment."

"It's obvious I was too lenient with both of them." Samson nodded again. "I will marry her to an oaf she'll loathe. It would serve her right, and Caroline has to be locked away too. Before her birthday."

"I would appreciate it if you could manage that small task. We can't lose out on the money that's vesting."

"I know, Gregory! I know!"

"It doesn't seem as if you do. You let her cry off from the engagement. You let her refuse to wed me. And now, you've let her run away. I should have Lucretia deal with this as well. You can denigrate her all you like, but she wouldn't flail around like this. Not when there is so much wealth hanging in the balance."

He stood and marched out, deeming it quite a pithy parting shot. He exited the room, but he snuck a final glance at his father.

Samson looked older and worn down, but Gregory wasn't sympathetic. His father had made one blunder after another, and he simply wanted to complain rather than take constructive action.

Gregory couldn't help him. He had his own difficulties to sort out. Most particularly, he had to shuck Caleb Ralston off his back. Of all the creditors harassing him, the fiends working for Ralston were the very worst.

How had Gregory ever assumed they were friends? It truly boggled the mind.

<hr />

CAROLINE WALKED DOWN THE stairs in Caleb's London house. It was early afternoon, so she'd definitely overslept. She was almost tiptoeing, feeling awkward in a way she hated. Caleb had suggested they meet for a late breakfast, but he couldn't have planned on it being this late.

He'd crept out of her bed as he'd promised he would, so she hadn't had to suffer the embarrassment of his being found with her. Yes, they were marrying, but they weren't married yet. His servants would soon be *her* servants, and she couldn't have their immediate impression be that she was very loose with her favors.

A housemaid had shown up to tend her, so she'd been bathed and dressed, and had had her hair pinned up. Then she'd been directed down to the dining room, with the assurance that the staff was waiting for her to arrive.

She'd yearned to pepper the girl with questions about Caleb: Where was he? What time had he risen and come down? Had he eaten already? But she hadn't thought she should seem too interested in him, so she'd politely, casually asked after him and Miss Jones. Miss Jones was out shopping, but the girl wasn't positive about Caleb, so Caroline was anxiously wondering when she'd bump into him.

She was so happy! She kept pinching herself to be certain she wasn't dreaming.

A footman greeted her in the foyer and guided her to the dining room. She strolled slowly so she could furtively assess Caleb's home. The prior day, she'd been too distraught to notice much of it. It was spacious and comfortable, with big windows, thick rugs, and colorful paintings on the walls. She'd be very content residing in it.

As she entered the room, she was surprised to find Blake Ralston in it too, and he'd just finished his meal. In all her musings about Caleb and when she might cross paths with him, she hadn't pondered his brother who was obviously still on furlough.

"Miss Grey!" he said. "I heard you were here."

"Hello, Ensign Ralston."

"That sounds terribly formal. You should call me Blake."

"I'd like that, and please call me Caroline."

She nearly added, *You're about to be my brother-in-law, so we can be on familiar terms*, but she didn't. Caleb should explain the situation to his brother.

"There's a rumor circulating," he said, "that you experienced some problems after Caleb and I departed your wedding celebration." He grinned, appearing a tad wicked. "It's the gossip the servants are spreading anyway."

"Yes, I had some trouble. I cried off from my betrothal, but my uncle and fiancé were vexed about it."

"I can imagine. Have you been looking for Janet?"

It was an odd query, and it startled her. "Well...ah...yes, I have been looking for her. She left before I learned of her address in town. I had hoped to locate her, but I couldn't figure out how."

"She saw your advertisement in the newspaper, but she was scared to reply. She was afraid it might be her father tricking her so he could catch her and drag her away."

Caroline was astonished. "How do you know all that?"

He leaned in, as if they were conspirators sharing secrets. "Don't tell my brother—he'd wring my neck—but I helped her run away."

"You scamp! It never occurred to me that she had help *or* that it might have been from you. Where is she living?"

"She's renting an apartment over in the theater district."

Caroline was stunned. "Is she all right?"

"She's grand."

There was a desk in the corner with a writing tray on it. He jotted down the directions, and she tucked them into her skirt.

"We could visit her later this afternoon," he said. "I could take you to her. How about around five?"

"Five would be fine."

"She'll faint when you waltz in." Blake lowered his voice. "Don't forget: Not a word to my brother."

"My lips are sealed."

He gave a mock salute and sauntered out, and once the air settled behind him, she realized she was ravenous. A pair of footmen seated her and plied her with food until she was filled to bursting. She thanked them profusely, then fled, but she wasn't entirely sure how to keep herself busy.

She spent some time snooping through the various parlors, but despite how she lingered, there was no sign of Caleb or Sybil Jones. She decided to head up to her bedchamber. The housemaids had laundered and mended the dress she'd worn the previous day, and she had to check how badly it had been damaged.

The inspection only took a minute though, then she was at loose ends again. She went out to the hall to investigate the other bedrooms. It would be her home very soon, and she doubted Caleb would mind.

She started up the stairs to the next floor, and when she was nearly at the top, she noted two people were talking. She stopped and listened, discovering it was Caleb and his brother.

She considered marching up the rest of the way and blustering into the middle of their conversation. She almost stepped toward them, when suddenly, Blake said, "Miss Grey is here. What a coincidence."

They were discussing her! Would Caleb mention their engagement? What would he say? How would his brother respond?

The old adage rang out: *Eavesdroppers never hear anything good about themselves.* Yet she couldn't tear herself away.

"After we left Grey's Corner," Caleb said, "some problems arose for her. She sought my assistance, and I'm happy to give it."

His brother snorted. "Is that what you're calling it? A bit of assistance?"

"What is that supposed to mean?"

"I *mean* I walked by your bedchamber last night, and I conveniently noticed you weren't in it. It's interesting how *her* door was closed tight. Would I be surprised to learn you were in there with her?"

There was a painful silence, then Caleb said, "Watch your mouth. I won't have you denigrating her."

"Who's denigrating her? I like her. You know that. I just find the situation curious. Was it her wedding night? Did you win your bet with Gregory?"

She frowned, as Caleb warned, "Shut up, Blake!"

"I never assumed you'd collect on that stupid wager. You weren't planning on it, were you?"

There was a loud crash, and a grunt of dismay. It sounded as if someone had been punched, then Caleb said, "I told you to shut your mouth."

"I think you broke my nose!" Blake complained. "It's bleeding like a cracked pipe, and you've ruined a perfectly good shirt besides."

"Get out of here or I'll hit you again."

"She invited you to join her? Seriously? The wager had naught to do with it?" There was another loud crash, then Blake said, "Sorry! Sorry! You're such a prick anymore. Your sense of humor has completely vanished."

She was frozen in her spot, too shocked to creep away as she ought, and before she could blink, Blake was on the landing above her. He had a kerchief pressed to his nose, and blood was splattered down the front of his shirt.

"Dammit," he muttered on seeing her. "My apologies for any offense I might have caused."

He kept on down the hall, probably to his own bedroom, and the door closed.

She stood there forever, urging herself to slink away. The humiliating predicament was her own fault for listening when she shouldn't have. Shouldn't she ignore what had occurred?

Finally, she grabbed the bannister and pulled herself up the stairs, feeling as if she had ice in her veins. She went to the only open door and entered the sitting room of what had to be Caleb's bedroom suite.

He was over by the hearth, picking up a decorative table that had been smashed in his altercation with his brother. He straightened and glanced over his shoulder. They stared for an eternity, then he forced a smile and said, "I was about to inquire if you were up yet. I was hoping we could have breakfast together."

"I heard the two of you arguing," was her reply.

He turned to face her. "We weren't arguing. Blake was simply being his usual obnoxious self."

"You wagered over me with Gregory?"

"No, don't be silly. I never would have."

He couldn't hold her gaze, providing galling evidence that he was lying.

She stomped over, approaching until they were toe to toe. "Tell me you never gambled with him over me."

He appeared flummoxed and frantic to devise a response that wouldn't infuriate her. Ultimately, he claimed, "It only happened once."

"Once!" she fumed.

"It was my last night at Grey's Corner. He was very drunk, and he was being belligerent. I didn't care to dicker with him when he was so intoxicated."

"What were the terms?"

He fussed with the decorative table, his movements very deliberate. He was buying time, struggling to settle on a remark that would paint him in the best light, so the debacle would seem less horrid.

"Let it go, Caro," he quietly said.

"I won't. I can't." More vehemently, she demanded, "What were the terms?"

"There's no point in hashing it out."

"I suggest you inform me immediately or I shall walk down and accost your brother. I'll nag at him until he spits it out. I'm certain he will. Shall I ask him?"

He sighed. "Gregory had lost everything he had, even the clothes on his back, but he wanted to keep playing."

"And you being such an ethical fellow, you continued even though he was beggared."

His rage flared. "I've told you this before: I am not Gregory Grey's nanny. Nor am I his mother. I have no duty to control his behavior, so don't try to make me feel guilty. You can't."

"Fine, you had no duty. What was the wager?"

She braced herself, as if for a hard blow, recognizing that he should never speak the terrible words she was insisting he impart.

"He had nothing left to bet," he said, "so he bet *you*."

"I have no idea what that means. You're talking in riddles. I need you to be very, very clear, so let's use plain English."

A muscle ticked in his cheek. "I won your virginity with a shuffle of the cards."

She was so stunned she was amazed she didn't faint. "You discussed my virginity with him? You gambled over it?"

"*He* gambled over it. I was protecting you from him. I was afraid—if I didn't jump in—he'd hand you over to someone else."

"You were doing me a…a…favor? Is that how you view it?"

"Yes, Caro, I was doing you a huge favor, so stop glowering at me as if I'm a monster. You don't understand the world where I live. You don't understand the kind of men who wallow in it with me."

"Obviously not."

"Men constantly raise the stakes when they're desperate. They toss out their daughters, sisters, and wives with nary a ripple in their corrupt consciences. He was desperate, so he tossed out *you*."

"I don't believe this," she mumbled, feeling sick at heart.

"I swear to you, if I hadn't consented, he'd have rushed to London and thrown you into a pot with some fiend who was much more debauched than me. You wouldn't have been notified, and one day—when you weren't expecting it—you'd have been kidnapped off the lane and forced to supply what your cousin had offered."

"I'd have been kidnapped and forced? The entire notion is despicable. Who would dabble in such filth?"

He shrugged, as if it was the most ordinary of circumstances. "It happens, and I tried my best to ensure it didn't happen to you."

"You made that bet with him, then you packed up the next morning and abandoned me there. Didn't it occur to you that I might have liked to be apprised?"

"I couldn't explain it. I realized how much it would hurt you, and if I remember correctly, I warned you to be careful."

She studied him, as she assessed the various sentiments pummeling her. She was very angry with him, and she was right to be, wasn't she? She was also offended and shocked. Those were appropriate reactions, weren't they?

He was so calm, so nonchalant, they might have been conferring about the weather. She grasped that he carried on in a spot where rules and morals were different, but what type of rogue wagered over a woman's virginity? What did it indicate about his genuine character?

Because they shared such a potent attraction, she'd convinced herself that she knew him better than she'd ever known anyone, but that wasn't true. They were barely acquainted, and she possessed scant facts about his history, his ancestry, his upbringing.

Every aspect of their relationship was now called into question.

He'd told her he'd resigned from the navy due to his *brother* being swept up in mischief, and he'd protected Blake by taking the blame himself. What if *he* had actually committed the crimes? How was she to guess?

This was precisely why a girl's parents picked her husband. They could evaluate a candidate in a cool, rational manner, without heated emotions being stirred into the mix.

He was glaring at her as if she was being a pest, as if she was deliberately failing to comprehend what he'd clarified. How could he think she would ever understand it?

"Let me ask you this," she said, "and don't lie to me."

"I won't lie to you. I haven't been."

He looked sincere, but how was she to judge his veracity? "Why did you climb into my bed? Was it because of the wager?"

"Oh, for pity's sake." He threw up his hands as if she was being ridiculous. "No, I didn't spend the night there because of the wager."

"Why did you do it then?"

"It just seemed. . . right, I suppose."

"That's it? It seemed *right*?"

"Yes."

It was the most tepid, exasperating word he could have selected. She'd wanted him to say it was because he loved her, because he couldn't live without her. But it had merely been. . . *right*?

"Your bet with Gregory was irrelevant?" she asked.

"Of course it was. I'm currently on a path to completely ruining him. He has no hold over me, and he has no power over you."

She gaped with dismay. "You're ruining my cousin?"

"Yes, and after how he imperiled you, he deserves it too. Don't you dare claim I should show him some mercy. I won't listen to any nonsense."

A hard gleam had entered his gaze, so he appeared cold and cruel, and she suspected she was seeing the *real* Caleb Ralston. He was a man who owned a gambling club, who watched dispassionately as dissolute idiots destroyed themselves. He felt no remorse about the role he played in the downfall of so many unfortunate souls.

"What about me?" she asked. "What is it I deserve?"

He rubbed a palm over his brow. "Could we not fight? I'm very busy today, and it's a mystery to me why we're quarreling."

"You sat in my home and dickered over my virginity with my drunken fiancé."

"Would you get it through your thick head? *He* dickered with me. My only involvement with his foul suggestion was that I saved you from his being able to raise it elsewhere."

"Aren't you a saint?" she snidely said. "You talk about it as if it's a common occurrence, as if it was no different from any other of your many entertainments."

"It wasn't different, Caro. You're correct about that."

Her pulse began to pound. Her anxiety was spiraling, and she couldn't breathe. She was so confused by what she'd just learned. They'd spent a perfect night together. He'd proposed, and she'd accepted, but she was conflicted about what had really transpired.

Their joining had been very special—on her end—but then, maybe it hadn't been on his. She'd given him a gift he'd won in an appalling manner, and he was so blasé about it, as if he couldn't figure out why she was upset, but she was hideously incensed and wondering if she should wed him. Was he the husband to whom she should bind herself?

The problem for her was that they'd engaged in the marital act. They'd proceeded to the worst conclusion of all, but he'd persuaded her to participate because they would marry soon. But should they?

She had to contemplate so many issues. Was she being too fussy or critical? She definitely had to calm down or she might say things she didn't mean and couldn't retract.

She spun away, and he asked, "Where are you going?"

"I need some time alone to think."

"About what?"

"About whether we should wed."

"Don't tell me we're not marrying. Your cousin doesn't have any bearing on you and me, and I have no idea why you're so furious. I don't intend to worry about him, and you shouldn't either."

"It's too late for you to claim Gregory doesn't matter."

She would have kept on, but he sighed dramatically, his frustration clear. "Would you hold on just a damned minute?"

"No, and don't you curse at me. I won't tolerate that kind of rough language."

"Well, you're being silly, and you're trying my patience."

"I'm trying *your* patience? You ought to pause for a second and ponder which one of us is more vexed. I'm quite sure it's me."

She stepped into the hall, and he actually shouted at her. "Caro! We're not finished discussing this. Don't you walk out on me."

She whipped around. "I'm not your servant or your employee, so don't order me about. As my uncle could confirm, that sort of male posturing doesn't have any effect on me at all."

She marched away and headed for the stairs, and Blake peeked out his door, saying, "Are you all right, Miss Grey?"

"I'm just dandy, Blake, but I've had enough of you Ralston men for one day. Leave me be."

She didn't tarry to see if he obeyed. She simply dashed down to her bedchamber. She slammed the door and locked it, and she couldn't help but notice that Caleb hadn't chased after her. She couldn't decide if she was glad about it or not.

Didn't he care to mend their rift? Yet why would they mend it? She'd never been so angry, and she truly thought, if he'd blustered in and she'd been clutching a pistol, she'd have shot him in the middle of his cold, black heart.

She was shaking and couldn't catch her breath. Her old claustrophobia was rising, and she had to get out into the fresh air before she suffocated.

Sybil had provided her with clothes, but she yanked them off and donned her own, more tattered garments. Then she grabbed the directions Blake had penned to Janet's apartment. She was suffering from a desperate hankering to be with a female, to confide what had happened.

Caleb still hadn't bothered to come down after her. The conceited ass! She stomped out of her room and down to the foyer. No servants were hovering, so there was no one to observe her departure. She speculated over how long it would take Caleb to realize she'd left.

She stormed out and down the street, and she stopped the first person she encountered and showed him Janet's address. According to the information he supplied, her cousin lived a lengthy distance away, but Caroline was healthy and perfectly capable of walking.

She rushed off, but as she arrived at the corner where Caleb's house would vanish from view, she glanced back.

She'd assumed he'd be standing in the window and frowning down at her, but he wasn't there. She whirled away, wondering if she'd ever see him again, and wondering too why she'd ever want to.

Chapter

21

JANET HEARD SOMEONE KNOCKING on her door, but she didn't answer. She was seated on her sofa and too lost in thought to worry about who it might be.

A maid stopped by in the mornings to tidy up and cook the day's food, but she'd left already. Other than her, it could only be Blake, but he'd visited earlier and wouldn't stop by twice.

There wasn't another person in the world she was interested in seeing except for him. His furlough was over in a week, so he was about to climb onto his navy ship and sail away. He would be posted to the Mediterranean and based out of Gibraltar, so it wasn't as if he'd be on the other side of the globe. But still, it felt as if he was about to fall off the edge of the Earth.

He couldn't guess when he'd be back in England, and she suspected—if it was months or years—he'd have trifled with a hundred different girls and likely wouldn't even remember her.

The prospect was depressing and galling. She no longer wanted to be a lonely spinster with no husband to share her life. She wanted to be Mrs. Blake Ralston, but she couldn't imagine how to achieve that conclusion. Blake snuck in frequently, and they'd immediately rush into her bedchamber and misbehave in decadent ways, but they never discussed private issues.

He never mentioned heightened affection, so she didn't mention it either. He was about to leave, but he hadn't evinced the slightest indication that he would miss her. He hadn't suggested they wed or even that they correspond after he departed. She was sick with dread and regret and growing terribly afraid she might be with child.

She wasn't positive of the symptoms, and it wasn't as if she'd had a mother in her home to supply those sorts of details. But she was nauseous in the morning and smells made her queasy. Weren't those pertinent signs?

What if she was increasing? What then? Dare she confide in Blake? What if she apprised him, and he shrugged off her condition? Or what if he learned of it and refused to marry her?

The knock sounded again, and she ignored it and sifted through a stack of documents she had balanced on her lap. She'd spoken to an attorney Blake had recommended, and she'd received a letter from him that she didn't understand.

She'd been eager to investigate her inheritance from her grandmother. She had to remove her father as trustee so he couldn't cut off her money.

Her attorney had researched the matter, and he insisted there was no record of Janet having a trust fund. According to court records, the only trust attached to her family was one created by Caroline's deceased father, and it had been filed as the *Caroline Grey Mining Trust*.

There had never been talk about it, and she'd never been informed that Caroline had any money. Caroline had joined them as an indigent orphan, and Janet's father had regularly teased her about being a financial burden they were happy to assume.

Janet simply had a bank account rather than a trust fund—as her father had always claimed—and she was sent monthly stipends from it. It wasn't a trust disbursement, which was very perplexing, and she was frightened by it.

The account was listed in her father's name, so he could shut it down whenever he wished. It meant she was in enormous fiscal jeopardy.

The knocking became more incessant, and she tossed the papers aside and stomped over to find out who was so adamant. She pulled the door open with a particularly irritated yank, and her jaw dropped in astonishment.

"Caroline!" she said to her cousin. "What are you doing on my stoop?"

"I hope you're glad to see me," Caroline replied. "Please tell me you are."

They fell into each other's arms, and Janet began to cry.

"AM I WRONG TO be angry? I'm not, am I?"

"No. You're not wrong."

Caroline gazed at Janet and said, "I'm so confused. I thought he and I were in love, but now, I'm not sure of what occurred between us. How should I proceed?"

"Let the problem fester for a few days. Once you're calmer, we can settle on the best course."

"That's very wise advice and much more logical than my plan. My solution was to buy a pistol and shoot him dead."

"It wouldn't necessarily be the worst ending."

"With how Gregory and your father treated me, then with Caleb turning out to be so depraved, I'd like to sail off to an island where there were no men. It would be marvelous to simply live around women."

They were in Janet's apartment and seated on the small sofa. There were three rooms: a sitting room, bedroom, and dining room. The ceilings were high, the windows big and facing south so plenty of sunlight filtered in.

Caroline couldn't get over how quickly and easily Janet had landed on her feet, but then, she'd had Blake to assist her, and a man always provided a buffer against catastrophe.

"Can I mention something awful?" Janet asked, and she looked very glum.

"You'd better. Considering our dicey circumstances, we shouldn't have any secrets."

"Blake and I... that is... he and I have been... ah... we've... ah..."

Janet couldn't spit it out, and Caroline said, "Apparently, it's too humiliating to voice aloud."

"Maybe." Janet flushed bright red and peered down at her hands.

"Should I guess what's happened? Blake is a handsome scoundrel, and with how he prances about in that uniform of his, I suspect he hasn't behaved honorably."

"It's my own fault," Janet hastily insisted. "He's just so... so... amazing, and I couldn't resist."

"What now? What future are you envisioning?"

"I'd like to marry him," Janet admitted, "but it's probably never crossed his mind."

"I'm certain it hasn't. As I've learned the hard way, the Ralston brothers aren't exactly pillars of the community."

"His furlough is over next week, and he's leaving for the Mediterranean."

"Well..." Caroline sighed. "That throws a wrench in your choices."

"I might be increasing." Janet started crying again. She'd been weeping on and off ever since Caroline had arrived.

"If you are, you shouldn't be surprised. A baby is the expected result for this type of conduct."

The comment made Caroline's stomach clench with dismay. What if *she* was increasing? Caleb had said it was a possibility every time a couple fornicated, and she'd never been lucky. What if she was pregnant? What then?

No, no, don't worry about it yet. It was too soon for symptoms, and Janet needed to be her focus. Later on, she could deal with her own dilemma—if it turned out there was one.

"What should I do?" Janet asked.

"As with my situation regarding Caleb, it can fester for a bit. We'll figure it out once we're not quite so livid."

"I'm so relieved that you're with me. I've been dying to hear a woman's perspective."

"I was thinking the same when I was walking over here. We never had a female in our lives, so we don't have anyone to guide us through these sorts of issues. If your father was even remotely rational, we could have him speak to Blake. Uncle Samson could force him to marry you."

"I couldn't bear to have Blake *forced* into it. He should marry me because he's madly in love with me."

Caroline recalled Blake as she'd last seen him in the hall outside his bedchamber. He'd appeared elegant and sophisticated—and a tad wicked—and she didn't suppose he ever thought about Janet. Why would he?

Janet had furnished him with what he shouldn't have had until after he'd put a ring on her finger. He'd received a huge gift he shouldn't have accepted. Caroline could have chastised her cousin for her moral lapse, but she was disgraced herself, so she was in no position to judge.

"We're a sorry pair, aren't we?" she said instead.

"Yes. I'm especially wretched because my fondness for him runs counter to my views about men and relationships. It's mortifying to confess that I simply want what all women want. I believed I was different, but I'm not."

"Don't mock the chance to wed and have children. Nearly every female who's ever marched down that road winds up happy. You will be too."

"How will I get him to propose though?"

Caroline knew how it could be accomplished. *She* could go to Caleb and inform him of his brother's mischief. He could pressure Blake. Or Caroline could confer with naval authorities, and they'd demand he step up. She doubted they would allow such turpitude to remain unchecked.

At the moment though, when her spirits were terribly low, she couldn't imagine pursuing those courses of action. She wished her uncle wasn't such a fiend. *He* should have handled it.

"We'll fuss over Blake Ralston tomorrow," she said. "We just managed to find each other, and with all our calamities, we're fortunate we're still in one piece. Let's concentrate on ourselves and ignore the men who've stirred such anguish."

Janet laughed miserably, then she rose and trudged to the bedroom. Caroline listened as she poured water and washed her face. When she came back, she gave Caroline some papers.

"I need your opinion about this," Janet said. "I've been working with a lawyer to gain control of my trust fund, but I found out there hasn't ever been one."

Caroline frowned. "That can't be right. You have that inheritance from your grandmother."

"No, I don't. Not that my lawyer could locate anyway. And look down toward the bottom. Our family has one trust fund, and it's in your name."

Caroline studied the words over and over: *Caroline Grey Mining Trust.*

It made no sense to her. She didn't have any money. Her uncle had always told her that, and there had never been any evidence to the contrary. "This is too strange to be credible. Are you sure your attorney is competent?"

"I think so. Blake's friend, Sybil Jones, recommended him."

"He's probably skilled then, so perhaps, he's simply mistaken."

"It just seems odd to me. Maybe your father left you a bequest, and it's been quietly sitting somewhere, but we were never apprised."

"I can't fathom it. If there's one fact about which Grandfather Walter was very firm, it was that my father was a lazy, negligent spendthrift."

Another knock sounded on the door, and Janet braced as if expecting a hard blow. "It might be Blake," she whispered, "but I can't talk to him. I'm too upset."

Caroline waved her away. "I'll see who it is. You hide in the bedroom, and if it's him, I'll claim you're not here."

Janet dashed out as Caroline pulled the door open. A messenger was standing there. He handed Caroline a letter for Janet, then he hovered, as if hoping she'd slip him a penny, but she didn't have a penny.

She shrugged an apology and sent him on his way. She went to the bedroom and gave the envelope to Janet, then she sat on the sofa again. A few minutes later, Janet joined her. She was holding the letter, and she appeared stricken.

"What's happened?" Caroline asked. "Don't tell me it's more bad news."

"It's from my attorney. He spoke to a banker about my allowance, and the account has been closed. The money was withdrawn yesterday."

"All of it?"

"Yes. There's not a single farthing remaining."

"Who removed it?"

"The banker wouldn't say, but it had to be Father. He's trying to punish me and force me home."

"So...you're out of money, and I never had any in the first place. How much rent have you paid on this apartment? How long can we stay in it?"

"Two more weeks. Two weeks, and then, we'll be out on the street."

"Unless you can convince Blake to marry you. Or we could go to Grey's Corner."

Janet cringed. "I would be more likely to fly to the moon than to have either of those things occur."

⌒〜

"WHERE COULD SHE BE?"

Caleb peered out the window, but no matter how fervidly he stared, he never saw Caro returning. It was dark outside, and she was out in the city alone, with no friends to assist her. Any mishap could befall her, and if she wound up imperiled, he might strangle Blake.

It had taken several hours for them to realize she was missing. After Caleb had quarreled with her, he'd assumed she was fuming in her bedchamber. He hadn't been overly keen to re-ignite their spat, so he'd waited for her to calm down and come downstairs, but she hadn't.

Finally, when supper had been served, he'd had a housemaid check on her, only to discover she wasn't there. Apparently, she'd crept away while no one was watching.

She'd shucked off the gown Sybil had provided to her, and instead, she'd donned the tattered garment she'd been wearing when she'd stumbled into his gambling club. He comprehended her message: She didn't want anything from him. Not even a loaned dress.

He whirled on Blake. His brother was over on the sofa, looking maltreated and a tad gallant, as if he was a scuffed hero in a theatrical drama. The skin under his eyes was black and blue, and he had a chunk of ice wrapped in a cloth. He was pressing it to his swollen nose.

"She's vanished, probably for good," Caleb said to him. "Are you happy now?"

"Don't blame me for your stupid bet with Gregory Grey."

"I don't blame you for that. I blame you for talking about it as Caroline was lurking down the hall."

"How was I supposed to know she was eavesdropping? The bloody woman had some nerve, sneaking up on us like that."

"I swear, if you utter one more idiotic comment about her, I'll bash out a few of your teeth too."

Blake scoffed. "Someday, I'll learn how to fight dirty, so you won't be able to pummel me anymore."

"Keep hope alive, Blake."

They'd often resolved their differences with fisticuffs, but Caleb always won any skirmish. Blake never thought he was in the wrong, so he was never prepared for Caleb to lash out. Blake was like a stubborn mule, and he wouldn't pay attention unless he was whacked right between the eyes.

"I can't imagine how you'll ever persuade her to forgive you," Blake said.

"I can't either."

"I'm sorry about all of this. I like Miss Grey, and I hate that I upset her. I apologize to you too. I was trying to make a joke, but I guess it wasn't funny."

"That is the understatement of the century."

Blake mumbled into his pack of ice, "I might know where she is."

"You *might* know? You've been sitting there like a bump on a log, and it didn't dawn on you that I might like to hear your theory?"

"I wasn't sure if I should confess it or not."

Caleb walked over, yanked the ice away, and tossed it on the floor. "Where is it you presume she might be? And don't you dare lie to me!"

"Her cousin, Janet, ran away from Grey's Corner, and at breakfast, I might have mentioned to Miss Grey where Janet is living. I wrote down the directions, so she likely went there. Wouldn't she have?"

Caleb's temper flared. "How would you just happen to be cognizant of where Janet Grey is living?"

"Well, I *might* have helped her move to town."

Caleb's rage bubbled so hotly he was surprised the top of his head didn't blow off. "Why, pray tell, would you have involved yourself?"

"You remember that I was flirting with her in the country, and she's very fond of me. As I was leaving, she might have begged to come along."

"Why would you have listened to her?"

"She can be very adamant."

"She's an unmarried maiden, Blake! Do you understand the ramifications that may be approaching? You'll be lucky if her father doesn't show up to escort you to the altar, and he will have a very big gun pointed at your backside."

"Nobody knows about us."

"Famous last words." Caleb bristled. "Have you ruined her?"

"No, no, we're just friends," Blake insisted much too hastily. "I was worried about her being in the city all alone, so I assisted her. That's it."

Blake struggled valiantly to hold Caleb's gaze, but he was so bad at prevarication. It was why his mischief constantly unraveled.

"Might she be increasing?" Caleb asked.

Blake blanched—as if the notion had never occurred to him. He'd trifled with paramours in the past, but Caleb had demanded he pick loose doxies who were adept in the bedchamber. He wasn't to ever choose reputable women where he might be ensnared by a carnal calamity.

What was he thinking? He was scheduled to return to his post in another week. Would they be having a quick wedding before he sailed?

"She's not increasing," Blake said, but he gulped with dismay.

"You're not God, so how can you be certain? If she is, the navy won't let you slink away like the cur you are. Nor will I. If you refuse to step up, they'll drum you out of the service, and after the trouble I suffered to keep you *in* it, I'm not about to have you destroy your career over a female."

"You're making too much of this."

"In my view, I'm not making nearly enough. You're about to put a ring on her finger. Are you ready to be a husband? Why am I convinced that the answer to that question is a resounding *no*?"

"She'd never agree to wed me," Blake blithely stated, "despite how you nag."

"Oh, really?" Caleb snidely inquired. "Why is that?"

"She's a radical intellectual who plans to carry on outside the bounds of normal society. She reads books by those blue-stocking spinsters, and she believes marriage is a trap. She'd never allow herself to be caught in it."

Caleb gaped at his brother, then he laughed miserably. "If that's what you suppose, then you're even more of a dunce than I realized."

"She's very firm in her attitudes."

"A *woman* doesn't get to decide. A *woman* can't fornicate until she spits out a bastard. It's a crime, Blake. Her opinion is irrelevant, and I'm predicting, when her belly swells, and she's faced with the shame of being an unwed mother, she won't be quite so opposed to matrimony."

Blake scowled. "You expect she'd change her mind? If that's what you imagine, you're deranged."

"She can't behave this way, and *you* can't either. You'd best prepare yourself, for I'm mortally afraid you're about to be a husband—whether you like it or not."

⌒

CAROLINE WAS IN BED when there was a knock on the door. It was very late, and she and Janet were snuggled on Janet's bed, but Janet wasn't roused by the noise. She'd expended so much energy weeping and fretting that she was worn out.

Caroline slipped off the mattress and tiptoed to the front room as Blake Ralston murmured, "Janet, are you in there?" There was a pause, then he said, "Janet! I have to talk to you. Open up."

Caroline bit down on all the caustic remarks that were yearning to spill out. She was attired in one of Janet's nightgowns, so she wasn't dressed, but that wasn't the reason she didn't respond.

He could converse with them in the light of day, and she was in no mood to argue about it. She would muster the courage to confer with Caleb or with officials at the navy. She would have Janet wed to the bounder shortly, but she wouldn't debate the issue with him in the middle of the night.

A pair of footsteps pounded up the stairs, and her pulse raced as Caleb said, "Is she there?"

"No one's answering," Blake replied. "They're probably asleep or they might have departed."

Caleb wasn't as reticent as Blake about being too loud. He banged on the wood very hard and called, "Caroline! I know you're in there. Open the bloody door!"

She steadied her breathing so she didn't march out and punch him in the nose. As with Blake harassing Janet, she was in no mood to bicker with Caleb, and she wouldn't let the brothers in. They'd caused enough trouble for ten lifetimes, and she was so furious she was practically dizzy with offense.

Caleb knocked more vehemently. "I can feel you hovering, so it's clear you're listening to me. Stop being ridiculous. I'm here to take you home."

A neighbor's patience must have been exhausted. From down the hall, a man hissed, "Do you mind? Some of us have to work in the morning!"

Blake mumbled, "Sorry."

The brothers whispered heatedly, then they crept away.

She waited until it was silent again, then she walked to the window and peeked down into the street, watching as they climbed into their carriage and drove away.

She received some solace from Caleb's arrival. She told herself to be glad about it. It was an indication that he regretted their quarrel, so they would likely be able to resolve their differences, but it wouldn't transpire right away.

She was still in love with him, and they needed to wed—it was the only proper outcome—but she would have to extract some guarantees prior to it occurring. He would have to clean up his wicked ways and become a better man. He couldn't continue to wallow in the gutter with fiends. Not if he wanted her to be his bride.

He would have to make some promises, and she would have to believe he would keep them.

Their carriage vanished around a corner, and she went back to bed. As she crawled under the blankets, Janet stirred and asked, "Why are you up?"

"I'm anxious, and I couldn't rest, but I'm fine now. Go to sleep."

Janet was so fatigued that she complied immediately. Caroline stared at the ceiling, wondering what would happen next. She couldn't imagine a good ending for them. Not with the Ralston brothers being the ones who would have to supply a viable conclusion.

It would be a very long night.

⁓

CAROLINE STOOD IN FRONT of the theater where Libby Carstairs was supposed to be performing. There was a poster by the door that listed the actors in the current show, but Libby wasn't on it.

The news was inordinately depressing, and it exacerbated Caroline's perception of being adrift. By her finding Janet, she should have shucked off her sense of gloom and dread, but they'd been worsened by her cousin's insane attachment to Blake Ralston.

When Caroline had been out of the apartment, the dashing scoundrel had visited Janet. He'd sweet-talked her until she didn't know up from down. She was merrily eager to delay awhile in order to discover if she was increasing.

Blake had spewed a few magic words, and she'd lost her ability to judge her predicament with a jaundiced eye. If she was with child, and Blake sailed away, what was her plan? It wasn't as if they could cast a spell and force him to reappear in England.

In the meantime, Blake was packing his bags and, like the most despicable cad, he was preparing to flee the country. Janet had forbidden Caroline to speak with Caleb or the navy, and apparently, Janet would engage in any deranged behavior if she thought it would make him happy.

Janet had told Blake about her father emptying her bank account, and the dastardly cur had given her money sufficient to pay six months of rent. With the funds stuffed in a drawer, she'd persuaded herself that she was no longer in a dicey situation, so she didn't need to *do* anything about Blake.

Caroline couldn't convince her otherwise. Despite Janet's plea that Caroline remain silent about Blake, she should have tattled to Caleb, but she hadn't seen him. Blake had instructed Caleb—at Janet's urging—to leave Caroline alone, that she would contact him if and when she felt like discussing their issues.

He'd heeded Caroline's request, and she was relieved that he'd stayed away, but she was incensed too. Why hadn't he ignored her edict? Could he be so easily dissuaded? His lack of interest had her suspecting he didn't really care if they wed or not.

His proposal had been voiced in the heat of passion, so maybe he hadn't been that serious about it. Maybe he hadn't actually intended to proceed. If that was the case, she'd certainly helped him achieve his goal when she'd stomped off in a huff.

As she'd learned from how Blake had treated Janet, the Ralston brothers weren't the marrying *kind*. No, they would have to be dragged to the altar, her problem being that she had no idea how to accomplish it.

Ooh, how she wished her father were still alive! If he'd been present, she'd already be a bride, and she wouldn't be standing on a busy street and worrying about the future. Her father would have settled it for her.

The entire mess had left her too exasperated to think straight, and she simply wanted to connect with Libby once more. For a few delicious minutes, she wanted to focus on someone other than herself and her myriad of difficulties.

She rattled the theater door, but it was the middle of the afternoon and there was no matinee scheduled, so it was locked. She knocked, her ear pressed to the wood to hear footsteps inside, but the place appeared to be deserted.

She dawdled, debating her next move when a man walked up. He was neatly dressed in a brown suit and wearing a bowler hat and spectacles, so he might have been a lawyer or a banker.

"Did you knock?" he asked her. "Is anyone here?"

"They don't seem to be."

"They usually arrive later in the day, but occasionally, there are people in this early. We could walk to the alley. The rear entrance is nearly always unlocked."

She pondered, then sighed. "I shouldn't bother anybody. I was looking for one of the actresses, but I'm not sure she's even performing. Her name isn't on the playbill."

"Who is the actress? I'm cordial with many of them."

"It's Libby Carstairs. The Mystery Girl of the Caribbean? She's so famous though. I likely wouldn't have been allowed to speak with her."

"Miss Carstairs is very approachable, and she loves to chat with her admirers. She'd have been thrilled to meet you."

"I'm not an admirer. I'm an old friend. A very *old* friend. I haven't seen her since we were little."

"Were you in a traveling troupe with her as she toured the country?"

"It was nothing like that. I was...was..."

She considered admitting her identity, but in the end, she didn't mention it. No one ever believed she was a Mystery Girl too.

"Never mind," Caroline murmured. "It doesn't matter now."

"She's not here anyway."

"Where did she go?"

"She's in the country. With Lord Barrett? They're about to have a quick wedding. It's the rumor that's circulating."

Caroline scowled. "Libby is marrying?"

"Yes, it's why I stopped by—to pry out some comments from some of her fellow actors. Since it's been revealed that she's Little Henrietta, the whole kingdom is enthralled by her all over again."

Caroline smiled, thinking Libby's marrying was the prettiest news in ages, but it made her sad too. Why had they been yanked apart? Why couldn't their families have permitted them to stay in touch over the years? What could it have hurt?

That sort of rumination was pointless though. It merely left her angry over all that had been lost, and she never gained any ground in stabilizing the floundering ship that was her problematic life.

He pulled a card from his coat and presented it to her with a flourish. "I write for the London Times."

"You're a newspaper reporter? My, my, that must be a very fun job."

"I'm the one who figured out that Miss Carstairs is Henrietta. I penned all the important articles."

"This must be a very exciting period for you."

"It's been very exciting." He grinned. "I earned myself a hefty raise too."

She chuckled. "Good for you."

He bowed to her. "Howard Periwinkle."

"Caroline Grey."

"I'm delighted to..." His sentence trailed off, and he studied her strangely. "*You* are Caroline Grey? Little Caro?"

"Ah...yes?"

"I've been searching for you!"

"Whatever for?"

"It's the twentieth anniversary of the shipwreck."

"Yes, it is. I've been reflecting on it quite a lot."

"So have I. So have our readers. Especially with Miss Carstairs being Henrietta. I've been hoping to schedule a reunion for the three of you."

"That's a marvelous idea. I'd like it very much."

"I've already talked to Joanna James, and she's agreed."

"You've talked to Joanna?" Caroline was surprised she didn't faint.

"We have to get Miss Carstairs to agree too. I would arrange it, and you'd simply have to show up."

"Libby is probably busy, what with her wedding and all. She might not like us to bother her."

"Miss Carstairs had a hard life, Miss Grey. I'm betting she'd be incredibly pleased to see you again—despite how busy she is. She'd receive great comfort from spending time with you and Joanna."

Tears surged into Caroline's eyes, and Mr. Periwinkle appeared stricken. He kindly patted her hand.

"Don't be sad about it, Miss Grey."

"I'm not sad. I'm happy and relieved! When we arrived in England, we were so young and so closely bonded. Then we were separated, and we weren't allowed to say goodbye to each other. I've had no information about either of them."

"Well, I have plenty—about their lives and what they've been doing. Would you like to hear some of it?"

"I would love to hear every detail you can possibly share."

"And if you're amenable, I have a plan for you and Miss Carstairs."

"What plan?"

"Let's find a restaurant and have a cup of tea. I'll tell you what it is."

Chapter

22

"Would you sit down? You're nervous as a cat in a thunderstorm."

Luke Watson, Lord Barrett, glared as his soon-to-be bride, Libby Carstairs. She glared back and said, "I can't relax. I'm too anxious. I feel as if something is about to happen."

"Will it be bad or good?"

"I can't decide."

"Well, something *is* about to happen."

"What?"

"We're marrying next week."

"Oh, that."

She pronounced *that* as if their getting married was of no consequence.

He was an earl, a retired navy commander, a hero of the Crown, a rich aristocrat, and a handsome rogue. Any female in the kingdom would have cut off her right arm to wed him, but not Libby Carstairs.

She pictured herself as being much more important than he was, so she believed he was the lucky one in their pathetic duo.

She was beautiful, dynamic, and flamboyant—and famous to the point of being notorious. Since she'd returned from the Caribbean at age five, she'd been the kingdom's darling, and with the revelation that she was Little Henrietta too, her acclaim had soared to astounding heights.

He had a very large ego, so he should have been incensed over the situation, but when he'd proposed, he'd been forced to acknowledge that life with her would never be boring. She'd never behave as a typical spouse would behave, would never do as was expected of her as his countess.

No, she was Libby Carstairs, Mystery Girl of the Caribbean, and she'd grown up in an unconventional manner, so she acted however she pleased. There would be no changing her, and he wouldn't want to change her. He loved her just the way she was—even when she was maddening and impossible to tolerate or manage.

They were at Barrett, his country estate, and loafing in the front parlor. There was chaos surrounding them, but they were ignoring it. The wedding was in ten days, but Libby had no feminine inclinations that would have made her a competent person to handle the arrangements.

Her half-sister, Penny, had stepped forward to supervise the event. Penny had been raised to be an aristocrat's wife, so she was the perfect candidate to be in charge. It was incredibly hectic. Servants were running to and fro. Tradesmen and merchants were delivering goods and offering services, and Penny was shouting orders like an army sergeant.

The wedding would be a very grand affair, with a week of parties and balls. The fact that he was an earl guaranteed it had to be fancy, but he was marrying Libby Carstairs. The whole country yearned to be included, so he was working valiantly to control the size and the cost.

The ceremony itself would be small, held in the village church that had pews for only a few dozen people, so they'd had to be meticulous about who they invited. They would compensate for the tiny amount of guests by hosting enormous celebrations afterward.

They probably should have tied the knot at the cathedral in London, but he wasn't an ostentatious fellow. He'd recently inherited his title, and he didn't like mobs or mayhem, so it definitely had him questioning—yet again—why he was so determined to proceed with her.

She couldn't stroll down the street without a crowd gathering. She relished being the center of attention and having audiences drool over her. When standing by her side, he was completely out of his element.

"Let's take a ride," he said to her. "I'll get you out into the fresh air, and it will help to calm you."

She had problems with anxiety and claustrophobia. They were symptoms left over from the shipwreck she'd survived, and he was adept at assessing the signs of her escalating discomfort.

"I can't leave right now," she said.

"Why not?"

"I just... can't."

She looked bewildered by her reply, and he laughed. "Because something is about to happen?"

"Yes."

"The only thing about to *happen* in this house is more havoc erupting."

He went to the sideboard and poured her a whiskey. She possessed numerous habits that no gently-bred female would ever dream of exhibiting. A taste for hard spirits was one of her oddities.

He handed her the glass, and she downed a hefty swallow. Alcohol soothed her quickly, and he studied her as she visibly relaxed, and it was definitely no great chore to stare at her. She was the most gorgeous woman in the world, and he was about to bind her forever.

For quite awhile, he couldn't have predicted if he'd win her or not. She'd certainly had no burning desire to be a wife, but he'd pestered her until she'd relented.

"Go by yourself," she said, and she rose on tiptoe and kissed him. "You need to escape this nonsense. I'll be fine by myself for a bit."

He pondered his route, thinking he'd visit her father, Charles Pendleton, who was Lord Roland. His estate adjoined Barrett, and he and Luke were cordial. They could chat about how much they hated weddings.

"Will you sing for me when I return?" he asked. "May I have a private concert."

"I might sing for you—if you're very, very nice to me once you're back."

"I shall view that as a challenge."

He initiated a kiss of his own, then pulled away. She overwhelmed him, and if he wasn't careful, he'd dawdle all afternoon, gaping at her like a halfwit. He was besotted as a green boy, and his infatuation sizzled hotter every day.

He walked out to the foyer. It was teeming with stacks of boxes and trunks that were filled with nuptial supplies. Servants were riffling through the boxes to note what had arrived.

He'd planned to skirt all of it and climb the stairs to his room so he could don his riding boots and fetch his coat, but when he passed the front door, his butler, Mr. Hobbs, was arguing with a man who seemed familiar to Luke. For some reason, Luke was instantly annoyed.

He stopped to focus on why he'd be irked, and the reason swiftly occurred to him: It was Howard Periwinkle, the oafish reporter who'd been harassing Libby about the shipwreck anniversary. He was also the infuriating tattle who'd written the stories about her being Little Henrietta. The articles had set off a wave of pandemonium that hadn't been totally quelled.

Luke had ended up being glad about the revelations, glad that Libby's identity had been discovered. If it hadn't been for Periwinkle being so dogged at his task, the truth likely would never have been exposed. Still though, Periwinkle had some nerve showing up at Luke's home. The last time they'd spoken, Luke had volunteered to thrash him for being so obnoxious.

He marched over and said to Hobbs, "I'll deal with this, Hobbs, and please take a good look at this lout. If he ever knocks in the future, grab several footmen to hog-tie him and drag him off the property."

At the command, Hobbs couldn't hide a shocked grimace, then he said, "The man's face is memorable, my lord. I won't soon forget him."

Hobbs eased away as Periwinkle doffed his hat and said, "Hello, Lord Barrett. We meet again."

"You have some gall to bluster in, Periwinkle."

"I've heard that about myself," the cheeky dolt agreed. "I have so much gall."

"I'll give you exactly thirty seconds to tell me why you're here, and it better not be because you're hoping to bother my fiancée."

"I don't intend to bother Miss Carstairs. I've brought her a surprise."

Periwinkle stepped to the side, and Luke could see a pretty, dark-haired woman had been concealed behind him. He scrutinized her, then frowned. "Should I know you? You're awfully familiar, but I can't place you."

She blanched. "You're Lord Barrett?"

"Yes, I'm Barrett." Recognition dawned, and he blanched too. "You were at the prison the day Libby was released from jail."

"I talked to you," the woman said, "but I didn't realize who you were."

Periwinkle puffed himself up. "This is Miss Carstairs's surprise. This is Little Caro." Luke glared at him, the name meaning nothing, and Periwinkle added, "Caro? Caroline Grey? From the shipwreck? She's a Lost Girl too."

Luke jumped as if he'd been poked with a pin. He recalled Miss Grey from the prison. She'd been bedraggled, as if she'd been experiencing personal difficulties, and he'd worried she was a tad unbalanced, so he'd been very abrupt with her.

She'd told him who she was, but the import hadn't registered, and the encounter had slipped his mind. To his great dismay, he hadn't mentioned it to Libby.

He was feeling discombobulated, amazed at how Fate worked in such strange ways. He was about to head over to apprise Libby about her visitor, but when he turned, she'd emerged from the parlor and was staring at them.

"Caro. . .?" she murmured. "Is it you? It's you, isn't it?"

"Yes, I'm Caro. Do you remember me, Libby? If you say you don't, I couldn't bear it."

Libby was still holding the glass of liquor he'd poured for her. It slid from her fingers, the contents splashing onto the rug. Then she ran across the room, and she slammed into Miss Grey so hard that they nearly fell to the floor. He and Periwinkle leapt to steady them.

The two women were hugging, crying, and through her tears, Libby said, "I've been waiting for you to arrive. Every minute since we were separated, I've been waiting."

"I've been waiting too," Miss Grey replied, "but I didn't know how to find you."

"Everything will be all right now," Libby said to her. "In fact, everything will be perfect."

<hr />

CAROLINE WAS BRIMMING WITH gladness. It was very late, and she and Libby had been sequestered for hours. Lord Barrett had locked them in Libby's bedroom suite. A housemaid had snuck in and out occasionally to check on them, but other than her quiet monitoring, they'd been alone.

Caroline had told Libby her entire history, starting with her being sent to live with her grandfather. She described how dreadful those years had been, how she'd been abused and mistreated and maligned.

Then she'd explained how her life had improved after her grandfather had died, how her Uncle Samson had taken charge of the family, but that it had never been particularly good. She talked about being engaged to Gregory whom she didn't like very much and didn't wish to wed.

She confessed how her relatives viewed her as a peculiar and damaged person merely because she'd endured a tragedy, and it was marvelous to have Libby listen and commiserate. As Caroline had suspected, Libby understood how terribly distressing her return to England had been.

Libby had told Caroline her entire history too, starting with her Uncle Harry claiming her from the authorities. He'd been allowed to waltz off with her, but he hadn't been a relative. He'd simply been acquainted with her mother, and for reasons no one could clarify, he'd pretended to be her kin.

He'd been aware that she was Lord Roland's missing daughter, but he'd hidden the truth and had raised her as his own child. Having recognized her flamboyant tendencies, he'd trained her for the stage, and she'd grown up, traveling around the country, regaling audiences with tales of the shipwreck and their survival after it.

It was such a relief to confer over what they recollected, to jog their memories and fill in the blanks. They'd been so young when the disaster had happened, so they'd forgotten many details.

"Mr. Periwinkle has met with Joanna," Caroline said.

Libby gasped. "You're joking."

"He asked her to join us for a reunion, and she's agreed."

"I thought I hated Periwinkle, but maybe I don't."

"He was kind to me, and if it wasn't for him, I wouldn't be here."

Libby smirked at the notion. "I'll send Joanna an invitation to the wedding. If need be, Luke can have someone fetch her to Barrett."

Caroline's pulse raced at the prospect. "What a spectacular ending that would be for the three of us."

"I have to show you something."

They were stretched out on the bed, lying on their sides, nose to nose. Libby slid away and went to the dresser. She retrieved a page that had been cut from a very old newspaper. It was yellowed with age, the paper tattered and brittle from being folded and unfolded.

It was an artist's sketch of them from when they were first back in England, and Caroline said, "What a precious picture. Where did you get it?"

"When the navy was searching for our kin, they disseminated a story about us."

"I don't recall it being drawn."

"Neither do I, but my Uncle Harry kept this copy. He'd pull it out occasionally, and he'd snicker over how it didn't look like me. One morning when he wasn't home, I stole it. I'd gaze at it when I was feeling low, and I'd think of you and Joanna and wonder if you might be thinking of me."

"I pondered you constantly. I used to dream that I could run away to the island, and you and Joanna would be there."

Libby chuckled. "I fantasized about the very same scenario, but I put Captain Ralston in the middle of it. Do you remember him?"

"Of course! The day his ship dropped anchor in the bay? It remains the most thrilling and alarming moment of my life."

"I would imagine he was my father and that he was hunting for me. He'd find me and carry me to the island so we could be there with you and Joanna." Libby sighed. "Should we try to locate him? We could invite him to the wedding too."

Caroline smiled, but sadly. "He's passed on, Libby. Not long after he stumbled on us."

Tears flooded Libby's eyes. "Oh, no! I can't stand that he's not out there in the world somewhere. I'd convinced myself that he was fretting over me and regretting how he let the navy whisk me away from him."

"I yearned for him to rescue me too. The years with my grandfather were especially gloomy, and I'd pray that he'd arrive to save me."

"I wish your grandfather was still alive so I could punish him for how he treated you."

"Should I have the same opinion about your Uncle Harry?"

"I had issues with Harry, but deep down, he was a terrific fellow. He pushed me to become who I am, and it was just what I needed. I couldn't have been shackled to some dolt and forced to stagger around in a hovel with a dozen children."

"No, you certainly wouldn't have fit in a small existence like that."

They laughed, then Libby said, "How did you learn about Captain Ralston's death? I thought you'd never heard any news about any of us after you were returned to Grey's Corner."

"I met his two sons recently. They're acquainted with my cousin, Gregory."

"I recall Captain Ralston being incredibly dashing. Are they anything like him?"

"They're exactly like him."

"What are their names?"

"Caleb and Blake."

"Caleb and Blake Ralston..." Libby mused. "Would they visit Barrett if I asked them to? I would love to speak to them about their father."

Caroline blew out a heavy breath, realizing she shouldn't have mentioned the wily pair. "Could I tell you a secret about them?"

"Yes," Libby replied, "but from your dour expression, I'm guessing it won't be a positive report. I hope they're not cads or wastrels."

"I wouldn't describe them as wastrels, but they're definitely cads."

Caroline paused to consider her next comment. There would be such relief to admit her situation with the Ralston brothers, and Libby wouldn't judge her for her moral lapse with Caleb. Lord Barrett might be able to help too, but she'd only just walked in his door, and she would hate to be a burden.

She was worried about so many problems: her uncle, the family's mysterious trust fund, her fling with Caleb, Janet's affair with Blake, Caleb's gambling business and it being such a dubious source of income.

Lord Barrett was a sophisticated navy veteran, so he might have some idea of where to start in addressing all of it. And wasn't confession good for the soul? It's what the papists believed.

Caroline opened her mouth and began to spill all.

<hr />

"Are you feeling better? Now that Caro has arrived, is your anxiety gone?"

"Completely gone."

Libby smiled at Luke. They were in the dining room, having breakfast. She and Caro had chatted late into the night, then they'd dozed off on her bed, snuggled together like puppies—as they had on their deserted island.

She'd left Caro sleeping, and she'd come down to eat without her. She was brimming with stories, with excitement, with joy, and she was eager to share every detail of their lengthy conversation with Luke.

"I waited up for you," he said, "but after the clock struck midnight, I went to bed."

"We couldn't stop talking!"

"I assumed that was the case."

She was seated at the table, and he was dishing up her food, pouring her tea. He fussed over her incessantly, as if—should he glance away—she'd vanish.

Initially, his hovering had annoyed her, but gradually, she'd decided it was extremely pleasant. While she was very famous and people gushed over her, she'd never had anyone in her private life show much interest in her condition.

Her Uncle Harry hadn't exactly been a warm and cuddly person. He'd raised her to be tough and strong, and whenever she'd protested any issue, he'd told her to buck up and stop whining. He'd always warned her that no one liked a complainer.

His stern attitude had taught her to swallow her grievances and present a contented mask to others, but internally, she'd seethed over many indignities. It was lovely to have Luke notice how she was faring, to have him ensure she was happy and comfortable. She could vent any frustration, and he never ordered her to be silent.

"How was her upbringing?" he asked. "Was it splendid or awful or somewhere in between? Were her relatives kind to her? Or were they horrid?"

"Oh, Luke, she was so miserable! She was sent to live with her grandfather, and he was a violent ogre. He used to lock her in her room, and he constantly railed that her father was burning in Hell, and eventually, she would too."

"That's terrible."

"She spent years alone, being quiet and playing by herself. I'm amazed she grew up to be so sweet. She has an uncle. Samson Grey?"

Luke shook his head. "Never heard of him."

"He moved to their estate after her grandfather died, and he's a bit of a fiend too. I can't bear to have her male kin in charge of her. Not with how she's been treated."

"I'm glad she travelled to Barrett then. Much as I loathe Periwinkle, I suppose I'll have to reward him in some fashion."

Mr. Periwinkle had stayed the night with them, and he was likely still in the house, but she hadn't seen him after she'd gone upstairs with Caro.

"Why didn't you tell me you spoke to her at the prison?" Libby asked. "If I'd known she was searching for me, I'd have worked harder to find her."

"We shouldn't discuss the debacle at the prison."

It was still a sore subject between them. He'd posted her bail and had arranged for her release, but they'd been fighting, and she'd been so angry with him that she'd climbed in her carriage and had driven away without him. It was a testament to his fond feelings for her that they'd ended up together. He'd definitely struggled to win her.

"Besides," he said, "she was positively disheveled. I was afraid she might have been a tad unhinged, so you wouldn't have wanted to have her chase you down. What had happened to her anyway? It appeared to me that she'd suffered a dozen calamities. When she strolled in our door, she was so improved that I barely recognized her. I'm stunned that she's the same woman."

"You won't believe what she's recently endured." She studied him, and his mood was very calm, so she asked, "May I request a favor?"

"From your impish grin, I should probably say *no*, but as you're aware, I can't refuse you. What is it you require? Let's discover if I can force myself to be amenable."

"I'd like Caro to remain with us at Barrett. I can't toss her out into the big, wide world. I'd worry about her too much."

"Of course she can tarry—for as long as she likes. Is that it?"

"No. I need you to do a few things for her. And for me."

"What things?"

"Her uncle has been threatening to lock her in an asylum."

Luke scowled. "Are you subtly informing me that she's deranged after all? Was my earlier assessment correct?"

"No! She's as stable as I am."

He laughed. "I wouldn't necessarily deem that to be a stellar endorsement of her sanity. I've always viewed you to be a bit mad."

"Don't joke."

"Who's joking? You're a menace, and I have no idea why I put up with you."

"You're lucky you have to put up with me, and don't you forget it."

He smiled a devastating smile. "I won't ever forget it. Why do you imagine I've insisted we rush the wedding? I'm not about to let you get away from me."

Fate could be so strange. She'd never planned to marry, but look at her now! Almost a bride and so eager to be his wife that she couldn't stand it.

He reached across the table and clasped her hand. "What are the other favors on your list? We'll figure out which ones I'll allow, and which ones I won't, then we can move on to more interesting topics."

"Like what?"

"Like my bed was very empty without you last night."

"I'm not sneaking up there with you in the middle of the morning. I won't have the servants gossiping about my loose morals."

"Too late, Libby. You're an actress. They assume you're a doxy."

"They do not. They adore me, and we'll keep it that way."

"You are a cruel vixen."

"I want to have you panting after me until our wedding. You should never be too complacent."

He snickered with amusement. "Trust me. I've never been complacent about you. I still can't fathom why you agreed to have me."

"Neither can I."

He leaned over and kissed her, and they sighed with pleasure.

"What are your other favors?" he asked again.

"Caro's uncle has been harassing her to wed a wastrel cousin. She doesn't understand why he's being such a beast about it, and I'd like you to find out what's motivating him."

"How would I?"

"I thought you could hire lawyers or investigators or something."

"I could hire someone. It's no problem."

"The men in her family shouldn't have control over her in the future."

"We should be able to fix that situation."

"And finally, she's in love, and I need to learn more about this fellow who's tantalized her. He's proposed, but she can't decide if she should consent or not. I'm concerned over whether he'd be worthy of her."

"What's his name? Did she tell you?"

"Caleb Ralston? He was in the navy for years, so I was wondering if you might know him. I guess he landed himself in some trouble though, so he was drummed out. He owns a gambling club in London now."

Luke snorted with dismay. "Yes, I know Caleb Ralston."

"You're frowning, so I can't deduce if that's good news or bad."

"It depends on what assistance you're asking me to provide."

"He seduced her, but she's confused if it was with wicked intent or not."

"She confided all of that? You two certainly aired plenty of your dirty laundry. I hope you were more reticent in the stories you shared about me."

"Maybe I was and maybe I wasn't," Libby saucily said.

"Is she ruined?"

"Yes."

"Then *my* opinion about him doesn't matter. He's about to be a husband."

"There's an issue with his brother, Blake, too. Do you know him as well?"

Luke blanched. "What sort of issue? She wasn't seduced by both of them, was she? That might be more of a problem than I could solve."

Libby chuckled. "No! Blake seduced her cousin, Janet, but he's about to sail away to the Mediterranean. The idiot doesn't believe he should have to tie the knot, and Caro has no power to make him proceed."

"His brother can make him. Or the navy can make him."

"It's what I suspected."

Libby was finished eating. She pushed her plate away, then she stood and patted him on the shoulder. He pulled her down and whispered, "Are you sure you won't come upstairs with me?"

"I'm very sure, and your answers about Caro were all the right ones. It has me thinking that it might not be horrid to have a husband in my life."

"I'm growing on you. I told you I would."

CALEB'S CARRIAGE RATTLED TO a halt in front of his London house. He dawdled on the seat, waiting for a footman to open the door. He wasn't usually a snob and didn't need his servants treating him like a baby. He could exit a carriage without having them hold his hand, but he was too aggravated to climb out.

After Caro had snuck away, he'd been brusquely informed by Blake that she didn't want to talk to him. Apparently, she presumed a quarrel could be mended by *not* speaking. It was the stupidest notion ever, but he should have expected it from such an absurd female.

Blake had claimed that *she* would contact Caleb if and when she felt like it, and because he was embarrassed over how he'd hurt her, he'd complied with her edict.

He'd spent several days, cooling his heels, trying to oblige her, but eventually, he'd been too irked to behave rationally. If she wasn't so stubborn, they could have been married already. Didn't she understand that fact? Why was she being so ridiculous?

He'd dragged himself to Janet's apartment and had been prepared to grovel, to offer whatever emasculating comment was required to be forgiven. Except when Janet had finally responded to his incessant knocking, she'd apprised him that Caro wasn't even in London any longer. While he'd been fretting over their rift, she'd packed her bags and departed! She'd been that unconcerned by what had happened.

How was he to evaluate such an exhausting decision? After their hideous fight, he'd felt as if she'd ripped out his heart and stomped it into the dirt. What had she felt? Evidently, not much of anything.

She'd fled the city, and that little snot, Janet, had refused to tell him where she'd gone. It was enough to make a bachelor swear off matrimony.

A footman arrived to attend him, but Caleb didn't emerge from the vehicle. He was so sad! When he'd hurried off to fetch Caro, he'd been determined to bring her back with him, and his failure had left him inordinately depressed.

Ultimately, the footman stuck his head in and asked, "Are you all right, sir? Will you be getting out?"

Caleb sighed. "Yes, I'm getting out."

He trudged down and went inside, and the butler greeted him with, "You have a visitor, Mr. Ralston."

Caleb's initial reaction was ecstasy. "Is it Miss Grey?"

"No, sir, it's an old acquaintance of yours from the navy."

Caleb turned around as a man stepped into view and said, "Hello, Ralston."

"Luke Watson?" Caleb asked. "Or must I call you Barrett? I heard that you'd inherited your family's title."

"Yes, my brother died last year. I've become what I never wanted to be."

"You're land-locked."

"I had to muster out and sail home to manage things."

Caleb gestured into the parlor, and they walked in together. He had the butler pour them a whiskey, then shooed him out and shut the door. The man had been hovering, eager to eavesdrop, but Caleb had no idea what was occurring. Until he figured it out, he wouldn't have the servants hanging on their every word.

Lucas Watson was Caleb's same age of thirty. They'd joined the navy at sixteen, and they'd served with distinction—until Caleb had been run off in disgrace. They'd moved in the same circles, with the same people.

In a different world, they might have been friends, but they weren't friends, and he couldn't imagine why Barrett would stop by. It had better not be to pry into the details of Caleb's split from the navy, and just as he caught himself praying that wouldn't be the topic, Barrett said, "Rumor has it that you had some trouble and had to retire."

"Yes, I retired rather than be court marshalled, but if that's what you'd like to discuss, it was a wasted trip. I'm not about to delve into it with you."

"I don't intend to pester you about it, but I will admit to being surprised that you'd get yourself in a jam like that."

Caleb shrugged. "It was an…unfortunate circumstance."

"You bounced back though. With your gambling club?"

Caleb studied Barrett as if he were an alien creature never previously encountered in England. "I hate to be blunt, Barrett, but we were never chums, so why are you here? I'm dealing with a huge dilemma today, so I'm very busy."

"I'm marrying next week."

Caleb was perplexed as to why Barrett would mention it. It wasn't as if Caleb would suddenly find himself on the guest list.

"Well…congratulations," he said. "Are congratulations in order? Should I be glad for you? Are you happy about it?"

"My fiancée is Libby Carstairs. You've heard of her, haven't you? The Mystery Girl of the Caribbean? She's definitely a handful, so I can't guess if you should be glad for me or not. She's not exactly the sort of meek, modest female a man seeks in a bride, so it's possible I've lost my mind."

"*You* are marrying Libby Carstairs?"

"It's wild, isn't it? From your expression, it's clear I've shocked you."

"That's putting it mildly."

Caleb was thinking of Fate again—and of his father. Libby Carstairs was a Lost Girl, as was Caro. What were the odds that Miss Carstairs would wedge herself into Caleb's life like this? It was eerie and bizarre.

"Libby is the most stubborn woman ever," Barrett said. "Have you met her? Or have you seen her on the stage?"

"No, I always wanted to, but...but..."

He wasn't about to explain how his father had rescued Miss Carstairs in the Caribbean or how he, Caleb, had yearned for an introduction, but how he'd been afraid of what she might impart.

Barrett saved him from having to clarify. "If you've never met her, then you could never comprehend why I couldn't resist shackling myself. I didn't stand a chance, not from the very first minute."

"Poor you," Caleb commiserated.

They smirked in a thoroughly male fashion, then Barrett said, "She sent me to speak to you. I'm carrying out a mission at her request."

"I'm confused. Since I don't know her, I can't fathom why she'd bother."

"We had a visitor show up at my home in the country. I'm told she's a friend of yours."

Caleb scowled. "Who was it?"

"Caroline Grey."

"Caroline is at Barrett?"

"Yes."

"I will wring her neck," Caleb fumed. "I've been looking everywhere for her, and I've been frantic with worry."

"I take it you have plans with regard to her."

"Yes, I have bloody plans. *Marriage* plans, but we quarreled, so she's been in a snit. I haven't been able to calm her down so we could head to Scotland."

"I'm delighted that matrimony is on your schedule. It means I won't have to drag you to the altar, but why are you eloping? Why not proceed in a church?"

"We're in a bit of a rush, but I doubted there was a bishop in the kingdom who would grant me a Special License."

"I can obtain a Special License for you. What about your brother?"

"My... brother?" Caleb asked, feeling even more perplexed.

"According to Libby, he needs to have his own wedding before he ships out. Is he still in London? Or has he left already?"

"He's still here."

"Then he's about to be a husband too."

"The young lady in question isn't interested. She assumes she can ruin herself without consequence."

"You listened to her?" Barrett said. "You let *her* decide?"

"I have no authority over her, so I'm in no position to make her behave."

"Well, Ralston, my fiancée and yours expect a wedding between the pair, so we have to accomplish it. Then you and I will ride to Barrett and complete your own nuptials. I must confess though that with all these marriages taking place, I may break out in hives."

"I warned my brother that he couldn't avoid it. It's the girl who's being silly."

"You and I will fix that situation straight away."

"And as to Caro," Caleb said, "she's so angry with me. If I stagger in at Barrett, she'll likely throw me out a window."

"Again, Ralston, *she* doesn't get to decide. You and I will handle it, and perhaps we can arrive with a few incentives that will convince her to like you again."

"What did you have in mind?"

"How about if you summon your brother? We have to inform him that his bachelor days are over. While we wait for him, I'll tell you what I was thinking."

Chapter

23

"Tomorrow?"

"Yes, tomorrow."

Janet gaped at Blake, and she felt something crack in the center of her chest. It had to be her heart breaking.

"What time do you sail?" she asked. "Could I come down to the dock and wave goodbye?"

"The tide turns around eleven in the morning."

She noticed that he hadn't answered her question about whether she could come to the dock or not. Would he like that? Was it allowed?

She supposed she ought to simply be glad he'd bothered to tell her he was leaving. He could have just boarded his ship and traipsed off. She wouldn't have figured out what had happened until he'd stopped visiting.

He grinned his devil's grin. "Will you miss me?"

"You're much too vain, so I won't admit it. It would merely inflate your ego."

"I'll miss you," he thrilled her by saying.

"If you can bring yourself to confess it, then *I* shall confess the same. I will miss you too."

He chuckled. "We had quite a go of it, didn't we? I'll always be proud of how brave you are."

She wasn't brave though. She was young and scared and very stupid. She needed to inform him she might be increasing, and she was desperately anxious to ask him for some more money, but he'd already given her so much. Dare she beg for more?

They were in her London apartment, and she yearned to drag him into the bedroom like the worst doxy. She wanted to hold him close one last time, but he couldn't tarry.

Again, she had to remember she was lucky he'd stopped by. He could have vanished with no warning. If he had, she truly believed she might have perished from despair.

She'd known the end was approaching, but she'd been living in a bubble, watching as his departure date neared, but pretending it wasn't about to arrive.

Now what...?

She wished Caroline hadn't left for the country to stay with Miss Carstairs. Or she wished she'd accompanied her cousin. It would have been better than listening to the quiet that would descend once he walked out.

"If I had to contact you for some reason," she said, "is there a way I could do it?"

"I'll get mail in Gibraltar, so feel free to write. I'd like to hear from you, but it will take forever for me to receive a letter."

"I see..." She forced a smile. "I guess I'm a bit fonder of you than I realized."

"Could I tell you a secret?"

"Of course. You can tell me anything."

"My brother learned about our affair, and he suggested we marry, but I told him you'd never settle for such a dreary conclusion."

On having him repeat her words back to her, she could have wept with regret and insisted she hadn't meant any of them.

She didn't want to wind up alone and forsaken. She didn't want to birth a child when she had no husband to give it a name. There might be a world in the future where a woman could carry on like that, but it wasn't here yet. And though she liked to picture herself in a different light, she was no courageous radical.

She was just Janet Grey from Grey's Corner, and she didn't have the maturity required to face down society as a pariah.

"Could I tell *you* a secret?" she asked.

She gazed into his beautiful blue eyes, and there were so many comments struggling to burst out that she might have been choking on them.

How did a girl propose marriage? It was why fathers dealt with the situation. A man could confer with another man and fix the dilemma. A man could coax another man to behave appropriately. What could a woman do?

She started to tremble, and he frowned and said, "Caleb was probably correct. Maybe we should wed. It's the expected path for us, but I would never pressure you into it. It would have to be your idea."

She was saved from responding by a brisk knock on the door. "Hold that thought. Let me see who it is."

She peeked out, being surprised to discover his brother standing there. There was another man with him. They appeared large and important, and she couldn't imagine what their purpose might be.

"If you're looking for Caroline," she said to him, "she's still not here."

"We're not looking for Caroline," he replied. "I know where she is. I have to find my brother."

Blake stepped into view. "You found me."

"Have you resolved the matter?" Mr. Ralston asked him.

"She's too adamant in her opinions. I can't convince her."

"We've debated that issue," Mr. Ralston said. "*She* doesn't get to decide."

Janet scowled. "What are you talking about? And I would appreciate it if you wouldn't discuss me as if I'm not present."

Mr. Ralston pointed to the man who was with him. "Miss Grey, this is Lucas Watson, Lord Barrett. He's engaged to Libby Carstairs."

Janet's scowl deepened. Lord Barrett's engagement to Miss Carstairs had no bearing on Janet at all. She gave him the fleetest curtsy ever, then peered up at Blake and asked, "What matter were you supposed to resolve with me?"

"I told you," Blake said. "Caleb thinks we should wed."

Caleb Ralston interrupted. "I don't *think* it, Blake. I demand it."

"So do I," Lord Barrett added.

Then she saw what she hadn't initially noticed. There was a third man lurking in the hall. He was wearing a cleric's collar and clutching a prayer book.

"This is Vicar Thompson," Caleb Ralston said, "and since Blake is shipping out tomorrow, we've obtained a Special License. There's no reason to delay the ceremony."

"Hello, Miss Grey," the vicar said.

Caleb Ralston gestured to Blake. "He's the groom."

"You certainly arranged this fast," Blake said to his brother, appearing a bit green around the gills.

"Lord Barrett and I weren't about to brook any nonsense. Not from either of you. You're departing in a few hours, and when you sail away, I'm sorry to report that you'll be a husband." Mr. Ralston shifted his caustic focus to Janet and said, "And *you*, Miss Grey, will be a bride."

Blake glowered at his brother. "I thought you were going to let me handle this."

"If I'd let *you* handle it, you'd still be a bachelor in the morning."

"Janet doesn't want to wed me, and I won't force her into it."

"I'll force her," Lord Barrett said. "I don't have a problem playing the part of bully in this fiasco."

"You don't even know her," Blake complained, "and you definitely have no authority over her. You can't make her do anything."

The vicar was listening to the argument, his head swinging from person to person as they bickered.

Finally, there was a break in the conversation, and he said to Janet, "Is this true, Miss Grey? Are you being forced? Despite how Lord Barrett commands me to proceed, I won't be a party to any coercion. Is it your wish to marry Blake Ralston? Considering the disagreement that was just aired, you'll have to persuade me that you'd speak the vows of your own free will."

Janet glared at Caleb Ralston, then at Lord Barrett. She still couldn't figure out why he was there. They were doggedly determined to get their way. Then she peeked up at her dear, adored Blake. He was dressed in his uniform, and he was dashing and handsome and too delicious for words. Who wouldn't want to be his wife?

"I've seriously pondered the notion," she said, and the four men stiffened as they wondered how she'd finish her sentence, "and I would *love* to marry Blake."

Blake gulped. "Are you sure? It's never been your goal."

"That was before I met you."

"There were to be no strings attached. Wasn't that your choice?"

"Yes, but I was being stupid. I didn't comprehend how much I'd come to cherish you."

Caleb Ralston snorted with disgust. "There you have it, Blake. She *cherishes* you—though I can't for the life of me understand why."

Janet jumped to Blake's defense. "Who wouldn't cherish him, Mr. Ralston? If he'll have me, I might be the luckiest girl in the world."

"It's marriage, Janet," Blake said, as if she needed reminding. "It's matrimony, which you claim to despise. It's *forever*."

"I know it's forever," she told him, "and I hate that they're insisting. I hate that I've consented. I hope you'll forgive me someday."

"It's not a matter of forgiveness. You simply have such different views about females. I was helping you realize them."

"I guess I wasn't quite so independent after all. You're not angry, are you? Please tell me you won't be."

"He won't be angry," Caleb Ralston firmly stated, "and if he ever seems to be, you can contact me, and I'll set him straight."

Blake stared down at her, and a long pause spread out between them. It was possible that he might utter any terrible comment. He might disparage Janet. He might order them to the Devil and march out.

But to her great relief, he said, "I'm not angry, and I'm betting we'll be fine."

"There you have it," Lord Barrett said to the vicar. "Let's get this over with."

The vicar spun to Janet. "I'll inquire a final time, Miss Grey. Will you proceed?"

Janet flashed a smile at each of them in turn, then she clasped Blake's hand and said, "Yes, I'd like to proceed, and could you hurry? I can't wait to be his bride."

On hearing her remark, Blake looked as if he might faint, then he squared his shoulders and said, "I'm ready too."

～⁘～

"Mr. Ralston? I'm surprised to see you back in the country. What brings you by?"

On having Caleb Ralston strut into his front foyer, Samson tried to be cordial, but he held Ralston personally liable for Caroline crying off from her betrothal, so he couldn't bear to chat.

Though it was strange, Ralston had a bevy of men with him. One man appeared rich and important, and two of them were probably clerks. The others were tough and unruly, as if they might be criminals. What could their purpose be in accompanying Ralston to Grey's Corner?

Samson was dealing with too many problems, so he couldn't fuss with Ralston. They still hadn't found Caroline or Janet. Since they'd snuck away, there hadn't been a single sighting, so he had no clue where they were.

He'd emptied Janet's bank account, so she was out of money, and he'd assumed it would force them to slither home, but it hadn't.

Gregory was vexing him too—worse than ever. He was convinced the wedding was off for good, so he felt he ought to marry Mrs. Starling. He swore it was his idea, but Samson thought it sounded like a ploy Mrs. Starling had cooked up. When Gregory had first mentioned the prospect, Samson was amazed he hadn't suffered an apoplexy. He'd been that aghast.

The foul pair was at Grey's Corner, with Gregory having to hide from creditors. Unfortunately, they'd begun to knock on Samson's door to ask if Gregory was staying with him, and Samson was receiving demand letters by the hour, where Gregory had signed over chattels and property to which he had no ownership.

With those issues plaguing him, he didn't have the energy to be polite to Caleb Ralston.

"I'm very busy today," he said to Ralston, "so what is it you need? Can you be quick about it?"

"No," the cocky oaf replied. "We should confer in your library. This may require a bit of discussion to get it resolved."

Samson wished he was strong enough to toss Ralston out bodily, but he couldn't have. Nor would Ralston's flock of guards have allowed it.

"I can give you thirty minutes," Samson said, "but that's it."

The rich-looking fellow said to Ralston, "While you're talking to him, I'll find Gregory."

"I'd like to have a word with him before they take him away," Ralston said.

Samson was so shocked that he was frozen into a stupor, then he physically shook himself and said to the man, "Why must you find Gregory?"

"We're here to arrest your son as a debtor. These gentlemen"—he flicked a thumb at the vicious group—"will be escorting him to town for trial."

Samson puffed himself up. "You have some gall to spew such outrageous claims. Who are you, sir?"

Ralston smirked. "Oh, didn't I introduce him? This is Lucas Watson, Lord Barrett. He's recently become very interested in Gregory."

"Who has accused him of being a debtor?" Samson tried to seem stern and upset, as if Gregory had never wasted a penny. "Tell me that—if you can!"

"*I* accuse him," Ralston said. "I have dozens of judgments, and I aim to see that he spends many, many years in prison for fraud."

Samson was worried he might faint. Lord Barrett started up the stairs, all but one of the felons tromping after him. The one who'd lagged behind walked over to stand beside Samson, as if to prevent Samson's escape. Ralston clasped Samson's arm and marched down the hall toward the library. The clerks traipsed after them, the felon too.

Samson recovered his wits and struggled to squirm away, but Ralston tightened his grip and kept on. They entered the room, and Ralston flung Samson onto a chair, then seated himself at the desk—as if it and the library belonged to him.

"I won't tolerate this abuse," Samson blustered.

Ralston ignored him and told the clerks, "Search every drawer and ledger. Confiscate it all—even if you're not sure it applies. Pack it and take it."

Samson rose to his feet, and Ralston shouted, "Sit down, Mr. Grey!"

The criminal put a hand on Samson's shoulder and pushed until Samson slunk down like a whipped dog.

"I'll be brief," Ralston said. "Your daughter, Janet, has wed my brother, Blake."

"What?" It was the last topic Samson had expected Ralston to address, and it was such an odd comment that he was certain he'd misheard.

"She's been misbehaving with him in London. I guess they pursued an amour while he was here, and when he left, she followed him to town."

"I can't believe it!"

"Believe it. It's over and done."

"She's only twenty. She can't have proceeded without my permission."

"We couldn't wait. I'm not positive, but it's likely she's increasing."

Samson felt as if he'd been pole-axed. For the remainder of his life, he'd be connected to the Ralston brothers by Janet's marriage. It was enough to make him want to weep like a baby.

Ralston continued speaking. "Blake is posted to the Mediterranean, and he's based out of Gibraltar. She'll join him there in a few weeks. There's a ship for navy wives that goes back and forth regularly. She'll be on it."

"Will I. . . I. . . have a chance to talk to her before she sails?"

"No. She's not interested in talking to you, and I wouldn't let her anyway. She's my sister-in-law, and I am declaring her to be under my protection now."

"Bastard," Samson muttered.

"Yes, I definitely can be."

"I don't agree to any of this."

"I don't care."

One of the clerks bustled over and said, "Look at this document, Mr. Ralston. It spells it out in plain English."

Ralston scanned the papers, then said, "Good work. See what other evidence he's stashed away."

Samson leapt up so he could peek at what Ralston had perused, but he'd forgotten the thug was lurking behind him. The man grabbed Samson by his coat and yanked him down so hard that his teeth clacked together.

He bent down and warned, "If you stand up again, I'll beat you bloody."

Samson was quite afraid, and he wondered where Gregory was. Why hadn't he raced down to investigate what was occurring? Samson deemed it perfectly typical that, the moment Samson needed his son, the slothful boy would vanish.

"After her wedding," Ralston said, "Janet showed me the strangest letter from a lawyer. She'd been trying to wrest control of her trust fund from you, and she was stunned to discover that she's never had one."

Samson lied with aplomb. "If that's what she told you, then she's gravely mistaken. Or she's confused for some reason I can't fathom."

"Her lawyer advises that your family has only ever had *one* trust fund, and the name conveniently happens to be, *The Caroline Grey Mining Trust.*" Ralston stood and braced his palms on the desktop. He leaned toward Samson, his glare ferocious. "Would you like to explain that situation to me?"

"No, I would not. My finances are none of your business."

"First of all, nothing in this house is yours any longer. Gregory has attached it as collateral for his promissory notes."

"As he doesn't *own* the property, he couldn't have attached it."

"He has guaranteed it as your heir, so after you pass away, everything will be mine. I've sued him in the courts to obtain it immediately—and won."

Samson scowled, his bewilderment growing. Could a creditor get judgment on a son's future inheritance? Was it possible? He supposed it was, but where did that leave Samson?

"I'll confer with my own attorney," he said, his smile tight. "He'll fix this for me, so don't be too confident."

"I'm not concerned about this paltry estate. I'd like to address the main issue that intrigues me." Ralston eased down into his chair again. "What excuse will you use to justify your lengthy embezzlement from your niece?"

"What are you saying?" Samson paled. "You can't spew slander without consequence."

"Truth is a defense." Ralston was very smug.

Samson shifted nervously, watching as the clerks came over to skulk behind Ralston. Their condemning glowers left him even more rattled.

"What is your point?" he asked Ralston. "May I suggest you be very clear?"

"Your theft from her trust fund has been exposed," Ralston blithely responded, "and you've been removed as trustee."

"What? What?"

"Lord Barrett will take your place temporarily, but I'll be in charge of it after I wed Caroline."

Ralston had spewed so many bizarre comments that Samson couldn't keep track of them all. He'd been removed as trustee? Barrett had taken his place? Ralston assumed he was marrying Caroline?

"You're mad," Samson blurted out.

Ralston nodded. "Many people have always thought so."

"That money is...is...mine. You can't merely swoop in and seize it."

"It's not yours, you deluded fiend. It's *never* been yours, and I've already seized it. Your fingers have been yanked out of that fiscal pie, and you'll never be able to stick them back into it. You've stolen your last farthing from Caroline."

"I demand to speak to her!" Samson blustered. "Produce her at once so she can inform you of how happy she's been with how I've managed her affairs."

"You have the gall to claim she's been happy? Is that your position? She was *happy* with how you stole from her?" Ralston gestured to the clerks. "These two fellows are very good with numbers, and they'll be delving into your records. Eventually, they'll apprise me—down to the penny—how much you pilfered."

"I spent all of it for Caroline's benefit! I spent it to make her life better! Just ask anyone. She lived like a princess in my home!"

Ralston clucked his tongue with offense, and the clerks bristled. The thug whacked Samson alongside the head and said, "Shut up. We're sick of listening to you."

Samson might have chastised the cretin, but he looked so fierce that Samson didn't dare. He gazed at Ralston instead and insisted, "You can't do this. You can't!"

"The switch of trustees is complete," Ralston said with a grim finality, "and now, you simply need to prepare for your arrest."

"My arrest!"

"Yes, you and your son. After I've notified Caroline of your malfeasance, I can't predict if she'll seek revenge or not. She's a very kind person, so she may request leniency on your behalf, but until then, you'll be incarcerated." Ralston rose to his full height, like a judge about to pass sentence. "If *I* am the man to decide your fate, I shall ask that you be hanged and that I be allowed to pull the rope that breaks your neck."

Samson forced out, "Caroline wouldn't want you to treat me this way."

"I don't plan to tell her. I'll keep her in the dark—as you have. I'll arrange to have you executed, and she'll never learn what happened."

Samson gulped with terror and fainted dead away.

"RALSTON! WHAT THE BLOODY hell is going on?"

Gregory stormed into the library, but with his wrists shackled, it was difficult to muster much bravado.

He'd been napping, sleeping off his hangover, when a group of ruffians had barged into his bedchamber. He'd recognized Lord Barrett from socializing in town, but he hadn't known any of the others. They'd dragged him off the bed and attached his fetters without uttering a word as to their purpose.

He'd been marched down the stairs without being permitted to make himself more presentable, so he was barefoot, not wearing a coat, his hair standing on end.

"Hello, Gregory," Caleb Ralston said. "Thank you for joining us. Have a seat."

Ralston was behind his father's desk, comfortably relaxed as if it belonged to him. Lord Barrett grabbed Gregory and was hauling him across the room when he saw his father unconscious on the floor.

He blanched. "You deranged lunatic! Have you killed my father?"

"Not yet." Ralston smiled an evil smile.

At hearing their voices, Samson stirred and sat up. He was swaying, off balance, and Gregory helped him to his feet, then Samson staggered to a chair, his eyes wide with alarm.

"They've taken the money from us!" Samson wailed.

"What?"

Gregory plopped onto his own chair and scowled at his father, but before the man could clarify his comment, Ralston said, "Your sister, Janet, has married my brother, Blake."

Gregory's jaw dropped in astonishment. "I don't believe it."

"It's true, and after the wedding, she provided me with some very interesting information."

Samson was gesturing oddly, as if warning Gregory to be careful. Gregory received his message. "My sister is flighty as a mockingbird."

"Most women are," Ralston agreed, "but in this instance, I felt compelled to investigate her story. Lord Barrett and I did some digging into the *Caroline Grey Mining Trust*."

"Oh..." Gregory murmured, then the import settled in, and he said more firmly, "Oh!"

"You can imagine our surprise when we realized that it was created by Caroline's late father and that Caroline is the sole beneficiary."

"I don't know much about it," Gregory claimed, "so I can't really furnish any details."

Ralston scoffed in an eerie way. "You don't know *much* about it? How peculiar then that so many of the quarterly disbursements have been shifted into your own bank account."

"You're mistaken," Gregory said. "I've obtained no such disbursements."

Ralston ignored him and continued. "We were stunned by the amounts that have poured into the trust over the years. If you and your father hadn't pilfered so much of it, she'd be one of the richest women in England, but the money is still flowing in. With some tidy management, it will grow back quickly."

"Well, good for Caroline," Gregory said, "but I'm confused over what any of it has to do with me."

"You're being charged with fraud and embezzlement."

"Now see here, Ralston!" Gregory huffed. "If there are funds missing from that stupid trust, pester my father about it. Not me. *He* is the trustee. I never had any authority over it."

Samson sucked in a sharp breath. "You little shit! You're blaming me for this debacle?"

"Of course, Father. How could I have glommed onto any of it?"

Samson studied Gregory, and his father looked defeated and disgusted. Then he straightened his shoulders and said to Ralston, "Gregory and I agreed to spend the money on ourselves, and we convinced ourselves that Caroline wouldn't mind. But Gregory is a wastrel, so he sought more and more, and I constantly gave it to him. He resided in London and pursued a style of living that was far beyond his means. Caroline has another fund vesting on her birthday—if she's wed by then—so we were pressuring her to marry him before it was too late."

"Ah...so that was your motive," Ralston mused. "We've been curious about it."

Gregory fumed, "Father! Shut your mouth!"

"I'm not listening to you anymore," Samson furiously said to Gregory, then to Ralston, "She decided to back out of her betrothal, and we couldn't let her. Gregory suggested we have her declared incompetent and locked in an asylum so we could garner control of her fortune without ever having to worry about her in the future."

"Father! Stop lying! I would never have behaved so abominably toward her."

Samson added, "Somehow, Caroline learned what we were planning, and she ran away. I'm ashamed that we debated the idea, and I most humbly apologize."

Every eye in the room swung to Gregory, and he said, "My father can beg your pardon and pretend remorse all he wants, but *he* acquired the court order. Not me! He was fully prepared to have her committed."

There was a shocked silence, and into it, Lord Barrett said, "You two are the sorriest pair of men I've ever met."

Gregory knew he had to brazen it out. "Are we finished? I could use some breakfast." He stood and extended his wrists. "Would someone remove these blasted ropes? I'd like to get on with my day."

A ruffian yanked him down onto his seat, and he muttered in Gregory's ear, "Be quiet, you dirty dog, or I'll gag you. And if you stand up again before Mr. Ralston gives you permission, I'll break your leg so you can't stand."

Gregory gulped with dismay, and he glared at his father, his expression beseeching Samson to *do* something, but his father wouldn't even look at Gregory. Gregory glanced at the door, wishing Lucretia would stomp in. She was a termagant when riled. She'd put them in their places.

"Gregory Grey," Ralston said, "I have bought up your markers in town. Every debt. Every promissory note you've ever signed. They're mine now. I also hold every loss from your wagering, both at my gambling club and with me personally. I demand immediate payment."

They were the most frightening words Gregory had ever heard. "I can't pay. Don't be ridiculous."

"Is it your admission," Ralston said, "in front of these witnesses, that you haven't the money to cover what you owe?"

"You're aware that I don't. If I'd had it, I'd have paid my bills when they were first due."

Ralston nodded as if it was the precise answer he'd been expecting. "I accuse you of deliberately defrauding me. I accuse you of accumulating financial liabilities you shouldn't have assumed. I accuse you of premeditated deceit."

"I didn't deceive anyone," Gregory insisted. "London is dreadfully expensive, and I simply couldn't keep up."

Samson smirked. "Gregory, you're already in a very deep hole. You should quit digging."

A thug approached, and he slapped some papers into Gregory's hand. "I arrest you for embezzlement from your cousin, Caroline Grey, but also for the swindling of dozens of merchants and vendors who have conveyed their legal rights to Caleb Ralston. Come with me."

"Come...where?" Gregory asked.

"You'll be in jail in London until your trial. I can't imagine you'll have much of a defense, so I can't predict what will occur after it ends."

Ralston grinned malevolently. "I shall argue that you be hanged, but I suspect Caroline will be content with a lesser penalty. You'll likely be transported to the penal colonies. I'll be fine with that conclusion—just so long as you never show your pathetic face in England ever again."

"Caroline wouldn't want you to treat me this way," Gregory said.

His father snickered. "I tried the same tactic, Gregory. It doesn't work with him." Samson fell to his knees, his hands folded as if in prayer, and he said to Ralston, "I sincerely regret my behavior toward Caroline. Please tell her how sorry I am. Have her visit me in prison, so I can apologize to her directly. I need her to know how mortified I am."

"Caroline will *never* visit you," Ralston replied. "I will never allow it. Not ever."

Gregory frowned. "Why would you suppose you'd have any authority over Caroline?"

"Didn't I mention?" Ralston said. "She's my fiancée, and soon, she'll be my wife."

Samson unhelpfully explained, "He intends to take control of our money—by becoming her husband."

Gregory blanched. Ralston was marrying Caroline? How had that happened? When had it happened? Why would they have enjoyed more than a passing acquaintance?

"You've stolen my fiancée?" he said. "And you've stolen our money? This is an outrage!"

He hoped he looked nobly aggrieved, but his bluster was cut short when the thug who'd previously threatened him stuffed a kerchief into his mouth.

"I warned you to shut up," the cretin said.

Gregory was dragged out, and he peered over his shoulder, visually seeking his father's intervention, but Samson was still on his knees and begging Ralston for mercy. Not that he was having any luck. He was lifted to his feet and marched out behind Gregory.

"Where am I going?" Samson asked Ralston. "Where are you taking me?"

"To jail in London to await trial with your son."

"May I pack a bag? May I fetch my purse so I have some money to defray expenses once we arrive?"

"You don't have any money," Ralston said. "It's all Caroline's, and it's our opinion that she wouldn't like you to get your grubby fingers on what's left of it."

LUCRETIA TIPTOED TO THE stairs and peeked over the railing. She couldn't see anyone, but angry voices drifted up from a parlor.

Ever since Gregory had been physically carried from their bedchamber, she'd been hiding in the dressing room, wondering what to do.

It appeared his creditors had caught him, and she was kicking herself for being such an idiot. Why had she tarried by his side? Why hadn't she snuck away the instant she'd noticed trouble brewing?

Her only excuse was that she'd grown complacent. They'd been together for years, and they'd lived in a posh manner. The funds had magically flowed in, and she'd never had to worry about where they came from or where they went.

Gregory was on a sinking ship. Should she dawdle and throw him a rope? Or should she swim to safety and let him drown?

Even as she posed the question, the answer was obvious: She wasn't about to have any of Gregory's consequences land on her. That very minute, he might be under arrest. What if her name was on a warrant somewhere? What then?

She hurried back to their bedchamber, and she grabbed a satchel and crammed her jewelry into it. Gregory had a few pounds stashed in a drawer, and she took that too. Then she rushed out, her mind awhirl with plans.

She'd head straight to London and begin to pack. Before any of them moved to attach their house, she'd be gone with all the items of value. If she was thrifty, she'd be fine. She would gradually pawn baubles and support herself until she could find a new paramour. She was young and beautiful, and she had no doubt she'd succeed in tempting a worthy candidate.

She smirked with satisfaction. Goodbye Gregory Grey! He was a reckless fool whose chickens had come home to roost, and she'd stayed much longer than she should have.

She dashed down the hall and was about to start down the stairs when she noted the housekeeper, Mrs. Scruggs, lurking in the shadows. The shrew glared at Lucretia in a condemning way, and in a different world, Lucretia would have paused to scold her for being impertinent. She might even have fired her, but there was no time to fret over a snooty, incompetent employee.

No, Lucretia had to get away while the *getting* was good.

She flitted down to the foyer, but her luck didn't hold. A mob of men flooded out of Samson's library. Gregory was at the front, with two criminals gripping his arms so he couldn't escape. He was gagged, his wrists fettered.

They marched by her, and Gregory was straining against his guards, trying to tell her something, but with the kerchief in his mouth, she had no idea what it was.

His father was brought out next, and he stared morosely at Lucretia and said, "We've been arrested. We're being transported to London to be jailed."

"Dear me!" she said, feigning alarm.

"Would you contact a lawyer for me please? Have him visit me so we can discuss his posting my bail."

"I will hire one for you," she lied. Once Gregory and Samson were whisked away, it was her specific intent that she would never see either of them ever again.

Samson was yanked out the door, and she breathed a sigh of relief, but it was short-lived.

Caleb Ralston and Lord Barrett strolled toward her. She couldn't figure out why Barrett was present, but she didn't have to ponder what part

Ralston had played in Gregory's downfall. Gregory owed the oaf a bloody fortune, and Lucretia had warned him over and over about Ralston.

Caleb Ralston was not a man to be tricked or cheated, and lesser men defrauded him at their peril.

"What's happened to Gregory and his father?" she asked Ralston, hoping she looked innocent and concerned.

"I've bought Gregory's debt, and he can't pay me, so he's been swept up as a debtor."

"How awful—for both of you."

"Yes, I'm sure you're devastated," Ralston sarcastically said. "They're also accused of stealing from Caroline Grey."

Lucretia frowned. "What could they have stolen from Miss Grey? As far as I'm aware, she doesn't have a penny to her name."

Lord Barrett scoffed with derision, as Ralston said, "We haven't requested a warrant for *you*. Yet."

She quailed, her knees suddenly so weak that she had to grab the bannister. "Why would you have suspicions about me? I'm simply Gregory's devoted friend. What crime could I have committed?"

"In case you're expecting to slither to your London home, you should know that we've seized it. Even as we speak, I have investigators there who are tabulating the contents."

She gasped. "What?"

"I'm certain every chattel in the place, as well as the house itself, was purchased with Caroline's money. We'll sort it out, but in the meantime, you're not welcome there."

His words pummeled her, and she shivered with terror. She didn't have anything of her own. Every little piece of her life had been acquired with what Gregory had taken from his cousin's trust fund. If Ralston had custody of all of it, what would she do?

"I should be going," she said. "Mr. Grey has asked me to hire a lawyer for him. I should rush to town to see if I can help him."

She might have walked on, but the old bat, Mrs. Scruggs, called from up on the landing, "Mr. Ralston, would you check the satchel Mrs. Starling is carrying? I believe it's stuffed full of jewelry. As long as you're seizing Miss Caroline's possessions, it's probably hers."

Lucretia's first instinct was always self-preservation. She bolted, but Ralston was a large man, and in two quick strides, he'd restrained her.

He held her while Lord Barrett peeked into the pouch. They were *her* jewels, gifts from Gregory over the years, but with her concealing them in the bag as she had, she appeared horribly guilty.

"We'll just be keeping these," Lord Barrett said.

"They're mine!" she insisted. "You can't have them."

"Tell it to the judge," Barrett snidely retorted.

Ralston marched Lucretia outside. He was still clutching her arm, and though she struggled to free herself, she couldn't.

There was a carriage in the drive, the door open, Gregory and his father slouched on the seats. Ralston dragged her over to one of the ruffians.

"This woman is Gregory's paramour," Ralston said. "She should be arrested too."

Lord Barrett approached and showed the satchel to the men. On their observing what she'd hoarded, she was met with reproachful glowers, and Barrett said, "She's as big a thief as Samson and Gregory Grey. She might be even worse."

Lucretia's wrists and ankles were bound, then she was lifted into the carriage. Despite how she protested, despite how she cursed them and their descendants forever, no one listened. The door was shut and latched so she couldn't jump out. The driver shouted to the horses, and they lurched away so rapidly she was nearly flung to the floor.

"Mmm, mmm," Gregory mumbled through his gag, his eyes wide with panic.

Samson said, "This is a fine pickle, isn't it, Mrs. Starling? How shall we fix it?"

She shot a glare that could have melted lead. "Don't lump me into your pathetic problem."

Samson laughed viciously. "You're in a deeper hole than I am. I, at least, can beg Caroline for mercy. What can you do?"

He snorted with contempt, then peered out the window, and the vehicle grew very quiet. The only sound was wheels crunching on gravel.

She gaped at Gregory, gaped at his father, but neither of them would look back at her. She was on her own, and it was the loneliest spot in the world.

<hr />

CALEB STOOD IN THE driveway as the carriage rolled off. Gregory, Samson, and Mrs. Starling were locked inside.

It had been a whirlwind of days, and he never ceased to be amazed at the power an aristocrat like Luke Watson could wield. Caleb might have wasted months, obtaining the documents to have Gregory and Samson arrested. Luke had accomplished it in a matter of hours.

The sole task left was to marry Caro, the trick being to get her to consent without too much arguing.

Luke sauntered up and said, "That trio of scoundrels just might be the most disgusting people I've ever encountered."

"You'd be right."

"Caroline seems very normal and pleasant to me. I can't imagine how she could possibly be related to them."

"I'm told her father was very different from the rest of them. She must take after him."

"Thank goodness," Luke said. "Will you have them hanged?"

"*I* would love that punishment, but Janet and Caro would never want them executed. They're kinder and much more forgiving than I am."

"What will you do with the manor?" Luke asked.

"I'll leave the housekeeper, Mrs. Scruggs, in charge. She's plenty fierce, and she'll keep things on an even keel until I can come back with Caroline. Then I'll let Caro decide about the property."

While Caleb didn't have all the records yet, it appeared Caroline's grandfather had taken out numerous mortgages on Grey's Corner. When Samson had inherited, he'd used a huge chunk of Caroline's trust to pay off what his father had borrowed.

Caleb supposed that made it Caroline's estate. If it wasn't already, it would be when the court hearings were concluded.

"Will you live here after you're wed?" Luke asked.

"I have no idea. I have to convince her to have me first. I'm not all that certain she will."

"Libby is expecting it," Luke said like a threat, "and I have no ability to disappoint her."

"You poor man. I see a humiliating life ahead of you, where you never wear the trousers in your own home."

Luke chuckled. "Just wait until Caroline puts that ring on your finger. You'll discover how low you'll stoop to keep her happy."

The carriage carrying the three fiends vanished in the trees, and Luke whipped away and stared up at the manor.

"This is a fine residence," he said. "There are worse places you could end up."

"I know."

"Will you give up your gambling club for her? I'm afraid you might have to. From the comments she shared with Libby, she's not keen to have a gambler for a husband."

"Gad, I hadn't thought about my club."

"You'll be marrying an heiress, so it's not as if you'll be a pauper. You could manage her fortune. You're adept at handling money, so maybe that could be your new job."

"I'd be my wife's accountant?"

"It's better than *not* winning her and being nothing to her at all."

"*Touché,*" Caleb said.

"Have we dealt with all your problems? We haven't forgotten any issues, have we?"

"I don't believe we have."

"Then can we return to Barrett? My nuptials are in a few days, and Libby will be starting to wonder if I've gotten cold feet and run away."

"You can't run away. We're both about to be leg-shackled. If I have to tie the knot, so do you."

"I complain about it, but I'm not serious," Luke said. "We're lucky they agreed to have us."

"Speak for yourself. I still have to persuade Caroline."

"I'd like to be a mouse in the corner to listen as you grovel."

"Isn't it interesting how we view ourselves as tough, virile men, but two pretty females have brought us to heel?"

"It's not interesting. It's embarrassing."

Caleb sighed with gladness. "Let's get you to Barrett. I'm suddenly desperate to talk to Caroline, and I'm eager to watch you walk down the aisle. I'm invited to the wedding, aren't I?"

"Yes, and Libby will probably demand you marry Caroline right after she and I finish reciting the vows."

"The church will be warmed up and the vicar ready. We could simply step to the altar after you step away."

"Don't muck this up, Ralston."

"I won't. She's never been able to resist me, and I'll wear her down."

"I will fervidly hope that turns out to still be true."

Chapter
24

"MY GOODNESS!"

Caroline peered over at Libby, her expression shocked and bewildered. They were in Caroline's bedchamber in Lord Barrett's home, and Libby had just brought a letter upstairs for her.

"Don't tell me it's bad news," Libby said. "With my wedding so close, I refuse to allow anything negative to occur."

"I can't decide if it's bad news or not. My cousin, Janet, has married Blake Ralston."

"Wasn't he mortally opposed to matrimony?"

"*She* was mortally opposed. She might be increasing though, so she had to set aside a few of her convictions."

"It sounds as if another scoundrel has been ensnared."

"He's definitely a scoundrel, so that's why I'm debating whether I'm glad for her or not. I imagine she'll have an exasperating life with him."

"Some women claim scoundrels end up being the best husbands."

"Who are the women claiming that? I'd like to learn how they arrived at such a ludicrous notion."

"Luke is an example."

"He is not. According to both of you, he was boring and normal until he met you. He had to develop wild habits so you'd assume he was intriguing."

Libby smirked. "You could be right about that."

"When you've been so gracious, it's rude of me to suggest it, but could Janet visit me? Blake is posted to the Mediterranean, and he's already left. She's going next week too, on a ship for navy wives, and she'd like to see me before she sails."

"She's going out onto the ocean—on a *ship*?" Libby asked.

"Yes."

They shuddered, their fear of ships and water deeply ingrained. They still had nightmares about the shipwreck, and they shared a hefty belief that humans should keep their feet firmly planted on dry ground.

"Perhaps you should warn her to reconsider," Libby said.

"She's young and in love. I could never persuade her to stay in England. Not with her being a newlywed."

"Probably not," Libby agreed, "and of course she can visit you."

"Are you sure? The manor is incredibly hectic, and I shouldn't be a burden."

"You're not a burden, and besides, *I* am not busy. I'm not organizing the wedding; I wouldn't have the faintest idea how. You must write to your cousin and have her come immediately."

"I will. Thank you."

"Now that we have that out of the way," Libby said, "your presence is requested downstairs."

"Why?"

"I have a surprise for you."

"I hate surprises."

"No one hates surprises."

"Well, in my experience, there are fun ones and awful ones. I've only ever suffered the awful kind."

"I declare that—with our crossing paths again—you shall just suffer the fun ones in the future." Libby started out, tossing over her shoulder, "Let's get this over with."

Caroline scowled and followed her out. "Your comment doesn't exactly fill me with excitement."

"You will be excited. Eventually. I hope. This is Luke's mischief, so if it blows up into a huge morass, I'll simply blame him."

"He's back?"

"Yes, he just rode in, and he's anxious to talk to you."

They reached the front foyer, and Mr. Periwinkle was there and dressed for traveling. Since he'd conveyed Caroline to Barrett, he'd been loafing in the house and ingratiating himself. Caroline suspected he was scribbling furtive notes and would earn a fortune penning articles about Libby's nuptial celebrations. Was Caroline the only one who'd realized that fact?

"Are you leaving us, Mr. Periwinkle?" Libby asked.

He tugged off his cap and bowed to her. "With your permission, Miss Carstairs, I thought I'd confer with Joanna James and escort her to Barrett. Or would you rather I wait until after the wedding? It's so chaotic here. Would it be too much?"

Libby asked Caroline, "What's your opinion, Caro?"

"I'd like it to be right away. She and I can sit together at the church."

"It will be quite the ending for the three of us." Libby peered at Mr. Periwinkle and said, "Bring a competent artist with you too, so there's a good drawing of us for your newspaper. I don't want a sketch where we look old and haggard."

Mr. Periwinkle was Libby's biggest admirer, and he gushed, "There's no chance of that, Miss Carstairs."

Caroline extended her hands, and he clasped hold.

"I'll see you soon," she said to him, "and when I do, I will expect Joanna to be with you."

"I vow to you that I will not return without her."

He pulled away, bowed to Libby again, and walked out. They observed until the door was shut behind him, and Caroline said, "That poor man is madly in love with you."

"Every man I've ever met is in love with me."

"How will Luke stand to be your husband? He'll constantly wander around in a jealous haze."

Libby grinned. "It will keep him on his toes. He'll always be afraid— if he's not careful—some other rogue will step in to take his place."

"You are horrid."

"And he doesn't mind that I am."

They went down the hall toward the earl's library. Luke was hovering and impatiently watching for them.

"I didn't think you two would ever arrive," he said.

"You know me," Libby replied. "I'm never in a hurry."

"It's just one of your many quirks that drives me insane." He shifted his focus to Caroline. "Did Libby inform you of what's happening?"

"No. She merely told me it was a surprise."

"I intend that this situation will be swiftly resolved, so don't dawdle or quarrel. I'm locking you in, and I won't let you out until I receive the answer I insist on having."

Libby sniffed with offense. "You can be so exhausting." Then she said to Caroline, "I'll be outside. If you grow too aggravated, call to me, and *I* will let you out."

Luke glowered at Libby. "Barrett is my home, so it's my castle. You're in residence now, so will I ever be in charge?"

"No, not ever," Libby cheekily retorted.

She shoved Caroline into the room, and before Caroline could protest the move, the key was spun.

"For pity's sake," she complained, then, braced for anything, she glanced around to discover what they'd arranged.

"I warned them not to lock you in," Caleb said. "I was certain you wouldn't like it, but Barrett can be an ogre when he's riled."

"What are you doing here?"

"What do you suppose?"

"I have no idea. I could have sworn I was very clear in London: I'm not ready to smooth over our differences."

He shrugged from over by the hearth. "I told Barrett you were still too angry, but he wouldn't listen to me."

A flood of emotions washed through her. She was ecstatically happy to see him, but she was also still incredibly furious over his behavior with Gregory. The dueling viewpoints warred inside her, and she couldn't decide which one should control her portion of the conversation.

With every fiber of her being, she yearned to race over and fall into his arms. She'd wax on about how much she'd missed him, how sorry she was that they'd fought, how desperately she'd prayed that he would chase her down in the country.

Yet at the same time, she wasn't prepared to address any of the issues separating them. She feared she'd make concessions she shouldn't make, that she would accept apologies she shouldn't heed.

She whirled away and pounded on the door. "Luke, would you let me out? I can't talk to Mr. Ralston at the moment. I'm too livid."

"I can't oblige you, Caroline," Luke said. "You have to exert more effort than this."

"Libby! How about you? Will you release me?"

"Luke won't give me the key," Libby claimed.

Behind her, Caleb snorted with annoyance. "It's futile to argue with Barrett. From what I've witnessed recently, it's a waste of breath."

She glared at him, but her severe look had no effect. He walked to the sideboard and poured himself a whiskey. He leaned against it, sipping his liquor, studying her as a hawk studies a mouse.

The silence stretched out, and finally, he said, "So...here we are."

She pushed away from the door. If they would be forced to chat, she couldn't bear to have Luke and Libby eavesdropping on the other side.

"It appears you have something to tell me," she said. "Why don't you begin, so we can wrap up this farce."

"You are still so irate. I'm amazed to observe so much temper from you."

"It's a secret about me people don't realize. I have an enormous temper, but I tamp it down and pretend to be content. I must admit that it's quite refreshing to allow it to fly free."

"I will confess to deserving a bit of your ire."

"A bit!" she huffed.

"All right, all right, perhaps *more* than a bit."

"Call me mad, but I thought we'd developed a strong bond."

"I thought so too."

"Then I discovered I don't know any details about you that matter."

"What you see with me is what you get. I spent a decade as a sailor, and I assumed I would die in the navy, but I was swept up in my brother's mischief, and I had to resign. To support myself—and Sybil—I opened a gambling club. It's the sum total of my biography. I wish you'd quit blaming me for landing on my feet."

"I don't blame you. I simply feel that a man who earns a living as you do—by ruining other men—isn't a person I should esteem."

He made a waffling motion with his hand, as if her remark was merely frivolous female babbling. "You constantly chastise me for other men being weak fools, so it's pointless to mention yet again that *I* have never ruined anyone. They ruin themselves."

"You pave the road for their destruction."

He considered the accusation, then nodded. "I guess that's a valid assessment."

"After you left the navy, you could have started any business, but you picked wagering. Why? If you could explain such a corrupt choice, I might not be so judgmental."

"I'm skilled with numbers and money. It seemed a natural path for me."

She clucked her tongue with disapproval. She was eager to delve to the heart of whatever topic he'd come to discuss, but their main problem would always be his club. It sat in the center of the room like a huge elephant that wouldn't move.

"Would you like to hear what I've been doing the past few days?" he said.

"Not really," she replied, when in fact, she'd been pondering him incessantly.

From the minute he'd stopped by Janet's in the middle of the night and had demanded Caroline answer the door, she'd been anxious for him to return and try again. She'd figured Janet would relent and tell him where she was, and every second she'd loafed at Barrett, she'd wondered when he'd ride up the lane.

In the meantime, she'd pictured him in town, where he was surrounded by rich, elegant people, and she'd been terribly afraid he would decide she wasn't worth the trouble she'd caused him.

Now he'd blustered in, and apparently, he was determined to hash out their differences. She wanted that. Or maybe she didn't. Ooh, she was so confused!

"First off," he said, ignoring her comment that she wasn't interested in his recent activities, "I got your cousin, Janet, married to my brother."

"*You* did it?"

"Yes. I was worried I'd never be able to force them, but Barrett helped me. Between the two of us, they didn't stand a chance." There was a pause, where he waited for her response, then he said, "Well? Are you going to thank me?"

"Your brother is an immoral libertine, and ultimately, he behaved in the only appropriate way. Should I be grateful that it took significant effort to accomplish it?"

He scoffed. "You are a hard nut to crack, Caroline Grey."

"Not usually. I've only been obstinate since I met you."

"I don't believe that. I think you were always obstinate, and I've simply given you excuses to unleash it."

There was quite a bit of truth to the statement, so she wouldn't argue about it. Instead, she asked, "Will Blake be a good husband to her? Or will he make her miserable forever?"

"He'll probably make her miserable forever, but *she* was delighted. That has to count for something, I suppose."

"And your brother? What was his opinion?"

"He was a tad nauseous, but he spoke the vows and wrote his name on the license without my having to beat him bloody."

Blake Ralston was a charming rogue who'd likely seduced women around the globe. He was a sailor, but he happened to have a very wealthy sibling. No doubt Caleb provided him with an allowance to supplement his wages, so Janet would never want for money, but Caroline suspected her cousin would frequently fret over exhausting issues like monogamy and adultery.

"Janet is my sister-in-law," he said.

"So she is," Caroline murmured, hating that it bound Caleb to her family when she wasn't certain he should be bound to it.

"She's heading to Gibraltar, to live at the British compound there, so she'll see Blake when he's in port."

"I hope it works out for her. She had other goals for herself, but she's ended up picking the most normal path of all."

"It won't kill her to be a wife and mother. There are worse conclusions." He gestured to the sofa. "Would you please sit down? I have to explain some shocking news, and you should be sitting when you hear it."

"I'll try to bear up," she sarcastically said.

"Yes, well, this might be more astonishing than you're expecting."

"Spit it out, Caleb. Stop being so irritating."

"Fine. Here goes: After Janet's wedding, she told me about her lawyer and the missing inheritance from her grandmother. It was an odd story, so Barrett and I investigated."

She frowned. "Investigated what?"

"It turns out, Caroline Grey, that there is only one person in your family who ever had an inheritance."

"Who is it?"

"It's *you*. You are a great heiress."

She cocked her head, thinking he might have babbled in a foreign language she didn't understand. "I could swear you said I'm an heiress."

"I did and you are." He pointed to a nearby table that was strewn with documents. "I brought the papers that prove it."

"What are you talking about? You could be speaking Chinese."

"It seems, dear Caro, that your father once traveled to Africa with famed explorer, Sir Sidney Sinclair."

"I know that."

"While he was there, he became the proud owner of a diamond mine."

Her jaw dropped. "Are you serious?"

"Yes. When he died in the shipwreck, his ownership fell into a trust fund, with the assets belonging to you. Originally, your grandfather was the trustee, and he refused to spend any of it, but when the role passed to your uncle, he had no such reservations."

"Uncle Samson has been spending *my* money?"

"Yes, Samson and Gregory. They were incredibly extravagant too."

"Am I. . . I. . . beggared?"

He chuckled. "They tried their best, but no. You're not beggared. You're *so* rich; the diamonds keep being mined, and the money keeps flowing in."

"I'm an heiress," she muttered. "A mining heiress. . ."

"Yes."

"Uncle Samson constantly joked about how poor I was. He used to tease me about it."

"He was a lying, greedy fiend."

Her mind was racing, struggling to process the information. "Is this why Gregory was so eager to marry me?"

"Yes. He needed to be in control of the trust as your husband, so if you ever found out about their mischief, you'd be his wife, and you wouldn't be able to complain."

"What about my Uncle Samson? Is that why he was pushing it?"

"Yes—that and the fact that you have another fund vesting on your birthday. You have to be wed by then, or you won't receive it."

He'd warned her to sit down before he began, and she'd declined, yet suddenly, her knees were weak. She staggered over to a chair and eased down. She gazed at the floor, her mind whirring at an even faster pace.

"They were...were...stealing from me!"

"That's putting it mildly."

"They planned to continue forever, but to ensure I never learned of it."

"You've just about covered it."

Fury blazed through her. They'd ceaselessly and relentlessly made her feel beholden, as if she was a vagabond begging for alms. How dare they!

"I want to go to Grey's Corner," she fumed. "I want to confront them."

"They aren't there anymore. They're in jail in London."

She froze, keen to deduce if that was the correct ending. They'd behaved despicably, but they were her only kin besides Janet.

"Who had them arrested?" she asked.

"Lord Barrett and I decided on it, and before you lament over how you pity them or would like them released, you should be aware that it's thousands and thousands of pounds."

She simply couldn't fathom such an amount belonging to her or that her uncle and cousin had frittered it away without her realizing. She'd thought it was *family* money, that it had been Grandfather Walter's money. It's what Uncle Samson had always claimed.

"Thousands and thousands?" she wanly said.

"Yes, and if it will help to stir your rage, Gregory has been supporting Lucretia Starling with it. He wasn't the least bit ashamed about it either. He's developed quite an affinity for your fortune, and he'd started to act as if it was his own."

"What about Mrs. Starling?" Caroline asked. "Please tell me she's in trouble too."

"She's in jail with them. We've seized the house they bought, and I've confiscated most of her jewels. All that I could find anyway in such a short period. We're still searching." He went to the table where the documents were stacked, and he grabbed a satchel off a chair. He brought it back and handed it too her. "Look at this."

She was almost afraid to peek into it and was trembling so hard she could barely untie the ribbon on the front. When she finally managed to open it, she gasped. The pouch was full of necklaces, rings, and bracelets. There were even two tiaras, one that was studded with emeralds and one with diamonds.

He plucked out the one with diamonds and set it in her hair, fussing with it until it was balanced just right. She was too stunned to swat him away. She dawdled like a statue, too bewildered to protest.

"I never saw it on Mrs. Starling," he said, "but I'm betting it's much prettier on you."

He was grinning, as if the situation was funny, but she didn't deem it to be amusing in the slightest. She removed the tiara and scrutinized the gems, tracing her thumb over them, wondering how someone even shopped for such a thing. It was beyond her comprehension.

How had Gregory become involved with a woman who would relish such pricey trinkets? They'd been poor when they were children, living under her grandfather's miserly thumb. What had changed him? The money? Or, deep down, had he always been greedy and corrupt?

The satchel slid off her lap, and she was too dumbfounded to reach for it. Caleb snatched it away, the tiara too, and placed them on the table. Then he leaned against the sideboard and stared at her from across the room.

"This is too bizarre to be true," she ultimately said.

"I agree, except that it is true."

"I'm speechless."

"You could shake yourself out of your stupor and say, *Thank you, Caleb.*"

In a mocking tone, she repeated, "Thank you, Caleb."

"You should exhibit more sincerity. I mean, let's review what I've done for you the past week: I forced my brother to marry Janet. I unraveled the mystery of Janet's nonexistent trust fund. I learned *you* are an heiress. I discovered the massive theft committed by your relatives. I yanked their fingers out of your accounts, so they can never steal from you again. I had them arrested, and I guarantee they'll be prosecuted and receive appropriate sentences. *And* I evicted them from Grey's Corner."

"Who's in charge at home?"

"Mrs. Scruggs is holding down the fort until you arrive to take charge."

"Why would *I* take charge at Grey's Corner?"

"Keep up with me, Caro." He scoffed with exasperation. "Your grandfather mortgaged the property over and over, and after he died, your uncle used your trust fund to pay off the debts your grandfather had incurred."

"The property is mine?"

"Probably. We have to work out the details, but Gregory and Samson can't make a claim to it. It was *your* money that saved it from foreclosure." He put a palm to his ear. "Was there a *thank you* in there somewhere? A genuine thank you? If so, I didn't hear it."

She smirked. "Yes. Thank you."

She was completely befuddled, trying to absorb what he'd shared. She was rich. Grey's Corner was hers. Her uncle and cousin were incarcerated. Everything she'd believed about herself, everything she'd ever been told, was a lie.

"Would you pinch me?" She extended her arm. "I need to be sure I'm not dreaming."

"You're not dreaming. This is really happening."

"What now?" she asked. "How am I to handle all of this?"

"I have some ideas about it."

She snorted. "Why am I not surprised?"

He poured himself another whiskey, and he sipped it, both of them quiet. He'd imparted a thousand wild facts that had altered every aspect of her life, but they hadn't delved into any of the issues that separated them. He still owned a gambling club. He still helped men ruin themselves.

He was still the kind of scoundrel who would wager over a maiden's virginity.

"You're obscenely wealthy," he eventually said, "so monumental changes are on the horizon for you."

"I don't necessarily concur. I'll still be plain old Caroline Grey, from Grey's Corner."

"No, you'll be heiress, Caroline Grey, a prosperous spinster who resides at her ostentatious manor in the country."

She chuckled at that. "Who will know? I can't exactly picture me strolling around the kingdom and blabbing it to people."

"The news will leak out. This type of secret is difficult to keep. Especially if your uncle and cousin have a public trial. You'll be in the newspapers, and I can see it now." He gestured theatrically, as if reading a large headline. "*'Little Caro, Mystery Girl of the Caribbean, is an Heiress! Little Caro Betrayed by her Male Kin!'*"

"I couldn't bear to be in the newspapers. My first experience when I was five wasn't all that thrilling."

"You're about to have suitors swarming."

She sputtered with amusement. "I doubt that very much."

"Every scapegrace, wastrel, and aristocrat's son in the land will beat a path to your door." He downed his drink and set the glass on the sideboard with a loud thud. "And *that,* Caro, is a situation I simply can't permit."

"What situation? Me, having suitors? You're being even more ridiculous than usual."

"Here is what we're going to do."

"What *we* are going to do?"

"Yes, and I won't argue about it."

He went over to the satchel, and he searched in it and pulled out a ring. He walked over and waved it under her nose. It was a modest piece of jewelry, a gold band with a pretty diamond in the center, and precisely the design she'd have selected for herself if given the opportunity.

"I didn't think to bring one of my own," he said, "so this one will have to satisfy you for the moment."

She scowled. "What are you talking about?"

To her consternation, he dropped to a knee and clasped her hand. A man only placed himself in that position for one reason, and her scowl deepened. She was actually quite aghast.

"Are you about to propose?"

"Yes, so be silent and listen to me for once."

"You're awfully confident that you can persuade me, but we should review a few pertinent facts. Namely, that you asked me previously, and I decided I'm not interested."

"Yes, but you were being absurd, so you don't get to have an opinion about it."

She tried to yank away, but he tightened his grip and wouldn't release her. Before she realized what he intended, he'd slid the ring onto her finger. The blasted thing fit perfectly.

"We've been fighting," she said, "and you're being a bully."

"We're done fighting," he ludicrously replied, "so how could I be bullying you?"

"I don't want to marry you!"

She was shocked that the words had spilled out of her mouth. She wasn't certain what she wanted and what she didn't, but of course, the rude oaf ignored her.

"You're dying to wed me," he insisted. "You've been hoping for it from the minute we met."

"If that's what you assume, you're insane. You run a gambling club! You destroy men's lives for sport."

"I repeat: *I* don't ruin anybody. They're all irresponsible wretches."

"Fine, I stand corrected. You're a veritable saint."

He grinned his devil's grin. "That's more like it."

"Don't tease me, and don't be flippant. My life is on the line over this."

"So is mine, and you can't deny me what I'm yearning to have."

"And what is that?"

"You, you silly girl, so this is what I'm willing to do for you."

"I'm on pins and needles waiting to hear." Her tone was much too snide.

"I'm giving my business to Sybil. I'll sign the whole enterprise over to her."

She gasped. "You'll...what?"

"I'll give it away. It appears to be a sticking point for you, so I'll relinquish it."

"Why would you?"

"Can't you guess? I swear, Caro, you are being an absolute dunce today. If that stupid club means I can't have you as my wife, why bother with it?"

"It's made you rich. It's how you earn your income."

"Yes, but I agree with you: It's a foul profession. Sybil is much better at managing the dolts who are members. She can have it all, then *I* can have you."

"If you get rid of it, you'll be poor."

"I was poor before I started it. It won't kill me to be poor again. Besides, if I dispose of it, I can try my hand at something else."

"What else?"

"I can glom onto you like the worst sort of fortune hunter and be a *kept* man. I'm actually looking forward to it." He kissed the center of her palm. "Dearest Caroline, will you marry me?"

She blanched. "No."

"That's not the right answer. You might as well tell me you'll have me. I won't stop pestering you until you give me what I want."

"You're a committed bachelor."

"Yes, I am, but I'm ready to change that situation."

He had her trapped in the chair, and he overwhelmed her with his physical presence. When he was touching her, she couldn't think straight. She pushed away and jumped to her feet, leaving him off balance so he nearly fell to the floor.

She dashed across the room to dawdle by the hearth. He was still on his knees, and he glared at her, a hint of temper showing, but it was swiftly masked. He pushed himself up and asked, "What's wrong now?"

"I'm confused about what kind of person you are. I presumed I knew, but I really don't, and I can't decide what's best."

"I'll decide for you then. *I* am best. I am precisely who you need in your life to be happy."

"What about you?" she asked. "What do you need to be happy?"

"Haven't you figured that out?"

"I thought it was *me,* but I'm so bewildered that I'm not sure of anything."

"First off, I should clarify a paltry detail I neglected to explain previously."

"What is it?"

"You have a new guardian."

"Who?"

"Lord Barrett. He had himself installed when the judge removed your uncle from the trust accounts."

"I'm barely acquainted with Lord Barrett. How could he assume any control over me?"

"You might not be acquainted with him, but he's an honorable fellow, and *he* has determined that you'll wed me. If you saunter over and ask him, I believe he'll say he insists on it."

"What gall for him—and you—to dicker over me like a cow at the market."

"At least we haven't robbed you blind."

"Not yet anyway."

As they'd been talking, he'd been slyly sidling closer. She should have fled the room, but she was glued to her spot and could only watch him approach—like a rabbit watching a viper.

"Fate is guiding my steps," he said. "I can't avoid you."

She'd sensed Fate's interference too, but wouldn't admit it. She wouldn't give him more leverage. "I wouldn't peg you as a superstitious type."

"Usually, I'm not, but if it's not Fate guiding me, then it must be my father. He's hovering constantly."

"Why would your father be hovering?"

"I think he wanted me to find you. I think he's been worried about you, and he wanted me to take care of you for him."

"That's a ludicrous idea."

"Maybe. Or maybe not. What are the chances we would cross paths? What are the chances my father would be Captain Miles Ralston and *you* would be a Lost Girl? Can't you feel how we've been drawn together?"

"I *might* feel it. Occasionally."

"I've tried to stay away from you, but no matter what I do, I'm dragged back to your side. It's my destiny to wed you, Caro. How can you imagine Fate—and my father's ghost—will permit me to escape your steady pull?"

She been gradually retreating, and finally, she bumped into the stones of the fireplace. He realized she could go no farther, and he swooped in and wrapped her in his arms, his blue eyes filled with anguish.

"Don't turn me away, Caro," he said. "If you won't be mine, if you won't have me, what will become of me?"

"Would you really give up your gambling club?"

"Yes, yes, yes! A thousand times *yes*. I would give up the world for you."

With that, he swept her into a torrid kiss that was wild and debauched. The passion they generated was like an explosion, like a detonation that could incinerate the whole kingdom. It was fiery and raw, and she shouldn't have participated, but the sorry fact was that she'd never been able to resist him, and she couldn't now.

He continued on, wearing her down until her limbs were rubbery, as if her bones had melted. If he hadn't been holding her up, she might have sunk to the floor in a stunned heap.

The information he'd shared had left her dazed and perplexed, so on the spur of the moment, she shouldn't agree to wed. She should ponder and debate in a rational way. Yet how could she *not* agree?

She always conveniently forgot that she'd lain with him, so it was possible she was increasing with his child. They'd sinned and marriage was the sole remedy that would save them. Could she remain stupidly proud and reject him?

He'd proposed that night in London, and he'd just proposed again. What if she refused him, and he had enough of her stubbornness? He was proud too. What if he stomped out? Could she bear to suffer that conclusion?

Her fit of pique had been fueled by his gambling, by his owning his wicked club, but he'd offered to relinquish it. For her. So she'd be happy. So she'd trust him. When he was prepared to make such a sacrifice, could she ignore it? Could she walk away?

No, she couldn't.

Eventually, he slowed and their lips parted. He gazed down at her and said, "You still haven't answered my question. Will you marry me, Caro? Will you let me be your *kept* man? If you won't have me, if you force me to carry on without you, how will I survive the loss?"

"Oh, Caleb…"

"I love you, Caro."

The declaration burst out of him, and they were the last words she'd ever expected to hear. Before she could stop herself, she said, "I love you too."

"Then why are we arguing? Say *yes*. Say you'll have me as your husband."

She stared up at him, and she was deluged by a river of images. She recalled the first day they'd met out on the lane at Grey's Corner. He'd instantly tantalized her, and since then, her infatuation had only grown.

Her entire life, she'd simply wanted one thing: She'd wanted someone to have for her very own. She'd wanted someone to cherish. And here he was! Caleb Ralston! The one man who would be hers forever.

She inhaled a deep breath and held it, then, feeling as if she was running toward a cliff and about to jump over, she said, "Yes, Caleb, I will marry you. I will have you as my husband."

"Do you mean it? I won't allow you to change your mind later on."

"I won't ever change my mind."

A knock sounded on the door, and Libby hollered, "What's happening in there? It's awfully quiet. You two haven't murdered each other, have you?"

A key was stuck in the lock, and Libby peeked in, seeing them huddled in each other's arms over by the hearth.

She raised a brow. "I take it everything is fine."

"Yes, Libby," Caro said, "everything is perfect."

Lord Barrett followed Libby in and asked, "Are we having another wedding?"

Caleb responded, "Yes, we are."

Lord Barrett shuddered. "The air is brimming with matrimony, and I can't fathom why it's occurring or what's causing it."

"It's easy to figure it out," Libby told him. "After too many years of searching, the Lost Girls have found the men of their dreams."

Caroline smiled up at Caleb and said, "Aren't we lucky?"

THE END

❦

Don't miss Book #3 of the
Lost Girls Trilogy!

Someone To Wed

the story of
Miss Joanna James
and
Mr. Jacob Ralston

❦

Available now!

About the Author

CHERYL HOLT IS A *New York Times*, *USA Today*, and Amazon "Top 100" bestselling author who has published over fifty novels.

She's also a lawyer and mom, and at age forty, with two babies at home, she started a new career as a commercial fiction writer. She'd hoped to be a suspense novelist, but couldn't sell any of her manuscripts, so she ended up taking a detour into romance where she was stunned to discover that she has a knack for writing some of the world's greatest love stories.

Her books have been released to wide acclaim, and she has won or been nominated for many national awards. She is considered to be one of the masters of the romance genre. For many years, she was hailed as "The Queen of Erotic Romance," and she's also revered as "The International Queen of Villains." She is particularly proud to have been named "Best Storyteller of the Year" by the trade magazine Romantic Times BOOK Reviews.

She lives and writes in Hollywood, California, and she loves to hear from fans. Visit her website at www.cherylholt.com.

CPSIA information can be obtained
at www.ICGtesting.com
Printed in the USA
LVHW031453241220
675096LV00001B/69

9 781648 711732